CW01658597

STOCKHOLM TEXT

KARIN WAHLBERG

DEATH OF A CARPET DEALER

This book is part of Stockholm Text's Scandinavian Crime series.
To find more titles in the series, make sure to regularly visit http://stockholmtext.com.

Stockholm Text
www.stockholmtext.com
stockholm@stockholmtext.com

Translation: Neil Betteridge
Editing: Deborah Halverson
Cover: Dorian Mabb & Simon Svéd
ISBN e-book: 978-91-87173-14-1
ISBN print book: 978-91-87173-21-9

CHAPTER 1

CARL-IVAR OLSSON SAT on deck, thoroughly enjoying himself. It was Saturday afternoon and the boat's motors were throbbing soothingly and lulling him into an agreeable state of calm. The fresh air was also doing its bit.

Well, there's fresh and there's fresh, of course, he corrected himself quickly. The atmosphere over a city of Istanbul's size was perhaps not the most salubrious. Around ten million people in one chaotic throng, exhaust fumes and a thin ozone layer to boot, and your handkerchief spattered with black when you blew your nose. It couldn't be doing anyone any good at all.

But anyway, what did he care? He liked it here. Part of his soul had taken root in Istanbul.

And he understood perfectly what had happened. As if by some kind of reflex, he had internalized his wife's thoughts and comments and made then his own, as if she were sitting there beside him. As so easily happened when two people spent their lives together, they rubbed off on each other, for better or worse.

He didn't actually want to let his wife in at that moment, but he was forced to remind himself to call her that evening to tell her he'd have to stay for a few more days. Tuesday was the offer he'd made her when she flew back to Sweden the day before, but even then he'd already made his mind up to stay until the following Saturday. Another whole week.

Although he couldn't make himself tell her straight out. She'd have glared at him and demanded an explanation without even opening her mouth. It was naturally easier to call her and tell her a little cursorily about an old, close friend from Syria who had just happened to turn up in Istanbul. She'd be busy with whatever she was up to at home and say something along the lines of, "Do as you like, Carl-Ivar. Just as long as you get home in one piece…" She probably wouldn't even sound put out. Possibly a hint of weary resignation in her voice, as to a child begging for candy.

She should have seen through him by now. But on the other hand – people see what they want to see.

Yeah, well, they weren't kids any more either, neither he nor Birgitta. Life has to be enjoyed for as long as it lasts, he thought gloomily as a sea breeze tickled his nose.

He was on the wrong side of sixty-five. He loved life. A lot. He had a lot to look forward to. He had to make sure to live life as wisely as possible and to watch out for that pot in his belly.

He suddenly felt that sidelong look from his wife again, and his dander rose. Her censorious gaze that had landed at the bottom of his bowl of creamy white yogurt at the hotel breakfast table. Mild and tasty, but too fatty here in Turkey. That's what the eyes had told him, he could read her mind with ease. The black olives and sun-dried tomatoes had, however, won her approval. He always made little piles on his pate, and she said nothing. Not about the cucumber sticks, feta cheese, and honey, either. Or the butter for that matter. Maybe she hadn't seen it.

But the bread was too flimsy, not fibrous enough. She'd gotten so upset that she tossed out a comment to whoever cared to listen: "Do you really not have any wholemeal bread in this place?"

That little word *really* had clung to him and disturbed him even now as he sat in peace and quiet on the ferry, stupidly enough. He should know better than to let her always-knows-best attitude eat away at him. As it was, he'd taken a sesame seed bun, poured himself a black coffee, and sat down at a brown varnished table for four. They'd eaten in silence. Her teeth clopped together, even though they weren't false.

As for Carl-Ivar, he adored these morning meals in Turkey.

The memory elicited a little cough as he sat there with the waves in front of him. As if in the end he wanted to cough away the image of his wife. But the irritation had already left something torn inside him.

Our lives persecute us, he thought philosophically as they were overtaken by a smaller, faster ferry. They're called sea buses here in Istanbul. The steely green water frothed richly along the hull and whipped up a half-fusty smell of seawater. The traffic on the

Marmara Sea was lively, with a continual shoal of boats crisscrossing their way to their destinations.

He scratched his neck with an index finger under his shirt collar and shifted his position, feeling all the while the soft bag against his body on the bench beside him.

He'd positioned himself so that no one could come between him and the bag. On the other side were the lashed-down lifeboats. When his hand left his collar it brushed quickly and almost imperceptibly over the front left side of his coat. He just wanted to make sure that the contents of his inside pocket were still there, which of course they were.

He then remained motionless until he had regained his self-control and could once again cope with the pleasure of passive sensuality. He had many nice things to get up to in his thoughts.

They were on their way to the Eminönü quayside in the heart of Istanbul. The ferry was traveling at a steady speed and made the slightest of yaws as he watched the waves. His thoughts whirled to a stop, ending up like dispersed leaves clinging stubbornly to their twigs despite the ravages of the autumn storms, until finally they too let go, dancing slowly to the ground. Fell to become leaf mold. Nature's eternal cycle, he thought dreamily.

Music pounded from a ferry that was just coming toward them. He started. Alas, that was the end of that pleasant drowsiness.

Instead, his wife, stupidly enough, popped up again. Perhaps it was a way for him to process things, as they said nowadays. To rearrange the soul, to stand to account, so that he could at last be free.

There was nothing really wrong with Birgitta, she was a capable and industrious person. He took it back. He heard for himself how this is exactly what he did. He took it back by defending her, thereby defending himself and his own frustration. And his own bad conscience.

He knew what he was up to, alright. He was someone who often spent time doing penance. If he was to show generosity toward her convictions, he could hope that she did the same. By being fair rather than black-and-white or judgmental in thought, he cleared his conscience. From experience he knew that this would make it easier for him to keep his wife at a distance. But without being cruel. He was not a cruel person. He refused to see himself as such, but as a person who radiated respect and honesty, generally speaking.

But without being too critical he could, in spite of everything, note that for the past few years quite a lot of their life together had revolved around what was good and healthy. What riled him especially was her passion for what was *not* wholesome. The unhealthy had taken on its own lure in her life. Something to nail herself down with, to condemn, like his youthful fornicating and boozing.

But one could, of course, wonder why he put so much time into getting himself into a lather about his wife's private mortal fears. She meant well, of course, with her exercise and low fat and fewer carbs. She wanted him to live as long as possible, too. The two of them, the rest of their lives on the same perch, like two old budgies. Should one die, the other would soon topple off to join it.

He gave a chuckle. Say what you will, a healthy lifestyle was a rather innocent occupation on the whole.

But now she wasn't here.

The sun, which had been slowly edging its way down, was still hot. His cheeks burned. He peered out over piercing reflections on the water. He could just possibly make out the Prince Islands on the horizon, since he knew their location. He then followed the coastline on the Asiatic side, until it dissolved and vanished into a steely green heat haze.

He sat there with a longing that already ached, which was undoubtedly why his thoughts headed off in the wrong direction – toward his wife. But he'd sort it out, After all, he had another few days to himself in Istanbul. A whole week, to be more accurate.

He was now on the way to dispersing the heavy clouds that had piled up in his life. It would cost him dearly, but it was worth it.

That would have to do for the time being. He'd have to work something out later.

The herd of American tourists that had been sitting beside him bleating loudly got up and went inside. At once his body settled down into an even deeper torpor. He was sitting comfortably, despite his being on a hard wooden bench. A reconciliatory mildness touched him. He succumbed to doziness again, a dreamlike tranquility that had his head bobbing to and fro before finally tipping backwards. His eyelids shut, his jaw fell open.

The boat glided onward. The clucking of the waves against the hull and the monotonous shrieks of the gulls lay now beyond the corporeal.

A heavy shadow had just fallen across carpet dealer Olsson.

CHAPTER 2

IT WAS A SATURDAY MORNING in May and Oskarshamn wallowed in white spring light. But the wind's tail was cool, and the air hadn't yet had time to warm up. Veronika Lundborg had found a sheltered spot on a bench in the middle of Flanaden, the only pedestrian street of the town center, and not a very long one at that. She sat leaning comfortably back with her legs splayed to make room for her belly, which swelled, huge and heavy. She was counting on sitting there a good long while in peace and quiet. Claes and Klara were off buying sandals. Klara had pleaded that *only* Daddy deal with this important purchase.

Kids, she thought.

The girl had, of course, worked out that her father was more compliant than she. With gentle eyes she'd watched them as they went their way, Klara skipping ahead and Claes looking down at their daughter, no doubt saying something funny while squeezing her hand a little tighter.

Veronika glowed inside before this trusting bonding between father and daughter, which was so strong as to be visible from the outside. Enjoy it! she told herself. The past winter had otherwise been a nightmare.

But that was then. She was no Doctor Death. She smiled crookedly at the thought. How easily pure madness could be elevated to truth. And in the small town world, mud quickly sticks to leave an indelible stain. She could hear them now: "You know, her, that doctor who killed that patient. Though I bet it was the husband, that corporate bigwig, and his lover, you know that pretty, young…"

But you had to be famous for something!

Cecilia, she thought then. The other tragedy. A day didn't go by without her thinking of Cecilia. The thoughts came in little portions. The anxiety that nagged, but also the relief that it had gone as well as it had. In spite of everything. But naturally she wished everything to be *exactly* as it was before. Almost wasn't enough.

She shut her eyes and bent her face upwards. The sun's rays rested gently on her skin and her features softened. She unbuttoned the neck of her ample top and laid a hand over the stove in her stomach. She could feel shifting, listless movements, mostly on the right-hand side. Soon her belly would be gone. She was neither scared nor particularly worried, just normally apprehensive. And curious, of course. The Caesarean was planned, everything under control, but major events should not pass without trace. A great strain came and went like holiday jitters, or the tingling harbinger of love.

Her last child, incontrovertibly so. She wasn't going to be like Sarah in Genesis, Abraham's wife who fell pregnant at a very old age. At least a hundred.

Just then she heard her cell phone vibrate. And so at last, the call she'd been waiting for and on one level hoping she'd be spared. She didn't even sigh when she fished the phone out of the tight trouser pocket and looked at the display. Yep, Cecilia.

Her throat suddenly burned, she cleared it and swallowed and pressed the phone against her ear, looking down at the pavement in order to concentrate better.

"Hi, sweetheart!" she said cheerfully.

"What are you up to?" wondered Cecilia tonelessly.

"Sitting on Flanaden, thinking of you," said Veronika, truthfully. "How about you?"

There was silence at the other end. Veronika regretted the question; why ask her daughter when she knew the answer only too well? But what could she say?

"Nothing special," answered Cecilia.

No, exactly. Nothing special. That was why she called. She called up just to pass the time in that uneventful and virtually desolate life that was hers since the tragic head injury. How long would it last? Forever, maybe? For life – it sounded awful.

Less than a year had passed since Cecilia was brutally knocked down one early dawn by a stranger in one of the more peaceable quarters of Lund. She'd probably been lying there a good while before a passerby had found her. That man Veronika had often silently thanked. She'd also, of course, thanked him in real life. He grew embarrassed, though moved, about saving the young woman, and equally tearful over their actually thanking him. You can't take being thanked for granted these days, he said.

All in all, there was a lot about Cecilia to be thankful for: that it didn't happen in the middle of the woods, that it was hours rather than days that she had lain defenselessly, that it had been August and the night relatively mild and not mid-winter with a bitterly cold, damp wind cutting through marrow and bone, like down in Skåne. Cecilia was rushed to the neurosurgical clinic at University Hospital in Lund. The best care imaginable just around the corner. Another stroke of luck. But nonetheless, things were as they were.

But why strike someone in the head, of all places?

To lay the victim out, naturally. To be sure that the injury is lasting, should the violence not be fatal.

The scarring on the scalp was no longer visible, her hair had regrown, blonde and thick, but they were just trifles in the bigger picture. What remained in all its pitiableness was that little difference, that which everyone who knew Cecilia before the accident found a tiny but nonetheless unfamiliar feature of her previously so complex and "normal" personality. We're like seismographs, thought Veronika. Detecting the slightest tremor in the earth's crust.

Brain injuries took time to heal, often years. Those two pallid hemispheres encased within a fragile skull were a source of fascination. No one who worked with the human body could think otherwise of this comparatively soft mass comprising densely packed nerve cells surrounded by connective tissue.

Have patience! she'd told herself, as she'd said thousands of times to her patients. The body needs time to heal. It was rarely as simple as replacing a nut or a screw.

Her phone grew hot against her ear. Eagerly, she furnished her daughter with assorted suggestions for how she could pass the day. Take a walk, try to read a book, go and buy a tasty treat and make some tea or coffee.

Cecilia breathed apathetically into her phone. Said effectively nothing at all. Just gave off some little passive whimpers.

"Maybe you could try going to the movies or watching a DVD?" said Veronika, unrelenting in her efforts to pepper her with suggestions.

"Naa… Can't be bothered."

"Why not?"

"It's just too much."

"But can't you call one of your friends?" Veronika managed at last.

Cecilia's lethargic breathing down the line.

"Like who?" she said, finally.

Jesus Christ! Had everyone given up on her? Cecilia had been such a popular girl!

And this raised a bitter question, one that Veronika had been putting off for a long time: What if these friends never came back? Seeing her child live like a recluse pained her. Deviant, odd, alone.

No!

But even an odd life was a life worth living, she thought then. Things weren't that bad, after all! And who has the right to judge? Humans are made to adapt, she'd seen it so many times – without breasts, colon, hair, or an arm or leg. Still, the thought was an unpleasant one.

Now she was making small talk. She could hear herself. Words, words, words. Sorting things and cheering up with a cheerful, steady voice. It somehow made things easier. She was doing what she was good at, even professional. But she should lower her voice. Soften, quieten down. My darling baby.

But when she aired her plans to move Cecilia to Oskarshamn so that she could support her more actively, her daughter had protested. She didn't want to, which was a blessing in a way. A momentary sign of recovery twinkled crystal clear.

And anyway, much could still happen, they'd said at the rehab clinic in Orup. The frontal lobes that controlled the ability to fine-tune social interaction were still developing well into the late twenties. Much of the personality was located there, too. It sounded comforting. Cecilia was only twenty-four.

When they hung up, Veronika was just as dispirited as she always was after talking to Cecilia. She stared vacantly ahead.

After a while, she pulled herself together and called Claes to ask if she should come and find them, but they were in the toy shop and hadn't even made it to the shoes, so he saw no reason for her to get up.

Kids! thought Veronika again.

"Make the best of it and take it easy, for Pete's sake," said Claes. "It might be your last chance for years. I promise…"

So she bought an ice cream from the cart beside her, sat down again, and bit pleasurably into the thick chocolate coating, splintering it into large chunks that she deftly caught with the tip of her tongue. Concealing itself underneath was creamy vanilla ice cream, rich and filling. The ice cream was simply too big, the calories would settle on completely the wrong places, especially now when she was less mobile. Then again, no one was making her eat the whole thing. But she was only human!

Once she'd thrown the stick into the trash can, she grew bored and wondered whether she should saunter off to the carpet shop to ask if the rug she'd brought in for repair had been returned. They'd probably have called or texted her, but you never knew. It would be nice to have everything ready before the baby arrived.

But no. She couldn't summon the energy to get up. It wasn't a big rug, but rather a prayer mat that even she, with her heavy body, could carry without difficulty. It came from Claes's family home. She'd found it rolled up amongst his moving boxes when they'd move in together. He hadn't wanted it on the floor of his ultra-modernly furnished bachelor pad, but she fell for it immediately – there was something poignant about its threadbare pile and faded colors, so she rolled it out onto the upstairs hallway. Where it had lain until the edge started to fray so badly that she caught her toe in the warp and almost fell flat on her face.

"It's a shame it's so shabby," she said.

"Chuck the horrible old thing," said Claes without hesitation.

It wasn't that she knew anything about rugs, but she couldn't bring herself to throw it out. It had come a long way and had a long history, perhaps it was worth having it valued just for the sake of it? She asked Birgitta Olsson, a nurse at the clinic, what she thought. And she didn't think anything. Rugs were her husband's province, not hers: "But it wouldn't hurt to take it to the shop and let Carl-Ivar have a look at it."

Carpet dealer Carl-Ivar Olsson was a genial fellow, one of those older gentlemen that she so readily fell for. Perhaps because he reminded her of her father.

Olsson's eyes had lit up when he saw the rug. It was an antique, he said, and that meant it was over a hundred years old. "No way!" she blurted out. He asked where she'd got it from, and she told him what she knew of the rug's provenance, and that went no further back than her husband's family. There were many fine mats in Sweden, he said then, owing to our early contacts with the Orient. At the end of the nineteenth century and into the early twentieth, Swedes helped to build railways and bridges, or started industries and erected public administrations in many countries to the east. It wasn't always possible for them to take out the money they'd earned, and so they invested in rugs and carpets that they brought home to Sweden. It therefore became fashionable in the better class of home to cover the floor in huge, expensive Oriental carpets or to dress the walls of the gentlemen's studies with Turkish *kilims*.

The carpet dealer seemed to have oceans of time, and Veronika was in no hurry either on that day when she'd handed in her prayer mat for repair. She'd sat down in the cozy little shop that stood on a corner with windows facing two directions, while he'd told her that the rug was a typical prayer mat – that was obvious by the large central section, called the prayer niche, which in this case was so worn from use that the pile had almost been rubbed away. This was definitely not to be remedied. The prayer section was of a beautiful turquoise, and if she stroked the side gently with her fingertips where there was a little pile left, she'd feel that it was angled from the feet up to the head. This indicated that it was a Turkish rug, said the carpet dealer. Persian prayer mats had the pile facing the other direction. He guessed that the rug came from a village somewhere near Sivas, a town in central Anatolia. Turkey, that is. He had a large map on the wall, and pointed obligingly to the location, and Veronika tried to make a mental note of it. It was as if the rug had acquired even more life than it already had. The carpet dealer stroked the pile with the same soft hands as a cat lover stokes fur, the only difference being that the rug didn't start purring. Surrounding the prayer niche were rows of borders in yellow, warm red, and lime green. The colors harmonized exquisitely, he wanted to say.

"Repairing the damaged section won't be a problem at all," Olsson explained. "Repairs will lend the rug character and this little beauty is definitely worth spending some money on… Not necessarily because it's valuable in monetary terms, which, incidentally, I believe it is, but mainly because of its splendor."

For a moment, Veronika had felt like someone on *Antiques Roadshow*. Naturally it was on the tip of her tongue to ask just *how* much the rug might be worth. But she didn't, and so didn't get the chance to sputter an astonished, "Wow, that much! Who would've guessed?"

Rugs are personal, and one should own them out of affection. Also, Oriental rugs make a great pairing with Nordic pine furniture, said Olsson, and she agreed and recalled suddenly how Claes's greedy little brother had tried to lay his hands on the rug a while ago, claiming that it was a waste to have it lying in the upstairs hall where no one could see it. It would go better on the floor of his study at home, he said.

Ha!

But that time even Claes had become wary and refused. Not least to put his little brother in his place. He didn't want Markus to think that he could wrap everyone around his little finger. And of course there was also Liljan standing yapping in the background. The sister-in-law, who was always sniffing around for a freebie.

Veronika arched her back and adjusted her waistband, which was cutting into her. She was disgustingly full, verging on nauseous. Damn ice cream! Everything was too big these days. Cinnamon buns, muffins, and tubs of popcorn at the movies. They were living in the era of surplus, surfeit, and obesity. She could find many perfect examples, herself excluded, without difficulty, just by looking around. They often talked about it at work. About how fat caused problems. It was much trickier, technically speaking, to operate on fat people, and anesthetizing them was not without its risks. There were more short and long-term complications. And it was nothing to shrug off. It was serious.

And really sad to think about. So instead she stared straight into a shop window, yearning for her skinny jeans.

At that moment she noticed the reflection of someone she knew. He all but crept past her behind the bench, clearly trying to make himself as invisible as he could. She turned her head unmercifully. Narrow but heavy purple plastic bags hung from each hand. The telltale clinking of bottle against bottle.

Göran Bladh. He knew that she'd spotted him, she could tell by the way he walked. He hurried his steps, which he was able to without looking as though he was fleeing.

But it wasn't her life he was ruining, Veronika thought. What he was doing was just so unnecessary and tragic. Well-dressed, good job, nice-looking, and interesting to talk to. Well, up till now at least. And that was exactly what she had said to him the last time he was in for pancreatitis.

"Someone has to say it. Your inflamed pancreas can't take any more. I know you know that. But you have a life to live," she told him, holding his gaze.

It was so worthless and pointless and demoralizing talking to alcoholics. Like talking to deaf ears, she knew that. But still, she wanted it said. For her own sake, perhaps. Because trying to save a person made her fingers itch.

"The life I have to live is not yours," he retorted dryly. "Maybe it'll be shorter. Can you respect that?"

Sure, she thought. No problem. She was only a doctor – as, incidentally, was he – not a savior. But she didn't say that. Antabuse, the twelve-step program, and alcohol rehab had no effect on him, he said. So there, now she knew! Poor thing.

And his job was obviously swimming along. Many days off sick, but according to the rumors not as many as one would have thought. He not only had numerous lives, like a cat, but also several overdrive gears. They probably turned a blind eye at the clinic, good radiologists were few and far between. He was skilled and engaged when on the right side of life and held himself erect. This was the upper-class alcoholic's suicide precipice. The polished façade.

She watched him as he hurried off to Besväret, the pretty area of old houses overlooking the harbor. He lived enviably well, not exactly under a damp tarp in the harbor. The question was how long he'd be able to hold down his job without making any serious blunders. He was not the only one he was responsible for.

No, she had to get up and move around, the small of her back ached. She rose laboriously and decided to visit the carpet dealer's shop after all.

CHAPTER 3

ANNELIE DAUN SAT BEHIND the plush walnut table with its gracefully carved legs that served as both counter and writing desk. She was reading, a language course in Italian. Barely audibly she mumbled phrases to herself, over and over again, as if unwilling to break the silence. The traffic outside wasn't noisy. Hardly a car drove past.

She'd put on some tight, small-checkered trousers in old pink and pistachio green, and a short-sleeved cotton blouse in a matching coral tone. She'd even ironed it this morning, and its cotton was soft and smooth. She felt pretty, yet smart. She made an effort, even though customers wouldn't be flooding into the shop. If, that is, anyone came at all. She dressed up mainly for her own sake.

The Italian phrases were starting to bore her. She broke off her studies, took a mirror out of her natural leather Mulberry bag, and applied her shocking pink lip gloss. She also managed a quick glance at her freckly nose, peaking out from under her blonde fringe. The sun had done its job, as Carl-Ivar would have said if he hadn't been in Turkey. He said things like that without sounding at all flirty or dirty-old-mannish. She looked *fresh and healthy*, she confirmed to herself with self-content, but that expression would never pass the lips of Carl-Ivar. In his world, fresh might refer to lettuce leaves or cut flowers. She'd been to the hairdresser's earlier in the week, and her hair was soft and shoulder-length, and cut in layers. She ran her finger through it so that it fell back a little less flat.

It was a Saturday, so she'd not be staying in the shop all day. Her neighbor had promised to pick her up at just after two. "Us country folk help each other out, of course I can give you a lift," Birthe had said when she'd called last night. If she locked up at one o'clock even, she'd have time to do a bit of window shopping until Birthe turned up. Her own car was at the mechanic's with a dead engine. Luckily it had managed to cough and splutter all the way there, sparing her the inconvenience of calling a tow truck.

The carpet shop was on a corner, and so the daylight fell agreeably in from two directions. The building was from the last century and had atmosphere, a pleasant feel that put her in a good mood every morning when she unlocked the door and stepped inside.

The table where Annelie sat was turned toward the door and the two windows. Behind her was a wall decorated with rugs, and on the floor was a low shelving unit containing heavy volumes, most in English, with gorgeous pictures of flat-woven and knotted rugs and carpets from all four corners of the globe. She could lose herself for hours thumbing through these magnificent tomes. What the human hand – and when it came to rugs and carpets primarily the female human hand – had managed to achieve was nothing short of miraculous.

Where the bookshelf ended, a spiral staircase descended to the storeroom. The premises were not that large, but altogether surveyable and cozy.

Annelie raised her head and looked out. The street corner was partly shaded, but the sun still managed to poke a bright finger of light through half of one of the shop windows, so she'd laid out some protective paper over the rugs to prevent them bleaching. She left her desk and walked over to adjust the brown paper, wondering whether she should switch the radio on, but the silence was addictive. She almost ate silence as her favorite dish. It was her years of failure as a substitute teacher in boisterous classrooms that more or less had made her nauseous and that had made her a little more careful about what she subjected herself to.

She stood now a little indecisive, her arms folded over her chest, gazing out the window. People in light shoes, their coats off. She smiled and turned back into the shop while trying to memorize some Italian. The phrases had completely slipped out of her mind. This happened only too frequently. She made an effort to retrieve a few words and join them together into a sentence, but pretty much all she got was a verbal risotto. She realized that she'd never learn to speak Italian with any real success. And yet on she struggled. Some projects, stupidly enough, were harder to let go of, she thought and watched as some specks of dust danced in the illuminated air.

Should she get the duster out? No, the cleaning was quickly done and could wait until Monday so that everything would be nice for Carl-Ivar's return on the Tuesday. Even though he didn't happen to be the kind to notice if the place was freshly cleaned or not, it would feel good to have it newly done.

The shop's décor was simple, in order to help bring out the rugs and carpets. A terracotta tiled floor and white walls, that was all. The exhaust fumes that percolated through were moderate. It wasn't the most heavily trafficked street in town that Carl-Ivar's shop lay on, but everyone knew where it was. At least everyone who needed a beautiful floor covering of top quality, or who wanted to bring in a worn beloved one for repairs.

It wasn't as if the shop was packed floor-to-ceiling with rugs. Nor were there any stacked in large piles down in the basement, even though there were quite a few there. Instead, the rugs were hung with discrimination on the white walls or draped over the staircase banister. So there weren't that many, but what there was, was of high quality. No rubbish had ever found its way in.

Once upon a time, when Olsson's carpet shop was housed in larger premises on Köpmannagatan, it was another story. But now that Carl-Ivar had retired and had a little something put aside in the bank, she suspected, he had the carpet shop mainly for the sheer pleasure of it. For fun, he once told Annelie, who was probably the only person who really understood him, he'd said. His wife wasn't that crazy about rugs and his grown-up children preferred bare floors. It's like the cobbler's children. But since rugs hadn't shaped her childhood, she could enjoy them even more.

Rugs were undeniably more than just decorative. You built up a completely different relationship with a rug than you did with a… Windsor chair, for example. She'd thought about that many a time, despite being very partial to chairs herself, particularly old ones.

She tried to read up about them, when she wasn't at Carl-Ivar's carpet school. He never lectured, preferring to portion out a little of his knowledge of rugs and carpets now and again when the moment took him, like when they had received a rug or carpet for repairs. But he was careful not to overdo it. It was a sensitive matter, especially with the customers, many of whom might easily feel that they were being lectured. They wanted to see themselves as specialists, particularly if they were collectors. And the collectors were more in number than one might imagine, and usually men. I guess that's how it is when big bucks are involved, thought Annelie.

The oldest known preserved knotted rug, the Pazyryk Rug, was 2,500 years old and had been found frozen in the Siberian ice – which is why it had survived for so long. Nomad women had been the ones to develop the art of knotting rugs to have something to hang on walls and lay on floors as protection against the cold. But they also could not help making the rugs pleasing to the eye. A sense of the attractive and beautiful must be an inherited human characteristic, thought Annelie. The women cut wool from sheep and goats, spun it and colored it with natural dyes, and then tied or wove it as they saw fit or in accordance with their tribe's particular nomadic traditions. The patterns were handed down from generation to generation.

Since the Oriental rugs originated from widely disparate areas, from the Balkan Peninsula all the way to China, their appearance, for obvious reasons, varied greatly. If nothing else, it was an adventure in itself to be able to look at a rug or a carpet and guess where it came from. This took as much knowledge as experience. These days, Annelie yearned to go out into the world to get to see rugs in their true settings.

On the free floor space in front of her in the shop lay a typical medallion "tribal rug" of varying shades of madder red and indigo. It was a Hamadan rug, made in one of the countless villages around the city of Hamadan in northwest Iran, the country's largest carpet-knotting district. These rugs were highly popular, and sturdy and hard-wearing to boot. Nowadays, synthetically colored yarns were often used instead of naturally dyed, said Carl-Ivar, who didn't think it actually mattered that much. People started synthetically coloring the yarns back in the 1860s, and such a synthetic yarn could be just as beautiful as its vegetable counterpart. Both could run, or bleed as one said, depending on how they were made. The warp of modern Hamadan rugs was often cotton rather than wool, Annelie had also learned. It was also rare to find cotton warps in nomad rugs since the women had to make do with what was at hand, which was the wool from their own herds. They were self-subsistent or lived on barter; either way, they generally lacked the hard cash to buy cotton thread.

Hamadan rugs were manufactured as a rule in only two sizes. On her tiled floor lay the smaller "Zaronum" variety. The larger "Dozar" carpets were big enough for a living room. The rug that she stepped on daily was robust and able to take a lot of wear and tear. She liked it. Better to have a sturdy, knotted Oriental rug in the hall, was her advice to customers who popped into the shop. She particularly recommended them to the parents of young children who needed something to trap gravel and mud. A better alternative was not to be found. Easy to look after, hardy and beautiful, too.

The Oriental rugs could be divided into three categories depending on the circumstances of their manufacture: nomad rugs, tribal rugs, and urban or workshop rugs, which were also known as factory rugs. Unlike tribal rugs, which were often woven or knotted in the home, the workshop rugs were knotted in factories. The largest rug and carpet country was Iran, the former Persia. Annelie could still hear people say "Persian rug" when talking about Oriental rugs in general.

Another large rug country was Turkey, where Carl-Ivar was at this very moment. The collective name for rugs knotted there was Anatolian.

That rugs and carpets were the bearers of culture was easy to see. Anyone visiting Olsson's carpet shop understood that to be the case practically the moment they stepped inside. A rug purchase was not supposed to be a hasty affair. Naturally, it was perfectly acceptable for customers to take rugs home and roll them out to see if they matched their furniture. Annelie had learned that Oriental rugs go well virtually everywhere. If customers couldn't find what they were looking for, Carl-Ivar would promise to keep his eyes peeled to see what he could get his hands on. There was little that couldn't be ordered. The carpet dealer also had a warehouse, the location of which Annelie was still slightly uncertain of. He'd never taken her there, and this had, of course, fired her curiosity.

Annelie was surprised at how much she thoroughly enjoyed looking after rugs, answering the phone and delivering orders. Perhaps because it wasn't particularly stressful. The rest of the day she could devote to her thoughts. She was no "thousand irons in the fire" kind of person. She'd once believed that she was in her eagerness to be a young woman on the go. It was one of the conditions of her generation. To slave away for the reward of intervening indolence. But her body preferred a more even trot.

She was just about to start fantasizing about M – she could already feel the physical thrill of his touch – when she saw a woman slowly waddle toward the door. Her gait was precariously tilted backwards owing to an enormous pregnant stomach. Annelie recognized her, it was Veronika Lundborg who opened the door and puffed and panted into the shop.

"I brought in a rug for repair," she said, collapsing as she did so onto the German Chippendale chair that stood conveniently by the door.

Annelie knew exactly which rug she was talking about, a threadbare but lovely Sivas from Central Anatolia.

"Is it ready?"

"Afraid not."

"No matter. I was passing and just thought I'd pop in and ask."

Annelie nodded, but found it hard to believe that someone with a belly like that went anywhere at all unless they absolutely had to. She was sitting like a swollen inflatable doll there on the chair. Annelie tried not to stare at her belly, an exercise just as hopeless as avoiding a nose that was flaming red or blue. And yet it was somehow alluring. Annelie hadn't yet been subjected to that kind of physical deformity. Unfortunately.

Veronika sat motionless for half a minute just gazing at the walls.

"Nice place."

"It is, isn't it," said Annelie with a smile.

"I could sit here forever, but I guess I'd better toddle off. You'll get in touch when it comes in?"

Annelie promised, and Veronika groaned herself up from the chair and shuffled out through the door, but as she reached the second step down a man appeared on the pavement wanting to go in.

So the door opened and closed again.

Jeepers, we're busy today, thought Annelie. Before her stood a man with strikingly pale blue eyes.

"Is Carl-Ivar Olsson here?" he asked unsmilingly.

Veronika paused in Lilla Torget Square and took out her new sunglasses. A pair of Ray-Bans, the classic Wayfarer model that had come back into fashion and that suited her.

She set off for the mall again. Her visit to the carpet shop had been a waste of time, but pleasant. If Claes and Klara hadn't dawdled so much she wouldn't have gone. But she felt that she'd been sitting for such a long time that passersby might have started thinking she'd made a home for herself there on the bench on Flanaden.

On Västra Torggatan she bumped into Birgitta Olsson, and told her that she'd just been into her husband's shop, although she'd not met him but a young woman instead.

"Carl-Ivar's in Turkey," said Birgitta Olsson.

That explained it. They stood there chatting for a while, Veronika's swollen legs the cause of constant pain. Birgitta Olsson, by contrast, was a lithe and nimble woman and was probably in better shape than Veronika, even without the belly, despite being fifteen years older.

"Seize the day, as they say," said Birgitta suddenly, and gave a broad grin that prettified her finely defined wrinkles.

"That's exactly what I'm doing," laughed Veronika and thought how strange it was that certain people could say certain platitudes without it sounding in the slightest bit silly.

"When's it due?" wondered Birgitta in a maternal tone of voice that spread a warmth through Veronika.

"In a week. Caesarean in Kalmar."

"Lovely. Then you'll soon have your hands full. Good luck!"

Birgitta nodded and vanished into a shop on the corner that sold sporting goods. She needed to buy some new running shoes, she said.

Veronika was unhappy to see that the bench was full, so she sought out another, a little further east where Flanaden crossed Östra Torggatan to then merge with Besvärsgatan, which with its cobblestones and wonky, picturesque wooden houses represented a totally different epoch.

She collapsed onto the bench. Now she had a different view to survey.

There was no traffic to speak of on Besvärsgatan, which ended in a series of steps that climbed down the cliff face to the harbor. Veronika could at least see two figures that came from that direction, a man and a woman who could hardly be said to belong to the upper echelons of society. She recognized the man, who'd come into A&E a few years ago, high on something and causing havoc; the woman was younger and had a long-haired Alsatian that lumbered by her side on a loose leash.

Why do they always have to have such big dogs, these druggies? she thought. The couple made their way toward the park.

A kick inside her broke her train of thought. She rested her hand on her belly and felt how it bulged. A foot, or a hand. She curled her lips up in a stately and self-centered maternal smile.

Just then, Claes called to inform her that they had just started to buy the sandals. Their trip to the toy store had taken longer than expected, he said, a shade apologetically.

"No problem," she said generously. It was pointless to stress when it wasn't absolutely necessary.

The creature within gave another kick. She wasn't worried, a scheduled Caesarean was all ready to go. There'd been no quibbling, bearing in mind, above all, her age, and the relative stiffness of the pelvis, presumably. And besides, Klara had been born by Caesarean, but that hadn't been planned. The placenta had become detached. *Ablatio placentae.*

Many minor reasons converged to become a major, significant decision. That was how Veronika interpreted the obstetrician's judgment, and neither she nor Claes had cause to think otherwise.

Forty-seven, next year. She was "the mature mother."

They didn't say it aloud, but she suspected that the comments were primed and ready as soon as she was out of earshot. She would certainly have come out with similar opinions, back when she only had Cecilia and was young and knew best. A long time before she met Claes and became the mature mother, who, in spite of this, was now asserting her raison d'être.

Her thoughts passed to Cecilia. To when she was born one late night toward dawn at Karolinska Hospital in Stockholm. Veronika was twenty-three, a biologically favorable age for childbirth. She wasn't anxious that time, either. Hadn't the good sense to be. And it went fine the normal way, even though she'd been surprised at how much it hurt.

But still the opinions came. It was irresponsible of her to have a baby in the middle of her studies, she was informed. She sat there with her newborn daughter at her breast and tried to defend herself. Was told that one made a better parent with a little more maturity. So said her mother-in-law. What do you want me to do? she wanted to retort. You surely don't mean that I should get rid of her?

She remembered. Of course she did, for who forgets their births? In particular, they came to her as an almost physical sensation every time Cecilia or Klara had a birthday. The bewildering joy and pride. "You're a mom now," the midwife had said as she lay alone with her arms embracing Cecilia's naked body. The words made her cry. She was a mom.

But she also remembered the piercing, dark forlornness, which took its time melting. Where the father was that long night she lay in labor she didn't know. It was before the time of cell phones. And he was probably too drunk and tired to read the note that lay on the kitchen table once he'd stumbled home. He later claimed that he hadn't seen it.

Could she forgive him for not being there? She thought so, at first. Trusted in the gentle influence of reconciliation. And in time. She so wanted them to be a family of three, not of two. It had never struck her that two could also be a family.

But Dan continued to let her down more than she had the energy to forgive. She could still feel a little cold twist in her soul when she thought of those times. Almost enough for her to need to console herself. It was strangely mixed. A multi-colored confetti. Hard and heavy and black, and then the rose-red pride, joy, and happiness. Why yes, she was happy. Too happy.

This time, though, she wasn't alone. Just over-aged.

Before she'd taken her parental leave, she'd met a patient who lodged herself in the happy corner of her memory. The woman was a little over ninety and remarkably astute. She saw Veronika's belly stick out from under the green smock. They were in one of the smaller treatment rooms of the A&E clinic. The nurse had called Veronika there since she'd operated on the patient the week before, for the sake of continuity.

"So you're expecting," the woman said amicably. "A joyful event!"

Veronika nodded and smiled. She sat on an adjustable stainless steel stool by the bed where the patient lay, her stomach bared. The woman had undergone a stomach operation to remove parts of her small intestine, and she'd pulled through well. But now she had a palm-sized area below her naval that was a shocking red and warm, and that fluctuated and throbbed. An infection. The pus must out, as a good old maxim went.

Veronika removed some staples that she'd closed the edges of the wound with and drew some local anesthetic up into a syringe while, stupidly, blurting out that she was not exactly of child-bearing age. To be honest. Which the patient didn't need to know. It wasn't her, the doctor, whom they were meant to be focusing on.

"You'll manage, believe me," said the patient encouragingly. "In the old days it was almost shameful to expect a child at a late age. At least it is not like that now, thank the Lord."

Veronika carefully opened the wound with forceps. As the pus drained away, the pain receded. It reeked. She wiped away the gooey mess and pressed lightly on the swelling so that it emptied completely. A pleasant calm spread through the room.

"'Bringing mongoloid children into the world, whatever next!' That's what we used to say," continued the woman.

"You actually said that?"

"By golly, yes. When I got *in the family way* with a new chap I was over forty, you know. We didn't have the same methods of examination then as we do now. It was my first child… and my only, as it turned out. Abortion was also out of the question; it wasn't allowed unless under very special circumstances, that is. If you had mental issues or something. And mentally challenged, I was not. We were very happy, my husband and I."

Veronika could hear the obstinate blend of unadulterated joy and hope that lives beyond all anxiety and humiliation. She could hear something else, too, and hoped that the nurse wouldn't burst in and break the spell.

"The girl was christened Stina. She was a source of much delight for her parents."

Her eyes glittered like crystals under the diaphanous eyelids. And then the woman drew up short, as if she needed to catch her breath.

"And, well, sure enough she had Down's syndrome, as one says nowadays."

Her tone was lingering, and told Veronika that she had spoken those words many times, but had never felt really comfortable doing so.

"Stina passed away ten years ago from a congenital heart disease."

Veronika nodded almost imperceptibly. Silence hovered in the room and descended softly. They were still waiting for the dressings.

"Yes, it was a difficult time. How we missed her, my husband and I."

CHAPTER 4

ILYAS BANK CAST A GLANCE over the guardrail. It would've been impossible for anyone on board to miss the busy sea traffic. Small, high-speed ferries zigzagged between the larger vessels that lay still in the seaway as they waited to enter the Bosporus, the narrow strait leading into the Black Sea that he himself had just passed through.

He sold tea on the ferry; it was afternoon and he was starting to feel tired. But still his working day was far from over.

He filled the samovar with a practiced hand and switched it on for a new round of hot drinks. He then dipped the used small, tulip-shaped glasses crammed onto the tray into the sink, fished them quickly out again and placed them on a rack hanging on the wall to drip dry. He nodded in passing to Ergün, who, finding himself with an empty counter in front of his *kiosk*, could slip out at last from his booth to light a cigarette by the railing.

Ergün motioned that he wanted company. Ilyas didn't smoke, but went amenably to join him, his arms folded over his chest. Across the water they could see the city with its eroded quarters and the huge cupolas, one after the other, and all the slender minarets that pointed heavenward.

They said nothing. They didn't feel the need to.

The air vibrated, ever more saturated with diesel and exhaust fumes the closer they sailed to the quayside in Eminönü. The tourists, herd animals that they were, had already risen from their seats and shuffled off stemwards to make sure to disembark first. They were standing in clusters now, watching the approach. But some remained behind. A tall, well-built man in a white cap, who looked American, rose from his seat and wandered around until he leaned his hands against the guardrail so that Ilyas and Ergün could only see his back before he left the spot and continued fore. Three young women, obviously Turkish, stood in a little knot wearing thin coats and headscarves of the same checkered pattern but different color scales: a pink, a turquoise, and one that tended more toward lilac. They had all chosen matching makeup and were probably sisters, thought Ilyas. They were hot.

He returned his gaze to the sea and looked at the enormous Sülaimaniya Mosque and the Blue Mosque, with its six lean minarets, and between them the alleyways of the bazaar quarter scrambling up the hillside.

The berth was tight. The ferries lay hull to hull, as though hitched together in several rows out into the water. On the quayside, the chaotic throng was almost impenetrable, and the perpetual smell of grilled fresh fish was spread by the wind. At the quay edge, the terminals of the different ferry companies jostled together all the way to the Galata Bridge, which spanned the Golden Horn. Up on the bridge he could see a swarm of heads and fishing rods with their lines dangling in the water.

"The Golden Horn, it's a strange name when you think about it," said Ilyas eventually to break the silence. He was in a chatty mood.

"It's actually a broad estuary that goes in there, not a bay. I've heard that the name comes from the way seafarers were once so rich that they threw gold and shiny objects into the sea."

Ilyas fell silent. He wasn't sure if Ergün was mocking him or not.

Ergün flicked his cigarette.

"I don't know if it's true, though," he continued.

"Why do it?"

Ergün shrugged.

"Perhaps to show their gratitude to Allah for having arrived safely."

Ilyas decided not to believe everything that guy said, simultaneously regretting that he had shared his plans with Ergün. All the wonderful places, one after the other, that he intended to visit. Or move to for good. *If* he managed to scrape together the money, that is, here in Istanbul.

"How's the money situation?" asked Ergün, as if reading his thoughts.

"Not brilliant," answered Ilyas truthfully. "But I haven't been working for so long…"

"What's wrong with this place, anyway?" said Ergün, nodding out over the water. "You can stay here, no?"

"Nothing at all. Not a single thing wrong, except for the fact that it's absurdly expensive," Ilyas hastened to say, and felt that grindingly uncomfortable sensation that always sprang up as soon as they discussed his future plans.

Ergün obviously thought he should control himself and not let his imagination run away with him, and it made him feel callow and stupid, at the same time as he refused to let go of his faith in the future and its possibilities.

And, anyway, he didn't want to control himself. But it was impossible to get the money together. The frustration was magnificent. You had to walk blind through Beyoğlu's shopping district to avoid being sucked in. Hip t-shirts, cool shoes, and the latest cell phones. But everything cost far too much. Nothing for him. Not now.

But it was still hard to resist the temptations, and his money ran through his fingers. And his panic rose at the same pace. How was he going to make ends meet? Especially as he'd made his mind up to put a bit aside for his future departure.

It suddenly struck him just how simple and cheap everything at home in his village was. He said this to Ergün.

"Go home then!" said Ergün with a lopsided grin.

But going back wasn't in his game plan, not to the little village in eastern Turkey by the banks of the Tigris. Even if the memory of how they played by the river in the summer did feel nice and homely right now.

The village came to him now and then, strangely enough, even though he tried hard not to think backwards. As if his homesickness did as it wanted. He found a creeping comfort in seeing the huddle of dilapidated houses in front of him, the ancient settlement nestling in the river valley between steep rocky slopes. The road dust that whirled and constantly lodged itself in the nostrils, the thistles and dry grasses that doggedly survived in the cracked earth under the heat of the summer sun. In the evenings as darkness fell, lights could be seen glowing cozily in the caves where people still lived. By day, it was the satellite dishes that shone instead, like large white plates outside the cave mouths, announcing that the place had not been abandoned. People had been settled here for thousands of years. "The caves are cool in the summer and easy to heat in the winter," his mother often said dreamily. She remembered. Unlike the cheap buildings that the mayor had had erected in the village. "But one shouldn't complain," she also said.

Ilyas stood now a little embarrassed beside Ergün. A gentle sea breeze stoked his face. He thought of how he and his friends had sat in the Internet café, dreaming of a life beyond the mountains. How they practiced their English. Tossed hellos and how-nices to each other, so eager they could leave the stagnant existence with the old people and the goats and the spinsters, the ones that were never married off, and who had no choice but to bend to the life offered them. But the friends had Istanbul in their sights, or one of the larger resorts on the south coast: Alanya, Antalya, or Side.

His friends' faces fluttered past. He wondered what had become of some of them. He had mail contact with two, who had made it no further than Diyarbakir. It all hinged on getting a job. They had boasted about relatives around the world who would give them the world's best opportunities. They surfed the net and whipped up their dreams as soon as they had a little money to their names.

In the summers they arrived. The relatives, the ones who'd made it. They sat behind the steering wheels of glistening cars without dents or scratches in the bodywork. Mercedes, Audi, the latest Volvo. They'd driven through Europe, from Germany or Scandinavia. Home to their village to show themselves off.

Ilyas had hardly dared to even breathe that he wanted to venture further than one of Turkey's cities. He was looking at the USA or Germany. Or Sweden. Not Switzerland. Up there in the north he had relatives. It was good there, they'd said. Peaceful and clean and nice and most people had their own car. He might even be able to study at a university if he came up, said his cousins in Sweden.

"I want to go to Sweden," he suddenly heard himself say to Ergün. Talking about going to the USA would still be taking things a bit far.

Ergün looked at him from the corner of his eye, as if skeptical.

"Oh yes, and how do you think that'll happen?"

"My cousin Miro who lives in southern Sweden says it would be a good place for me to live."

"If you say so…"

"He's got a sister, who's also a cousin of mine and she's really pretty," continued Ilyas eagerly.

"Really," said Ergün. "And you're counting on getting married to her?"

Ilyas fell silent. He wasn't the only one to have thought of that. That the two of them would be a good match, but that probably didn't interest Ergün, he thought, and dropped the entire line of reasoning, which didn't really interest him that much, anyway. He didn't feel like getting married at all right now.

Everything depended on the English, he'd been led to understand. Without English you'd get nowhere. He worked hard at it, practicing on the tourists on the ferry. Naturally, he stumbled along and had to search feverishly for words, but most things resolved themselves with a good laugh, and he was quick to laugh. He noticed that people liked him. Making contact was therefore easy.

He was a good tea seller. One of the best they'd ever had on the ferry, joked Ergün, but he mainly said that to ingratiate himself. A little over three months had passed since he'd arrived in Istanbul. Three whole months in the heart of the action.

"You've at least got the water now," said Ergün, spitting over the railing.

"Hmm…"

It was true. He had the water. The Sea of Marmara and the Golden Horn and the Bosporus, through which he'd passed so many times by now that he'd lost count. The busiest straits in the world, which separated Europe and Asia and which even cleaved the throbbing city in two. The ferry made six stops on its route into the Black Sea before turning back. The boat trips were packed with tourists, his bread and butter, the ones that bought tea.

The engines eased off further. The gulls screeched in flocks overhead, the city din neared: streetcar wheels squealing, car horns blaring, and engines roaring, propelling themselves uphill.

Ergün had finished his cigarette long ago and flipped the butt overboard. They had remained standing.

"I guess we'd better get back to it," said Ergün at last.

They separated. Ilyas continued to bustle around, picking up tea glasses that people had left behind on seats and tables out on the deck and in the lounges.

He was grateful for the job. He really was. One day, after a long, slow month living partly off his sister and her husband out in the suburb, a relative had stepped in and offered it to him. For almost two months, he'd glided around among the tourists with his round tray balanced high on one hand, the tea sloshing around in tulip-shaped glasses, each on its own little saucer accompanied by a sugar cube. Piping hot China or apple tea, which were very popular here in Istanbul.

His white shirt was sticky under the arms and his collar chafed, but the fabric stayed clear of his body since he had put on a thin vest underneath. It was his sister who one morning threw him a bunch of freshly laundered cotton vests that would soak up the worst of the sweat. His sister was keen for him to look neat. He was as well, as far as this was achievable given the hectic job that he had.

He'd been to the barber's and tidied his neckline, but hadn't yet used the pass for a rather seedy gym near where his sister lived out in Avcilar. It pained him to fork out a bunch of money that they could only dream of back home in his village. He didn't have the heart to use the card, even though he liked to keep in shape. Carrying trays wasn't enough, even if his legs were taken to the limit of their endurance by his working the deck from morning to night.

They berthed at last. He watched the backs of the last passengers disappearing up the quay. And then a brief calm descended, before the next human cargo boarded.

But then he spotted a lingerer, a man sitting slumped on a bench that ran along the port guardrail, apparently asleep. He'd probably drunk too much raki or beer in the heat. It was easily done for some people, Ilyas had learned, and he sauntered off to wake the passenger up.

The man was seated as far aft as was possible on the long wooden bench, next to a frapped lifeboat, against which he was leaning like a sack of potatoes. A well-groomed gentleman, he looked like a German, with sunburned fair skin and thin ash-blonde hair, neatly trimmed at the neck. His head had lolled forwards and his slumber looked heavy. He was wearing light summer trousers, a beige poplin jacket, and a pair of brown shoes of a sporty design that few men of his age wore in Turkey.

All this was storing itself in Ilyas's memory while he hoped that the loiterer was not too drunk to prop up along the gangway and tip onto the quay without his taking it upon himself to tumble into the water. At worst, as he was already planning, he'd have to ask some of the sailors for help carrying him off. This wouldn't be the first time. There was always an element of reluctance in this task, mostly because the sight of these drunken gentlemen who were unable to grow old with dignity was both embarrassing and pathetic. The last one he'd helped off had even urinated in his pants. He would never get like that! he thought.

At that moment he saw something else far more worrisome. He had just lifted the tourist's arm to shake life back into him when his eyes landed on the breast of the man's pale blue shirt. A cascade of dark red blood had drenched virtually the entire shirtfront.

Ilyas blinked and snatched his hand back as if he'd just burned himself on a hot pot. At least five long seconds passed. Perplexed, horrified, and appalled, he stood as erect as a pole while his heart pounded.

But he didn't vomit. He controlled himself and leaned carefully forwards to clumsily lift one of the man's hands, which lay lifeless against his pant leg, in order to feel for a pulse. Perhaps he was still alive? The gulls continued to circle them. With nervous, damp fingertips, Ilyas squeezed the man's wrist and tried to remember if it was the upper or underside of his arm where the pulse could be detected. At least his hands were warm, as if living. Whatever it was, it wasn't right. He felt his flesh crawl, he had to get help. And those accursed birds were cawing and flapping ever more obtrusively.

His eyes, thought Ilyas. He'd managed to avoid looking at the man's face so far, but now he forced himself, with a curiosity polluted by disgust, to drop onto his knee so as to be able to look the man in the eyes.

And he was greeted by a pair of steely blue irises. But barely. For the gaze he was seeking had gotten stuck half way, and there was something at once moving and implacable in it. Ilyas dropped the hand as if it had the plague.

Everything then happened very quickly. The engines had dropped yet another tone, and the ferry lay still, but the screams of the gulls had reached such an ear-piercing level that Ilyas hardly dared leave the man's side.

Just then, he caught sight of a rectangular envelope poking out of the inside pocket of the man's jacket. Ilyas pinched one of the corners and managed to slide it out without getting blood on him. He squeezed it between his fingers. It was thick and unsealed. He inserted a finger into the opening and peered inside. His heart leapt. Without checking himself he quickly pulled in his stomach and stuffed the envelope under the waistband of his trousers, making sure to adjust his shirt to cover it.

Meanwhile, the gulls had grown almost feral, fighting over the meat. Human flesh from a body still warm. Perhaps still alive, what did he know? Powerful wings almost swept him over, and he had to throw his arms over his head for protection as he ran to fetch help.

At that very moment he realized that the man's killer could still be on board. His eyes swam as he flung himself toward the stern lounge and Ergün, who was standing behind the counter.

"A dead German!" he gasped.

"A dead German?" repeated Ergün, looking inappropriately jocular. "We must notify the captain!"

"I'll stay here," stammered Ilyas, who was scared of the captain.

Ergün set off for the wheelhouse. Ilyas paced up and down by the dazzlingly clean counter as if walking barefoot over hot coals. He realized, in spite of his nerves, that he had to hide the envelope so that no one would find it. Otherwise he'd be in big trouble. He almost regretted taking it.

The coast was clear, so he dashed swiftly over to his own little nook. He knew a good hiding place: under the table top, which was loose and tended to slide during heavy seas so that he had to hold it in place as he poured the tea.

But now he hastily moved the tray of glasses onto the floor, realizing that his bottom was sticking out through the door as he bent down. He had to hurry so that no one would see him. He lifted the little marble top and hid the envelope. But it was too thick and made the top wobbly, so he had to remove all the banknotes, euros all and of such high denominations that he became glassy-eyed with excitement. The marble slab now sat nicely in place, and he picked up the tray and set it down on top. He checked to make sure there was nothing poking out and went to look for Ergün.

Luckily, they didn't have to deal with the captain. It was the helmsman on his way down from the bridge who received the news. That was enough, and shortly afterwards there wasn't a member of the crew who didn't know what had happened. As they waited for the police to arrive, the diminutive captain set everyone to searching every corner of the boat. They had to make sure that no unauthorized person was hiding on board.

A man was detailed to guard the gangway so that no one could sneak off, or on, unseen.

The *MS Tirowor* would not be departing any more that day.

CHAPTER 5

CHIEF INSPECTOR CLAES CLAESSON strode into the shoe store, daughter in hand. They had gone first to the toy store and bought a jigsaw puzzle and a metal princess's tiara. She'd cast a longing eye at the pink princess dress, but after a while she swallowed her disappointment. They had then gone to the camera store to buy a new camera case and then to the sporting goods store to look at sandals, but there were none there to Klara's liking.

Adventures of this kind – sandal purchases for a child – he otherwise avoided; that was Veronika's department. But now Klara was so touchingly serious and determined about the task at hand that he was even grateful that the errand was his. A sallow sales clerk in her mid-twenties appeared immediately to help them. Perhaps he looked as awkward as he felt. Klara, on the other hand, did not dither one second. She found what she was after, and tore from the wall a pair of sandals that she declared loudly she wanted him to buy her.

They were pink. Claes wondered just how gender-inherited children's taste in colors actually was while turning over the sandals in his hand, mainly to give himself a little time to think. Should he let her get her way? Should he choose a different quality? Thicker soles and less plastic?

The clerk, clad in black jeans and a white top, was equally white-faced and raven-haired, dyed, with sooty rings around her eyes. Like a ghost, or like Snow White, if one wanted to be kind, for she was very much human, and smiled broadly, revealing a magnificent tongue stud that sparkled in her mouth. Klara stared at it.

"Daddy, I want one of those in my mouth, too," she said.

The clerk laughed and squatted obligingly to help Klara try the sandals on. She opened the straps with deft fingers, fastened them and said that there was just the right amount of room at the toes for them to grow during the summer, but not so much that she'd keep tripping up. Dumbfounded, Klara studied her broad feet in stripy socks that were now encased in marzipan pink straps.

When they paid at the counter, she watched with equal concentration as the shoes ended up in a bag that was then ceremoniously handed over to her.

"Hope you get a spring in your step this summer," said the white-powdered face with yet another metallically glistening grin aimed exclusively at Klara, struck dumb with rapture.

Even the soles were shocking pink, thought Claes. His daughter had gotten her wish. But why not? He smiled at his delighted little child.

Klara held tightly onto the bag as they made their way to the bench where Veronika was resting.

Daniel Skotte was standing in front of her, casually dressed in jeans, t-shirt, and a lightweight jacket. Klara spotted her mother and ran toward her. At that same moment, Daniel Skotte lifted a hand and left Veronika on the bench. They were both surgeons at Oskarshamn Hospital, a small but good hospital, as Veronika liked to say. But the local health authority in Kalmar was undergoing reorganization. Again. It was the natural state of things, and the purpose was, of course, well-intentioned: to provide effective healthcare as cheaply as possible. It was best just to grin and bear it.

Claes had time to nod at Skotte before the man vanished off toward Lilla Torget Square.

"Skotte looks relaxed," he said.

"Yeah, he's recharged his batteries," said Veronika.

As you have, he wanted to say. Veronika and Daniel Skotte, two surgeons at the same clinic that had taken a few knocks over the past year. But life went on.

Veronika kissed Klara on the cheek while her daughter eagerly tried to extract her sandals from the bag. Veronika had put on a pair of sunglasses. The light was sharp, although that was not the only reason, Claes suspected. They suited her but were also convenient for hiding behind, even though the time when Veronika was named and shamed as Doctor Death in every tabloid headline had passed.

The town had a population of eighteen thousand, the entire district almost twenty-seven thousand, including Misterhult, Kristdala, and Döderhult. Small towns had their pros and cons and Claes was a real local Oskarshamnian, self-secure and simple in many ways, even though, of course, the matrix of interacting lives could be suffocating. He was convinced that as long as Veronika remained in Oskarshamn, she'd have to live with the blame of having caused a patient's death on the operating table, even though it wasn't true. Denial never had the same impact as calamity. Yet another incident added to all the other stories of crime and punishment, disappointment, embezzlement, and other ill-assorted life destinies that made a place alive, even if most of it faded eventually. At the end of the day, everyone had enough concerns of their own.

Veronika rose from the bench. They were to continue their shopping tour, and then it was time for the garden on this wonderful day. But then she gave a sudden, violent jolt, doubled up and slumped back onto the bench again.

"Jesus," she whimpered, sounding winded.

Claes waited for the contraction to subside and it did. But then the screw took another turn, and even worse this time, so protracted and painful that he saw Veronika's face stiffen into an ashen mask.

At that moment, a slideshow of unpleasant images played out inside his head. Memories of pains and red fluid, blood and goo. Biological and necessary, but not at all to his taste. It had nothing to do with reason, he just found blood repulsive. And scary.

But his mind had run away with him. She wasn't bleeding now. On the other hand he was thinking of the roads and how it was fifty miles to Kalmar. If he stuck to the speed limit, it would take them fifty-five minutes to get there.

Shit!

The maternity clinic in Oskarshamn had closed down long ago, so the only other option was Västervik, and that was just as far away. And besides, it wasn't where they'd gone to discuss the planned Caesarean that had been scheduled for a little less than a week from now, barring mishaps. Anything else was off his mental radar. He wasn't in the frame of mind to be grateful that they didn't live in the north with at least 125 miles to the birthing room.

He hoisted Veronika up from the bench and relaxed a little when he saw that she was capable of walking on her own two legs. Her waters hadn't broken and she wasn't bleeding. Not this time. Not yet. He'd transformed one situation into another in the blink of an eye, as we humans tend to do when in a state of panic. As it was, he knew how he worked and quickly put the brakes on the images that were hurtling through his brain. Veronika was fully occupied, groaning and taking heavy, controlled breaths as he helped her back to the car.

His pained relationship with blood and mangled bodies was otherwise nothing to discuss. It was no secret at the police station; his facial expression usually betrayed him.

"And you a professional cop. Jeez, what a wimp!"

Yes, he'd had to learn to live with comments like that. Or rise above them, as one said nowadays. And it wasn't a problem at all, now that he was a little longer in the tooth and a man of certain rank. He'd felt enough shame in his time. Now enough's enough!

They'd come within a hair's breadth last time, he'd never forget that. The blood that suddenly started flowing thickly out of Veronika, someone in the room who pressed an alarm button, a horribly ringing sound filling the room and the door being flung open as a doctor rushed in to stand quietly by the bed to survey the situation. Red seconds ticked away in the agony of decision. Then she nodded curtly to the midwife, whose eyes took on a hunted look. Hands grabbed hold of the end of the bed and rolled Veronika away. And left him standing alone. Minutes passed, as cold as burnished steel and as long as infinity.

Until finally they came and fetched him. The green-clad. Led him to his execution. He, wearing the same green scrubs and a ridiculous light blue disposable shower cap. Walked to the room adjacent to the operating room, already the embodiment of calamity, and cautiously nosing the Inconceivable Grief.

And there she was, lying on the heated nursing table. Lovely and rosy, she searched tentatively with her newly awakened eyes, dark in their little slits, for something to latch them onto. And found his. It was love at first sight. The warm, soft baby in his arms. The eyes. His daughter.

Can such luck strike twice?

It had to!

He sped up, getting annoyed that Veronika couldn't walk any faster. She was pigeon-stepping her way along. Jesus Christ! He yanked whenever she came to a halt. Klara sat in the crook of his other arm, not making a peep. She clutched the bag containing the newly purchased sandals in her little fists, an unadulterated joy that had been far too short-lived for the three-year-old soul.

"They're probably just pre-term contractions," whimpered Veronika. "They'll pass soon."

"Like hell they will!" said Claes. "We're going to Kalmar!"

She nodded and he removed his hand from his wife while they lurched past the newsstand. He took out his cell phone and hoped that Janne Lundin and Mona could take pity on Klara. Otherwise she'd have to go along, too.

As the phone rang, he opened the car doors. Klara, who still hadn't let go of her bag of shoes, climbed into the rear child's seat herself and all he had to do was buckle her in. At last Mona answered. She was out of breath, having just come through the door after walking the dog.

"What are you up to today?" he asked.

"I've got people coming for coffee at three," she said.

Fuck, he thought to himself.

"Was there anything you wanted?" she wondered.

So he told her.

"Dear me, of course I can still take Klara!"

A weight fell from his shoulders.

"Are you sure?" he said.

"Absolutely sure."

He slammed the car door shut and started the engine.

"There are always decent people somewhere, we shouldn't forget that," said Veronika.

"I actually find women like Mona who say *'dear me'* a bit of a turn-on," he said. Veronika managed to smile and stoke his cheek before having to concentrate on her next contraction.

The Lundins lived just around the corner on Köpmannagatan. Mona was out on the sidewalk and waved. Klara was conveyed into her arms, still without making a peep. She knew Mona and Janne well and was even a bit spoiled by them. But she didn't wave when her parents drove away. She just stared after them.

They sat in silence as Claes turned out onto the E22.

"You can't go around thinking you can plan everything," Veronika eventually said, pulling at the seatbelt that lay tight and irritating over her belly, while bracing herself with her other hand against the dashboard when the contractions came.

They passed the exit to Påskallavik. She was still in control of the situation, Veronika maintained. Claes gave her the phone then squeezed the steering wheel tightly.

"Can't you call maternity in Kalmar when you're not contracting and warn them? I don't want to take my eyes off the road."

She did as he said and he could hear them ask her how frequently the contractions were coming, how long they lasted, and if her water had broken. It hadn't. Veronika hung up.

"They're ready," she said.

"I'd have taken you there, anyway," he said, steel-faced as they approached Mönsterås. There were dawdlers on the road, typical Saturday shoppers.

"I'm soaked through," said Veronika suddenly. They were just by the exit to Timmernabben.

The leather upholstery! he thought. A totally despicable, materialistic thought. At least he didn't voice it. Veronika was thinking likewise, apparently.

"It can be cleaned," she said coolly and fished a magazine out of her bag, folded it, and slid it under herself.

Her stomach had calmed down a little, she announced. The lull before the storm, he thought. And he was right. As they drove into Rockneby, it started up again and Claes started to wonder about what he might have to do. Taxi drivers managed it, normal married and unmarried other halves had managed it for generations in remote villages where the nearest maternity hospital was far away. He thought of his father. "You should set up your life so that you're always ready to cope on your own." He'd preached that so often that Claes no longer heard what he said.

However, a little of that spirit had presumably soaked into him, whether he'd wanted it to or not. He'd never been attracted to physical challenges as had his father, who'd been a lithe and fit man drawn to hardship, to long mountain hikes with heavy packsacks in crap weather. But what good did his father's good physique do once the cancer had dug its claws into him? And he hadn't been an old man, a mere fifty or so.

Claes had naturally endured the same schooling as his father, that had been inescapable, but as he grew up he'd opted out of the worst of the hardships. He'd wanted to become a policeman, and found good use for his physique during the entrance tests.

And now he thought he'd find good use for his optimistic disposition. Everything will be alright. Pretty much. If it wasn't for the blood. But even that he'd deal with. Nothing's impossible, he convinced himself.

"It'll be alright, don't worry," he said aloud.

Veronika didn't reply right away.

"In one way or another I guess it will," she managed once the pain had subsided.

They reached Lindsal. Not far to go. Veronika called maternity again. Groaned that they'd just passed the entrance to town. The person on the other end asked questions again. Lots of questions. Claes wished he could answer for her, help her along. She answered as obediently as she could and then hung up, placed both hands on the dashboard and let out a long, loud bellow the likes of which he'd never heard before. At least not from her throat.

By now they'd arrived at the exit to the bridge over to Öland and were heading toward the southern approach to Kalmar. The one marked with a red cross on a white background. Toward the hospital.

CHAPTER 6

ILYAS BANK SAT IN A HEATED room at the police station, which was located on a narrow, crowded street close to the Spice Bazaar. He'd been driven there, otherwise he would never have found it. The streets were like the tunnels of an anthill.

He was trying to tell himself to relax, but wasn't making a very good job of it. He was drumming his thumbs on his thigh where he sat, opposite an empty desk with a wooden top and steel legs and an impressive computer enthroned in one corner. He was waiting for the police to come and take his statement. And that was making him nervous.

All that mattered was that they didn't think he had anything to do with it. He wasn't a killer. The money… he thought. He regretted hiding it. What if he went down for murder because of it?

Although right now he was mainly grateful that this wasn't happening at home but in a city where he was virtually unknown. Curious glances had licked his neck both at the ferry terminal and outside the police station. How could anyone know that he was a mere witness? That he wasn't the murderer? That he wasn't any kind of criminal? That he had a conscience as white as snow? Well, almost.…

Please don't let them find the money! Why was he so stupid as to take the envelope?

He didn't like having to wait. The police officer had wandered off into the corridor to get something. She was taking her time. Ilyas wondered if it was some kind of trick to make him feel insecure and soften him up. His stomach cramped. He was only meant to give a witness's statement – that's what she said, the officer that is, they'd assigned a female cop to him – but obviously they had to treat everyone as a suspect until the opposite was proved.

She was called Merve something, he'd managed to read from her door. What a place to be a police officer; he fantasized and felt pangs of envy.

He was in an unfamiliar part of the city, somewhere in Eminönü. It was a tourist area and dead in the evenings except in the restaurants. The classic sights were here, and many hotels, of course. The moment he'd arrived in Istanbul his sister had shown him around.

Most famous was the Topkapi Palace, which he could see every day from the ferry. The palace was situated high up on Seraglio Point, where the Bosporus and Marmara Sea meet. The lines into it were always so long, and the entry fee so high that he and his sister skipped it. He knew that a wealthy sultan had chosen the site and built upon it with great extravagance and that there was a large harem there, which although admittedly out of use still fired his fantasy.

His chain of thought was broken by the door swinging open as the policewoman entered and sat across the desk from him in front of the humming computer. Hot on her heels came a man dressed in civilian attire with a tray containing two glasses of tea, which he set down before walking out again.

Ilyas tried hard not to stare at the police officer. She was of indeterminable age, somewhere between thirty and forty, perhaps. She had a pretty, curved nose, he noted, since he saw her mostly in profile. It was the computer that aroused her interest, not him. She was no doubt waiting to pull up the right document on the screen. Her nails were long and shiny, and rested on the keys while she stared into the monitor, whose light reflected against her cheekbones. She was wearing a freshly ironed light blue uniform blouse with dark pants, and had her thick black hair gathered at the neck.

His nerves hadn't yet settled, but now he had no time to regret his ruse with the money. He straightened his back and gratefully dropped a sugar cube into his tea, stirring it slowly with the spoon while trying to shed his cloak of shame. Still, the policewoman had made no effort to smile. But the almond eyes were friendly.

It could have been worse – as he persistently tried to convince himself. He wasn't in the hands of the notoriously hardboiled military police. The methods they used were no joke, that much everyone knew.

He sipped his tea. It tasted good and moistened his throat, which was as arid as the desert. The policewoman had made some progress and had started to key in his personal details, which he rattled off breathlessly: parents' names, place of birth, current address, cell phone number. There was no end to what they wanted to know. The questions came naturally and without pause, so he understood that she'd done this before. He was fascinated by her fingers, which danced over the keyboard.

Suddenly she turned away from the screen to look him in the eyes for the first time. For far too long, it felt.

"Ilyas," she said in a deep voice, and delivered an insufferably pregnant pause. "I know that what happened on the ferry was a nasty experience for you, but would you like to go through it all again just one more time? Take your time."

She prepared herself for his torrent of narrative by placing her fingers over the keys. He was thrown by the informality of her address, which made him at once embarrassed and nervous.

"Where shall I begin?"

He'll have to watch his tongue. Everything was whirling around his mind in one big jumble, his heart was thumping, his head buzzing.

"Start from when you discovered the man," she offered amicably.

At that moment, a color cascade of red blood and light-blue cotton flashed in front of his eyes and he could hear the wretched screeching and cawing of the gulls. Even now, he knew that these avian cries would pursue him for many years to come.

But he talked, and it went fine. She wrote, but didn't actually ask anything about the blood and that made it easier for him to continue.

He gradually started to settle down, as his voice stabilized and his tongue loosened. Yet he could feel how beads of sweat were forming on his scalp. The room had heated up during the day, and there were still many hours to go before the merciful cool of the evening. He looked up at the ceiling. The large fan rotating above his head was all but useless.

Ilyas didn't dare glance at the time, but a good while had passed since he heard the call to afternoon prayer echo over the quarter from the loudspeakers high up in the nearest minaret. It had, in other words, past five o'clock.

Istanbul was densely packed with mosques, very large ones and very small ones, and most very old. He still reacted to the metallic sound of the muezzin's voice, which was not as warmly inviting as the imam's soft tones that descended softly from the minaret in his home village.

As he talked and tried to answer her seemingly arbitrary questions, he stared at the emblem on her blouse breast. It was a little higher up than her bust, which was lucky, as she wouldn't have to suspect him of sitting staring at her tits. Which, incidentally, were ample, he'd been quick to note.

How cool to get to wear a uniform with that emblem on it, he thought. He'd check out the possibilities of his joining the force later.

His stomach started grumbling and rumbling. The tension and the discomfort had upset his belly. She heard it, of course – only the stone deaf could have missed it – and cast him a quick glance.

He felt as mortified as a dog and even more determined to get out of there as quickly as he could, and so began to babble with increasing speed while she miraculously kept up until the plasticky clicks of the keys resembled the backing track of a rap song.

When he was done, there was a moment or two's silence before she read aloud from the screen, pausing to ask one or two brief questions and writing in the amendments. He could tell by her dialect that she was probably from Istanbul. Now she was ready, and read out what she'd written one last time.

"Is this right?"

"Yes," he said with a nod.

"So you'd never seen the man that you found dead before?" she repeated with her eye fixed on him.

He shook his head. "Nah," he said. "But we get new passengers all the time."

"I realize that there are a great many people on the ferry. And you can't be sure where the man came aboard?"

"All I can think is that it was at one of the midway stops, in Yeniköy, maybe."

She turned and studied that map that hung on the wall behind her.

"On the European side, that is," explained Ilyas.

"I know," she said and continued to examine the map, as if to fix the point with her eyes. "There are some beautiful *yalis* there," she said dreamily, dropping for a second her formal air.

Ilyas nodded. The lavish multi-story villas that the wealthy once had built, often out of wood, were situated along the water's edge and were a delight to see from the approaching ferry. They evoked dreams of another world. Another life.

"You seem to have a pair of eyes on you," she said, smiling. "Do you remember if the man, in that case, was alone when he climbed on board?"

Ilyas felt flattered, naturally, and tried to squeeze his memory harder.

"He wasn't the only one to get on there, so I guess I didn't think too much about it. It doesn't often happen that only one passenger comes aboard. But he… him… that dead guy, I mean, he bought some tea after a while, by which time he was already sitting there by the railing… well, where I later found him. On the port side… And there was a crowd of Americans there, too, as I've already mentioned."

"So you can't say for sure if he was with someone?"

He shook his head.

"Did you notice anything during the trip that you think might be worth telling us? Something that happened or a person that you particularly noticed – anything?"

He searched his memory, but no, he couldn't think of anything.

"Did you see if the man had a bag of some kind?" she continued.

He stared at her desktop. "No," he said, and sounded honest. "At least he didn't have a bag when I found him… when he was dead, I mean… but I don't know if he had one before that."

"If we're really lucky, someone's taken a photo from the boat and caught him in the frame. We can find out more that way," she said, and it sounded like a piece of information, but Ilyas felt his stomach tighten again. "He didn't have anything in his pockets that you happened to see?" she asked as if to no one in particular, rolling her head as if to ease some tension in her neck.

"No," he replied with a rapidity that made her stop and face him with her arms folded across her chest.

Ilyas felt his stomach knotting itself with a frenzy of cramps that almost made him pale with pain.

"So you didn't happen to go through his pockets, then?"

"No. Why would I do that?"

"To find out who he was, for instance. To see if you could find a wallet with a drivers license in it or a passport or something," she said in a tone that was deviously smooth, but with such exaggerated stress on every syllable that Ilyas understood she was used to a much tougher approach.

This is a trap, he thought. I'd better watch my step.

"No," he insisted. "It was horrible. I ran to get help straight away."

"Without going through his pockets first, you mean?"

"Yes."

She stared briefly at him and then leaned back to her computer.

"We will, of course, be making a thorough search of the boat," she said.

Ilyas's pulse started to gallop. This was torture! His stomach was on fire, and he thought he was going to burst. He couldn't hold it back any more.

"I've got to go to the bathroom," he said, knocking over his chair as he shot up and rushed out.

"It's on the right," she called after him.

But he'd already locked himself in and was emptying the entire contents of his body, or so it felt.

She stood in the corridor and waited for him, and watched as he came out, shamefaced.

"You never know, sometimes things turn up much later," she said and actually smiled, and he noticed that her teeth were even and white. "I'd very much like you to get in touch," she continued and gave him a piece of paper with a phone number he could call.

He promised to do so, took the number, and left.

Chapter 7

SUNDAY TRANQUILITY, thought Birgitta Olsson, pulling up the blinds.

She stood by the window for a few seconds, looking out onto the garden. The sun was shining as heedlessly as it did yesterday. Another lovely day to take advantage of! She couldn't wait to thrust her fingers into the soil. She had the whole long day to herself and wasn't due to start her nightshift until nine o'clock.

The window stood ajar to let in the blackbird's song while she made the bed. Flowing in with it was the pleasant sound of hoes and spades. Her neighbors had already gotten started on their gardens. At least the Bromses, she thought, and pictured first Sven in her mind. That was natural. She knew him best. Not that that was known to Nettan, whose real name was Agneta. Birgitta had never got used to calling her Nettan, the two of them weren't intimate enough for that. The Bromses would no doubt be taking off to Skorpetorp's golf course later, she thought. They were *golfers*, as Carl-Ivar said, sounding as if he were talking about some lower species of human. Or perhaps higher.

She'd just smoothed down the bedspread when the peace was shattered by the rumble of a powerful motor that seared through the serenity and lay over the neighborhood like a carpet.

How rude, she thought, and then went to put the coffee on. There was once a time when Sunday was a day of rest, when maybe you mowed the lawn if absolutely necessary, but you did so with a quiet push mower, and then after mass. But now times were different, with evening shopping and round-the-clock gas stations and TV or Internet entertainment when you wanted it. A new generation had grown up and thought differently and more selfishly.

She noticed that her brain was working, but wrongly. She wanted to stay in her state of harmony.

Of course she knew who it was who was being disrespectful and cutting their grass this early morning. Everyone in the neighborhood knew. A weasel among the ermines. She grew irritated with herself over the way she couldn't help getting worked up by it. For *letting* herself be irritated.

She turned into the bathroom, splashed her face quickly, and then squeezed out a blob of suntan lotion that had been sitting in her medicine cabinet for God knew how many years. She rubbed it into her face with small, habitual circular movements, while her thoughts continued to snag on the lawn mower.

She entertained herself by working out how long she and Carl-Ivar had lived on Holmhälleväg. Thirty-four years this September, she concluded. They'd moved from a cramped little one-bedroom apartment on Borgmästargatan. They were delighted with their solid, spacious 1960's house. They repapered and painted it, but they kept the walls where they were.

The house was no flimsy knock-up; builders knew their stuff back then! She and Carl-Ivar could even live there when they were old enough to use walkers, they sometimes talked about that. It was a bungalow, but that didn't bother them when they bought it. Of course not. When you're young, you're immortal.

They moved in at a time when it was quiet here, almost rural. For a moment she could hear once more the silence that then prevailed.

But now a generational shift was underway. The house that their neighbors down the road had taken over a few years back hadn't been that cheap. These days she and Carl-Ivar would never have been able to afford a house here. Nor the kind of renovations that their new neighbors were subjecting their property to. They lived three plots down, closer to the sea. The husband was in the IT business, as many people were nowadays. Or they were consultants. Whatever they did, they earned a lot of money. Or had nothing against taking huge loans. That was something that people in her and Carl-Ivar's generation were more cautious about. Borrowing. What if you couldn't pay it back?

They'd renovated the house out of all recognition, rendered the walls smooth, dug up the garden – massive machines had rumbled down to their little piece of territory – and cleared everything away. Birgitta had heard that the purple lilacs didn't match the façade, but if the little sprays had been white they'd have been kept. The wife was some kind of landscape gardener. There was no accounting for taste! Almost anything goes with gray, Birgitta had thought, and actually felt sorry for the bushes as they were hauled away to an incinerator: dog rose bushes, bird-cherries, hardhacks, spiraea, mock orange.

Then even more machines had trundled down the road to lay out a sterile landscape with gravel and grass in neat little rows, piquantly interspersed with the odd low, topiaried, evergreen bush.

She went into the hall and opened the door of the walk-in closet, in which cast-off but clean clothes lay waiting to be used in the garden. As she stepped inside, she tripped over a bag that she had herself placed on the floor the moment she came home from Turkey. It was a soft, roomy black cloth holdall that Carl-Ivar had asked her to take home with her. Jokingly, she and her husband called these types of holdall "smuggler bags." The carpet traders in Turkey kept plying you with them and there were different sizes depending on the size of rug purchased. The traders were phenomenal at folding and compressing rugs, even carpets, so that they could be taken home. Otherwise they'd send them on by courier. Carl-Ivar had never known of a rug that had failed to arrive.

However, this particular bag wasn't very large. She had no idea what Carl-Ivar had bought, but it was doubtlessly something remarkable, that much she understood since she'd been given detailed instructions about keeping it with her at all times. She wasn't to check it as luggage, in other words, but to take it with her to her cabin.

She thought about Carl-Ivar while she lifted the bag and squished it into place above her husband's shoes and underneath all the jackets and suits. He had shoe trees in most pairs, so they could take it.

It struck her that he hadn't called her that evening.

They used to talk to each other once a day. Not necessarily a long conversation, it was enough to hear that the other was alive and that everything was fine. There wasn't much they had to say to each other after so many years together. And it was nice. She could be her on her own.

She thought about giving him a call after breakfast as she grabbed herself a short-sleeved top and a pair of over-washed faded blue jeans from the pile of clothes, which was large enough to last the rest of her life. She'd have to deal with it one day, she thought. Liberation by rejection.

The lawn mower engine was still rumbling away as she stepped out of the closet. She got dressed and looked at the man down the street in front of her. How he sat on the four-wheel drive mower, sweating fatly.

She didn't even need to force his image, it arrived on its own accord with the noise he was making. The man was one big warning sign about what an unhealthy lifestyle could do to a body. Around forty-five and already magnificently pot-bellied. What would become of his heart in the future she couldn't imagine.

She went into the kitchen, poured the hot coffee into a thermos, quickly prepared two rye bread sandwiches – the same breakfast every morning – filled a glass with juice, took out the coffee cup, and sat down. There was no paper on Sunday, and so instead she stared out through the window, crunching audibly. In a sequence of images she imagined her neighbor down the street suddenly clutching his chest as his face twisted in agony and pain.

Her imagination was vivid, it always had been. She let the neighbor with the mower suffer. He gasped for breath and called for help, but his voice was drowned out by the din of the engine. He made a few clumsy attempts to stop the infernal machine, but failed and fell headlong over the steering wheel, while the mower continued on its own expedition through the low bushes marking the boundary of his garden and into his neighbor's. The machine chewed its way along, leaving behind it stubble and a shiny, well-mown strip along the neighbor's lawn as it approached the pool, the lifeless body hanging like a mountain of sunburned flesh over the steering wheel.

Just when the contraption and its driver were about to tip into the water – she could already hear the splash and then the sudden silence as the engine came to an abrupt stop – she blinked.

What on earth was she doing, imagining this? She exhaled and sipped her coffee.

Just how the neighbor with the swimming pool further down the street reacted when he found the lawn mower in it, and a corpse, she didn't find out. That would have to wait for a later occasion.

The heat struck her. She peered into the garden, which was bathed in bright spring light. Yesterday's breeze had abated and the air was balmy.

The shed smelled of dry earth and gasoline. The pruning shears were hanging on their hook and the long gardening gloves lay in their place. She put them on right away to protect her forearms from scratches, as she was going to start by pruning the roses. A task she enjoyed.

At last!

She took a deep and blissful breath and squatted down. It was a rather bushy rose that they had planted when they bought the house. It came into bloom with clusters of deep red flowers, made even more beautiful by their appearance only once a season.

The phone rang. She had the portable in her pocket and stood up to retrieve it. It must be Carl-Ivar, she thought. She had mixed feelings. He was no doubt going to tell her that he was intending to stay a few extra days and wouldn't be home on Tuesday.

But it was Magnus. Their son-in-law.

"Hey, Birgitta," he said in his Stockholm dialect.

Well now, he sounds ingratiating, she thought.

"Hi," she answered, more neutrally.

"Is Carl-Ivar at home?"

"No. He won't be back till Tuesday."

"Is that so? That's a pity."

"Was there something special you wanted?"

"Well, it's about a rug that he'd promised to get me from Turkey."

"What rug?" she said, her ears now pricking up. She thought she could hear fairly heavy traffic in the background. Magnus and Lotta lived on Sibyllegatan on Östermalm in Stockholm, but it was a quiet street, especially on Sundays.

"I can take it up with Carl-Ivar when he gets back," he said.

I bet you will, she thought.

"Can I speak to Lotta?" She mainly just wanted to hear her daughter's voice.

"She's not actually here at the moment. I'm in Germany, in Munich, on a job."

They hung up. She stood motionless for a while with the sun on her back to let the conversation sink in before she returned to the flowerbed. She snipped away the dead twigs with a practiced hand.

After a while her knees started to ache. She pulled herself up and stood by the flowerbed, swaying to bring the life back to her hips. Spotting her, her neighbor yoo-hooed at her over the hedge.

It was Agneta Bromse and she was always happy.

"Isn't it lovely?" she chirped. She was called Nettan by her husband, but Birgitta couldn't make herself say it. It was far too intimate. "Real summer weather here already!"

Birgitta assumed that Agneta was smiling but couldn't actually see to make sure as her face was shaded by the broad peak of one of those caps that people otherwise wore when playing golf.

She tried to spy Sven. The sight of him produced a soft tingle in her body. She didn't feel guilty. She had nothing to feel guilty about. No actions, at least.

But Sven didn't seem to be at home, otherwise he probably would have popped up from behind the hedge and given her his crafty yet warm smile. She was definitely not going to ask Agneta were he was. There were limits to her fervor.

"Yes, it certainly is," she agreed instead, placing her hand over her eyes so as not to have to squint. Her head was bare, although probably shouldn't have been.

"But to make up for it, midsummer will be cold and rainy," she heard Agneta sigh under her peak. The straggly wad of graying, formerly blonde hair that stuck out from a slit in the back of the cap vibrated merrily.

"By the way, did you have a nice time in Turkey?"

"Oh, yes! Carl-Ivar's still there. He'll be home this week."

"So you're enjoying the single life," chuckled Agneta and they smiled like two conspirators. "Sven's not at home, either. He's away on some business thing, but he'll be home tonight."

Not much more was said and they each got on with her own work.

Some relationships never quite fully develop, even if it doesn't mean you're constantly at odds, thought Birgitta and returned to her weeding.

She had to call her parents, she reminded herself. Perhaps she'd travel over there tomorrow when she'd had a good night's sleep.

They were old now. Every time she paid them a visit, she thought that it might be the last time she saw them alive.

Her dear little mom. She remembered her voice from her childhood: "I think I'll go across to the salon," she'd say, meaning that she'd be stepping into the salon she'd set up in one of the rooms on the ground floor. She was continually shuttling between the kitchen sink and local female heads. She had the only hairdresser in Brådbygden. The men worked the soil or toiled in the forest. The women generally tended to the animals, milking and mucking out.

They kept them all fed, animals and people alike. But her mother also took care of the vanity and beauty.

Birgitta remembered the laughter and voices that bounced around the walls as they tried to make themselves heard above the drone of the hair dryer hoods. As a little girl, she'd love to hang around here, in the world of joy and beauty among the chamois curlers and the pungent odors of the perming fluids and various packs and hair dyes. Among women who walked away, freshly coifed, waving and happy.

She wondered if most of the profits went straight into the farm. Although her mother did squirrel away a little in the tin behind the floral-patterned cloth that hung from the shelf with the large mirror above it.

At times, she'd take out the tin and give Birgitta a coin or two for a new hair slide or a lemonade down at the café where she hung out as a teenager. She'd never asked her mother about the money. Her childhood long pre-dated the "talk-about-everything" era.

The leaf basket was full again. She struggled upright and went to empty it onto the compost.

The phone rang again. She no longer took the phone out with her as it chafed in her pants pocket. The door was wide open so she heard the signals and rushed inside. It was Lotta, wondering how things were with them.

"Fine," said Birgitta.

"Has Dad come home?"

"No, he's staying a couple of days extra. You know him, he likes being in Turkey, but I'm working nights now and don't want to take out all my vacation time just yet. Anyway, where are you?"

"At home in Stockholm. Why d'you ask?"

Birgitta thought. Should she say that Magnus had called?

"Pah, it was nothing," she said, realizing that it would only lead to questions. Things were so delicate between Lotta and Magnus, but she couldn't put her finger on just what. That's just how it was, and you had to go along with it. "How are the kids?" she asked instead.

The two beloved grandchildren, who were unfortunately the source of considerable disquiet. Were they really doing alright?

"They're doing just fine," said Lotta, sounding as businesslike as usual. How had she given birth to such an efficient daughter?

"Don't they want to talk to Nan?" wondered Birgitta and tried not to sound needy.

"I don't think so," said Lotta. "We're just on our way out."

"I see... Well, give my love to them and Magnus, won't you?"

She went into the kitchen, ran the cold tap, then drank a couple of glasses as she thought about Magnus. About how he had developed a recent interest in carpets. She supposed it was just part of the upper class thing: attractive apartment, antiques, sailing.

Of course, it was nice for Carl-Ivar to have someone listen to his detailed accounts of his trips to the Orient and rug purchases. To be sure, there was money in rugs and carpets, but you had to be a player in the higher divisions to access it, and Carl-Ivar wasn't there. He bought rugs for the simple reason that he loved them. And he'd made a success of it because he was a customarily parsimonious Smålander, who'd grown up in rather meager circumstances and had thus developed a sense of and respect for money.

Magnus, on the other hand, worked with the big companies. Helped with advertising and marketing and whatnot, Birgitta had never really grasped what it was he did. Nor had Carl-Ivar. Anyway, modest sums it wasn't – that much they'd understood.

Magnus held a master's degree from the Royal Institute of Technology in Stockholm. And that counted for something, especially in Oskarshamn. These days he ran his own company, and according to Lotta it was doing just fine. He was a good catch, as they said. Birgitta could see her son-in-law in front of her, always looking shiny and new from head to toe: the shoes, the pants, the shirt underneath the blazer or the lamb's wool jersey – even his glasses shone. And he liked to smile. From one corner of his mouth. He always had done.

They'd known Magnus since he was a boy, and his family, during the summers, but mostly from a distance. "The Stockholmers," as they were known locally in Klintemåla. The disparities and differences between them were so overwhelming that no one even tried to bridge them. The Stockholmers in their "wedding cake," as the villagers called their summer residence, with its towers and pinnacles and a glazed veranda overlooking the sea.

And to think that it would all go to pot.... The father had been playing the stock market. But then the recession hit in the nineties and he practically lost everything. He'd taken too many risks, thought Carl-Ivar. The mother had never worked, and they were used to living in luxury; and Magnus had always had the best of everything. Now this backup was no longer there.

Carl-Ivar and she had always found the Öbergs somewhat aloof. The father was erratic, warm at times but could quickly become irascible.

The parents moved to Spain and Magnus did his best to keep up appearances, but Birgitta suspected that his contact with them was rather sparse these days.

She placed the glass on the sink and went back out into the sunlight.

She thought about the grandchildren, about little Olivia and Ludvig. About their tough upbringing.

A lump appeared in her belly. Perhaps they had just as tough an upbringing as Magnus once had, she guessed. But she'd never ask him that, what his childhood was really like. Their relationship wasn't of that kind, more politely distanced.

Instead, her mind turned to one of her patients. Some of them were unforgettable.

The image of that little boy still pained her. They'd been remarkably similar, he and Magnus, and of the same age. The dark, curly hair and little freckles straddling the fair-skinned nose. Both were fearful of the strap, too. You could feel it.

It was at that time when corporal punishment was banned, at the end of the seventies.

She was almost ashamed now, but back then she was one of those who thought the law was unnecessary. She and Carl-Ivar didn't need it at least, they never beat their children. A light slap on the bottom or an ear-boxing could hardly be considered violent. It hadn't done her any harm, she always liked to add.

And in a way it hadn't, at least compared to her brother, who their father had been stricter with. The son that was to be disciplined, as was the thing to do in those days. She felt sorry for Lasse.

But she swiftly changed her mind when the boy was admitted to the clinic, beaten half to death by his frenzied father, who refused to believe that his son would suffer from a good hiding.

Everyone who, with gentle hands, helped to care for that little child's body was openly thankful that a law had been passed against such horrors. The boy had lost a finger, the father having snipped it off with pincers because his four-year-old son had picked up a bottle and dropped it on the floor. He'd screamed like a stuck pig, enough to bring the neighbors running to his rescue, otherwise he probably would have lost more. What the bottle had contained was never recorded, but there were convincing rumors that it had been alcohol of some kind.

The otherwise so amenable and hardworking doctor was furious, almost unrecognizably so. Birgitta remembered it with tenderness. If the doctor hadn't been a man of little physical strength, he probably would have gone to the father's house and thumped him.

Over the years, she'd wondered now and again what had become of the boy. The boy that hadn't been born under a cloudless sky and with a silver spoon, like Magnus Öberg. The father no doubt received some sort of punishment and the child welfare agency probably did its bit in accordance with the arrangements of the time. Perhaps a foster home or a children's home, both were a gamble. She'd never know.

Her hair was sticky and the sweat was streaming even more profusely. She'd forgotten both time and space. Her tummy grumbled. She got up and went inside to make herself a late lunch.

CHAPTER 8

THE ROAD WAS DRY, the sun hot overhead.

Claes Claesson had folded down the sunshade, but the light was still piercing and so he groped around in the compartment between the front seats for his sunglasses. He found then and placed them on his nose.

Klara was not making a sound. She was sitting belted into the child's seat in the back, listening intensely. Lennart Hellsing's "Cackle Cackle Spectacle" was playing out of the car's speakers. To think that his lyrics still worked!

"Let's sing, Daddy," she said. "Play it again!"

He backed up the CD, cleared his throat and joined in:

Cackle cackle spectacle
Cousin Girton
Swinging from a curtain
With a scream and a shout
Come out! Come out!
Cackle cackle spectacle
What are you thinking about?

He and Klara both knew it by heart. Two generations with the same heritage. After a while, Klara made do with just listening.

So there he was on the E22 again on his way to Kalmar. He'd passed Mönsterås, but this time without his heart in his throat. The sky was so bright it was nudging white.

When he saw the sign for Timmernabben, a whim struck him to take the old coast road to Kalmar. It had to be years since he last went that way – Pataholm, Korpemåla, Slakmöre – but it really wasn't an option just now. He could see the pretty oak groves down by the sea. The coast changed south of Oskarshamn as the granite rocks made way for grassy fields that stretched all the way to the shoreline, populated by countless ruminating cows.

"Are we there yet, Daddy?"

"Not long now," he said while trying to catch her eye in the rear-view mirror, but failing, naturally, given that she was seated in a backward-facing child seat. She contented herself with his reply.

He'd put the baby seat in the trunk and was now on his way to fetch his wife and yet another offspring. Veronika had actually wanted to go home the day before, just a few hours after the birth, but had been persuaded to stay overnight to give the doctor time to examine their newborn baby girl.

He was at ease. He glanced at the seat beside him. The stain was very faint, barely noticeable, in fact, if you didn't know it was there. Let it stay, he thought. As a memento.

He grinned broadly.

CHAPTER 9

MERVE TURPAN WAS a detective inspector, although not a detective chief inspector. Yet.

She thought about it at times, that she had a goal, and that she'd have to let reaching it take its time. She was content with her life as it was – but still she drove herself ever onward.

The only one who was displeased with her life was her mother, but that was another story.

Merve was very well aware that she was smart and capable. Not only because she'd often gained the highest grades and the most lavish praise, but also because she'd been told as much, by her boss foremost of all. True, this was partly to do with his occasional tiredness. Or indolence, perhaps. Or maybe he genuinely did have as much on his plate as he made out – her boss, Superintendent Fuat Karaoğlu, a head shorter than her and with a singular ability to supply her with work.

But he took her seriously. That was attractive and she liked him. A lot, even.

Right now, though, she would have given anything for a shower. Refreshing water streaming down over her body. As it was, cold or possibly lukewarm water was all there was available, despite the recent renovations on the apartment she'd bought a year back. She didn't dare even think what it would be like come the winter. The landlord was definitely not a man to trust.

It was a Sunday and the narrow corridor outside her office was deserted. Through the open window she could hear someone on the floor below talking on the phone. Possibly Cem, but if he wanted her for something, he'd stop by.

Cem was the youngest forensic investigator, who'd now been given an entire boat to rummage around in. It would no doubt be a fruitless exercise; Karaoğlu thought so, too, he'd even said so aloud. Cem and the two other forensic technicians had only had Saturday evening to do their thing. The captain had grumbled over the serious losses he was making with the ferry temporarily berthed, and anyway, all that was needed was for the wind to change and the rain to come for any clues to be washed away, no matter how carefully the scene had been covered by a tarp.

The traffic outside barely penetrated her room, and the calm was pleasant. She needed to concentrate.

Her boss would be turning up in an hour to read through her report to Interpol so that it could be sent off today. Hopefully, it would reach Sweden tomorrow.

Fuat Karaoğlu owned a small apartment that was almost disgustingly centrally located behind Hagia Sofia. Cem, who'd been there, said that Karaoğlu even had a view of the Marmara Sea from his roof terrace. Unfortunately, Karaoğlu's wife was seriously ill, and couldn't leave the apartment. That was his cross to bear, thought Merve. Maybe that was why he was always so tired, even preoccupied at times. He had help with his wife, but more often than not he had to go home to look after her.

She stood up and went to rinse her thin cotton washcloth in cold water. She wiped her face and neck. This was nothing compared to the heat of the summer, but she was tired and her mind was sluggish.

Her cell phone rang. She noted who it was, the only source of dread in her life at the present time.

"Hello, Mama."

"What are you doing?" asked her mother, at once tender and stern.

"I'm at work just finishing something off."

"But my dear girl, Sunday is not a day for working! You must go out and enjoy yourself. Meet some friends… maybe one of them has a brother….?"

Merve didn't even sigh. Her mother called her twice a day from Iznik, and that was definitely once too often. She should give up. The main problem was that Merve wasn't married. She was an only child, and her mother longed for grandchildren.

"I don't have time for men," she said in an irksome tone to her mother, whose worry had been escalating ever since Merve had turned thirty-three. "Turkish men don't want an educated, independent woman."

But her mother was inured to all this. She sighed heavily and only after a host of endearments was she able to hang up.

"You're my mother, you're my best mother in the world. Goodbye!" she'd said.

Notes and reports lay scattered over her desk. The report was to be a summary, not long but concise, and partly a notification of death and partly a request that the Swedish police notify relatives of this death.

She was also meant to compose an application for the personal details on the victim, one Carl-Ivar Olsson, according to the driver's license inside the wallet that they'd found in his back pocket. Inside had also been a wad of bank notes, both Turkish lira and euros, to a total value that would've been enough to fit her out from head to toe.

Her boss was, moreover, not averse to her adding an elegant postscript to the effect that help with the investigation from the Swedish police would be welcomed.

"Very much welcomed," he'd said at first, but then checked himself. "Alright, strike *very much*, it might make us sound incompetent, but…" He'd been twisting his moustache, a habit of his, and was regarding her with his different-colored eyes: one blue, one brown. "This case probably won't be that easy to solve, no matter who is working on it. It's just too messy."

She agreed. A murder on a boat full of people, mostly unknown passengers that they'd never track down, was indeed *too messy*.

Just questioning the entire crew had worn them out. It had taken all yesterday evening, plus today.

She wrote in Turkish, and then the whole thing would be translated into English in Ankara before being sent to the Interpol headquarters in Lyon, and from there to Stockholm.

Beyond that it was out of her control, the dead man's homeland lying well beyond her radar.

He'd looked pathetic, somehow, she thought. A dapper elderly gentleman. But there was nothing pathetic or dapper about the way he'd been murdered. Or executed, more like.

CHAPTER 10

IT HAD TURNED SEVENTEEN MINUTES past nine in the evening, and it was still Sunday.

Birgitta Olsson was the duty nurse for the night and was sitting, face aglow, on a chair in the unit office. Her arms and legs, unaccustomed as they were to gardening, were aching, but it was a pleasant tenderness that testified to her having used her body for something.

She'd even had time to snatch an afternoon nap and was feeling on top of the world. And she'd called Carl-Ivar, although he hadn't answered.

She'd then received yet another call from Magnus, roughly an hour before she'd left for work, wondering if Carl-Ivar had been in touch and if she'd possibly spotted a carpet in the hotel room or something, back there in Istanbul. She couldn't say that she had, she said, and managed to end the conversation by telling him she had to get cycling to work. It was like she was standing treading water, she joked. She felt tempted to ask if he'd called Annelie to find out if Carl-Ivar had contacted her first.

It would, admittedly, have been embarrassing if Carl-Ivar had called his temporary help, his niece Annelie, rather than her, but there was a certain logic to it. Annelie and Carl-Ivar worked together these days, and if it was a matter of carpets then Annelie was more at home than she was.

These days… , she thought. Carl-Ivar had been looking after his little lost niece temporarily. It had been a good solution for everyone, she thought. But Annelie wasn't that little or lost any more. Oh no, not like when she was growing up. And her son-in-law Magnus doubtless had nothing against talking to Annelie! But he would've been able to work all that out for himself alright without her sticking her nose in.

Down in the hospital's basement changing room she'd discovered that she wasn't the only one to have failed to balance exposure time and sunscreen factor. She and her colleagues had laughed at their porky pink faces and then sauntered off to their respective wards.

Now, sitting up straight with her shoulders relaxed, her hands resting in her lap, she turned her head so that she could see out through the window.

Since the children had left home, she'd started to make a habit of arriving at the ward early. She considered the few extra minutes a luxury rather than a waste of time.

She'd attended neither yoga classes nor group training in meditation, so possibly she had a natural gift for relaxation, in the same way that Carl-Ivar had a gift for working in naps now and then, preferably in front of the TV news.

She at once experienced a powerful sensation of presence. True, it was worrying that Carl-Ivar hadn't gotten in touch, the old fool, but he no doubt had his reasons. He almost always did. He'd probably forgotten to recharge his phone. Or perhaps he turned it off or chose not to recharge so as not to be disturbed?

Doing whatever it was he was doing, that is....

Something of course could've happened to him, but that was a possibility she didn't care to entertain.

She noticed that Anne-Sofie slipped into the office, and dropped her bag on the desk with a thud. But Sofa, as everyone called her, was a together and considerate person who didn't demand everyone's attention for herself, so she left Birgitta in peace and disappeared out into the corridor again.

"Shall we get started?"

Tina Rosenkvist, nicknamed Rosie, slumped down panting into a chair. It was time for her to clock out for the day. Birgitta gave a start but smiled benignly. Sofa quickly joined them and together they rolled on their office chairs closer to Rosie. In their hands were reports that they'd printed out from the computer listing the patients' room numbers and beds, each accompanied by a series of abbreviations that helped them immediately identify the care that needed to be given and the tests that needed to be taken. GBU meant that a patient "gets by unaided," HWE that they needed "help with everything," SBR stood for "strictly bedridden," LD for "log drinking," LDU for "log drinking and urine." The list went on and on, no abbreviation causing any interpretative difficulties. What was hard, on certain nights, was getting it all done.

Rosie was hardly a whiz at reporting systematically; in fact, she was more muddled than anything, but Birgitta let it go. She knew that Rosie wanted to go home. She lived near Kristdala, not many doors down from her childhood home, and her husband was probably already outside the hospital with the engine running. Everyone knew that he always made a point of picking her up, sometimes in a freezing car with both kids strapped into the back seat. Rosie said it was because they could only afford one car and that her husband needed it for work during the day. The bus wasn't much use when you had irregular working hours, everyone knew that. But some people whispered that he just wanted to keep tabs on her.

Birgitta let Rosie babble on to make the procedure as brief as possible and counted on being able to read up on the rest. Or talk to the patients. The older she got, the more use she made of this simple method: to go to primary sources.

And it was these chats with the patients that she enjoyed most these days. In the early days of her career, there was much to get in the way. Lush doctors, among other things. And her fear of making a mistake. The coffee-break chat and all the plans for the kids back at home also drained much of her energy. They were constantly competing, the young mothers, measuring their own value with their children's successes.

Once Rosie had fluttered out – she was of that dainty butterfly mold, with a head of thick, bushy hair – Birgitta sat herself down at the computer and skimmed through which pills or drips were to be administered at 10 pm. The more detailed reading she'd save until later. Looking over her shoulder, Anne-Sofie checked who she was to take the temperatures of so she could get that over and done with.

They then did their medication round at their easy pace, working as usual in perfect harmony.

They'd completed a few rooms when the on call doctor called asking to admit a patient. Birgitta went out into the corridor to take the call so that no one in the room would overhear anything by mistake. Rashly spoken words were easily caught and given wings that flew far beyond the hospital walls.

Acute abdominal pain, said the doctor. She heard by his voice who it was. Christoffer Daun. Annelie had married up, having netted a doctor. But her husband was not the sharpest scalpel in the box, none of them would claim that. He was popular with the patients, though. Especially the female ones. He was a good listener, they said. He definitely had a personal need to be liked or at least admired, but as long as everyone was happy and no one reported him for making improper advances, there was nothing for it but to let it pass. And she guessed that he knew exactly how far he could go. He was an intuitive plucker of the female heartstrings.

Calling now, he said that he didn't think it was the appendix; so the patient was just in for observation, in other words. The tests hadn't all come back but, hey, he couldn't send her home, could he? he said, with a diffidence that Birgitta immediately detected.

"Given that her dog's just been run over..."

"Her dog?"

"Right. That's kind of why she needs a bed. You'll see what I mean when you see her."

He was of a compassionate cut, and that was good. But sometimes it was perhaps more about passing the problem onto someone else, about their not having time down in A&E, and about there being precious few other places that were open 24/7 for people in need.

Birgitta breathed as silently as she could down the phone so that he wouldn't think she was sighing.

"And if anyone can handle her, you can!" he said with emphasis. He knew that flattery would get him somewhere.

Birgitta wasn't one to protest openly. She hung up and continued with Sofa to a woman who'd undergone gall bladder surgery and was due to be discharged the next day. She'd pressed the alarm because she was in pain again, and she showed them with her hand where – high up, although on the left side where her gall bladder had not been. Apart from the operation she was in full health and only fifty-three years old. She looked a little ashen, possibly in a cold sweat. They talked a while.

"Look, I think we'll run an ECG on you. Just to be on the safe side, really," said Birgitta. "I'll call the doctor later and ask him to take a look at you."

Her tone was calm, as she saw no reason to cause the patient unnecessary worry. She asked Sofa to take her temperature – 100.2 – and then took a fresh blood count.

"Just a little prick on your finger," she told the patient, thinking to herself that the problem might be a hemorrhage. Or a nascent infection. Unless it was her heart, which seemed a bit far-fetched given how bright and alert the patient had appeared earlier.

"Pah, it's probably not that bad," said the woman in the bed. "I feel a lot better just having had a chat with you."

Sofa went away to fetch the ECG machine and came rolling it along in the corridor just as they heard the door at the end open. By then, Birgitta had noted that the woman's blood count had dropped slightly, but not alarmingly so. She'd take it up with the on call doctor later. The AAP with the dead dog appeared, supported by one of the A&E nurses. Doubled up and moaning, her face twisted, she came hobbling along. At least she wasn't on a stretcher.

Birgitta walked up to her, and Anne-Sofie let go of the ECG to join them. The girl was twenty-something and wailed in Birgitta's face as she removed her coat – which was heavy, as if she'd filled her pockets with rocks or everything but the kitchen sink – and led her to a bed. It was clear from her hold on the patient's upper arm that she was emaciated. Greasy, streaked hair hid her face and her clothes fit poorly. Her body language gave off two simultaneous messages: Don't touch me! Take care of me!

"I don't wanna live any more," sniffed the young girl loudly.

"There, there, come with me," said Birgitta, and placed a finger over her lips to indicate that she should tone it down, other patients were trying to sleep.

"Fucking hell, how can I be quiet when my belly's killing me? You can't make me! Jesus H Chriiiist! I wish I was deeeead!" She screamed until her face turned red, doubled up again, and collapsed into a kind of squat.

Oh my God, thought Birgitta. She shouldn't be lying here wasting away, she should be in psychiatric care in Västervik.

She exchanged a knowing glance with Sofa. Both were trained in keeping their heads and not getting worked up.

It was the pain in her stomach. The doctor wanted them to keep the patient under observation over night, anyway, and then they'd see what was to be done with her. It could, after all, be her appendix. Appendixes could be deceptive.

They helped the young woman out of her clothes, which reeked of cigarette smoke and needed a good run through a washing machine. They chatted with her and she eventually began to calm down. She was indeed thin, and her nails woefully bitten down to the quicks. I wonder if she's a junkie, thought Birgitta as she scanned the girl's arms for needle punctures. There was already a large bandage covering the crook of one her arms from the blood test she'd been given in A&E, and her forearms were covered in discreet scratches and bruises. It looked like she had a tough life. Birgitta assumed that they'd screened her for blood infections down at A&E, and she'd soon be getting the results.

The patient's name was Nilla Söder.

"You've gotta give me something for my stomach," she whined, then folded up like a penknife in the bed. "I need a shot of something!"

"The doctor wants us to wait a little before giving you any powerful painkillers to give us time to see how things turn out with your tummy," said Birgitta. "Since you're fasting, we can give you a couple of Panadol suppositories to insert in your bottom."

"That won't help!" wailed Nilla. "I can't believe Softie's dead! I want something stronger!"

I bet you do, thought Birgitta.

Softie, that was the dog. Nilla continued to sob pathetically as she exorcised her angst. Birgitta and Anne-Sofie both avoided asking too many questions. They would have to wait, they had all night. They even avoided looking at each other, as it would make it all to clear exactly what they were both suspecting.

"Does anyone in your family know you're here?" asked Birgitta, and the young patient shook her head. "You know, I have to make a note of a next of kin in case we have to call them."

"You don't have to call anyone," Nilla Söder said curtly.

Birgitta pretended not to hear. "You think about who I can write down, alright? We'll be back in a bit."

Twenty-two years old and single, they got out of her later that evening. Nilla Söder hadn't had contact with her mother in years. She was an alcoholic, Nilla finally informed them. Anne-Sofie's expression said that she knew of her.

"Nothing's worked on that woman, she's a wreck," she said afterwards when she and Birgitta had exited into the corridor. Out here in the country, the social awareness was great, but the safety net had its holes.

The next time they went to see Nilla, she'd thought about a possible next of kin.

"You could write Adde, but I don't know if he can afford to buy any minutes for his phone, if you're thinking of calling him," she managed.

"Adde. What's his full name?" wondered Birgitta.

"Andreas Gustavsson."

Birgitta wrote. She also took down the number of that cell phone that was possibly stone dead. Nilla Söder's address was already in the patient records, although Nilla said it wasn't right without going into any greater detail about where she usually crashed.

"Homeless, probably," said Anne-Sofie later. She, who was dependability personified, could not think of anything worse. She rolled her eyes over that fate countless times that evening.

But the way she did it was always so innocent, and she rarely got on Birgitta's nerves. Anne-Sofie was warm-hearted and if there was work to do, she'd do it rather than simply plonk herself down onto the staff sofa like some apathetic, inert lump, as some people did. Or in front of the computer, the new entertainment center where several of her colleagues would sit glued to the screen as soon as they had a spare moment, playing solitaire or mah-jong, doing quizzes or dreaming of a new home on property sites.

Birgitta didn't like forcing people out of their chairs and would rather do most of the work herself, which left her both tired and cranky. But there were also those who'd never dream of sitting in front of the computer – they cleared up, emptied boxes, tidies shelves, and generally puttered about. Birgitta wished that the unit manager spent more time out on the wards and less in the office so she'd be more informed about who the time-wasters were; it was her job to give people a dressing down, not Birgitta's. To go to her behind their backs was unthinkable.

Sofa had another great advantage: she didn't smoke and so wasn't forever popping out to the balcony to get "a little fresh air." All in all, it was a huge bonus to share the night shift with Anne-Sofie.

Birgitta knew that the pleasure was also mutual, and this certainly didn't make matters worse. All that stuff about personal chemistry was interesting. Anyway, it was wonderful when it worked.

"I'd imagine that Nilla's had to manage as best she could ever since she was little," said Birgitta with pity in her voice.

"Some kids have it so tough," Sofa agreed.

Birgitta felt a sharp sting inside her. She thought of her own grandchildren. True, it wasn't as if they were going without shelter or clothing; but they were being raised strictly. They were quite simply too well-brought up. She *had* to take this up with Lotta, she thought.

As the evening wore on, they also found out that Softie had been a mongrel. An Alsatian with much else besides in him, and he was the world's sweetest dog with lovely brown eyes.

"He just took off across the road. He's never done that before. Ran right over Döderhultsvägen and never saw the bus."

Maybe he smelled a rabbit, thought Birgitta. Nilla also has nice eyes. Her heart ached.

Sofa then stuck the ECG under Birgitta's nose. She called Christoffer Daun and gave him the lowdown, that the gall bladder who was due to go home had chest pains and that she'd had an ECG run on her, but that it wasn't up to her to interpret it. He asked her to read out the mechanical assessment; it would do as a rough measure but couldn't be taken as fully reliable. And it didn't sound alarming.

"She's sub-feverish with a temperature of 100.2, the Hb has dropped a bit, but the first reading was before the operation and taken venously. Shall I take it again venously?"

"Yeah, that'd be a good idea."

"But you'll be up later, right?" she said. "She's got a headache, too."

"Let me just clear up down here. But it doesn't sound too serious. She's got a healthy heart."

At least she did earlier, thought Birgitta Olsson. She made a note in the report that she'd contacted the on call doctor and why.

Before the midnight round, Birgitta and Sofa sat down to eat. It was a matter or principle for Birgitta to never eat dinner after twelve, so as not to lose her rhythm. Today she'd brought chicken fillets filled with mozzarella and potato wedges, which she popped into the microwave. She also had a fresh salad in a plastic bag, with dressing and all.

"That looks delicious!" said Anne-Sofie when she saw the food on the plate. For her own part, she had a frozen ready-made Weight Watchers dish that was nowhere near as enticing. After all, it was spring, the time when the hospital staff lived on carrot sticks, cottage cheese, bananas, and fruit salad so as to get into shape for the beach.

They then placed their plates and cutlery in the dishwasher and Birgitta sank down by the side of Nilla Söder's bed, thinking what it was like when Lotta lived at home, and feeling a pang of yearning.

Nilla admitted that the pain in her stomach had eased off a little and she was calmer. More like normal misery, thought Birgitta.

The patient with the pain in her chest was still not fully recovered, but the worst of the pain had subsided. Birgitta felt stupid and a little duplicitous as she stood there reassuring the patient. She'd called Christoffer again; the time had been half past one, his voice had sounded thick and he'd no doubt been asleep. He'd forgotten to do a round of the ward before going to bed and asked her to read out the ECG again.

"It doesn't sound so bad," he said, just as he did the first time. "Let her get some sleep tonight, and I bet it'll all be over in the morning."

Yeah, right! Sure, a good night's sleep was good for lots of things, but not everything.

Birgitta was dissatisfied with his reply, but she could hardly go to the on call room and yank him out of bed.

The breaking dawn found Birgitta and Sofa in the office looking out of the window. They were tired and cold and had pulled their blue hospital cardigans over their shoulders while they looked out over Döderhultsdalen, which was slowly coming to life. There was mist in the valleys and the spruce-covered ridge far away in the backdrop was still darkly toned in indigo. Over in the east was a fringe of yellow-blushed sunlight. The mild sparkles of the morning sun tickling the waves of the Baltic they couldn't see, merely imagine.

There they stood, shoulder to shoulder.

"My goodness, it's so pretty," said Anne-Sofie.

"Isn't it," said Birgitta, with serene emphasis.

CHAPTER 11

IT WAS HALF PAST EIGHT, and Christoffer Daun had just filed his report for the night in the radiology unit, where they had their Monday morning meetings. He'd run an apathetic eye over radius and hip fractures and a dislocated shoulder. The orthopedists would be taking a proper look at the X-rays later. Then he just had to file his report. What he remembered of it.

With heavy steps, he made his way back to the unit on the sixth floor. He'd promised to call on two patients before leaving for home. No one stopped him to ask him anything, patients or staff. And *she* wasn't there.

He cursed himself. It was far too easy to promise to call patients, and unfortunately just as easy to forget. He hadn't come up yet with a foolproof system, but he was working on it. The regular telephone hours didn't stretch that far, not for him, anyway. There were always people wanting to speak to him, mostly women. He was such a good listener, they said. He *saw* them, they said. When boxes of chocolates and bouquets of flowers came tumbling into the clinic, his colleagues wondered tauntingly what he'd really been up to. Nothing special, he'd say, smiling bashfully. He just took time, looked them in the eye, and listened instead of harping on himself. "Was it really that easy?" wondered José Fuentes.

Yes, it was that easy.

But it wasn't just a matter of just shutting up. You had to listen with presence, too, thought Christoffer, but it would be totally pointless to explain to Fuentes how to do it. He was a man of big words and wild gestures.

He sat down in the office, picked up the phone, and opened the file where he had Post-it notes with telephone numbers, which he proceeded to throw away. It felt like his eyelids were going to drop like opera curtains. Tired, tired, tired! He envied the colleagues who shrugged their shoulders at night duty. Why was he so sensitive? He wanted to be more robust. Wanted to be made of different stuff.

He heard the phone ringing, but no one answered. He keyed in the cell phone number. The phone rang again as his foot wagged nervously. He hoped that no one would answer this time, either. So he wouldn't have to go through with it.

Sleep, heavenly sleep!

The man, a patient of his, finally answered, but had such bad hearing that his wife had to take over. It was about his medication. How was it to be taken? Had he been so unclear when he prescribed it?

"It says on the package," he said.

"I see," said the wife, sounding as if she wasn't quite on the ball.

Christoffer was unsure that they'd sorted everything out when he hung up, but what more could he do than patiently explain? He dictated. Then it was time for the next one. She, on the other hand, answered immediately but asked him to call back in five minutes, and she hung up before he had time to say that it wasn't possible. Was she on the toilet?

He checked the time. Five minutes, not a second longer. The demands people made these days! Expecting him to sit and wait before calling. Jesus.

What he didn't know about stress wasn't worth knowing. Both theory and personal experience had given him thorough insight. He was the man who had run like a mad thing in a hamster wheel. Two years in Stockholm at the main university hospital. For many, it was nothing but stimulating. But all that "positive stress" wasn't just beneficial. Naturally, negative stress was worse, but pressure is always dose-related, regardless of how pleasant it is. Some people can take more, others less, but an overdose is never without its side effects.

It was an experience to have to acknowledge his limitations at such a relatively young age. His need for rest. That simple need to get a proper night's sleep, every night. Most people needed six to nine hours of uninterrupted sleep, when their metabolisms had a chance to ease off, their body temperatures to drop, and their pulses and respiration rate to slow.

But what good was it to know that fact if you couldn't settle yourself down?

For the two years or so he was in Stockholm he'd awakened every morning with the feeling of having to scale a mountain. Again and again. Things got so bad, in fact, that he seriously started to think about the meaning of life in a way that was less than healthy. About how he might just as well put an end to his anguish.

Eventually, he would wake with a grinding nausea every morning, day in and day out. He recalled how he struggled with his breakfast. How Annelie would sit watching him from across the table with worried eyes.

But he couldn't be talked into doing something about it. He wasn't ready for that, despite never managing breakfast and vomiting after the morning coffee at the clinic. If, that is, he made it anywhere near a cafeteria.

Believing that he could change the extrinsic conditions at the capital's main hospital was pure idiocy.

"You've just got to grin and bear it," he was told. "Those who can't stand the heat don't hang around."

He blinked and looked at his watch. Five minutes had passed, almost. But now he had neither the will nor the energy to call up the old biddy on the toilet. Well, she only had herself to blame, he'd given her a chance. She'd have to wait till tomorrow.

He stood up and left the ward.

Five minutes later, Christoffer Daun was making his way down through the hospital two steps at a time. Jeans and short-sleeved shirt. His private self.

He almost collided with Ronny Alexandersson, who was on his way up.

"Good night!" Ronny called after him as Daun continued down.

Ronny was Christoffer's guru. He looked up to him. It was Ronny who'd taught him alternative rules of life when he first arrived at the clinic in Oskarshamn and was worried about how he'd cope with the job.

"Don't worry about coping," said Ronny without a hint of critical undertone. "Self-pity takes up too much space. Just get working and we'll take things as they come. There's room for all sorts here."

Afterwards, Christoffer found that he was right.

"Here we work to live, not live to work," said Ronny a while later. "It's a choice you make."

Ronnyisms was what Christoffer called these words of wisdom. There came more, and he collected them in the small green notepad that he always carried with him in the spacious pocket of his doctor's coat. For Ronny had much to give, his knowledge seemed inexhaustible. He wasn't the type to go strutting around. He just *was*.

The ground floor was full of morning activity, as people streamed in through the main entrance. Christoffer slowed down and directed his gaze onto the steps so as not to have to meet people's eyes and greet them. Besides, there was someone he wanted to avoid, and he'd managed so far.

Hunger wrung his stomach as he was greeted by the aroma of coffee from the cafeteria, but he passed through the glass doors at the same time as radiology consultant Göran Bladh passed in. At least he wasn't swaying, even if his gait was a little bow-legged, Christoffer noted. But Bladh's visage was extremely bright red and he was late. He'd probably been on a bender the entire weekend and had had trouble dragging himself out of bed.

The air that ricocheted off him was chilly, and he should have been wearing his coat, but it was in the car.

He rummaged around for his car keys in the outer pocket of his packsack, unlocked the red Passat and plonked himself down behind the wheel.

Just as he was about to start the engine he spotted a slip of red paper flapping under the windshield wiper.

"Crap!" he said half aloud to himself and climbed out far enough to snatch up the note. He sank back behind the wheel, tossed the piece of paper onto the passenger seat, then turned, at last, the ignition key.

The note was a half-sheet of paper, and out of sheer defiance he refused to read what was on it. He'd made it this far. But she was craftier!

But when he threw the car into reverse and was about to pull out from his parking spot, he couldn't help casting a quick glance at the text. Easy-to-read print with soft curves that suggested care, tenderness even. A hand that until recently could make him weak at the knees now only inspired aversion. A sense of cloying. He wanted out. The duplicity depressed him. It was complicated.

And yet it was hard to avoid the thrill. It so easily fired him up. It was *life*. And the woman who put the note there knew that only too well.

He scrunched the note up into a tight little ball and threw it crossly onto the floor by the passenger seat. And regretted it immediately. It couldn't lie around there, for God's sake!

But by then he was already on his way out of his parking place and couldn't reach that far down with his hand while driving. The Santa-red paper ball rolled up and down as the car swung out onto route 37.

I mustn't forget to pick it up and throw it away before I get home, he said to himself as he drove westward.

As he passed the town boundary, the clouds started to build up, but the spring light was still strong enough for him to put his sunglasses on. The road was almost empty.

The car knew the way. Soon it would turn toward Kristdala at the Århult junction and continue northward on a minor road.

It had never been his intention to settle in Småland, the plan had been to stay in Stockholm after his specialist training. He was a Stockholmer, after all, of course that was what he'd do! What would a city boy do out in the wilds of Småland? Pick blueberries and stare at cows?

The property that he and Annelie had already bought out in the sticks in Bråbo, bought because they'd both fallen for it, they'd intended to keep as a summer retreat. A red-painted two-story cottage with the obligatory white corners, a barn, a henhouse – sans hens – and a wonky outhouse that seemed to be praying to the gods not to be demolished.

Something like that.

"If it was at least Kalmar," his mother had sighed.

She was passionate about the pretty medieval town fifty miles to the south, which even boasted a magnificent castle. It was a town steeped in history. Kalmar was just that little bit more classy.

"Oskarshamn, Christoffer dear! What do you want to be going there for?"

Quite. What was he going there for?

The birches in their groves were just coming into leaf. He and Annelie lived in one of Sweden's largest uninterrupted stretches of cultivated countryside. It was so beautiful that he thought about it every day, regardless of season, as he drove the fifteen miles to work. Today, too, in spite of his feeling tired and irritated.

He saw stone walls and natural log fences and small lots. Bråbygden was no longer a depopulated area. The permanent residents were growing in number, and there were Germans and Dutch here who liked to take care of their property. The houses were a radiant white and the glazed verandas shiny and new.

The last leg of the journey was uphill. The villages, which consisted largely of a collection of farms, were high up. They lived in Bråbo. And there was Äshult, Kärrhult, Bjälebo, Fallebo, Applekulla, and Krokshult, plus a handful of other villages with equally wholesome names.

Their neighbor was repairing his fence, he saw from afar. The old boy had been at it for days. His son, who was called Lars and nudging sixty, would probably be lending a hand. There was something about that man, not just the fact that an accident – which very few people actually knew the details of but still liked to speculate about – had left him with one leg shorter than the other. Lars kept himself to himself, but was kind-hearted, as Annelie said. They were distant relatives, Annelie and the neighbors.

Christoffer parked in the courtyard outside the barn and, opening the car door, was met by fresh, soil-steeped air and birdsong. A car drove past on the road, probably the neighbor who lived further down toward Bäljebo giving the kids a lift to preschool.

Kids, he thought. Would things have been different had they had kids?

There was no point checking the mailbox, the postman wouldn't have come yet and Annelie had no doubt already gone to get the newspaper.

As he walked toward the kitchen door, his eyes traveled to the slope behind the house. The fairies were still dancing in the dale, and now the sun was starting to burst its way through white fluffs of cloud that had started to form in an azure sky.

He gave a little smile, took a deep breath, and opened the door.

Again he was greeted by the aroma of coffee. Annelie had finished her breakfast, dressed, and put on her work face, having applied just the right amount of makeup, particularly around the eyes, to turn them a clear, sparkling blue.

She was busy stacking the dishwasher. She was pretty, his Annelie. He knew, of course, that she was pretty, but hadn't registered it for a while. A heart-shaped face, blonde bangs and soft shoulder-length hair. She'd always been curvy and moaned constantly about not being rake thin, but he liked the fact that she had shoulders, boobs, and a butt.

"I'm glad you're back," she said giving him a fleeting stroke of the cheek. "How was your night?"

"The same," he answered thickly and half absently, wondering whether to make some oatmeal in the microwave or to have cereal instead.

It'd have to be the cereal. He opened the fridge and shook the carton of milk. It'd do. But no coffee, however tempting it smelled. He wouldn't get to sleep. And not being able to sleep was hell on earth.

"Then I'll take the car," she said. "I called the garage, and they said they won't be ready with mine till tomorrow. Call me if there's something you want me to pick up."

Right, of course! Her car was at the garage. She was helping her uncle out in his shop in Oskarshamn now that she was out of work. She'd never got a permanent teaching post in Oskarshamn. In Stockholm, there was lots of substitute work, even for longer periods than normal, lasting whole terms.

"Are the keys in it?" she asked from the doorway.

"Er… yeah."

He heard her footsteps on the gravel, the car door slam, and the engine start and drone as she drove out onto the road.

The sun had now broken through fully. He wolfed down his cereal. The morning light was shining brightly over the courtyard. It was really a day for him to be outside. Digging, planting, pruning. It always felt such a waste to sleep away a radiantly beautiful day.

He planned to go for a long leisurely jog once he'd had a few hours' sleep. He usually found it difficult to get the body going at any kind of pace the day after night duty.

The house was liberatingly quiet. He mostly thumbed through the paper, unable to focus on the text. His tension eased, his muscles softened, and doziness came creeping. This lethargy that was so agreeable.

Less than five minutes later he was in bed. Annelie hadn't made the bed, knowing that he'd snuggle down as soon as he got home. He lay naked on the cool sheet. A window was on its hook and he'd pulled down the dark blinds that he'd hung up when he'd started to develop insomnia.

The spring sun had a tendency to slip through where it could, especially through the gaps down the side, so he turned over and pulled the comforter across his face.

Just as his body was starting to drift away and his mind to doze off, the red paper ball came rolling back. Like a warning signal that seared the inside of his eyelids.

Fuck! He'd forgotten to pick it up from the floor of the car!

His heart started to race. He leapt out of bed and stood naked on the pine floorboards, his teeth rattling as the first panic attack flooded through his body.

CHAPTER 12

I HAVE TWO DAUGHTERS who are my flesh and blood.

Claes Claesson didn't say it loud, but he thought it. He was lying outstretched on the sofa with little Cannon Ball on his chest.

And then there's Cecilia, too, he thought, because he couldn't just ignore her. She wasn't his flesh and blood, but she was his all the same.

His newest daughter lay on him like a frog with her round cheek pressed against his chest. He'd put on a faded, soft cotton top. Relaxed, they lay there, he and Nora, two days old, with legs and arms still spindly. They'd soon fill out and get those lovely folds. Now she was sleeping the innocent sleep of the newborn, giving the occasional jerk; she whimpered, fell silent, and went back to sleep.

Klara had wanted her mom to drop her off at preschool, needing Veronika to herself for a while. "My mommy," she said, taking Veronika by the hand and leading her away. She could have stayed at home, but she was dying to tell her playmates about her new sister. Now that one of her parents was expected to be at home each day, the rules limited her preschool time to three hours, between eight and eleven, and that was probably more generous that elsewhere in the world. Women in Sweden who wanted to stay working dared to have babies without the fear of ending up at the kitchen sink.

But she wasn't allowed to stay over lunch; eating at preschool was apparently regarded as lacking pedagogical value, according to the rules.

The newspaper lay spread out over his legs and he picked it up and started reading it over Nora's little body. The house was strangely quiet. He skimmed through half an article about a man who'd adeptly plundered a company and was now living in Latin America.

His eyes grew at once heavy, for it had been a tough night, and he let them fall, dropping the paper onto the floor and descending one level of consciousness. He could hear birdsong, too, a whole orchestra that squeezed its way in through the opening in the veranda door. The blackbird was the loudest. Later in the season, the lark would start to warble. He would hear it now that they'd moved out to the tranquil housing estates in Kolberga. When he lived more centrally, birdsong was not something he was particularly fond of.

Nora whimpered. He raised his level of awareness a notch and laid a hand over her head. She fell silent.

His leave from work felt good. He'd called Louise Jasinski already yesterday, Sunday. She congratulated him and didn't even sigh at the prospect of having to shuffle the schedule around a week earlier. Unforeseen things happened all the time, that's just how things were. He'd also called and told his sister Gunilla, but not his brother.

Veronika and he really were two very lucky people to have first had Klara and then another one! There'd been no guarantee that they could've had children, having met so late in life.

He'd have to go and see his mother in the home and give her the news about Nora, he thought. He wanted to, even though she'd just stare blankly at him. Perhaps frown, as if deep down, as something was moving after all; dull and sluggish to be sure, but still an indication that she'd understood that she'd got another grandchild. And that it was he who'd gratified his demanding mother with it. He still had his primitive need to win her support and approval. It was something he could smile at these days.

Life had been good to him these past years. He could see himself when he was hung up on the crazy notion that the neurotic was exciting. The women in his life had made it a quagmire. Capriciousness and the veiled and dark sides had a magnetic pull, and life was rarely tedious. But at the same time, the constant swings between fighting and reconciling wore him down. Gastric pain gnawed at him, his sleep was periodically shallow, and he was constantly tired. But he thought that was what it was meant to be like.

The women in his life had all been strong, but in different ways. Veronika, who was certainly strong, was reasonable with it. Just think how wrong he'd been, and for all that time! How stupid can you get?

Veronika called and wondered if Nora was holding up. If all was well she'd get a bit of shopping done. Nora was sleeping like a little piglet, he said.

Five minutes later, Louise Jasinski called, and he could tell at once that she wasn't interested in hearing about if he'd filled in his application for leave.

A murdered carpet dealer! Would he mind traveling to Istanbul?

You've pushed your luck too far, was his spontaneous thought. At the same time, he began to wonder whether it was the same dealer he'd given his handed-down rug to for repair. Was he dead? That'd be terrible!

And a very brutal death it had been, too. Sheer butchery, in fact, and it had occurred last Saturday, just before four o'clock on a ferry in Istanbul as it came in to dock. According to the Turkish documents, there'd been fresh blood from his belly when they found him, and they assumed he'd been murdered just before the passengers were due to disembark. His Swedish driver's license was in his wallet, but a relative was still needed to go there and confirm his identity.

"It was one of the crew that found him, the report don't say exactly where, but I guess a ferry's got lots of places to hide a body in," said Louise. "There's no suspect, or a murder weapon, which was probably a knife, but all the killer had to do, I suppose, was chuck whatever it was into the sea," she continued.

Claesson could see the bloody mess in front of him. The associations also brought up images of bustling crowds, traffic noise, and gangs. Easy to make a getaway, in other words.

He'd been away before, but only to Europe. Istanbul was right on the border. Searches and investigations, as well as autopsies, were always conducted in the country where the crime had been committed, that was crime-school ABC. The same went for trials, if things ever went to court. When the foreign country requested help from the victim's own country, it was always on their terms. Things didn't always go smoothly, that he knew from before. The world had many a tender toe.

Louise read from the document she'd received from Interpol in Stockholm. He could see her now, her head slightly jutted forwards and tilted in affected humility. And then bang, a sudden broad smile and the sparkle-eyes on full power.

"I mean, Istanbul, Claesson. I don't want to go myself. Please don't ask me why," she said in a mild, pleading tone, and he figured it might have had something to do with her new man. "That's just the way it is. And I know that you've got a newborn baby at home, but you won't have to be away for more than a few days. We have to plan carefully to make sure things go as well as they can…"

Peter Berg was tied up as preliminary investigator on another case that he couldn't drop, and Janne Lundin felt that his language skills weren't up to scratch – he was referring to his English. Erika Ljung was working in Malmö trying her hand at a reassignment. That Martin Lerde wasn't dry enough behind the ears was patently obvious, and his name hadn't even been mentioned, even if he probably thought he was the best man for the job, she added bitingly.

On the other hand, Mustafa Özen had been pegged as the man to go under *all* circumstances. He was pretty new in CID, but he knew the lingo and the culture.

"Good stuff, as Lundin said," laughed Louise, mimicking their colleague. She revealed that Martin Lerde's mood had thoroughly darkened when he heard the rumor. "During coffee this morning, he was so pissed off he slammed his cup down and the handle broke off!"

Claesson gave a smile.

"But how much Turkish can Özen actually speak? Wasn't he just a little kid when he came here?" he asked.

He was six, Claesson was told. He didn't know Mustafa Özen that well, and that was all well and good, he thought. They were not a family here, just colleagues, even though some were closer to him than others, such as Janne Lundin. Özen, who was called Musty by his closest colleagues, claimed that he was totally familiar with Turkish, that it was what they spoke at home, Louise informed him. Özen was, naturally, raring to go.

"Don't they have many languages in Turkey?" asked Claesson.

"How on Earth would I know? What is this, twenty questions? Anyway, isn't that a bit more to the east, Kurdish and other languages? I'd imagine it's like in Sweden, with Sami and Finnish, minority languages and stuff… But as I've learned, Turkish is the majority language and is what's used by the national administration. Although…"

"Although what?"

"I'm not a hundred percent certain that we managed to outplay the National boys, and naturally they want to go down. I'm doing what I can, but it's a grabfest, as you know," Louise said, and he nodded on the other end of the line. It was always like this, particularly for the bigger, more prestigious investigations, like airplane crashes or shipwrecks.

"Of course, the chances of us getting to go are greater if we say we're sending people with knowledge of the victim's home town and who can speak the local lingo. But our trump card will be that the other one is a highly experienced violent crime investigator, someone with gravitas," she said.

"And that person is me, you mean?" he said with a grin.

"Yes. I mean, you realize yourself that…" he heard Louise continue as if she could read his mind.

He was still lying flat on the sofa. His pulse had quickened, and his heart was thumping so violently from decision anxiety that he feared Nora would be awakened by the noise. Under normal circumstances it would've been good-bye and thanks for the ticket. Exciting and educational.

But now…

It wasn't just that he didn't want to leave Veronika on her own with the new baby and everything. It was more about his not wanting to miss that downy period, the very tenderest and so very ephemeral. For purely selfish reasons he wanted to watch over his new daughter. To be home, all of them together, a time that would never come again…

Though of course Nora would be with him for a long time, forever, until he died. And after all, the trip was only for a few days.

Veronika, he thought then. The prospect of even brining it up with her felt leaden. Not because she'd get angry or disappointed, but because the very question begged a yes.

"We'll first have to look into what can be investigated here at home, of course, and then you'll have to take that to Istanbul, but we… or rather, you and Özen, will have to get over there as quickly as you can," she said coaxingly.

And he couldn't help smiling as he lay there on the sofa with the cordless to his ear. It wasn't hard to understand that Louise had made it far up the career ladder. At first, her efficiency and unconcealed ambition had rubbed him up the wrong way. Capable women were easily seen as officious by men, said Veronika. It was a way of bringing them down, a defense mechanism against competition that didn't come from another man, which was easier to tackle, more established, more familiar, she said.

He wasn't always that thrilled when the feminist wave cascaded over the kitchen table, but he was trying to learn.

And he'd doubtlessly tried to bring Louise down himself at times over the years. A woman who didn't just want to work with domestic violence, what can you do? Janne Lundin took on a great many such cases these days, he was mature – soon due to retire – and sensible, and made people feel calm and able to put their trust in him, but he didn't pull his punches. It worked out well, and Janne was happy.

Louise was like a terrier. "We've checked the records, and the carpet dealer's clean, and never been under surveillance. Ludvigsson and Özen have just gone to see his widow to give her the news before the media runs with the ball. If she's home, that is."

Claesson had a vague memory of Veronika saying that she knew the carpet dealer's wife. That she worked at Veronika's clinic, or something along those lines.

"We're counting on the wife being willing to go down and identify."

"Has he got children?"

"Two, grown up."

He could hear that he was asking far too many questions. But he could still back out. He had his statutory right to parental leave. Ten days. Guaranteed!

"You've got a valid passport, I assume?" asked Louise and gave him the name of the Turkish preliminary investigator. It was on the encrypted Interpol report. She tried pronouncing it. The first name was easy, Fuat, but the surname wasn't one easily committed to memory. Something beginning with K. But it sounded Asian and evoked images of a dark-haired man with inscrutable velvety eyes and a neat, jet black moustache.

Louise continued to talk about the widow and the two adult children and about coordinating their identification of the body with his and Özen's trip down. He listened with half an ear.

Louise fell silent on the other end. "Are you listening to me?"

"Of course," he said quickly. "But you're talking as if it's already been decided that I'm going. Can't I at least run it by Veronika first?"

Claes heard Veronika's bike trundle into the garden. Tire against gravel. She opened the door. Nora whimpered.

"Jesus, the stress," she said, checking the time. "We've got just over an hour before we have to fetch her again."

She picked up Nora and sat down to breast-feed.

"What's up?"

She looked at him.

"Louise Jasinski just called."

That was all he said.

"Yes? And?"

His divided loyalty sat like a brand on his forehead.

"Did she want you to go in to work?"

Veronika smiled crookedly.

"What would you say if I went to Istanbul for a few days?"

"Oh." She fell silent.

He said nothing, either.

"Are you out of your mind?" she finally said. "What do you have to go there for?"

"You know that carpet dealer?"

"Who?"

"The one who's got our rug."

"Well, yes, and?"

"He's been murdered in Istanbul… Nah, forget it. You're right. It'd be crazy to go," he said resignedly, following it with the world's deepest sigh.

A mite feigned it was, he could admit that. A bit of emotional blackmail.

"Oh dear, oh dear, oh dear," she said teasingly. "Hold your horses, why don't you? Come on, you have to let me get used to the idea. I guess I'll survive a few days. Me and the girls… I could ask Cecilia to come over. She's not totally useless, you know… It'll just be a pity for you to miss out being with Nora, now that she's changing so much from day to day. But I can be terribly nice and kind and sweet and all that, you know I can be, and take photos of her every day and text you over there in the far east."

"Come on, it's not that far…"

He tried to make the trip shorter. Shrink the journey.

"A three- or four-hour flight, I'd imagine," she said. "It's not exactly a return trip to Kalmar. If I put it like that."

CHAPTER 13

NETTAN BROMSE HAD Mondays free, it was a way of prolonging the weekend. Sven was always free. He'd reached that age.

They'd just come home from Skorpetorp golf club and it was getting close to midday. They were starving.

Nettan had, conveniently enough, some leftovers from the weekend – roast pork with wine sauce – that she popped into the microwave while she chopped up a salad and set the kitchen table. Sven was in the shower. He didn't hang around; she intended to have her shower after lunch.

She left the wine box where it was in the cupboard under the little working top. It felt slightly "uncouth" to put the entire box on the table, and filling a carafe and decanting on a normal weekday like this would be making an unnecessary show of things. And anyway, she was the only one drinking.

She'd already squirted a wine-red jet into the glass as silently as she could while preparing the food. She drank in shamefaced gulps and then rinsed out and wiped the glass before placing it on the table by her plate. A small glass with lunch you could treat yourself to, it's what almost everyone she knew did. There was no reason to hold back when you'd passed the sixty mark. The Mediterranean diet with its olive oil, shellfish, and a glass of wine a day, at least, was good for the circulation and what's more it helped to ward off Alzheimer's, she'd read recently.

Or was it coffee that counteracted this depressing dementia disease? She'd have to google it or ask Birgitta the next time they had a chat over the garden hedge. Pooh, what the hell!

Sven was a beer man, and she didn't want to put his can on the table before it was time to eat so it'd be nice and cold from the fridge.

The bathroom door opened. Steam puffed from Sven as he chugged his way into the bedroom with a towel around his hips.

"Lunch is ready!" she called merrily. She liked being merry, with or without wine coursing through her body.

"Smells nice," he called back just as affectionately as he entered the bedroom, where he quickly dressed himself and returned in a pair of khaki pants and an orange piqué top that Nettan had given him that week and that was apparently that summer's color.

When they'd seated themselves and laid the paper napkins on their laps – they were *royal blue*, according to the packaging – their gaze drifted naturally out through the window. As it always did, since the only things that ever chanced to happen did so on the street outside. Of each other they had their visual fill, although without becoming indifferent.

The street outside was as calm as ever. There was, in other words, nothing more exciting to look at than the odd dog owner out exercising their mutt, or Enoksson's driving school car creeping by at a snail's pace.

They chewed on. Nettan took another sip of wine and wondered if she dared pour herself another glass and risk one of Sven's dirty looks. Sven drank his beer in large gulps, acquiring a froth moustache that he wiped away with his napkin. He then got up and went to fetch another beer as if it was the most natural thing in the world. Nettan dished up some more salad and splashed some dressing over it. The salad filled out the stomach. They were heading toward the summer season.

"Golf sucks," said Sven, reseating himself.

Their gaze was drawn again to the street. Another car came slowly cruising, but without the Enoksson logo. It was a police car. It drove past their garden and stopped right outside the Olsson's driveway.

"Oh my, I hope something hasn't happened," said Nettan when they saw two police officers, a short blonde woman and a large, red-faced man, step out. They both walked toward the door and out of sight. Nettan and Sven Bromse heard Birgitta Olsson's door shut.

"Well, at least she's at home," said Sven.

They looked at each other.

Birgitta Olsson was sleeping soundly, but still not as deeply as when she slept at night.

Now a distant thudding sound penetrated her dreams. She didn't like it and hoped it would stop. Someone was knocking on her door, but she didn't want to get up and turned over in her bed to find a position in which she could get back to sleep.

But the door knocker stubbornly continued, so she rose drowsily and walked to the front door, tying her robe around her as she went. The sunlight immediately stabbed at her eyes, and without her sunglasses on she was forced to squint. But it didn't require much clarity of vision to understand that something terrible had happened.

"Are you Birgitta Olsson?" asked the man outside, inviting himself in.

The moment she stepped aside to let the two officers pass, she realized that someone was dead.

"Is it Carl-Ivar?" she asked, lips taught.

"Yes, your husband has been found dead in Istanbul," said the strawberry blonde one.

He hadn't called as he usually did, and she'd suspected but suppressed the feeling that something was wrong. What more could she have done to try to get hold of him?

They sat in the kitchen. No, she certainly didn't feel like putting some coffee on, she said and offered them none, either. Her mind had come to a standstill. The police officers were both silent. The one, a women, was so young that Birgitta almost wanted to spare her from the kind of misery that the dead caused. Even more, she wanted to stop her life when the male officer continued to relate the brutal facts. He was called Lennie and did his best. Lennie was the kind of name that was easy to remember, unusual yet soft and kind.

Carl-Ivar had been sitting on a ferry and someone had stabbed him to death, she was told.

"It can't be true!" she spluttered.

They didn't answer "well it is," but left the truth of **it hang**ing in the air.

"But we don't know who did it or why. It happened last Saturday. We didn't hear about it at the station in Oskarshamn until now."

He needed to explain himself, she recognized it from her own job. And it was true that Carl-Ivar hadn't been in touch, she said, and the young policewomen opened a little notebook and made notes.

It was preposterous for Carl-Ivar to be murdered, she thought. It wasn't his style to die so dramatically.

Her heart thumped but her brain insisted on remaining inert. The tears didn't come – although it would have been the right thing to cry, to be inconsolable in front of these two police officers.

But she'd have to do her blubbering later, when she wasn't in her shock phase, as they said at work. The reaction phase would come sooner or later, she knew that. As for her, it could come when it saw fit. She wouldn't be feeling particularly good for a while, that's just how it was.

Did he often travel by ferry?

"I've no idea," she said, and felt a little foolish for not having had a better idea of what her husband was up to. It occurred to her to ask, "But what ferry was it?"

"As we understand it, it went from Istanbul up through the Bosporus," said Lennie, sounding a little out of his geographical comfort zone. The police officers had only been asked to announce the death, and she knew what that was like. But she couldn't help wondering where Carl-Ivar had been going.

"Was he alone?" she asked warily.

"We don't really know, but he was alone when he was found."

No, she had no idea of anything at all, she said. He'd been due home the next day. No enemies, as far as she was aware.

"Carl-Ivar isn't… wasn't the kind of person to make enemies. One or two people he might have fallen out with perhaps… but… I can't actually think of anyone right now."

She told them that she, too, had been in Istanbul. They'd traveled there with the carpet dealer in Kalmar and his wife, but she'd come back home alone on Friday in order to work. She'd been working last night, she said, which was why she was in her robe this late in the day. She gave them the name of the carpet dealer in Kalmar. Lennie Ludvigsson squirmed awkwardly as he explained that in the case of a death such as this, one that wasn't *natural*, they had to question everyone involved.

"So… do you by any chance have anything to show when you left Istanbul?"

She'd flown by e-ticket, and might have the printout and the flight number somewhere, she said. Her bag was in the hall, so she went to fetch it and dug out a folded printout that she said they could keep.

"And yesterday morning I was in town, and there are lots of people who can vouch for me. Veronika Lundborg, as a matter of fact, you know her, right?"

They nodded. Claesson's wife.

"I can't believe that when I left, it was the last time I saw Carl-Ivar." She gave a sniff and stared out through the window. "Alive, at least…"

"You can call us later if you think of anything," said Lennie Ludvigsson.

"But are you completely sure it really is Carl-Ivar? I'd like to go there and confirm it with my own eyes. I'm sure the children will want to come, too… maybe… if they can get away."

Yes, they'd thought of that, said the officers. Two of their colleagues from Oskarshamn would probably go down to help with the investigation. "It still hasn't been decided which of our colleagues, but whoever it is they'll try to be with you when you identify your husband. But according to the driver's license he was carrying, it is him. There'll be an investigation, of course… We don't know how hard it will be to catch his killer, but we'll do what we can."

"Have you got someone who can be with you?" asked the blonde woman.

"I'll be fine," she said, still completely empty inside, bewildered almost. "I'll manage, I'll call and tell the children."

To think that Carl-Ivar would mess things up and go and get himself murdered! The only comfort she had was that he was probably happy up there in heaven that it had at least happened in Turkey. In his beloved Istanbul.

A streak of something like jealousy shot through her.

CHAPTER 14

CLAESSON HAD JUST PASSED the police reception desk and received a big hug from Nina.

Always a man of habit, he ran up the stairs and opened the glass door to the CID section. The sofas in the little waiting room immediately off the corridor were empty. The time was five past twelve and people were at lunch. For his part, he'd wolfed down some milk and muesli before leaving home by bike.

He could hear someone talking on the phone; the voice came from Louise Jasinski's room, two doors down from his. Both their rooms were facing Slottsgatan. Lovely, big rooms they were, and right in the center of town. They were very privileged.

Just as he was stepping into his office, Benny Grahn appeared in the corridor.

"What you doin' here," Benny said with a teasing smile. "Shouldn't you be at home changin' diapers?"

"A little job's come up," Claesson said. "Turkey."

Benny nodded. He knew. "Soow anyrord…" he then said in his thickest regional dialect, scratching his scalp, "… heard that the lass shot out as if from a cannon. An' that you almost had to get the first aid kit and rubber gloves from the car an' play at bein' midwife?"

"Yeah…" Claesson chuckled. "We've seriously thought about calling her CB, for Cannon Ball."

"Though maybe it's not quite your thing," Benny pointed out. "What with the blood an' all…"

Louise Jasinski had heard their voices and came out of her room.

"I'm glad you've agreed to go," she said first, referring to the Istanbul investigation. "Janne's made sure that everyone knows it was an emergency," she continued, this time meaning the birth. "It's hard to believe, when everything had been so carefully planned and all."

Janne Lundin had, of course, elaborated a little on the story.

"I guess I've never been such a danger to other road users," he said. He enjoyed telling the tale. "You can imagine all the Saturday shoppers crawling along outside Mönsterås. So, sure, I thought a number of times… or rather, the whole time, that I'd have to get out and deliver the baby myself there by the side of the road. Veronika's contractions were coming constantly by this time, and she was resisting out of sheer will power… So once we'd got there and she ended up on a gurney and they were taking her into the elevator, it was as if someone had pulled out the plug. She groaned 'It's coming' and so the midwife had to deliver it on the run. So you could say that she was born to the cheers of the crowd, our Nora."

Claesson had been on a constant high since last Saturday. There was no reason for him to restrain his joy.

"Özen will be here soon, he's out on a routine call. We'll meet in your room," said Louise. She went back into her office to fetch the paper they'd printed out from Istanbul. She handed it to him: "In the meantime you can cast an eye over this."

He went into his office and opened the window. It was stuffy in there, and he sank down beside his desk and read. Nothing new here; Louise had gone over most of it on the phone.

The head of investigations in Istanbul was called Fuat Karaoğlu, however the hell that was pronounced. Holding the pen, or rather pressing the keys, for the report had been one Merve Turpan. Was that a man or a woman?

When he'd read the congenially disposed report – they were inviting them down, for Pete's sake – enough times that he pretty much knew it by heart, he turned to his computer. While it booted up and ran through all the security software, he started, a little absent-mindedly, to tear open his mail. He then got down to answering some emails and deleting others.

He noticed that his hands were fidgety and wanted to keep active, and that he felt it was pointless to sit there waiting, wasting away time that he really should be spending at home. So he shuffled a few documents and stacked them in a pile that he really would have to polish off very soon. Maybe I could take some back with me, he thought, procrastinatingly. Parental leave had hit him straight on.

But no, he changed his mind. He wouldn't lug home jobs that he'd only have to lug back undone. Had he been ten, fifteen years younger, possibly. Back then he was hungry and hunted like a man possessed, and always believed he had to be one step ahead. Which proved to be completely right in some situations, but completely wrong in others.

The original plan had been that he'd take out his ten days of parental leave after the birth, and the longer leave when Veronika started work around Christmas time. This time, he looked forward, with a degree of wariness, to it. The last time, with Klara, he'd initially been restless, felt alienated from society and life, and unable to identify with the role of stroller pusher. But once he'd relaxed and realized that he had to plan his days, a break from the rat race was just what he needed. The greatest discovery was finding how dispensable he was at work. This should have dented his ego, but to his surprise it didn't. On the contrary, it gave him a sense of freedom. If he wasn't there, there were others to fill his place.

Apart from just now, evidently!

He checked the time. Half an hour had passed. Hopefully, Ludvigsson and Jönsson would make it back in time from the widow's house for him to hear what she'd had to say, before he and Özen headed off to the carpet shop. They hadn't notified the woman who apparently looked after it while the carpet dealer was abroad, as they were keen to announce the death face-to-face to gauge her reaction.

Istanbul! He'd have to go to the bookstore to buy a travel guide on Turkey, and Istanbul in particular.

He got himself a cup of coffee from the coffee machine for want of anything better to do. The weekend had been relatively calm, he found out by hanging around the lunchroom. The usual stuff: fights, domestics, assaults, and some petty theft, including a break-in at an all-night store in Blomstermåla.

Then he heard the door out to the stairs open and shut, and shortly afterwards Mustafa Özen appeared. He was in uniform, the job he'd been on had required it.

"Come in," said Claesson, gesturing to a chair across the desk from him.

Özen looked uncomfortable. Claesson realized that he had to show a bit of initiative. He picked up the phone and called Louise.

"Jasinski is booking a flight for you and me, you know that, I take it?"

"Yes." His forehead was glistening, perhaps from the pressure of sitting in front of Chief Inspector Claesson.

"Good. You can go and get into your civvies later and perhaps get a bite to eat?"

"I grabbed a burger on the way in."

"Good. Have you been to Istanbul before?"

"Yes, many times."

"Are you from there?"

"No, I come from central Turkey."

"OK. If you and I really get our skates on here at home, we'll be leaving on Wednesday. And today's Monday. That'll mean a certain amount of planning."

Louise entered the room and stood with her back against a bookshelf. She listened.

"Your main job is to be a cultural and linguistic link between us and the Turks."

"I'd thought as much."

"Good."

"We'll get cracking as soon as you're changed."

"OK," said Özen and started to rise from his chair.

"What do you know about Oriental carpets?" said Claesson.

Özen swallowed.

"Not much, if I'm honest," he said.

OK, then, thought Claesson. They were both about to learn a lot about carpets.

CHAPTER 15

CLAESSON AND ÖZEN FOUND themselves crossing Lilla Torget Square five minutes later. They had no trouble locating the carpet shop on the corner a short way down Frejagatan. A sign in the door announced that the shop was open. The little handwritten card seemed a little old-fashioned at a time when everyone was designing their own signs on the computer in some charming yet sometimes overdone way, but it looked nice.

They ascended the short flight of steps and stepped inside. A relatively young woman in a pair of blue jeans and a tight white top with narrow red stripes, summer-fresh in Claesson's opinion, stood at a table, or counter or whatever you called it. She was out of place in a carpet shop, but he could be wrong, he thought as he introduced himself and Özen, noticing that her throat immediately began to blush a violent red and her eyes flit about anxiously.

"What's happened?"

"Carl-Ivar Olsson has been found dead in Istanbul," he said, and she collapsed over the table in a kind of dry weeping.

They stood in silence watching her for a minute or perhaps two – a long time when you're waiting – to give her time to recover a little. Meanwhile, Claesson's gaze swept over the walls. He saw nothing but carpets: blood red, ruddy, bluish, green toned, dark claret, and all richly patterned. Could these innocent floor coverings be a reason for murder? He found that hard to believe, but he recalled his brother's craving for the little threadbare rug that he'd happened to inherit from his parents when their mother moved out and that Veronika had brought in here for repair. Some carpets could, of course, be more valuable than others. But how much? Özen wasn't going to be much help, not knowing, by his own admission, a thing about carpets. He'd have to read up on them himself.

The woman introduced herself as Annelie Daun, with what Claesson would describe as a firm handshake despite the slenderness of the hand. She seemed very coherent, given what she'd just learned. Sufficiently sad, but still alert and on the ball. Özen noted down her personal details and kept the notebook open.

While Annelie Daun answered Claesson's questions as best she could, he noted the odd local or two walking slowly past on the street. People were curious. Had the news already spread? It was a mystery how it happened sometimes, but happen it did and quickly. Perhaps the local radio had already found out.

"I can't believe that Carl-Ivar's been killed so brutally. Who'd ever have thought of murdering *him* of all people? It must have been a case of mistaken identity!" she said firmly.

"Can you describe your relationship with him, apart from you being his employee? How long have you known him?"

"He's my uncle and he's always been incredibly kind to me. You could almost say that Carl-Ivar and Birgitta have been more like parents than my real ones. I've never met my dad."

There was some digging to do here, Claesson could tell – but not right now, given their hurry. They could always question her about details later.

"So if I've understood you right, Carl-Ivar Olsson was always good to you?"

"Oh, yes! There can't be anyone who doesn't like him. Apart from the one who's… who's done this terrible…"

They found out that she was a teacher, that she'd mostly done substitute work, and that they'd previously lived in Stockholm, she and her husband, who worked at the hospital. He was a doctor. She hadn't really enjoyed working with children in such a temporary way, and Carl-Ivar had rescued her by asking if she could help out in his shop a few hours now and then.

"What about his own children?"

She shook her head. "They've never been interested in carpets. They've got so much other stuff on their plates and they don't even live here. Lotta's in Stockholm and Johan's in Kalmar. I wasn't that interested in carpets either once, but I'm learning…" A pleased look flickered over her face. "Carl-Ivar was a good carpet mentor, you could say," she said, and her eyes glossed over, but she held back the tears.

"The carpets become your friends. It sounds weird, but that's how it is. This is, after all, Carl-Ivar's life work," she continued forlornly.

Carpets as friends!

Sure, thought Claesson, who'd heard worse expressions of loneliness. For lonely she must be, in her soul at least, he could feel it. He'd seen her wedding and engagement rings. He must be a boring husband. They'd run a check on her as soon as they got back to the police station.

No, she'd not noticed anything special about the shop or Carl-Ivar Olsson before he went to Turkey, she told them. Carl-Ivar was the same as normal, she wanted to add. He'd been off to a carpet conference or whatever it was for a few days. It was a meeting of some kind, at least; she wasn't so in on what was going on.

"You can ask the carpet dealer in Kalmar, he went down with him. And they had their wives with them, but I guess Birgitta's already told you that."

He said nothing. He had no reason to say what they did or didn't know. But right now he didn't have a clue what the wife had said.

Claesson informed Annelie Daun that they would like to have a look at the books and files that were in the shop, and that they might want to check telephone records as well.

"Do what you have to," she said wanly. "I promise to help you as much as I can."

There was a windowless room at the bottom of the spiral staircase, along with a bathroom and a little desk – where Olsson usually sat, apparently. The normal office equipment was there, too: computer, printer, phone, fax. They didn't find any address books: Olsson had probably taken them with him, the shop assistant called down. Özen, who'd been at Claesson's side like a calm shadow, had started to idly flip through a set of folders, which they'd already called and asked a colleague to drive over and collect. The file closest to the desk contained receipts and invoices. He picked up another, the back of which was worn and the red textile grimy from use, and skimmed through it. Claesson looked at the rugs and carpets on the floor. They weren't lying straight on the cement but on wooden pallets. There weren't that many, he thought, wondering how anyone could make a living as a dealer of quality carpets in little Oskarshamn. Some rag rugs stood rolled up against the wall.

Özen turned to Claesson and flashed him a broad but silent smile as he took out a sheet of paper. Claesson grew curious and, edging closer, saw a black and white photo of a shabby old rug. He looked inquiringly at Özen.

"Nothing, it's only that the rug comes from Cappadocia," Mustafa Özen said barely audibly. "From where my family comes from in central Turkey, or central Anatolia, as it's also called. Most of Turkey is actually a huge peninsula between the Black Sea and the Mediterranean. Some people say Asia Minor," he continued, as if he'd been quiet for so long that he needed to open his mouth.

Just as Özen went to replace the folder, Claesson stopped him. There had to be a reason why this very page should appear as soon as Özen opened the folder. There was something else written by hand in front of the word Cappadocia. He also noted that the paper was a little soiled and dog-eared, as if it had been repeatedly taken out and put back.

Ayvali it said. Özen said that he thought that it was a place, a small town, or rather village, in Cappadocia; he wasn't entirely sure but promised, of course, to find out.

Claesson asked the women, who'd stayed upstairs in the shop, to come down. "That's a fragment of an ancient Anatolian pile rug," she said.

"Pile rug?" asked Claesson.

"Yes, a kind that's knotted rather than flat woven… like this," she said, showing them a blood-red item with a rhomboidal pattern that lay on top of the pile on the floor. "You can imagine that animal skins had inspired nomads to knot carpets in this way in their tents a very, very long time ago." She ran her hand over the pile as if petting a horse, with long, harmonious strokes. "That," she then said, pointing at the picture, "is a preserved fragment of a rug from the fourteenth or fifteenth century, I think Carl-Ivar said."

Claesson stared at the rug with its unevenly ragged edging; half of it seemed to be missing. The moths had clearly found something to feast on. Fourteenth century, he thought. To think that rugs that old had survived. You could still see its patterning, even though the photograph was in black and white and hardly did the rug justice.

"Is there any demand for a rug like this?" he wondered. "It's in pretty bad condition."

"Sure there is. There's massive interest in really ancient fragments. They're sold at international auctions or through carpet dealers who've struck lucky," said Annelie Daun, her face turning thoughtful. "Perhaps not a huge amount of people," she said, changing her mind. "But some collectors are very rich. They can do almost anything to get their hands on a rare specimen."

She heard what she'd said and snapped her mouth shut.

Collectors were a very interesting breed, thought Claesson. Not all were fanatical, but some of them were prepared to go to any lengths to get hold of that special something. A document, a stump, a coin, a weapon, a potsherd, or a carpet fragment. He'd come across it before. The older and rarer, the better and more valuable.

Claesson said to Annelie Daun that he wanted to take the page with him and promised to arrange a copy for the shop. No problem, she said. The computer was also going to be requisitioned. He couldn't determine if it was an emailed picture or if it had been downloaded from the net – any name had been cut away, he noticed. If it had come by email, if must be possible to get hold of the sender. He'd leave that to the computer guys. It would be a slow process, and he'd probably have time to go all the way to Turkey and come home again before they were done.

They thanked Annelie and left. On their way back to the police station, Claesson asked a bit more about the place where the rug in the picture had originated from.

"We'd spend our summers in Cappadocia when I was a kid. My parents are from there. The terrain's very special, very beautiful... Maybe you've seen the tourist pictures of tall, slender rocky outcrops... which... ?" Özen grinned and formed an erect male member with his hands. "You can stay in a cave hotel and ride in a balloon. It's very popular with the tourists. There's lots to see there, really old underground cities and cliff churches and cave dwellings."

He liked telling people about Turkey, it was obvious from his voice. In the way that people tend to like taking about places that move them in one way or another.

Claesson asked him to call the carpet dealer in Kalmar. A visit there before it was time to head off to Turkey. It was a matter of squeezing in as much as they could.

"Maybe even today," he said with a glance at his watch. He'd just give Veronika a call first. It would mean he'd be late home, but perhaps he could make up for it by staying home a little longer tomorrow. Perhaps just have a little chat with the widow. One call from the police a day would have to do. He'd also have to make time to extract from Ludvigsson and Jönsson what they'd found out before he called on her.

CHAPTER 16

THE PARENTS.

Birgitta would have to tell them herself, she thought, before the news reached them from the radio or papers. They were old enough. And she couldn't cope with being all on her own in the house, but didn't even want the kids or a friend, let alone the neighbors, there with her. So she went round the house packing a little overnight bag, while the tears ran and blurred her vision. She wanted to go home. And home, that was her parents' farmhouse in Bråbo.

Five minutes earlier she'd replaced the receiver after having informed both her children that their father was no longer alive. Johan and Lotta would come over the next day, at some point in the afternoon, probably. She realized that everything would be getting a bit chaotic. They'd then no doubt spend the night down in Oskarshamn so that they could all fly down to Istanbul together by the Wednesday.

The police said they'd be in touch, but the tickets they'd have to book themselves. Magnus, her son-in-law, had immediately hurled himself at the computer and found that there were some seats available.

She'd also called her ward manager. She was due to go on night duty tomorrow, but that was naturally out of the question now. Birgitta could tell by the woman's voice that she wanted more exact details about when she thought she'd be back, but Birgitta managed to pre-empt this objectionable efficiency by saying that she'd be away for no less than a week. At least.

"Oh, yes, of course. Of course you have to take the time you need! And such a dramatic way to die, too. That must take time to digest!" said her manager. "So get in touch when you feel that you can conquer your grief."

Conquer her grief? Where had she got that from?

There was so much expert opinionating these days, even in something so fundamentally human as grief. As if the concept had become a term with a built-in action plan. Recipe-mindedness. How to go about things the right way, like how to bake a sponge cake to make it fluffy.

But this had nothing to do with the state she was currently in. Like Bambi on the ice, she could get no purchase. And the darkness would descend on her in time, she knew that.

There were many heavy conversations with the children, there was so much they wanted to know that she had no obvious answer to. Why? was their first question. A bloody death, how is that possible? Their dad? In Istanbul, what's more. "He wasn't up to anything dodgy, was he, Mom?" wondered Lotta. "I mean, Dad was mildness itself."

Both her children cried in turns, and she let them, trying all the while to keep a little distance, mostly for the sake of her own comfort. There would be lonely days and nights when she could weep her heart out in the solace of her own undisturbed solitude. The odd shoulder to lean on she could no doubt find, too, if she wanted and needed one.

And then there were all the practicalities, with details to be coordinated for the funeral. It was Lotta who raised the matter. Typical her! But Birgitta managed to put the brakes on all precision planning. They'd talk to the funeral home once they'd returned from Istanbul. They were sure to know what had to be done. They themselves had no clue how long the Istanbul police would have to keep Carl-Ivar, she said, and Lotta calmed down and started to sob again, like when she was a child. Johan was more restrained, and cried thick and throatily. His Malin was also easy and uncomplicated to deal with, and would undoubtedly support him. They were quite simply two down-to-earth people, Johan and Malin.

She needed to see with her own eyes that it really was Carl-Ivar who was dead and not some other person who'd got hold of his ID papers. She knew what it could be like down there.

Her head was spinning. Her thoughts were in chaos. All the practical things that had to be seen to. She tried to fend off the mental image of all the paperwork: files, insurances, taxes, accounts both private and business. She'd heard friends express their condolences. It's almost like you have to take a course just to handle all the purely administrative stuff when you become a widow, one of them said. But if she took one thing at a time, she was sure to get things sorted. Annelie would no doubt take care of the carpet shop for the time being if she asked her to. What luck that she already knew the ropes! Magnus, who was used to running a company, had also promised to help out with the paperwork if need be.

But right now, she was to do nothing, the police had said. Other than be available. They'd be in touch when they knew more.

"At the present time" – this phrase that was always heard spoken by police officers – "At the present time we have no idea of what's behind this," they said patiently in answer to her recurrent question. Without their saying it out loud, she was made to understand that she'd have to be very grateful if they ever found the guilty party.

It was the job of the Turkish police to handle the investigation and when she heard that she pictured Istanbul. She'd been there several times. Anarchic traffic and noise and bustle penetrated her as if she were there. Finding a killer there must be like looking for a needle in a haystack.

Just as she was about to lock up, she turned and went back in, opened the door to her wardrobe, groped around in the dark under Carl-Ivar's jackets and suits for the bag, took it with her, locked the door, and walked to the car.

As she pulled out onto Holmhälleväg she wondered whether she should call in at the Bromses to tell them what had happened. Mostly to nip things in the bud before the gossip got too wild – after all, they'd be reading the newspapers tomorrow. And possibly to derive a little empathetic cheer from Sven's friendly eyes.

But she couldn't be bothered and drove on toward Växjövägen. When she'd turned onto Kristdalavägen her shoulders relaxed. She saw birch, sallow, and alder in their delicate foliage against gray stone walls. Nature was so frail and newborn that she started to cry for real. The road wound on, and by the time she found herself driving up the long, gentle slope toward her parents' farmhouse, the tears had stopped.

The door of Lars' little side cottage was shut and the blinds drawn. Had he been drinking? After having been on the wagon for so long…

She picked up the little overnight bag but left the other bag behind in the car. She needed to get her mind straight. Think of a good hiding place until she knew what to do with its contents.

Her father, Albert, emerged from the chicken coop just as she knocked on the front door.

"Well, well, look who's 'ere!" he said. "Didn't she 'ear you? I reckon she be havin' one of 'er naps."

"Who is it?" she heard her mother call anxiously from inside the house once her father had unlocked the door.

"It's only our Birgitta," he called back, letting her into the kitchen.

He realized, of course, that something was up, otherwise she wouldn't have come rushing to see them like this. Her mother stood there in the doorway, small and thin, hair circling her head like a bushy halo. It was hard to believe that she'd run a hairdresser's salon, thought Birgitta, as she told them what had happened. "Carl-Ivar's been found dead in Istanbul."

It came blubbering out more quickly that she would have imagined. As if she was a little girl again.

"Oh, heaven help us," her mother said.

They let it sink in, and then they put some coffee on. It was just this kind of thing that coffee drinking was good for. Filling the coffee filter, setting out the cups, cutting the bread – a local Fliseryd loaf, as usual, she noted – arranging the butter and cheese and spotted salami. Birgitta found two pewter candlesticks with light blue candles in them in the sitting room, or the lounge as it had always been called. The wicks were white, the candles blotchily sun bleached. They'd stood there as ornaments, but now it felt right to light them and think of Carl-Ivar, even though it was light outside.

Chapter 17

CHRISTOFFER DAUN THOUGHT that he heard the Passat further down the hill. He was standing hollow-eyed at the back of the house. He'd been scraping the paint from an old wooden chair with moderately energetic strokes for a long while. He had to have something to occupy himself with. Anyway, it'd look better if he wasn't standing there with his arms dangling uselessly by his sides when Annelie finally returned. As if he'd been waiting for her.

He'd do anything for her right now. Needed to be accommodating. Had promised to fix up the chairs ages ago.

Was he afraid of her?

She was no monster. She wasn't the one who'd messed things up… but if she just hadn't been so… unengaged, or whatever the word was, then this would never have happened. It was like she didn't see him anymore. Maybe they'd just started to take each other for granted. The excitement was missing. He could also do with a little… extra… .

Baloney, he knew that. But he needed baloney as a defense.

Whatever, he was now making an effort to do his best to pour oil on the waters. Standing here, making a show of things, when things were already screwed up, he was also thinking. He should give up. What the hell *was* it that was holding him back?

It's not that he disliked Annelie. He didn't wish her ill. He'd long been trying to stop what he was getting up to. He wanted, quite frankly, to hang on to Annelie. But in a different way, more like it had been in the beginning.

And here he was, standing with a Windsor chair in his hand.

Those damn chairs were one long, never-ending saga. The division of labor was such that he'd scrape them bare, and Annelie would repaint them. She'd been intending to run a brush over them all in one go. All in all, it was a question of six chairs that they'd picked up for a bargain at an auction that previous summer. And if he knew Annelie, she'd roll her sleeves up when it was her turn to set to work. She'd paint them both quickly and well in just a couple of days. They'd argued about that, too. It was just before Christmas. About how he never got the job done. Never got anything done, she said. *Not a thing he ever got started on.*

"I might as well do everything myself," she'd said. "For Christ's sake, you just never pull your goddamned finger out."

Then all hell had broken loose, they'd screamed and they'd fought. When they'd calmed down – as they always did after half an hour or so – they decided that the expression "sharing each other's burdens" said quite a lot. They kissed and cried and made love, too, actually. They'd have to be careful not to make more demands on each other than life was already making, they promised. And she'd understood, once he'd explained, that in spite of everything the scraping of chairs was not one of life's great priorities. Or so she said. His work was more than enough.

And he realized, as he stood there now with birdsong in his ears, that he found these post-storm lulls worth all the arguing. They were so intimate, so sudden. They came so close, listened so tenderly to each other.

They belonged together then.

"It doesn't mean that I don't want to do everything you ask me to do," he'd said entreatingly back then, before Christmas. "I'm doing my best, Annelie! I just don't know what to do to really make you happy!"

He'd used his despairing voice. It crept out easily in such situations. He was also deeply ashamed that he didn't get his act together and do the chairs, it wasn't such a big deal if he really wanted to. But he was even more ashamed of the fact he was lying. Not just to her, but to himself, too.

And she'd not said a word. They had their given roles. Throughout their argument she hadn't said a word about his lack of fortitude. That he was what health professionals would call a *delicate person.* But the words hung in the air all the same. And he felt like a wimp. But it was a comfort that she'd never stoop to humiliating him. She never had. Not yet, anyway.

On the other hand, he was magnanimous and said nothing about who it was who made sure they had food on the table. That they were doing alright, moneywise. After all, she wasn't getting down to finding a proper job. The carpet shop paid nothing, no matter how much she liked it there. Good teaching jobs weren't exactly falling from the sky, but without the will, there was no way.

But he didn't say this. That's how nice he was.

And neither of them talked about that fact they were childless. They'd stopped all that. A typical dead topic, for these days they hardly ever slept with each other, which in a way made things easier, he thought.

The car he'd just heard passed by. It wasn't Annelie. He relaxed, but it wouldn't be long – she'd have to come home, sooner or later.

It was cooler than yesterday. The air was crystal clear. That was why he'd decided to stand outside rather than in the barn. His jaw muscles worked in pace with his hands over the seat of the chair. He heard another car, and this one came up onto the driveway and stopped its engine. His heart pounded. A car door opened.

It must be her.

Maybe the little ball of paper had hidden itself under the passenger seat? Could he have been so lucky that she hadn't seen it?

He put the scraper and brush down, ran his fingers through his hair and tried to set his expression to neutral. Just then, the cordless phone he had in his pocket rang. He fished it out just as he heard Annelie's footsteps on the gravel. He answered as he entered through the veranda door and passed through the sitting room into the kitchen. He'd meet her with the phone in his hand like a shock absorber. There was no intention behind it, if that's what she'd think.

"Hi. It's Ronny. I'm glad I've got hold of you."

"Right, hi," replied Christoffer, taken aback. Ronny Alexandersson had never called him at home before. Was he going to ask Christoffer to do an extra night?

The tone of his voice said not.

Annelie nodded to him in the kitchen. She looked serious. Angry?

"I was in charge of the ward this morning and discharged that gall bladder patient who'd not been seen to."

"Really?" said Christoffer curtly. The creeping sense of unease that he had was intensified by Annelie's clenched, grave air. She'd discovered the little red ball.

"The woman with the post-op stomach pain, if you recall?" said Ronny down the line. "Around fifty. And with a headache, too, so we wanted to keep her in for another 24 hours. It was planned that she'd go home today."

Christoffer felt how his cheeks started to burn.

"So the taxi came to pick her up around half ten," continued Ronny in a neutral voice. But it concealed something.

"I see."

Annelie had started to circle him. She'd placed two shopping bags on the counter and started to fill the fridge. Her movements were leisurely, lethargic even. It was like she was trying to avoid meeting his eye.

"She died exactly one hour after arriving home, according to her husband," said Ronny.

Time stopped.

Fuck! Christoffer was unable to utter a sound. He even forgot to breathe.

"Can you hear me?" asked Ronny.

"Yeah, sure…"

"Heart attack, we reckon," said Ronny, strangely enough without sounding accusatory.

Shit, thought Christoffer. Fucking shit!

"She'd suffered chest cramps during the night, as I later found out from a nurse. Or post-operative abdominal pain, they can be hard to tell apart. The night nurse reported it early this morning and entered it into the report, but I didn't read it, and as you know, it's total chaos in the mornings. Everyone on their way home. Anyway, no one said anything to me. Not the patient, either. Though as far as I recall you didn't report anything about it this morning, either. But I could be wrong."

His tongue was paralyzed. And that it was Ronny of all people who'd gotten sucked up in all this didn't help.

"I don't know what to say," he said finally.

"Did you examine her?"

The question was callous but warranted.

"No."

He could hear Ronny breathing down the line.

"Didn't Birgitta Olsson get in touch? It says in the notes that she took Hb, temp, and an ECG and called you."

"There was a hell of a lot to do last night… I don't really remember all the details. But I guess she did… Yeah, though it didn't sound as if the ECG was anything to get alarmed about. But we should of course have taken some blood tests for a heart attack. I would have made sure of that," he corrected himself when he realized who it was that had had medical responsibility for her.

Ronny made no reply.

"OK, Christoffer," he said then. "We don't need to talk about it now. I just wanted to let you know. It's just that it's bad news when something happens and the one it affects doesn't get to find out, you know how easily that can happen."

They were both, of course, familiar with that. That talk that went on behind your back while you yourself never got to hear a thing.

"We'll have to go through this properly later. Cardiology's had a look at the ECG now. It's possible it was normal, but as you know it's never easy to judge. Women and their hearts, you know. There'll be repercussions, of course," continued Ronny Alexandersson, still without sounding acerbic.

Christoffer was no longer listening. His head was spinning. Ronny finished up the call by saying they'd see each other the next day, and Christoffer hung up and remained standing.

"Has something happened?" Annelie had stopped what she was doing and was looking inquiringly at him. "I found out today that…"

"Gah," he said, cutting her off. He couldn't cope with any more right now, and certainly not her accusations. "I need the toilet."

He flushed after having evacuated virtually his entire intestines.

"I just have to get something," he said, and slunk out without looking at Annelie.

The fresh air cooled his face. He filled his lungs and exhaled slowly as he walked to the car. It stood so as not to be visible from the kitchen window. And yet still he turned just to check to make sure she wasn't spying on him.

He yanked open the front passenger door and stared down at the floor. It was empty except for the dark gray rubber mat and a little gravel. He bent down and felt under the seat. Nothing. Went down, just to be on the safe side, on all fours and laid his cheek against the rubber mat to have a proper look. He found a coin, which he pocketed. And a sweet wrapper, which he left. Nothing else. No red paper ball.

It was gone.

CHAPTER 18

BIRGITTA OLSSON FETCHED some sheets from the linen closet. They were freshly mangled.

"I suppose you should stay in your old room," said her mother. "We don't use the fireplace in there but it's not that chilly out now, anyway."

Imagine being over sixty and still having the bedroom you had when you were a little girl! Some things had been taken out or moved, but it was still her room. Faded flowers on the wallpaper and a browned water stain up in the corner that had been there even when she was a child. More than fifty years ago. Her mother and father had had their bedroom across the hall, but these days they slept in the old salon on the ground floor to avoid having to use the stairs. A large fixed mirror with a shelf under it remained from the time when her mother dressed hair. A while ago, Birgitta had found one of the old drying hoods out in the barn, and was acutely reminded of the years that had passed.

Nowadays, they didn't just pass; they sped.

She made the bed. The sheets were cool and soft to the touch. There was a top and a bottom sheet, her parents never having converted to a comforter. She ran her fingers gently over the border that her grandmother had once crocheted. The bedside lamp on the wall emitted the same yellowish glow that it always had.

When she sat on the narrow and overly soft bed to undress, her eyes fell on the photo on the chest of drawers, the one that had been there ever since it had been taken by a traveling photographer sometime in the fifties. A bleached color photo of Lasse, Harry, and herself.

Where her sister had been that day she didn't know. Iréne, who was later to move out into the big wide world with her successful husband, but who'd since returned to the security of Sweden after he dumped her for a young Brazilian. Iréne had sailed through life, thought Birgitta. Had never got herself a proper education, and instead had mostly just drunk cocktails by miscellaneous poolsides. Many a time Birgitta had been envious of her little sister when feeling stuck in the safe but small-minded life of Oskarshamn. But now Iréne wasn't having such a good time of things, what with having little money and aching joints. She lived outside Stockholm in Vallentuna.

Birgitta studied the photo again, immersed in the past. Lasse, Harry, and she were standing in a row in the middle of the narrow, winding lane between their homes, the farms opposite each other. They looked like children from some Astrid Lindgren story. Freckly, flaxen-haired cherubs with gaps between their teeth.

And then she snuggled down, feeling like a little girl again, back at home with Mommy and Daddy. And it was good.

Claesson was on the lounge sofa again with Nora on his tummy, but this time it was almost half past nine in the evening. Klara was sleeping and Veronika was tidying the kitchen.

He'd come home earlier than planned. Mustafa Özen and he hadn't gone to Kalmar as the carpet dealer was out and would see them the next day.

The widow hadn't been in, either; she'd gone to stay with her parents. Good idea, he thought. You could always be a little child again with your parents. If he didn't get around to talking to her before they went to Turkey on Wednesday, there wasn't much he could do about it. He'd have to talk to her in Istanbul, better late than never. According to Ludvigsson and Jönsson, she had no idea of what had happened. She seemed to be telling the truth, they said, however they could have known that.

Veronika came in and sank into the armchair. She looked bruised under the eyes.

"How do you actually go about finding out the details of a murder committed abroad?" she wondered, lacing her bare feet on the table.

"Well, you know, there are routines," he said. "The local investigator in the country where the crime was committed writes a report to the Interpol office in their capital… I suppose Ankara in this case. The report includes a notification of the death to the next of kin and the information needed to get the victim's personal details from his home country. Interpol has a computer system. You can actually find it on their website if you care to look…"

"I think I've got better things to do," she said, wiggling her toes. "What then?"

"The whole lot is then translated in Ankara, into English in this case, and then gets sent off to the Interpol HQ in Lyon, which then sends it on to our Interpol office in Stockholm. The boys in National CID are informed and are generally interested, depending on the case."

"So what can you do that they can't? They've got more resources, haven't they?"

"Well, they've got more forensic technicians to send out and the wherewithal to do the profiling, if it comes to that. We don't. But we're probably quicker at finding out the victim's background, if need be. We've got the local knowledge. And we've got…"

"What?"

"A cop who speaks Turkish. He was with me today. It's a feather in the cap to have a cop who's from the area – Oskarshamn, I mean – and who also knows the foreign lingo."

Nora tried to lift her heavy head and started crying. Veronika picked her up.

"Get yourself to bed," she said. "You can do the morning shift instead."

CHAPTER 19

CARPET DEALER ROLAND KARLGREN lived on Ängö, an island beautifully situated in the center of Kalmar, the skyline of which was dominated by the towering baroque church. It was actually a cathedral without a bishop, whose seat was in Växjö. Claesson didn't really know why it was still called a cathedral. They could see the bridge to Öland stretch into the distance in the background; visibility was good, and the eye could follow the bridge all the way to its abutments about four miles across the strait.

"Nice here, isn't it?" said Claesson as Özen turned onto Sparregatan. "You could just saunter down to the water in your bathrobe for an early morning dip if you wanted to."

They looked over an even lawn with a playground, and then came the sea.

"Sure is," said Mustafa Özen, turning off the engine.

Ängö consisted of a collection of wooden houses interspersed with rendered facades in harmonic tones, from white, pink, and light blue to warm yellow and ocher. There wasn't a single housing estate or modern creation in sight. At one end of the island by the bridge was a budget hotel.

Karlgren was waiting for them. He lived on the second floor. His sitting room was light and lived-in. His apartment wasn't wanting for carpets, of course, even if some of them were modern items rather than Oriental, as far as Claesson could tell. The place smelt of coffee. Claesson stood by the window.

"Nice view," he said, looking out over the Kalmar strait and over toward Öland.

"Quite, though it was nicer before they started building houses on Varvsholmen," Karlgren said as he made the coffee. He'd already laid a pretty dining table with a freshly mangled tablecloth in one end of the sitting room, a place for guests to sit at. The carpet underfoot felt thick and soft.

I just hope that Özen isn't one of those tea drinkers, thought Claesson. The host having to go back into the kitchen to boil some more water could throw a man off his rhythm.

But Mustafa accepted a cup of coffee.

"Terrible news about Olsson," said Karlgren, biting into his slice of bun and staring at the tablecloth. "Almost too hard to believe."

And then he started answering questions.

The two carpet dealers had known each other for a long time, thirty years. They had been in sparse but regular touch, once a year or every other year they'd call each other on the telephone or bump into each other at some carpet-related event. They never called each other without a purpose, said Karlgren. Men seldom, if ever, call each other just for a chat, thought Claesson.

They let Karlgren talk on for a while. Claesson "touched down," as it was so flatteringly called, and then wondered if it was OK for them to turn on a tape recorder. He promised Karlgren that he'd get to read the transcription afterwards.

"Fine by me," said the carpet dealer and Claesson fished his tape recorder out from his jacket pocket and checked the battery – which, admittedly, he should've done before he took it with him.

Karlgren said that they'd been in Turkey together before, him and Olsson. "But I got a feeling he goes there more often than I do."

"What makes you think that?"

"No, well, he'd sometimes speak as if he'd just been there." Karlgren ran his fingers over his chin. "Can't say exactly," he added in a tone that suggested that he regretted mentioning it at all.

"So what do you think he was doing there?"

"Haven't the foggiest. Looking at rugs, I suppose. Guess he liked it there."

"Business?"

"Carpet business, yeah, of course."

"Other kind of business?"

"You mean dodgy business? Drugs or something?"

Claesson said nothing.

"Nah, don't reckon Carl-Ivar was into that." The fingers around the chin again. "Though his getting brutally murdered like that, well, makes you wonder, of course…"

Claesson waited, but nothing more came. He didn't want to set the man's imagination running, that wouldn't do any good. He asked Karlgren to talk about the trip, about why they went. And found out that Karlgren and Olsson had slightly different itineraries, but that they'd been at the same meeting with other carpet people from around the world in an old former mosque that served nowadays as an exhibition and conference center. Claesson got the address and an information leaflet illustrated with delightful color photographs of the mosque and of carpets, which was in a plastic envelope on the table.

"You can take the whole file. I've put some things together for you."

Here's a man who needs no secretary, thought Claesson, taking a sip of the hot coffee before thanking Roland Karlgren for his consideration. Olsson and Karlgren had flown down together with their wives. Roland Karlgren's wife, Marianne, was away in Gothenburg, but of course she'd be pleased to help the Oskarshamn police with their investigation.

Claesson also learned that the Olssons and the Karlgrens had not stayed at the same hotel, but rather had been nearby each other in Sultanahmet, the part of Istanbul that was designated the old town and that lay inside the city wall that enclosed the famous and monumental buildings: churches, museums, mosques.

"Alleyways and passages, right chaotic but fascinating," he said. "Istanbul is an eternal city, like Rome," he added, getting a dreamy look in his eye.

Karlgren said that the four of them had gone out one evening for dinner.

"Can you remember the name of the restaurant?"

Karlgren shook his head.

"That's a tough one. Once you've been to Istanbul you'll see what I mean. Can't ever be sure to find your way back to the same place twice two evenings in a row, even if you wanted to. Maps are pretty useless. Parts of the city are a maze of unnamed streets. But hold on..."

Karlgren got up and went to fetch his wallet from the hall, out of which he produced a calling card.

"Forgot this," he said. "If you're lucky you might find it. If you ask a local for directions they'll likely take you to another restaurant which is pretty much the same. Though much better, they'll add. But they won't say that it's owned by a cousin. Everyone seems to have swarms of cousins. Family means a lot."

Karlgren looked curiously at Özen, who grinned back at him without a word.

Claesson slid the card into the plastic envelope.

"Otherwise nothing much special happened at the restaurant. We ate. Good food. Then went home and went to bed," continued Karlgren. "I've known Olsson a long time and never in my wildest dreams could I imagine Carl-Ivar getting himself murdered so cruelly, I tell you… If it's true what the papers said." Roland Karlgren sought the answer in Claesson's face, but it was totally blank. "Nothing short of an execution? But who in the name of thunder would want to execute him?"

Karlgren shook his head.

"Let's move on to the carpets. Do you know if Olsson had any deal going on? I'm not much of a rug expert, can you help us out here?"

Again the shake of the head.

"No. Carpet deals rarely lead to murder. I know every business has its bastards, but it's not exactly drug peddling," he said with a curl of his lips. "Must've been a mistake or about something completely different. Never actually heard of a murder in the carpet world, even though pretty large sums do exchange hands at times."

"How large?"

"Varies a lot. Rugs are cheap in a way if you compare them with other handmade objects, like antiques or newly made furniture and top notch goods."

"Seven figures, would that be unreasonable?" wondered Claesson.

"Of course there are rugs that fetch that kind of money, it depends on what kind of rug it is. But then we're talking the large global market, and the big auction houses like Sotheby's and Bukowski's. Nothing that me and Carl-Ivar are into… at least not me," he added after a brief pause.

"Is it just men in the business?"

"You could say, to put it simply, that it's the women that do the producing. They knot or weave the rugs at home or in special workshops, while the sales and repairs are done by men. It's hard work repairing rugs, you know. And when it comes to money… well, tradesmen have always been men. I mostly sell new rugs, and not top of the range ones, neither. Kalmar's no Mecca in that sense. A new rug that's densely knotted can, of course, be expensive, but won't fetch the kind of money you're asking about. Five-figures, more like. A lot of work goes into them. Take this one, for instance."

He got up and walked over to a rug on the floor, and turned up one of the corners. "You can see here how tightly knotted it is. Meticulous job. Takes time."

Karlgren looked up at Claesson, who bent down toward the rug and nodded. But he avoided the question of whether children also made rugs. Knotting with slender, nimble fingers in some murky sweatshop. That's how it was, of course, in some parts of the world.

"Knot density doesn't matter that much when it comes to old rugs, though," Karlgren continued. "There are other things that count when those ones are valued. You'd have to work with antique rugs pretty much full time to get a feel for them. Olsson was better at it than I am."

"Like at what to look for?"

"Well, age and the name of the carpet house that made it, color and design and originality, you know. Carl-Ivar's always been more interested in antique rugs than I am – I mean ones over a century old. Those that are older than fifty but younger than a hundred are called semi-antique. But I never got the feeling that he was doing million-dollar deals, exactly."

Claesson showed him the photograph of the fragment from Cappadocia. Roland Karlgren put his glasses on his nose and looked at it closely. He shook his head.

"Nothing I recognize," he said. "It looks quite old."

"Fifteenth century, apparently," said Claesson.

"You don't say," said Karlgren without a flicker of expression.

The silence hung in the air.

"How are rugs stored, generally speaking?" wondered Claesson.

"On the floor at home, or on the wall. Or as a cushion to sit on or as a pillow, like the nomads do and like the country folks did in Sweden back in the old days. Rugs are to be used, not stored in some safe somewhere, although I daresay there are some that do that with particularly remarkable items. Rugs are hardy. Feet, shoes, mud, just vacuum them clean. Otherwise, we dealers like to keep them in darkened rooms to preserve the colors. The room must be kept a constant temperature. Rugs should lie on shelves if they're to be kept long, and not on the floor, at least not in a basement where you can get rising damp."

That almost goes without saying, thought Claesson.

"Do you know who Olsson's contacts are in Istanbul?"

"I know he always went to a highly reputed carpet dealer, near the Grand Bazaar. They were old friends. Should think his son's taken over the business now, but I daresay he hangs around there during the day. I know him, too. I've got no card, but I can show you where it is on a map."

He got up and went into another room, returning with a book on Istanbul. He looked up Kapalı Çarşı, the Grand Bazaar.

"This particular carpet shop isn't in the bazaar itself but just next to it, in a courtyard that's right beautiful… Here!"

He pointed at the northeast part of the enormous area that filled a double-page spread in the tourist guide. "It's called Zincirli Hanı." Mustafa Özen made a note. "It is without doubt one of the most beautiful *hani* in the Grand Bazaar. Han means caravansary, or hotel. *Hani* is the definite form," explained carpet dealer Karlgren eruditely. "A peaceful oasis smack in the middle of alleys and boutiques. Not far from there, in the bazaar itself, is the oriental *kiosk*…here." He pointed to a photograph of a small, narrow building, rather comical in appearance. "It was a café at first, but now it's a jewel shop, I think. Did you know that the word *kiosk* comes from the Turkish? Originally means *little garden shed* or something like that… Anyway, the Grand Bazaar is an experience. You can easily get lost, but everyone knows where Zincirli Hanı is. Trust me."

"What should we make of this," asked Claesson as they drove back. "Nothing," he answered himself. "You can turn it into anything from drugs to carpet fraud to human trafficking to sheer bad luck!"

Özen didn't reply, just ran his hand uneasily over his neck.

"My God, we're going to know a lot about rugs after this," he continued. "Though perhaps you don't care about God?"

"No, not really," said Özen.

Claesson looked askance at him. Özen was driving. Claesson had been expecting a more detailed presentation of his confessional affiliation, but Özen said no more. He was presumably a Muslim, he thought. Or secular, like himself.

He glanced at his watch. A quarter to three. They ought to drive over to the widow and talk to her, but Claesson wanted to go home. They'd have time to talk to her in Istanbul, he said, making excuses for his laziness, or rather his disinclination. He wanted to go back to his family, especially given their current situation. He and Özen would have to go through Ludvigsson and Jönsson's report again carefully on the plane. A victim's closest circle of family and friends was always important in a murder inquiry, and was often where you'd eventually find the guilty party, but a better alibi than his wife's was hard to find. Birgitta Olsson had been seen in Oskarshamn on the day of the murder by none other than Claesson's own wife, and they'd had a chat.

"I don't think we'll have time to go and see the widow," he said aloud.

Again Özen said nothing. If he carries on like this, it's going to be a long trip, thought Claesson.

Özen parked the car in the police station's underground lot. They went up to get the tape transcribed immediately so that they could take it with them to Istanbul. Claesson flirted with one of the civilian secretaries.

Their hotel voucher and tickets lay on their desks. "*It's settled, it's you. Not the Nats or Kalmar. Have a nice trip! Louise,*" a note said.

Claesson saw that they'd be flying from Copenhagen and would have to take the Öresund train from Kalmar just after seven. It would mean an early start. They were to be picked up at half past five by a car that would take them to Kalmar. He raised his eyebrows and saw a sleepless night ahead of him. An early rise *and* a flight.

He didn't like it when planes shuddered – he got scared quite frankly – and long flights were always bumpy. He just hoped there weren't going to be problems with the train. They had a margin of error, he could see that from their itinerary, but not oceans of time if there were serious delays, which were a little too frequent for comfort.

He stuffed the documents into his briefcase as a rush of travel fever surged through him.

Claesson had printed out some information on Istanbul from the net and had bought a book on Turkey, which he also packed. He was intending to educate himself on the plane. He'd already learned from carpet dealer Karlgren that the word *kiosk* had been borrowed from Turkish. But there were more words he'd have to get straight in his mind, such as *sultan*, *harem*, *divan*, *Ottoman*, and *Byzantine*. Some of them weren't even Turkish. Maybe Persian or Arabic. Whatever they were, they certainly evoked images of foreign far-away lands in the Orient. Even the word *Orient* tasted nice on his tongue. Date palms swaying lazily in the breeze, the smell of aromatic spices and incense.

He pictured himself sitting on a rug, leaning against gaily-patterned cushions, puffing on a hookah as the dusk fell and the blistering heat of the day turned into a pleasant coolness. He could sense the tranquility.

He took the steps down, feeling elevated by the adventure that awaited him.

CHAPTER 20

ANNELIE DAUN LEFT the front door ajar for a while to let in a little fresh air. She dropped her shoulders, rolled her head, and felt a calm spread through her. She'd lock up in half an hour.

But yet her heart had started to beat that little bit faster. She was keyed up. There were so many questions, so many mysteries.

That nice Detective Inspector Claesson would do everything he could to catch the guilty party, she was sure of it. Even though it was all the way down in Turkey where the murder had taken place. Birgitta and the family would be traveling to Istanbul tomorrow, she'd learned. In one way, she'd have liked to have gone with them, but that, of course, was out of the question. Carl-Ivar hadn't been like a father to her, but close to it. Like an absent-minded but secure figure in the background.

She stared out of the window. Her thoughts were sluggish and slushy, and far from elevating. Although there was no reason to do so, she felt somehow dragged into things against her will. Felt guilty in a way that she'd often felt as a child and that she'd put a lot of energy into not feeling. Not every fault and mistake was her fault. It was very self-obsessed to think so.

But now here she was, slipping into that same rut again, that she was always to blame when things went wrong. She could hear her mother's admonitions: "You know your mother can't cope, Annelie. Why do you do things like this?"

And it had almost always been her mother herself who'd cause trouble. Of course sometimes it was Annelie, dropping a glass on the floor or forgetting to do the shopping on the way home from school – and then her mother would be all over her, pecking at her relentlessly. If she was sober, that is. There was no off button on her. If she was drunk, she'd just get querulous until she fell into a stupor.

During her childhood years, Annelie had spent a great deal of time thinking about which was worse, finding her mother drunk as a skunk, as the neighbor downstairs said, or sober and angry.

Whatever, she'd always be blamed, both for what she might have done and what her mother had done, or forgotten to do. Like the laundry, or the shopping and cooking, for instance. Other mothers did all that. But not hers. Only sometimes.

Christoffer had something of her mother's talents in him, she'd found herself thinking all the more frequently. He sighed over money or over her being too slow and in need of pulling her weight. "It's not easy to take care of everything on my own. Our finances and all that," he said, looking distraught at her as if she'd be able to vomit money.

And yet she could see that he enjoyed it. He who has money has power, it was as simple as that! He could spend it how he liked, she had no right to ask him why he'd bought a new computer. But he'd gladly feel entitled to ask her as soon as she came in through the door with a shopping bag. He did it even when she'd just been to H&M and the money was hers from the carpet shop. "Was that really necessary?" he'd wonder critically. "You know that we have to tighten our belts."

He spoke to her as if to a child.

It's none of your damn business what I do, she wanted to say. I'll buy what I like. But she said nothing. It was exactly the same with her mother. No statistics in the world had told her that it paid off to answer back. It just made things worse.

Carl-Ivar.

She was convinced that something had happened in front of her eyes that she wasn't getting. A strong feeling, like an unpleasant undercurrent, or like lies and cheating. Secrets. But about what? She wished she could pick up the phone and call the police and tell them something.

The murk that growled inside her wasn't only to do with Carl-Ivar's death, she knew that. Her own life was teetering, but she was managing for the moment to ignore it. Carl-Ivar's tragic death was timely, in a way, as it had given her something else to think about.

Although why had he been so broody?

But that was as far as she could get in her reveries, as the door swung open and in came Magnus Öberg.

She smiled in surprise.

"Hi, there!" he said, as undaunted as always. "Lotta and I are at Birgitta's. The kids are back in Stockholm with my parents. We're going to Istanbul tomorrow afternoon. Just thought I'd check in..."

She hadn't seen him since last Easter, when he and Lotta and the kids had been in Oskarshamn. Magnus has stopped by to see his father-in-law in the carpet shop, but she hadn't really had a chance to chat with him. Carl-Ivar had monopolized him completely.

She'd found it a little touching that Carl-Ivar had been so keen to show off to his strange son-in-law from Stockholm. He didn't have to do that, she thought. He was better than that.

"Well, hello!" she said, embracing him lightly so that her chest only barely brushed his own. She caught a whiff of his aftershave, and even knew that it was called Paul Smith. He ran an index finger over her neck. She shivered and tilted her head forwards.

How little it took, sometimes!

He hadn't changed, the summer boy from Klintemåla. The sea watered hair and the freckly nose. The eternal summers of childhood.

Why does hindsight make these summers seem so lovely? Because it wasn't true, at least not all of it. She could remember a good many boring times, too, when she'd been alone with her mother in the apartment and had to make do with what she could. Sometimes she'd bike to nearby Gunnarsö to look for friends. Though a lot of the time she was left alone while others went with their parents to vacation cottages by the sea or on driving trips or on formal vacation tours.

Magnus didn't have freckles any more, he'd grown out of them. He was the city boy who spoke a posher dialect than they, and who came down every summer with his rich parents to stay in the wedding cake. By winter, he and his family lived in a world far away from hers. The wealthy, simple, happy, and carefree life in Stockholm, she imagined.

But come the summers, and she and Magnus would share the same shoreline rocks and jetties. Birgitta and Carl-Ivar were kind and *took pity* on her. She'd heard someone say that once, a lady friend of Birgitta. She'd had plate-like feet that she'd squeeze into narrow, pointed shoes, that's what she could remember of her. Because she'd almost died when she heard it and just stood staring at the ground.

She and Lotta had to share the bunk beds, and Johan moved onto the wooden settee in the main room, which wasn't that big. And then all the summer visitors and sparkling waves and brackish water in the nose – long days sunbathing and swimming. They'd go fishing, too, and sailing, and in time they started making out. She'd fallen in love for the first time, and shortly afterwards really, unrequitedly in love.

The first big love of her life, the one who she'd cried her pillow soggy over, was now standing in front of her. It had been fairly obvious from the word go that Lotta would grab him for herself. She was a year older, no little girl like herself, and both prettier and more self-confident. It was a meeting of equals. She watched it happening and was powerless to do anything about it. Watched how Lotta sucked Magnus into her sphere. She'd seen Lotta do it before with others, but this time it was so patent. And terrible and unstoppable.

But that was all over now, she told herself reassuringly. Gone.

Magnus had a look around, smiling in the same way he always did, lifting one corner of his mouth higher than the other. Crooked, but very charming. Meanwhile his eyes darted over the walls, taking in the rugs.

"So how's business?"

The candidness of the question made her start, but he wasn't being serious, was he? She was about to say that he'd have to ask Carl-Ivar, but, of course, she couldn't. If nothing else, an estate inventory would be taken sooner or later, if he was that interested in the actual figures.

"I'm sure it's OK," she evaded.

Her heart started to pound. Damn the thing, she thought, but at the same time, the sensation was really quite delicious. It was like she'd come alive again. It was the same the time before, when they'd met last Easter, but it had had to stop at glances. And last summer when Birgitta and Carl-Ivar had a party in Klintemåla and everyone was in the cottage, she'd felt Magnus's eyes following her and their tangible warmth, which had never actually left them. It was as if nothing had disappeared or drifted away since the summer days in Klintemåla when they were teenagers.

"Carl-Ivar told me he was working on some big deals," said Magnus, making it sound as if he was really just keeping the conversation going.

"Is that so? So you and Carl-Ivar talked about the rug business?" she said, smiling.

"It happened… I've started to teach myself a little on the side, you could say. It was something we had in common, my father-in-law and I. He'd promised to procure some fine samples for me. Special items, if you know what I mean. I even gave him money. Incidentally, do you know anything about that?"

Now the smile was not so much crooked as broad. She decided to think quietly. It was a little odd for Carl-Ivar not to have said a word about this, but then he naturally wasn't obliged to tell her anything. No doubt these slightly bigger deals he managed on the side. After all, she was only a kind of helping hand in the shop.

So she said, "I've actually got no idea. It was nothing he'd mentioned to me, at least. The rugs that we have are here in the shop… or down in the basement."

Magnus held his sunglasses by one earpiece, spinning them in his hand while he continued to go around inspecting the rugs even more closely. The air thickened. Annelie swallowed. She took in his self-confidence and his open posture that she recognized so well. Not even when his parents went bankrupt, when the wedding cake was sold and everything went down the tubes for the well-heeled Stockholm family, did he lose his composure. He was born to own the world, whatever the weather.

"So how are things with you?" he wondered, pinning her with his eyes.

"Just fine."

"You've turned out so incredibly pretty, Annelie, do you know that? You've always been pretty, but now your beauty is quite simply unsurpassed."

He came straight for her, his forehead bowed. Like a bull, she thought. He came closer, smiling and affectionate, and placing a finger under her chin, pushed her head up half an inch or so. "You should hold your head like this. A little more erect. You're worth it. A little more self-confidence, please!"

She could feel her cheeks turn a violent red and her throat start to burn. He was a bastard at being candid, at drawing her into him.

They stood still, his eyes gazing deeply into hers.

"Damn it all, Annelie, I miss you so much sometimes. Can't you give me a little smile?"

His voice was at once soft and cocky, and betrayed a yearning, but still he was in total command of the situation. She smiled back at him and shuddered with pleasure. Why could she not stop wanting this? A single fingertip against her skin and then nothing was as it should be.

"Can't you lock up?" he whispered. "And then we can go down…"

She nodded, closed the door, locked it, and was then half way down the steel stairway.

By the time her back landed against a pile of Iranian carpets of the highest quality, she'd stopped thinking. She just existed.

But way back in the furthest reaches of her mind, another thought echoed.

We'll deal with that later, she thought. Not now.

CHAPTER 21

IT HAD GOTTEN BUMPY over the Alps, but not bad enough to interrupt the majority of passengers who were sleeping, eating, or drinking, apparently quite unperturbed. Except for Claesson, who'd been sitting as tense as a coiled spring, staring straight ahead and doing what he could to keep a grip on his self-control. In particular he'd been keeping a close eye on the behavior of the cabin crew. As long as they weren't flapping around like headless chickens or casting anxious glances, then everything was OK.

He wasn't of course the only one who had an apprehensive relationship with traveling through the air. Human beings belonged on the ground, it was simple as that, not up in the air or on the moon, that's what he believed.

But now they'd passed the most turbulent area, the co-pilot announced. The plane glided forwards as if on rails.

He sat thinking. Özen was sleeping deeply beside him, head lolled to one side, mouth open, and, thankfully, not dribbling. Özen wasn't afraid of flying.

They'd talked about Carl-Ivar Olsson over a beer at the airport. Once on board, they'd gone through the few documents they had from Istanbul and their own police station. It was stressful to have to make a good impression in a strange place. He wanted something to give the Turks, although really he didn't want to stay one day more than he had to. He was quite happy to go to Turkey and Istanbul, quite happy to collaborate across borders, but he'd rather it not get too convoluted or take too long. He wanted to go back home as soon as he could and with at least a little light shed on the case, because he didn't dare to hope that they'd solve it down there. It was easier to meet relatives in the knowledge that they'd done what they could.

So just who was this Olsson? He caught himself getting almost irritated by the man, but he figured that was more to do with the way his death had cut into his parental leave. Besides, people with irreproachable backgrounds made him slightly nervous. Consummate decency in a person always seemed unlikely.

No, that was wrong, he corrected himself, realizing how occupationally damaged he'd become. Most citizens were honest and the country safe, even though these days people didn't dare leave home with the door unlocked. Not like before, when he was growing up. He'd heard people go on about it ad nauseam, and thought the same thoughts himself. More and more people were installing alarms and locking the front door, even when they were at home. Otherwise, some lowlife would come and rob you blind while you were watching television in another room. The fifties were idyllic, said everyone who'd been around back then. You could trust each other. But there was nothing wrong with the sixties either, the decade of his own early memories.

He returned to Olsson. They'd struck his wife and children and their families off the list of possible suspects for the time being, since they'd been in Sweden at the time of the murder. And Annelie Daun, the niece who looked after the shop, had also been eliminated. Peter Berg and Martin Lerde had been with her mother, Olsson's sister, a well-known alcoholic in Oskarshamn. She'd been quite sober at the time, but had been completely ignorant of the fact that her brother had been in Turkey. Or so she claimed.

So no one in his immediate family, unless they'd hired an assassin, of course, but that was a highly improbably theory.

They'd have to draw up a list of everyone who'd had some kind of link with Turkey, they agreed.

The next question was whether the killer had been out to get Olsson personally or something he possessed – money or a valuable rug? Had a carpet deal gone wrong? Was someone in desperate need of money? In debt? There was a lot of digging to do here, no doubt about it.

Was the murder committed on impulse? It didn't seem so to judge by what they read. The risk of discovery on the crowded ferry was obvious, but still there was something audacious about the whole thing. Either it was a case of perfect timing or a well-planned murder by a cold-blooded killer who'd been shadowing Olsson and who'd struck when the risk of discovery was minimal. At the end of the day, it was a pretty exciting case!

But why Istanbul?

Drugs are what immediately come to mind, said Özen, and there might be something in that, Claesson thought. Drug running was always a dirty business. If they understood the report from Istanbul right, the intention hadn't been to warn, frighten, or injure Olsson but quite obviously to kill him. It was murder, in other words, rather than manslaughter.

Annelie Daun in the carpet shop had nothing to gain from the dealer's death, as far as they could tell at this point. She'd probably go on the dole, although that wouldn't be so bad for her since she had a relatively stable life with a husband able to provide for her.

They suspected that Olsson had had an unusually big carpet deal in the works. The paper copy they found in the file suggested it. Claesson had still not quite digested the fact that someone would be prepared to pay millions for a moth-eaten rug, even if it was six hundred years old. For whom was Olsson going to acquire this extremely special rug, if that was what he was up to? Had he gotten hold of it before getting himself killed? And if so, who had it now? How had the financial transaction taken place? Was Olsson just a middleman, a carpet courier who'd carry the rug through customs into Sweden while the millions took another route and into other people's accounts? Olsson would have been getting something out of the deal. Few people are outright idealists.

His colleagues back at home had been assigned to the bank accounts, both private and business, but things like that took time.

The likelihood that Olson was honesty incarnate was greater than his being a narcotics mule or dodgy carpet seller, Claesson finally concluded. Most people were, after all, sound-minded, as Veronika liked to say, although at times she found it hard to believe from her hospital perspective.

He could picture different scenarios. How Olsson was sitting on the ferry with an overly stuffed wallet. There were just two problems with this: his wallet wasn't missing or emptied, and rarely were pickpockets prepared to kill.

Otherwise it would've been much easier to pocket the money and toss the wallet overboard, he thought, squinting as he watched the episode play out against his eyelids. Olsson, sitting in peace and quiet on the boat as it slowly disgorges its passengers. The killer creeping up on him. Like a flash, he pulls out his knife and rams it deep into his stomach, placing a hand over Olsson's mouth to muffle his screams. The grunt that Olsson still manages to force out being drowned out by the engines that are revving up as the boat slows down, ready for docking. The blood flowing, Olsson slumping down unconscious. The killer throwing the knife into the sea and joining the rest of the passengers, walking calmly along the gangway to swiftly disappear in the crowd on the quayside.

But what had he been after?

The airline attendant rolled her cart ahead of her, collecting trash. She took the empty tomato juice can and smiled cheerily. What a crap job! Confined and hassled and constantly having to put on that genial smile.

The flight was still smooth. One and a half hours left. And there was Özen, sleeping like a log. And now snoring as well.

Claesson took his book on Turkey out of the seat pocket in front of him. The cover was adorned with a picture of a large mosque bordered by four minarets, which looked like rockets aimed at a bright blue sky. He opened the book and found a simple map that he studied carefully.

Özen had said that Turkey was roughly the size of Sweden, Norway, and half of Denmark combined. It had everything from the well-known summer tourist paradises to snowy mountains and ski lifts.

First was a thick chapter on Turkey's history, which seemed unusually long, pretty much as long as human history itself. People had lived in Turkey since the Stone Age, and tribes of various kinds had migrated in from the east, subjugating the ones already settled, and established new communities. He read on about the Fertile Crescent, which looped from Mesopotamia, the land between the Euphrates and the Tigris, down to Egypt.

Mesopotamia! He tasted the name. Wasn't that where Ur lay? The city from where the patriarch Abraham journeyed to the land of Canaan, according to the Book of Genesis. Claesson knew his biblical history, having had a very engaged teacher as a young boy.

Constantinople was founded in the fourteenth century on a site called Byzantium, which was a Greek colony. The city was long known as New Rome. In 1926, it changed its name once more to Istanbul.

Mongol hordes invaded the country in the 1200s, and many Christians converted to Islam when it turned out that the Mongols gave the Muslims tax breaks. Rebellious Turks took the country back, however, and the Ottoman Empire began to emerge. The country took part in the First World War on the German side. In 1915, under the shadow of the war, over a million Armenians were slaughtered, and according to the book, this was still a dark stain on Turkish history. The world war led to the collapse of the empire, and it was carved up between the victors. As part of the agreement, there was a massive exchange deal: over one million Greeks in Anatolia were swapped for half the number of Muslims, who were sent from Greece to Turkey. This was less than a hundred years ago, thought Claesson. Quite recent, actually!

But an army officer called Mustafa Kemal drove out the occupying Greek army after a war of liberation, then expelled the remaining foreign forces and declared Turkey a republic in 1923. Ankara became its new capital instead of Constantinople, and Kemal its new president. He adopted the name Kemal Atatürk, which means "the father of the nation." They were about to land at Atatürk's airport.

The country was ravaged. Atatürk carried out great and sweeping reforms. He looked askance to the West, toward the European lifestyle, and wanted to break ties with Islam as part of the country's modernization. Turkey was secularized, the road network was developed, industry, too, in an attempt to woo foreign investors. Atatürk wanted to prevent the emergence of the kind of fundamentalism that existed in neighboring Iran. The price had been, apart from genocide and gaping class differences, the persecution of different ethnic groups, including the Kurds. The military had always had a strong influence in Turkey.

The land was now being democratized, and a great deal of effort was being put into qualifying Turkey for accession to the EU.

Then the plane began its descent.

Claesson had always hated packing. The advantage of this was that he always traveled light. Veronika said that he was the best packer she'd ever met, in that sense.

He'd learned it from his father. Just put everything you intend to take with you on the bed and then discard half of it! Mustafa Özen seemed to have done the same. The upshot was that they didn't have to wait by baggage claim but could march straight through customs with their respective carry-ons.

Atatürk International Airport was large and modern. Everything proceeded according to plan, and outside stood a man with a sign. *Oskarshamn*, the printed letters said.

The young police officer in the dark blue jacket and light blue shirt who'd been sent to collect them looked inquisitively at the two Swedes, paying particular attention to Mustafa, who introduced them in Turkish.

In the car toward Istanbul, Claesson took out his cell phone and called home. No one answered. He called Veronika's cell phone.

"We've just landed."

"Was it a difficult journey?"

"Not at all. We're now on our way into Istanbul."

"Is it hot?"

"Oh yes, but not baking… How are things?"

The nagging conscience.

"It's going just fine."

The easing conscience.

"Kiss the girls for me."

"Do I also get a kiss?"

"You're my girl, too."

He hung up and felt at once a little embarrassed, wondering what Mustafa Özen had made of it all. But what the hell.

Özen sat up front so that he could keep chatting with his Turkish colleague. Claesson saw green water in the mist on his right – whether it was the product of heated air or exhaust fumes he couldn't tell. Probably both. People were walking along the beach or having picnics. Cargo ships lay alongside each other, riding at anchor. That must be the Marmara Sea, he guessed.

They'd arrived in Istanbul.

CHAPTER 22

ANNELIE DAUN HELD the post office slip in her hand, turned the "back soon" sign to face outwards, and stepped out onto the sunny stone steps and locked the shop. She had to pick up a package and she had a good idea which rug it contained. It wouldn't be too heavy for her to carry.

It was a gorgeous Anatolian prayer mat, if she wasn't mistaken. It could, of course, be another rug that Carl-Ivar had sent out for repair, or one that he'd bought in Turkey and asked to have sent home because it was heavy and cumbersome, but items like that were usually delivered by courier.

After a few steps down Frejagatan as she took the pavement toward Lilla Torget Square, she had a feeling that she was being followed. She looked back and saw a slim man in his forties. He was some way behind her. They were virtually the only two on the pavement.

When the man noticed her looking at him, he dropped his eyes to the asphalt, took out a cell phone and put it to his ear. She recognized him. He'd come into the shop late last week and asked for Carl-Ivar. Just another carpet junkie, she'd thought.

He'd spoken the dialect of the neighboring county, and had asked her if she was sure that Carl-Ivar was still in Turkey. What he wanted with him he didn't say. Just that he and Carl-Ivar had agreed that he'd show up in his shop when he was in the neighborhood.

Did he know that Carl-Ivar was dead? she wondered. Of course he did, it was all over the papers.

She'd been insistent and asked if he'd come on account of a rug, and he'd said he had, naturally, but he didn't go into which. She'd even asked if she should ask Carl-Ivar to call as soon as she'd gotten in touch with him, but it wasn't necessary. He was obviously in no hurry.

This had happened last Saturday, before she knew that Carl-Ivar had died that same day. Perhaps he'd even been alive just then?

The idea slammed into her there on the pavement, her throat thickened and she gave a sob.

Here come the tears, she thought. At last. There'd been extremely little of that. A drop in the car, but she didn't want to cry at home, she had enough on her plate keeping Christoffer on edge. She even quite enjoyed it. She'd seen him look at her and wonder if she'd found that red piece of paper. But she said nothing, that was the punishment. Did he think she was stupid? She'd figured out some time ago what kind of man he was. If nothing else, she remembered how he'd snared her once many moons ago.

The tears stopped, she swallowed and remained standing with the slip in her hand as though waiting for the man in order to ask him if he'd wanted anything from the shop. But he turned on his heel and started to walk in the opposite direction, still with his phone pressed against his ear.

With a nagging sense of discomfort prowling inside her, she continued on to Lilla Torget Square, following the row of planted trees arrayed in holes in the asphalt along the left-hand side of the pedestrian precinct. Deep in thought.

But once she'd picked up the rug that had been in for repair in Stockholm for one of Christoffer's colleagues, the one named Veronika, and carried it back to the shop, her unease had lifted, leaving only numb grief behind. As soon as she'd shut the door behind her in the shop, she intended to let the tears come.

The phone rang. Veronika Lundborg snatched up the receiver before the ringing could wake up Klara. The back door stood open, letting in yet another beautiful day. It was Cecilia.

"How are you, sweetheart?" she said, hearing how she was twittering a little over-zealously, sounding almost like one of the birds outside. Nothing new there, in other words.

"Good," said Cecilia, for once.

Veronika skipped a beat.

"That's great!" she burst out. "Has something special happened?"

"Nah… well, yeah, I guess… I've started going to the gym."

"Wow! So where do you go? You used to go a lot to the gym out in Orup, didn't you…" She almost bit her tongue. Why drag up Orup? Cecilia had left rehab. A new phase of her life had started, a return to normality. A normal, everyday life, eventually.

"Been going to Gerda," said Cecilia with in an unusually nuanced tone, albeit with a little of the monotone left.

"That's great!"

Veronika knew the place. A popular gym wedged in among old university departments and professors' houses in central Lund, not so far from the hospital, in fact. It was on Gerdagatan and so was called Gerda Gym. Its regulars were an eclectic mix: fat, thin, young, old, fit, not so fit, and pure rehab cases, apparently.

"What got you back into that?"

"I've got to do something," said Cecilia. "I was speaking to someone at the reception desk who thought I should start going to physical therapy. They're good at helping you move on… if you know what I mean. I've just come from there."

"Really?"

"I want to meet people, I told the physical therapist. She said I had good balance… I could take normal aerobics classes… but I should take it easy at first, perhaps. So I'm going to start gently with some light core classes."

"That's great! What fun!"

Veronika could hear how she was repeating herself like a parrot. This was big. A turning point.

She could picture it now, her daughter being greeted by the agreeable bustle of a locker room, with lines for the showers and then lots of people all sweating together. Just what her eldest daughter needed to bring herself out of her shell.

She asked if Cecilia wanted to come home to Oskarshamn. Claes was away.

"Nah," she said. "Not now. Later, maybe."

Veronika's first reaction was to feel affronted at this, as she'd more or less expected Cecilia to come running. But then she realized, once she'd given it a little thought, that it was actually news to rejoice about. Her daughter was growing independent again.

Veronika had popped into the local Coop corner shop on the way home from preschool and bought some fresh rolls. Sinful. You were supposed to eat whole wheat, she knew that, but the rolls' white fluffiness was just so yummy. Anyway, she was feeling just a tiny little bit sorry for herself, and she didn't know how long Claes would be away for, so surely she was entitled to treat herself?

Ugh! Why all these excuses? You could always find reason to sin if you wanted to, she thought, putting on some fresh coffee.

Her mood had swung. Maybe Cecilia wouldn't be calling any more today, she thought hopefully, looking out through the kitchen window. The weather had held out for a week now. Perhaps it would even feel empty without her daughter's calls?

Then Else-Britt Ek called from work, but not for an idle chat. She was off the next day and was wondering if Veronika and the girls wanted to come over in the evening for a bite to eat, given that her husband was away. They could sleep over if they wanted to.

Else-Britt lived on a farm run by her husband out in Applekulla. It was an old family estate that lay along a narrow, winding road not far from Bråbo and Bjälebo. Pretty as a picture!

They decided that Veronika would drive over herself with the kids. It was light long into the evenings now, and Klara would have time to brush the horses and perhaps even take a little ride on one of the ponies.

Veronika stood by the kitchen window, looking out at the apple tree. The blossom in bud, pinky white and stubby, ready to burst.

She lifted Nora up in her carrier and pulled the kitchen door closed, shutting in the rumble of the dishwasher, then walked into the sunlit sitting room.

CHAPTER 23

'SWEDISH GENERAL CONSULATE' the shiny plaque by the gate read. Ilyas Bank had gone past late the previous night and checked out the opening hours. Then the tall iron gates had been locked. Above them hung the Swedish national emblem, a large yellow crown, and underneath a blue field containing three smaller crowns. His stomach panged with respect even then, but he knew he had to go there.

So here he was, having passed through the big black gates just over half an hour ago – at exactly nine o'clock. The consulate had a nice, central location, right at the end of the long commercial street called Istiklal Caddesi, right beside the Tünel, whose carriages would whisk him underground down the hillside so that he didn't miss yet another ferry tour.

He'd be given a hard time by Ergün no matter what happened. Ergün would be at him, smiling and nonchalant, but unrelenting. There was no way he could tell Ergün that he was thinking of taking off. They weren't allowed to travel anywhere now. The police had said that they had to be contactable, both of them.

On the other hand, they both shared the experience of seeing a dead man, and that was nothing to shrug off. Someone who'd also heard the screeching gulls, and that was almost the worst part of it all – a jolt shot through his body at the mere thought of them. It had been a shock, and one that had bound them to each other, which was both good and bad. It was nice to have someone to talk to who'd also seen it with his own eyes, you didn't have to explain that much, to go into detail, like he had to do when he was sitting in the police station and she, that policewoman, wanted to know every little thing.

He'd decided not to say a word about it to his sister. She'd only get worked up and call their parents and then God knows what would happen. His whole family would pounce on him, protecting him and pressing him for details. And the cousin who'd gotten him the job would turn up like a hungry dog, sitting fat and bloated in his sister's sofa, chain-smoking cigarettes between coughing fits as he nailed him with his eyes. You haven't gone and done something stupid, have you? he'd ask. Think about me, about your family's reputation, he'd say. You could suck me into this, me, who got you the job in the first place! We're honest people in our family!

No, he hadn't done anything stupid, he'd have to lie.

Many years ago, back in his village, he'd dreamed about a situation like this – about being in the center of things. But it wasn't that great now that he was in it.

He just wanted one thing, and that was to disappear. The money, he thought. It made him both high and scared. He could go away somewhere. But there were things he'd have to work out first.

He'd talked to someone in the consulate called Yasemin, a rather stiff, tight-lipped Turkish woman who administered the visa applications. Swedes going to Turkey needed no visa, but Turks wanting to go to Sweden had to have one. It had to do with the Schengen Treaty, she explained.

There was no end to the papers he had to arrange. But it wasn't impossible. He was visiting family, he told Yasemin, and was planning to be away for three weeks.

She hardly even raised a shapely eyebrow. There were, of course, many Turks with family in Sweden, so he shouldn't be thinking he was unique in any way, she seemed to say. She gave him the creeps. But what the hell, all he had to do was take all the forms she lay in front of him. It would take a few days to arrange everything, he realized once he was outside by the gates again.

A passport he already had, and as luck would have it he'd brought it to Istanbul with him. Two color photos were the easiest things to check off his list. He also had to show that he had enough money to cover his visit, so he'd have to go to a bank and deposit the cash he'd need, but not too much, mind, as it would raise suspicions. Maybe he should open a new account?

And then he'd need a printout from the family register, from Nüfus, confirming his civil status, parents, and siblings. A streetcar rattled by along Istiklal Caddesi. He waited for it to pass and then took out his cell phone and called his sister to ask her to call their mother and tell her to get one and send it to him.

"What do you want it for?" she asked, naturally.

"You know that I've always wanted to travel..."

She breathed while her mind worked. He was building up for a long explanation, but then one of her children suddenly screamed and she had to go.

"OK, leave it to me," she said, and hung up.

There was no time to lose. He went to the Tünel and bought a *jeton* at the desk, and climbed into the train that took him downhill under the ground. With him were a mix of tourists and locals. Sumptuous tiling clad the walls of both stations.

He got off at Karaköy in the Galata neighborhood and exited into the sunlight. The city had awakened some hours ago, but the morning mist still shrouded the gray-green waters of the Golden Horn. With hurried steps he took off toward the Galata Bridge, rushing past all the men leaning over the railing with fishing rods in their hands. The traffic was moderate.

He could see his own ferry coming from the Bosporus, chugging toward its berth in Eminönü. A wave of apprehension came over him. He'd be held to account. He'd have to come up with an excuse. He'd overslept, that would do, he thought. If he went over the top with overly complicated excuses it would only make people suspicious, he realized.

When he reached the abutment on the other side, in Sultanahmet, he caught the whiff of grilled fish and realized that he hadn't eaten anything for a while. He sauntered up to a man with red eyes standing by his broiler and bought a freshly grilled fish in newly baked white bread and an orange Fanta. He was too restless to sit down at the long tables there, so he ate as he made his way toward the *SS Tirowor.*

The passengers were disembarking. He went on board full and contented, but felt eyes on him as he approached his niche. He'd avoided looking in the direction of the *kiosk*.

Just as he'd gotten the water ready for the samovar, he felt a soft finger press into his back. He spun round.

"Where have you been?" asked Ergün.

"I overslept," he said.

And despite having rehearsed this line quietly to himself the whole way along Eminönü's broad quayside, and although he knew very well that it was forgivable and even human to oversleep once in a while, he turned bright red.

"Right," was all that Ergün said, going back to doing what he was doing.

Which also felt a little overly blasé.

He then lifted the little tabletop and inserted his hand. And there at the back he could feel the notes spread out. The ones he'd left there and that not even the police's sniffer dogs had managed to uncover.

Actually, he didn't know if the police had brought dogs on board. Narcotics dogs in that case, maybe? Perhaps the dead Swede had been a drug dealer. Not that he looked like one. But you never knew!

It was all very exciting. But still mostly pretty grisly.

CHAPTER 24

IT WAS JUST AFTER DINNERTIME. The day crept along in restlessness. The radio was on at a low volume, and Annelie's ears were pricked up so as not to miss the local news. Perhaps they'd say something about Carl-Ivar today, too. Maybe they had some fresh information.

She turned it up and held her breath while the announcer's voice informed listeners that police officers from Oskarshamn were now on their way to Istanbul. Her heart was thumping with excitement. It soon passed and she was able to breathe again.

The tinkling of a piano then started to trickle out of the little transistor. She didn't have time to turn the volume back down and so was bathed in the delightful tones, which set her insides quivering. It was a commercial for a world-renowned pianist, who was to give a concert in Kalmar that coming Saturday.

She was just about to tear the brown wrapping off the rug that she'd just picked up from the post office, but the news about Carl-Ivar that had boomed out in such a dry, neutral manner, succeeded by this melting music, had made her head spin.

She burst out crying. She sobbed, and let the rolled-up rug lean in its protective plastic sheath against the table while the tears ran. She wiped her face with the back of her hands. I just hope no one comes in right now, she thought.

But what if they did? Everyone knew what had happened. Birgitta had told her that flowers had been pouring into the house on Holmhälleväg. Four chunky, beautiful bouquets had also turned up at the shop, sent by customers sending their condolences. She'd placed one of them on the table and the others in the windows. The rays of sunlight that fell on them made the petals gleam. Roses and lilies and sweet peas, a plump strain that must be foreign.

It was at once beautiful and simple, and brought a delicate perfume into the shop.

She'd put together a framed photo of Carl-Ivar and placed it in one of the windows. Christoffer had found that a bit over the top when she told him. He was surprised that she of all people would pay such emotional respect. "I mean, Carl-Ivar wasn't royalty," he said. "Just a common rug dealer."

She heard him and knew what he meant, and let it go. She was doing exactly what she wanted, and didn't even think about defending herself. She could detect a little jealousy in Christoffer. It didn't go down well that she spent time with someone other than him. But what was he doing?

She'd never really been the doting type, over and above when it came to him, and he knew that only too well and was content to have it that way. He interpreted it as her showing him both love and patience. But was it love? Sometimes she wondered. Did she know what real love was?

Whatever, she did her best. Copied women she'd seen who were only too happy to talk up their men and fuss around their sons, and go hard on their daughters.

Like her own mother. But then again, she was no normal mother.

And as for Christoffer, well, she could tire of him, she admitted to herself, and she sent her husband a thought that was ambivalent, to say the least.

The telephone rang.

It had been ringing quite a lot recently. For that reason alone it was good that she was holding down the fort. Especially now that Birgitta and the children had gone to Istanbul to say their final farewells to Carl-Ivar.

It was a woman on the other end who'd spilled red wine on her rug. There were many accidents of this kind happening all of a sudden, as people made up reasons for calling the shop, thought Annelie as she coughed quietly to clear the thickness in her throat.

No, it wasn't a big stain, said the woman on the phone, but how could she remove it?

Annelie said that she could take a towel and keep dabbing a little warm water mixed with a few drops of dish soap on it. She recommended that the woman pour the soapy water into a bowl and test a piece of the carpet carefully first to make sure that the dye in the wool wouldn't bleed.

"It's usually fine," she said in her professional voice, which had regained a temporary stability.

As she spoke, she straightened her back; it was as if the baton had been passed on. As if she'd become an extension of Carl-Ivar.

"Then do the same thing with a towel, but this time use some water in which you've added a few drops of vinegar instead to help bring the color out," she continued.

It could just as easily have been Carl-Ivar himself giving this practical advice. She could hear how she used his words, borrowed them but strung them together in her own way.

She cheered up at once. For the first time she saw herself seriously as Carl-Ivar Olsson's successor.

The woman was listening on the other end of the line. Annelie thought that she'd then hang up, but she clearly had something else to get off her chest.

"Tell me, what about vacuuming it?" she wondered, to prolong the conversation. "A neighbor told me it's better to beat the rug instead like you did in the old days when there were beating frames everywhere in people's gardens."

Annelie advised her against beating the rug. "People are so full of ideas," she said and they both laughed. "I'll send you some cleaning instructions. Feel free to use a vacuum cleaner, but go *with* the pile, not against it. However, the wool fibers contain a natural oil called lanolin that repels dirt and makes the rugs hardwearing. But gravel and muck you want to get rid of. Dirt like that can damage the roots of the fibers if you leave it lying around."

No, the woman didn't have the rug in the hallway, Annelie discovered. But there was nothing wrong with having them in the entrance hall if you looked after them properly, she felt the need to point out, and again made ready to hang up. She felt it was time.

But the woman continued to eagerly express her great joy at owning such a lovely rug.

"Nice to hear it," said Annelie, beginning to feel a little frazzled. But the woman was as obdurate as ever and went on about how she'd bought the rug a year back. And in the same breath launched into a vivid description: size, colors, and pattern, pretty much as if she were talking about a dog. Breed and coat.

Finally Annelie guessed which one she was talking about.

"Is it by any chance a Caucasian rug with a lot of green in it that you have? Where you can clearly see that the green changes tone, that the dyes aren't precise?" she asked eagerly.

"That's it! I think it's so lovely. You can really see that it's a work of craftsmanship and not some industrially manufactured thing…and if memory serves it's called an *abrash*," said the women, doubtlessly feeling a bit clever.

"That's right."

"That's what the carpet dealer said," continued the woman. "The one who died."

There. The line went silent.

"It's so tragic, isn't it," the woman continued in a hollow voice.

"Yes," said Annelie, feeling her throat suddenly thicken and her professional carpet-dealer self-crumbling away.

"You never know how long you've got," said the woman without sounding sentimental. "He was a good man, as far as I could tell. The best ones often go first."

That's another way of looking at it, thought Annelie.

They hung up and she stared vacantly out of the window.

Chapter 25

IT WAS WEDNESDAY and Christoffer Daun's first day back at work after the weekend. He'd had Monday off after having been on night duty, and yesterday he just couldn't drag himself in. He still felt like crap, but now at least he was at the clinic making an appearance.

He avoided Ronny Alexandersson. Didn't want to meet him alone. So at that morning's X-ray rounds, he snuck away while people were still in their chairs to dress himself in the surgery ward's locker room before everyone else: green trousers, shirt, and cap. So he popped his head into the operating room earlier than expected, much to everyone's happy surprise.

"Oh, terrific! Now we can get down to work more quickly," said the OR nurse.

The staff were busy preparing the patient, who had an inguinal hernia the size of an orange that Christoffer himself had placed on the schedule a few weeks before.

He had the sink to himself. He put on his surgical mask and rubbed his hands and forearms under running water, dried them, sterilized himself with alcohol, and dried himself again by wafting his arms and hands in the air.

So far, so good. He'd managed to keep out of the way and avoid anyone from his own clinic. The orthopedists were doing their thing, they had their own room down the corridor where they spent most of the time planning operations to replace the hips and knees of patients from around the whole Kalmar region.

Christoffer had sometimes felt tempted to study to become an orthopedist. There was something Inspector Gadget about it all, what with all the specially made instruments; but there were more rudimentary tools like hammers and chisels as well. As sturdy as anything. The orthopedists in Oskarshamn had also really gotten things moving there. If you needed a new joint, a new joint you got – and quickly, was their winning concept. The tax-paying citizenry should not need to wait years, and you gained nothing by putting off the inevitable. Waiting times had been reduced to two or three months for fully examined patients. There weren't many hospitals in Sweden that could beat that. It's that kind of thing that gives you job satisfaction, said his colleagues down the corridor.

He slipped into the room.

"Hi. Alright?" said OR nurse Susanne, smiling with her eyes above her surgical mask.

"OK."

His reply just popped out of him. It sounded more vapid than anything, but that didn't matter, they accepted him as he was and didn't try to cheer him up with jovial acclamations. Otherwise the nurses would have been only too happy to, mothering as they did their grumpy doctors as much as they did their children and husbands.

Susanne was laying out the instruments on the assistant table, called the "ass tab," and pumped it up to a suitable height. She had arranged the sterile instruments neatly in accordance with protocol.

She then helped him on with his surgical gown. He sat and waited at a short distance from the wall on a rotating stainless steel stool with his hands on his knees – he'd already put on his sterile gloves. He sat there as if enclosed within himself.

The patient was sedated, Susanne washed him and draped the body in a sterile covering with an opening over the incision site. Large paper sheets in light blue or green, colors that were thought to have a calming effect on the human psyche.

He stared at the second hand on the clock as it clicked around rhythmically, soporifically. All the same, he felt tense. Daylight was flooding in through the window at one end of the room, easing the sense of claustrophobia. Many operating rooms lacked windows; it was like working in a mine, forever underground. It eventually made you feel both sluggish and gray.

Susanne worked swiftly and rolled across the prepared ass tab, a domain over which she was lord and master. It was forbidden for him, the actual surgeon, to take instruments from it, the idea being that he should not have to take his eyes from the wound but just reach out a hand to get what he needed. Or ask for it. Susanne was a trained assistant who kept up with proceedings so that she'd know what he needed without his having to request it. He'd never forget the time when he was new and got barked at for swiping a scalpel off the table. The hag had gripped his hand, squeezing his fingers until he'd had to let go of it. He'd almost cut himself. It wasn't his fault that the scalpels were always placed conveniently at the edge of the table for impatient fingers to grab at.

"There you go," said Susanne.

He got up and went to stand beside the patient. Susanne hadn't washed away the entire black marking, so he could see where the incision was to be made. She handed him the scalpel and he inserted it into the flesh.

The operation was underway. A calm descended on the room.

No one asked him why he was early. No one asked him anything at all, for that matter. His fingers worked. He plowed on.

His plan was to lie low for the entire working day. But, of course, he couldn't continue like this forever. That would be pure madness, he knew that.

He needed time to build up the courage, he imagined. For how long and how much, he had no idea. His angst sat like an icy lump in his gut.

He'd rambled on at home about headaches and getting flu, talking in an extremely thick, croaky voice. Annelie appeared to fall for it. Although flu rarely broke out in May. But she was used to his not always feeling his best and would care for him and say cheery things and stroke his hair away from his forehead. Like his mother had never done, like he'd always yearned for her to do.

But Annelie hadn't done it this time. She hadn't even commented on his condition very much at all, in fact. As if there was something between them that had stopped. Or gone cold.

The red ball of paper! Why wasn't she saying anything?

Or maybe she hadn't seen it? If that was the case, he didn't want to ask. Perhaps it had been blown out of the car when she'd opened the door? No, unlikely. Anyway, he'd searched for it but it hadn't been there.

"Bad luck. I guess you'd better stay home until you're better," was all she'd said without hardly glancing at him, let alone touching him. No hugs, no brief pecks on the cheek.

There was clearly only one person going around in her head, and that was carpet dealer Olsson. You obviously have to be dead to get a little attention around here, he thought.

He missed and at the same time didn't miss her hand on his forehead. But he wanted things between them to be normal again. Not tense.

And yet he was ashamed, and that, of course, distanced him even further. He had no one to blame but himself. There were rats to be smelled here, and they were all his.

Ronny Alexandersson was not someone to talk behind people's backs, Christoffer knew that and trusted it. Ronny had the wherewithal to be direct when it was called for, demonstrating a civil courage possessed by few. Most people just kept silent.

But Ronny's fairness and honesty also had a scary side. You didn't get away with things. And this is why Christoffer Daun started and his heart began to thump when Ronny suddenly appeared in the doorway.

"Look, we might as well get this over with," he said.

The operation was over and Christoffer was sitting in the booth, dictating his surgical report into a humming computer. The thought of slipping away struck him, but how would he go about it? Ronny was blocking the narrow doorway. Not that he was fat – he was more the lean greyhound type, pale of skin and red-haired, at least originally. He was now turning gray, or rather, colorless.

So, Christoffer had no choice but to stay put. And whatever happened, he wanted to stay on good terms with Ronny Alexandersson. He also wanted to keep his job and not have to impress some other new employer.

"I presume that you're capable of understanding that if you're called up when you're on nights and a nurse asks you to come you have to go and make a medical assessment. You're the one with the medical responsibility," said Ronny, mercifully neutral in tone, neither supercilious nor chastising. A bully or someone with low self-esteem would have made a meal of this, thought Christoffer.

But still he felt the heat.

They're only words, he made himself think as he tried to swallow. But his mouth was as dry as the Sahara desert. Words, words, words. That's all they are, he said self-convincingly.

But the burning, stinging sensation remained.

"I've spoken to Birgitta Olsson… Her husband has just died, by the way… Maybe you've read about it," said Ronny, and Christoffer nodded but said nothing about his wife having worked for him. It wasn't the time or place. "And Birgitta claims that she's been perfectly clear about wanting you up there," continued Ronny. "She even noted it down in her report."

Christoffer nodded once more. It was best to confess. To expose his throat.

"Birgitta's right," he said, and felt like a hero. A fairly crestfallen one, to be sure, but befittingly remorseful.

It was his fault. He might as well admit it. He'd been tired and scared to death of not getting any sleep, but he let that pass. Didn't want to reveal that he lived with the constant fear of spinning out of control. His job was one in which panic attacks were hardly *de rigueur.*

"It won't happen again," he said in his best adult voice, sensing how the skin of his entire body grew hot under the green surgical clothes.

Ronny watched him, his gaze steady, as if he could see right through him.

"Tell me, how *are* things with you?" he said at last.

"Apart from the flu… Well, it's pretty much over now, so they're fine."

Ronny stared at him some more and then nodded.

"OK," he said. "At least we've found that the ECG was totally normal. That's all we know for now, the pathologist isn't done yet. Call me if there's something I can help you with."

What was he getting at? Christoffer wondered afterwards. What would I need help with? Does it show?

Christoffer finished his dictation, the words pouring out of him. Luckily, he didn't have to think. His concentration skills were set to zero.

At least Ronny had had the manners not to go on about it or to point any moral fingers.

He got changed, tearing off his green garments and tossing them into the laundry bin, and pulling on his jeans and top. He donned his white coat and walked into the ward, asking if everything was alright with his patients. And it was, on the whole, he found out.

He ought to get down to some paperwork. Signing reports, referral replies, and lab results on the computer. The "signing bin," as the software also called it, was full to bursting. It was a boring job. Maybe he could put it off a bit longer. Get down to it before the evening meeting on Monday, if nothing else.

And then he saw who it was standing down the corridor looking at him. The gaze flew its entire length, landing inside him with a metallic rattle, like a coin in a piggy bank.

He turned his head toward the staff room to avoid it.

Shit, he thought. How can I get rid of this pull, this passionate yearning that's like a glowing, all-engulfing fog?

He walked into the staff room and drank a glass of water, hoping that she'd be gone when he re-emerged.

Chapter 26

CARL-IVAR HAD BEEN A DECENT chap, that was for sure.

It was like Annelie was waiting for him to push open the door, wipe his shoes carefully on the doormat, which he'd do even if it was a nice day outside, and say "Good morning" in a loud, clear voice. And mean it: "I really hope you have a good morning!"

Then he'd switch on the computer and go around smoothing down or just stroking his rugs and carpets. Toward the afternoon, he'd ask her to pop down to Nilsson's and buy some buns to have with their coffee. Right now she was standing there almost waiting for it.

And he'd mean cream-filled buns. Never unfilled and preferably with a little powdered sugar on top.

But no companionable request for buns came.

The room was quiet. Dead quiet.

She shook her head and thought that probably the most important thing that Carl-Ivar had given her was not her in-depth knowledge of rugs and carpets, but the insight that one should let things take their time. He had neither caused a fuss nor moved heaven and earth for trifles, and that had been liberating for someone like her.

She could think of no situation in which Carl-Ivar had taken up space in the way that some people tended to do. Not even on his sixtieth birthday did he claim much attention. In fact, it was more like unease that he seemed to be feeling as he sat there comfortably in the dove-blue plush sofa at home in his sitting room, wearing his best red paisley-pattern tie and a paper napkin over one knee. He'd sipped the wine and had picked with tender fingers at the delicate little titbits that Birgitta had prepared.

Poor Birgitta, now all alone!

Carl-Ivar would naturally not have expected a big fuss to have been made, let alone demanded it. Satisfying people who harbored great expectations was rarely much fun, she thought. Rather, they tended to inspire scorn and antagonism, making you want to turn your back on them.

Like her mother.

Annelie screwed her lips together tightly.

When she was little she'd wished that Carl-Ivar had been her dad and Birgitta her mom. The typical survival dreams of a vulnerable child.

In her mind's eye she'd watch how the doorbell would ring and a dependable lady in a sensible skirt from some secure place that oversaw children's welfare would step inside to explain that a serious mix-up had been made. But she was here to put it right, the imaginary lady would say, smiling magnificently with lipstick on her teeth. As all the little more sensible ladies always had, those with influence. Unlike her mother, who mostly just drifted round in a fog of her own making.

And then she'd move in with Birgitta and Carl-Ivar instead.

But no ladies ever came wanting to rescue her from her mother. Nor anyone else, for that matter, not even Carl-Ivar and Birgitta. So she had to stay with her mother.

Like a tousled polar bear cub she'd once seen in a photo, that's how she felt. It was pressing its shivering little body up against the cozy security of its mother. But the mother bear was lying dead on the ice, a bullet in its still-warm body. Never again would she rise up to take care of her little cub.

Her own mother was always saying that she didn't have time for her. She had to go to work in the café or she had a headache and needed to rest, or she was sad and needed to cheer herself up with "a drop," as she put it. Then she'd get mushy in the head, and reel around singing loudly and badly until Annelie had to help her into bed so that she wouldn't wake the neighbors. If she hadn't collapsed into a heap on the carpet, that is.

Annelie thought that she should learn to give up. She wasn't good at it. Stubbornness had embedded itself in her. She couldn't give up neither her mother nor Christoffer.

Chapter 27

WHEN CHRISTOFFER DAUN had left the surgery ward, he went down to outpatients to empty his mailbox.

He inserted his index finger into the last of the brown internal envelopes, and opening it found yet another referral reply which he signed and placed on the pile for archiving. He then tore open a white envelope and pulled out an ad for hypertension medicine, which went straight into the trash. He rarely prescribed those kinds of drug. Anyway, he committed the brand name to memory as part of his general education, and if he wanted to find out more he could always look it up in the drug register.

And there, lying flat on the bottom, was a little white envelope of handmade paper with his name on it written in real ink. He picked open the envelope to remove the watermarked card. Everything had been done with the greatest care; in fact, it was almost over the top, but he was touched nonetheless.

Someone wanted to thank him with a naively drawn rose in black Indian ink colored in with red chalk and with a green stem. The drawing was touching, as if a child had done it or a dewy-eyed teenage girl. There were two lines of writing. Two lines about what a wonderful doctor he was. Exactly what he needed on a day like this.

He recognized the name, but couldn't put a face to it. He'd have to look her up on the computer later. He stuffed the letter into his jeans pocket and walked to the stairs. He had a patient to discharge.

When he'd done so he remembered the letter, so he took it out and brought up the report on the computer to find out who his admirer was. Suddenly he remembered her as if it were yesterday. What a case!

A woman, ten years his junior, who'd gotten her coat caught in the car door as she was getting out and been dragged a few yards before her husband had the presence of mind to stop. You'd think he was both blind and deaf! The woman had had a guardian angel and avoided ending up under the rear wheel. She'd also been spared any broken bones, but she was severely bruised and had slight concussion. He remembered that she couldn't stop crying with gratitude for their kindness, as he and a nurse stitched and dressed her wounds. She probably wasn't used to people being nice, he thought. Many people had learned to live on a tight rein.

Afterwards the woman said that she'd start a new life, without going into any detail about what she intended to change. He and the nurse recognized the reaction. When you've been given your life back after having been at death's door, obviously you wanted to do something about your future. "Wonder how long she's going to live with that man," the nurse had said dryly. It was Birgitta Olsson, if memory served.

He felt like calling the woman up to ask. But he encountered so many human destinies that his curiosity had become blunted. Despite his being a "savior type" or a real "people junkie," as Veronika jokingly called him, he managed to stop himself.

There was a knock at his door and he got up to open it. A fully dressed patient was standing in the corridor wondering when she could go home. He was always taken a little aback by the total transformation that occurred when the patients got out of their hospital gowns and into their regular clothes. Became themselves.

She was dark, slim, and stylish in her modern, slightly baggy jeans and a soft pink top and matching lipstick.

He began by giving her a few brief instructions about avoiding lifting heavy objects, ran off an e-prescription for painkillers from the computer, and filled in a form for a short period of sick leave.

And then he turned to her.

"Is there anything you're wondering?"

He sat completely still and silent and looked into her eyes. A large truck could be heard changing gear outside on Växjövägen far below them.

"Well, this is nice," she said, looking embarrassed. "Can I come and see you again… if something happened, I mean?"

She broke into a blood-red flush. He smiled to ease her discomfort.

"Of course, you have my name."

"If I needed to take out more sick leave…"

"Then just call the reception desk and ask for me."

He was still looking into her eyes, and smiled. Not flirtatiously, though, as that would be overdoing it.

"Are you sure it won't come back… The hernia, I mean?"

She didn't want to go. He could tell. She wanted to stay with him. Score!

"You can never be a hundred percent certain, but I wouldn't think so. Not if you're careful and look after yourself properly," he said in a familiar tone.

She smiled back but still showed no sign of wanting to get up from her chair and leave him. Not yet.

He didn't give off any such signals either, that he was short of time, that he was a busy person.

His cell phone buzzed. He put his hand in his pants pocket and turned it off. He'd brought the eyes in front of him to life and he was busy enjoying it. Like a warm breeze. Like a spring day. Like it was outside. The trust that grew. The thing we all yearn for, thought Christoffer Daun, content at being able to give. Even if he didn't always manage to receive. It was all to do with his lack of bonding as a child, said Annelie.

Who, incidentally, was off to a birthday party at Gabbi's tonight.

CHAPTER 28

ANNELIE PACED WITH slow, wavering steps back and forth on the soft carpets in the shop while her thoughts and feelings spun.

It was nice to move around, it made her better able to control the tears. She'd had more than enough of the complicated and neurotic in her thirty-four years, she thought. She liked the still, calm waters best, definitely. Like Carl-Ivar. Solid rocks.

Everything that Magnus wasn't, and still she was drawn to him. He pleased her. He'd always done so, strangely enough, but there had never been any talk of their being together in a more steady relationship. She'd dreamed about it. Quite a lot, once. What Magnus dreamed about was anyone's guess. He probably didn't even know himself.

But the sex worked, and she'd stopped asking herself why. All they had to do was touch each other and they were off, sucked into each other.

She could feel the pleasure rise in her where she stood. She'd sometimes divert herself when she was alone by shutting her eyes and fantasizing about Magnus coming to her. It usually worked. But she couldn't think about him when she was having sex with Christoffer. It would be as if she were completely ruining what she had with Magnus.

Her blonde hair had tumbled down, and her face was flushed and puffy. In the mirror she looked wild. She stroked away the hair, re-clasped it with the clasp at the neck, then fluffed her bangs. She glanced quickly at the photo of Carl-Ivar in the window, and a new attack of weeping forced her to drop her arms and bury her face in her hands.

Kind eyes, thin hair, friendly and somewhat droopy cheeks, a serious but not sullen mouth. He was wearing a striped shirt open at the neck and a burgundy V-neck cardigan. It was Birgitta who'd bought his clothes for him.

He never betrayed his age by making himself out to be younger than he was. He certainly hadn't been vain. More genuine and natural.

And yet she'd always suspected that he'd been up to something.

It had never occurred to her to interfere. She'd wanted to return some of the kindness he'd always shown her. He'd never poked his nose into her life. Not that he'd needed to, of course. He'd known about most of it. At least the important stuff, the things she was ashamed of. So she didn't have to tell him herself; or at least could choose to remain silent.

But he'd never asked questions.

She thought about those phone calls that came into the shop now and then. She'd always assumed they were from other carpet dealers. From Iran, Pakistan, Afghanistan, or Turkey. But it had always been the same voice. A woman's voice. A secretary, perhaps.

Carl-Ivar had always asked in English if he could call back, and would leave the shop, telling Annelie that he had an errand to run.

She'd always imagined that he just went round the corner and called back. Or that he sat in the car. She'd seen him in it with his phone pressed to his ear. He'd looked pretty upset that time.

The police wanted to check all the calls to and from the carpet shop, his home on Holmhällevägen, and his cell phone. It would take time to get a comprehensive list, but it could be done, she'd understood. Carl-Ivar had a cell phone service subscription rather than a pay-as-you-go card, so his calls were all traceable.

Just the simple fact that he had such a payment plan suggested that he hadn't been up to anything dodgy, Christoffer said. The real bad guys had disposable phones that could be topped up with minutes as needed and then just dumped as soon as they'd done a job.

She'd called her mother to tell her that Carl-Ivar was dead. She'd done so as soon as she herself had found out, but her mother had just started going on about herself, as usual. Annelie hadn't been surprised, just tired and a little irked for once, even though she knew it was a waste of energy.

Her mom had launched instinctively into a sermon about her lack of money, about having worked her fingers to the bone her whole life, about her aches and pains, and about losing her teeth. She'd begged and pleaded with Annelie to come home and help her. The least she could do was pay for a dentist; she who was, after all, married to a doctor and lived so well.

"It's the least a mother can ask of her daughter. All the times I've taken care of you," she said, her voice whiney.

"Don't you understand what I'm telling you, Mother?" she'd screamed at last.

"What?"

She sounded like an innocent babe.

"Your little brother's dead. Don't you get it? Carl-Ivar's been murdered."

"Oh, right, yes, how awful…"

Annelie could still hear how her mother had just breathed down the line then. The hamster wheel had probably stopped turning. She just didn't want to hear. Didn't want the outside world getting into her brain. Couldn't cope with other people's business; she was forever stuck in her own calamity. She was a victim on many levels. All levels, possibly.

Jesus Christ!

"Oh, my darling brother," she finally managed. "He was the nicest person on earth! Is it really true?"

"Yes, it is."

"Carl-Ivar, who is goodness itself… My little Anneling, tell me it's not so!"

"Mother, it's all over the papers…"

"Carl-Ivar, my darling brother! What'll I do without him? My little Anneling! You know that Mommy misses you, don't you? You must come home, now that this terrible thing has happened to me. My daaaarling brother is dead…"

Annelie could feel her heart grow cold. She refused. There was no way she was going to sit at her mother's kitchen table, listening to the woman, full ashtray in front of her, croaking on about herself. About not being able to afford her sixty cigarettes a day. And now she'd need even more because poor *her* had lost Carl-Ivar. Her beloved brother! That was something you didn't hear much otherwise.

But as soon as she hung up, Annelie was filled with regret. Of course it was a great loss to her mother that Carl-Ivar had died. They had, after all, always stuck together in some strange way, brother and sister. But mostly on the quiet.

She went down and splashed cold water on her tear-puffed face. When she heard the shop door pling open, she quickly blew her nose and ascended the stairs. But before she had time to stick her head up into the shop, the door jingled again as the visitor clearly left.

For heaven's sake, some people are so impatient, she thought.

She hurried over to the windows, first the one and then the other, to see if it had been a customer she recognized. She'd then be able to call after them, apologize and explain.

But the pavement was deserted in both directions, with the exception of a young couple in dark, baggy clothes, hair all tousled and dyed. Those two had definitely not come into the shop.

She turned around and was just about to turn down the radio when she noticed that the rug she'd just been busy unwrapping was gone.

She ran her eyes over the shop. She'd put the rolled-up rug by the table, hadn't she?

Chapter 29

At last Christoffer was able to leave the ward. He was heading home, but he made it no further than around the corner of the stairwell when his phone began to vibrate in his back pocket again.

An expected call, but not one he really wanted to take. On the other hand, he'd lived with his ambivalence for a long time, so why not a little longer?

And he'd already survived one blow today, once he'd finally dragged himself to work – the disastrous meeting with Ronny Alexandersson in the surgery unit, which hadn't, after all, been that bad. He brushed aside the thought of the woman who'd died at home and instead fished out his phone to check the display.

He was right. It was her. She was tenacious. But he got a kick out of it, nonetheless.

"Hiiii," she purred, voice silky and languid, with her usual intimacy. The hairs rose on the back of his neck. "I saaaw you earlier at the unit."

"Yes, I saw you, too," he said softly.

The red paper ball rolled once more over the rubber mat at the foot of his passenger seat. Minor panic. Where had it gone? He couldn't really cope with more contrition, most of what he had he'd consumed earlier that day when Ronny had come looking for him. But still it chewed him up. Gnawed, clawed, and sawed away.

"Are you leaving for home?" Tina asked. He didn't answer. "How are you?" she asked tenderly.

"Fine."

Her softness made the world stop spinning for a brief moment.

"Where are you?"

"On the stairs just about to leave for home. You know I don't want you calling me," he said in a low, guilty voice.

"But I couldn't help it… I love you so much," came the words, as quiet as a whisper.

He didn't respond in kind. Not there, where he was right now. He'd have to hide himself away to say things like that. So he said nothing now either, but nor did he hang up.

"Where are you?" he asked finally.

"I've shut myself into the washroom."

"OK."

He realized that someone would soon yank the door open and find her there, cheeks all flushed.

"So maybe I can catch a ride with you so I don't have to take the bus and Pär can get the job he's working on done and not have to pick me up? My mom's picking the kids up and is taking them back with her."

She was babbling. The coast was clear, in other words. She'd handed him this on a plate. He couldn't turn it down.

But still he didn't answer straight off. Didn't like people seeing her slide into his car. Tongues wagged so easily.

"But I was thinking of leaving this very second," he said, hoping that she wasn't ready to go home herself.

"Great. It's pretty quiet today on the ward, so I can leave a bit early. See you by the car?"

And so it was to be.

Just as he was getting changed, Michael Strong called. He was a man with a firm grasp of the pecking order, and so had a surname that suited him perfectly. Michael should have stayed in academia, Christoffer had often thought. Here in the country they didn't feel the need to keep pulling rank.

"I'm just about to sign off for the day," said Michael. "You'll have to go to the ward and discharge three patients for me," he continued without even asking if this was possible.

Christoffer's hackles were raised.

"You know, I'm on my way home, too, and have already changed. They're your patients, you discharge them."

He hung up before he could hear Michael snap at him. Only a year ago, he would have swallowed and gone to the ward and discharged the patients and been even more annoyed at Michael. If that was at all possible.

By now, the parking lot was half empty. The rowan trees that had been planted between the different sections were covered with new leaves and clusters of small white blossoms. He'd never noticed the little flowers before, but there wasn't much else to look at as he sat there behind the wheel waiting for Tina.

She was called Rosie by her colleagues, on account of her surname being Rosenkvist. She lived with some thuggish type, he'd understood from what Tina herself had told him.

He didn't know Pär more than from a distance. A good plumber, people said. She'd grumbled a lot when they first met, venting her frustration at his stupidity and rabid jealousy. But he thought that Pär seemed laid-back. He was the broad-shouldered, muscular type, a fact that Christoffer had noted with a pang of envy.

So why did she hang around?

Such questions never had simple answers, he'd learned that from experience. He couldn't live without Annelie. He stayed with her because he wanted to. All the other stuff was unimportant, really. All that which happened on the sly. But without it, life would be boring.

Anyway, he realized that Tina wasn't the woman who'd make him happy for the rest of his life. He'd need more. He was fussy. Needed a little friction now and then. Above all, his ambivalence meant that he didn't want to commit himself to any one person. But he needed Annelie. She was *there*. That's what he liked about her. She was smart and good to talk with about stuff other than love. She was nice company, even though he was bored with sleeping with her.

But you had to give to get. He'd learned that trick early in life. Practiced it on his old mom, and she'd been a tough nut to crack. She wasn't exactly the kind of person to clasp you to her breast without a second thought. No huggy-mommy, in other words.

Tina and he had talked quite a bit about Pär, as if he, Christoffer, could rescue her. He wanted to, at first. Wanted to be the knight in shining armor. He'd thought, Fuck it, she shouldn't have to take this crap! A man who threatens and beats his wife! Jesus!

These days, though, he didn't feel so worked up by it anymore. Tina didn't talk that much about leaving Pär. As if the man had become less of a control freak. More decent, perhaps.

She wanted to stay for the children's sake, they weren't that old, you know, she said. She wanted to hang around for a while, at least, she said in a little girl's voice so that he'd soften and understand. Meanwhile they could work on their relationship. It was like they were made for each other, she said, and he didn't object.

But time had done something to them. It was like they'd taken their relationship to a different level than when they'd first met. As if their relationships really could continue as it was forever. A kind of equilibrium, perhaps. In which case, having your cake and eating it was brilliant.

In the middle of all this thinking and waiting in the car for Tina, he was struck by the sudden urge to talk to Annelie. If nothing else, he wanted to be sure that the coast was clear – that she hadn't cancelled that evening's dinner with Gabbi.

She picked up right away.

"How are things?"

Fine, she guessed.

"Just wanted to say hi."

"So you didn't call for a particular reason?"

He had to confess that he hadn't. Her voice sounded odd, he thought, but he didn't ask why.

"So you're not coming home this evening?" he said instead.

"Nah, I reckoned on going to Gabbi's as planned… But is something up? Do you want me to come home?"

She sounded a little concerned.

"Not at all," he responded hastily. "Have a great time!"

He hung up.

What the hell was he doing? Was he getting paranoid? There was nothing strange about giving Tina Rosenkvist a ride home, was there? After all, they lived just a few houses down from each other. Good neighbors help each other out here in the countryside.

This realization calmed him, on that point at least. He had other things to worry about. He was going on report and there was no denying that he only had himself to blame. He sucked on that bitter thought for a while to accustom himself to the taste.

Or perhaps it'd be Ronny who'd take the brunt of it. They'd know once the autopsy was over, Ronny had said. The hospital was going to conduct an investigation into possible negligence. The wheels would start grinding. But they already knew, he thought. That he'd acted irresponsibly. That he *had* been negligent.

The very thought wearied him. The question was whether it wouldn't be best for his mental health to stand up and accept the blame. To don the heavy, sodden mantle of remorse and, of course, apologize. So that would be that and he'd be able to move on. Not because they'd be able to bring the woman back to life or that he could count on being forgiven. But really just to put an end to it all.

But on the other hand, it might not have made such a difference for the patient if they'd sauntered on up and had a look at her. What did they know? Damn it all, said Ronny. Only that she should have been sent for further examination rather than sent home. After all, it had only been a simple gall bladder case, and the patient herself had stated on her health declaration that she was in good physical shape and was not taking any medicine.

He saw Tina walking toward him. And then she was opening the passenger door and plonking herself down onto the seat beside him.

"Hi," she said, looking at him with intense eyes. A gaze that burned like a welding torch.

He reversed and drove out of the car park while scanning for anyone that might have spotted them.

Silence settled in the car. He held the wheel with both hands. Tina laid a hand on his thigh and gave it a squeeze. This rankled him at first, but he let it lie there, which it did all the way to the Århult junction. When they turned in toward Kristdala, the air was so thick that the car was fit to explode.

CHAPTER 30

THE POLICE CAR HAD LEFT the Sea of Marmara and turned onto a winding network of streets with ascending, densely-packed residential quarters.

Claesson sat silently in the back seat, taking in this indescribably thronging world that seemed to float in a faint blue afternoon fog. Or maybe it was exhaust fumes that made the air dense and shimmery.

They were driving alongside a narrow open space with a lawn in its center and tall obelisks rising at each end. Tourists stood in clusters around the flowerbeds adorning the bases of the obelisks, which they photographed with necks bent to get in the top. Buses stood parked in a line along the curb. Any fool could see that this was a historical place. Like an arena, thought Claesson.

The man behind the wheel said something to Özen, who then turned to Claesson in the back seat.

"The hippodrome," he explained in Swedish, pointing. "The stadium was built a long time ago by the Romans for horse racing. It was then developed by the Emperor Constantine…you know, the Greek… whenever he was…"

"The thirteen hundreds," Claesson offered. "I was reading about it while you slept. He was the one who founded the city. It was called Constantinople once. We in the north called it Miklagård during Viking times."

He felt like a school teacher, and was just about to wax descriptive about the Byzantine period when Özen interrupted him.

"And right next to it is the famous Blue Mosque. As you can see, it's not blue, but has blue tiles inside. It's easy to recognize because of its six minarets. It's unusual to have so many. Here in Istanbul people don't say the Blue Mosque but Sultan Ahmet Camii. It's high up and can be seen from the sea."

The car drove on, weaving between tourist shops and buses of all shapes and sizes. The smaller ones were normally white, he noted. The policeman, who was driving with an easy, accustomed hand through this maelstrom of human bodies, continued to supply facts, which Özen conveyed back to Claesson.

"And there's Hagia Sofia." Özen pointed at an imposing, brick-colored building with a domed roof and a conglomeration of annexes, flanked by four minarets pointing like sharpened pencils into the heavens.

"It's one of the real big tourist magnets alongside the Blue Mosque and the Topkapi Palace, which has harems, you know! The Sultan was busy…" Özen grinned as he listened again to his Turkish colleague. "When Hagia Sofia was built it was a Christian church, that was long ago… I don't know how long…"

"I can look it up," said Claesson, who was totally captivated by the unreal environment on the other side of the car window.

He didn't expect to have time to do any tourist stuff. The sights would, however, still be there for another visit, he thought, feeling a spontaneous urge to share all this with Veronika. But Istanbul was hardly a place to go to with small children. It'd have to wait.

"The guy here says that Hagia Sofia means the Church of Holy Wisdom," continued Özen, who'd put on a well-modulated guide's voice. "Now it's a museum. Always packed with tourists. There are even some runes there that were scratched into the walls by Vikings. The emperor employed Vikings as guards and soldiers because they were reliable and hard as nails."

Shortly afterwards, the marked police car rolled onto a narrow street untouched by the sunlight. Lining the pavement were workshops, small boutiques, and bars, like holes in the walls with a scattering of rickety plastic tables outside.

Then the car stopped by a large building with an old-looking façade but with modern-looking windows, noted Claesson. He and Özen took what little luggage they had, which for Claesson consisted of the smallest model of rolling suitcase and a shoulder bag containing a laptop and documents about the case.

The air inside the police station offered little succor from the heat, but Claesson was so tense that he didn't care. His forehead and cheeks were burning and his hands were moist.

He was wearing a short-sleeved checkered shirt of thin cotton and relatively new, slightly tidier chinos. He suddenly wondered if he should have dressed more appropriately. Many hours had passed since the shirt could have claimed to be freshly ironed. A jacket and pressed, sharply creased slacks might have looked better, but were not as comfortable to travel in. At least he had a navy blue linen jacket with him, neatly folded into his case, to put on when necessary. Although this need rarely arose as he found jackets uncomfortable these days.

Mustafa Özen was also casually but smartly dressed in jeans and a neat but more youthful piqué top in bright pink bearing the logo of a Swedish quality label on the breast. It suited his dark coloring and revealed the well-pumped biceps with their thick veins that snaked like mountain paths over the skin.

They were greeted by a high, shiny counter topped with a light-gray laminate. A man in a bright blue uniform shirt and a mournfully droopy moustache sat behind it. He picked up the phone as soon as Özen informed him of who they were.

Another unformed man soon appeared and ushered them through a locked door and up a flight of stairs and in through another locked door. They found themselves in an office environment, not completely unlike that at home, but more crowded. The city rumbled on outside.

A man and a woman came to meet them. The man was relatively short and clean-shaven, with a wreath of grizzled hair at his neck and, startlingly, one blue and one brown eye. He looked fit. This was Superintendent Fuat Karaoğlu. The first name posed no problem, and Özen had taught him how to pronounce his surname on the plane. A g with a little hat was swallowed, the hat indicating that the proceeding vowel was long. *Karaoolu*, in other words.

"*Hos geldiniz*," said Karaoğlu and took Claesson's hand. "Welcome!"

That Merve was a woman's name was something that Claesson had also learned on the plane. She was both younger and taller than her boss, and had large, friendly eyes with glossy black hair that she'd pulled back into a ponytail. She greeted them with the same phrase and introduced herself as DI Merve Turpan.

Unlike Fuat Karaoğlu, who was plainly dressed in short-sleeved shirt and pants, the DI wore a uniform consisting of dark slacks and a blue blouse bearing the police emblem on the breast, showing the white crescent moon and star against the red background. Both looked inquisitively at Mustafa Özen. A more detailed introduction was required, and that was done in Turkish.

Finally the introductions were out of the way.

"Very good," said Karaoğlu companionably to Claesson once he realized that they'd managed to find a Swedish detective with a Turkish background.

"Then let us get down to work. We must use the time well now that you have traveled so far," said Karaoğlu.

They were seated around a table in what served as the police station's conference room. Apart from a white screen that was stretched over part of one end and a large map showing Istanbul's myriad streets and alleys and sprawling suburbs, the walls were bare.

DI Turpan left the room. They were to wait a minute, Karaoğlu informed them. For what, he didn't explain – but Claesson could tell by Mustafa Özen's facial expression that he at least knew what was going on.

Karaoğlu also left the room. He returned shortly, walking in and out with armfuls of maps, and then fired up a laptop that was on the table. In the meantime, Claesson unpacked his briefcase and placed the papers on the desk in front of him, along with a notebook and pencil that he then proceeded to roll between his fingers.

His stomach panged and grumbled discreetly. Otherwise, he was of Dromadarian descent and could go for a few more hours without food.

He was also a wizard these days at waiting for babies to fall asleep. He was thinking of Klara, and of how sensitive she was. If she picked up on his restlessness when he was feeding her and on his intention to abandon her, her eyes would pop open and he'd have to start all over again.

He could at once feel her soft body beside him, and began to wonder how they were getting on back home.

Özen interrupted his reverie by explaining that they were preparing refreshments, and in Turkey that nearly always meant tea.

Tea was what invalids had with their toast, thought Claesson. But hey, when in Rome....

Karaoğlu returned and checked the quality of the image on the screen. Now they just had to wait for Merve Turpan.

Claesson couldn't properly gauge the size of the police station, but there was no doubt it was bigger than theirs in Oskarshamn. And it was more crowded here, too. The offices that he'd walked past were like cubbyholes, shared ones to boot. Now in Oskarshamn they were spoiled. They were housed in a former newspaper printer's that was both spacious and centrally located, but undisturbed by traffic.

He wondered what their clearance rate was. It was hardly appropriate at this initial stage of their partnership to ask. They were probably stuck with the same investigative backlog as they were at home, where some cases were written off right away owing to lack of time: thefts, break-ins, even robberies. But murder inquiries they always put resources into. They were rare at home, one or two a year in Oskarshamn, but the cases could still run aground and go cold.

Nowadays, Sweden had special cold-case teams for unsolved crimes; its forensics experts were making huge strides and were able to provide answers to what were once unanswerable questions.

He thought of the victims' relatives. It was easier not only for them but also for him to tackle the feeling of emptiness that an unsolved murder could often elicit if a genuine attempt had been made to find the killer, at least. Some would call now and again, wondering if there were any developments in the case. *Crimewatch* was a regular feature of the TV schedules. The need for closure was deep.

He'd primed Özen as the pen holder – or tape recorder operator, as it turned out – since he could speak Turkish and English as well as Swedish, and would therefore probably grasp most of what was said.

Or rather miss less of it.

The door opened and in walked a man carrying a circular tray of tea and round buns coated with sesame seeds.

"These buns are called *simit*," said Özen.

Claesson broke off a piece and found it tasty.

It was now time for business. There were four of them in the room: Superintendent Fuat Karaoğlu, DI Merve Turpan, cadet-detective Özen, and Claesson himself.

You could hardly accuse Karaoğlu of beating about the bush, Claesson thought. He prattled away in English with a frenzy enough to inspire envy in the best of them. He had an accent, naturally, a thick one even, but that didn't stop him, which on one level made Claesson relax. At least his own regionally inspired English accent would cause him no shame.

"We were called to Eminönü ferry terminal at twenty-three minutes past four pm, about eight minutes after the ferry had docked and the passengers had left. We were there about seven minutes later. It was one of the crew who had called us...."

He turned to Özen and said something in Turkish.

"Helmsman, I think it's called," translated Özen and Claesson nodded.

Karaoğlu then turned to Merve, who showed them on the map behind them where the ferry had its berth. Claesson thought that Özen and he should pop down there later, if they had time.

Karaoğlu pulled up a picture onto the screen. It showed a young man, around twenty with slightly drooping eyelids and a totally expressionless face.

"This is the witness who found Olsson. His name's Ilyas Bank," he said.

Merve wrote the name on the white board and Özen copied it down.

"He sells tea on board, walking around among the passengers with a tray. He worked in telemarketing for a few months, but says he wants to make a future for himself. When the ferry was docking and all the passengers were crowding through the exit, he went around collecting glasses."

Claesson nodded, lifted his own glass of tea and sipped.

"Then he found Olsson by the railing on the... port... on, er... which is it... the left side in the direction of travel. Anyway, he was on the side facing the Marmara Sea rather than that facing Istanbul and the Galata Bridge."

A new picture appeared on the screen.

Claesson and Özen both gave a start. The color photo was exceptionally high quality. There was something tender yet grotesque about the neatly dressed gentleman who sat with head hanging heavily and the entire front of his shirt saturated with blood. You could see his intestines slipping out through a gash in the material.

The silence that had descended on the room was allowed to settle for a few seconds as a kind of homage to this aged Swede whose life had been so brutally taken, here in Istanbul.

"Yes...so this is how the witness found Olsson," said Karaoğlu in a hushed tone. "He tried to feel for a pulse in his wrists, he told us, before he understood just how bad things were. The body had actually not had time to become cold before we arrived. It was also quite a hot day, around sixty-eight degrees. According to the coroner, Olsson died minutes before he was found, no more than half an hour before, but we suspect that he was killed just as the boat was emptying."

"There is a good deal of confusion then," continued Karaoğlu. "If you are planning to kill someone that is probably the best time, even if it is also very risky.... If nothing else, someone might catch the murderer in the act. Even from one of the passing boats, the quay is very busy, you understand. But just at that time there was apparently no boat passing. We have asked around, but we have no information that someone saw something. Anyway, his wallet was still in his back pocket. Driver's license and a little money, but nothing to kill for... If, that is, it is the same man on the driver's license, of course."

"His wife and two children are due to arrive tonight," said Claesson.

"Then they can identify the body tomorrow. Very good! Can you be present?" wondered Karaoğlu, peering at them over the rim of his glasses with his different-colored eyes.

Claesson and Özen nodded.

"Merve will help you, also."

This she confirmed with a nod as Karaoğlu gathered his breath.

"Have you ever heard of Wasp knives?" he asked.

"I know what they are but that's about it," said Claesson, and looked at Mustafa Özen. "We've heard about this knife from our forensics guys, but never seen the effects of it, not where we come from. But I guess it's just a matter of time..."

"A great nuisance," sighed Karaoğlu with a shake of his head. "An American knife, originally made to be used against aggressive sharks and other wild animals, so the manufacturer says."

He brought up a picture of a knife on the screen with a matchstick under it. The handle was thick and sturdy.

"But it works just as well against two-legged animals, too," he continued. "The handle conceals a carbon dioxide cartridge that is triggered when the knife is stuck in its victim... and... then there is a..."

He was searching for words. Merve Turpan tried to help him. They had to resort to Turkish and were saved by Özen.

"Overpressure," he said in Swedish.

"Thank you. Inside the body this has a terrible effect," he continued. "The carbon dioxide then leaves the body. This causes trouble for the pathologist, an agent that cannot be measured is always a problem. According to the autopsy report, Olsson died from abdominal tearing. His intestines and major blood vessels were punctured in many places. The blood emptied quickly. But now we have seen this type of injury so many times that we can see a pattern and can hazard a guess at the weapon," Karaoğlu continued. "We suspect that it was this type of knife that was used to kill the victim. The knife causes an effective and quick death. Olsson would hardly have had time to catch his breath before it was all over."

Mercifully, thought Claesson.

"It is also true that we at this police station, and, yes, at other police stations in Istanbul, have confiscated copies of this knife that are made in Russia and a bit easier to handle. Smaller, quite simply... lighter to carry, and I suppose cheaper to buy. One might suspect that the manufacturer did not intend it to be used so much against four-legged animals as against two-legged."

A new picture on the screen showed a somewhat slimmer version of the same knife.

"You can order them on the Internet and hope that the customs people are blind that day. Or buy one almost anywhere here in Turkey. I do not know how it is in Sweden with illegal weapons?"

"They're common," replied Claesson curtly.

Karaoğlu drew a breath. He had a warm voice that mingled pathos with strength.

"Why?" he said in a slow exhale, and then fell silent, as if he had taken a course in dramatic effect. "Do you have any ideas?"

What, in other words, was the motive?

"No, not yet," said Claesson.

His head started to get muggy. As far as he knew, Carl-Ivar Olsson had never been involved in any kind of criminal activity, and he said so.

"But we are not ruling out drugs," said Karaoğlu.

"Drugs?" repeated Claesson and exchanged glances with Özen.

You had to keep an open mind for any eventuality, even if it seemed a little far-fetched. After all, it wasn't that long ago that they'd busted a sixty-year-old man dressed as a Catholic priest at the border crossing on the Öresund bridge. He'd claimed that he was going to be traveling around looking at medieval Swedish churches. He had double-lined underpants stuffed with heroin.

"Nah, I shouldn't think so," said Claesson evasively. "We've got no reports of Olsson being involved in drug smuggling. But sure, there's a lot we don't know. But on the other hand, we've got quite a bit on a rug. Or rather a fragment of a very old and valuable rug from central Turkey, but we can take that later."

Karaoğlu nodded to Merve Turpan, who took over the keyboard. Her fingers flitted while she focused on the white screen until she had brought up a detailed map of the Bosporus.

"Here is Yeniköy," she said. "Our witness Ilyas Bank thought it possible that the carpet dealer boarded here. Other witnesses think so, too."

The place was on the European side a little upstream.

"Yeniköy is a very, very old place." Something dreamy came into her eyes. "It is from the Byzantine era. There are *yalis* there, beautiful nineteenth-century villas down by the water. Very, very beautiful."

Claesson had picked up on Merve Turpan's way of expressing pleasure. Very, very nice, old, beautiful…

She's a good ambassador for her city, Claesson thought. A manifest pride and not that blunt matter-of-factness that some people suffered from at home among all the sights there. Was he as good an ambassador for Oskarshamn?

"Excuse me, but I'll go and see to some more tea," Merve said suddenly and walked out.

She might need to go to the bathroom, thought Claesson. He needed to himself, and stood up with a slightly embarrassed air. Karaoğlu read his mind and pointed down the corridor.

When Claesson had returned, Karaoğlu told them that they had questioned every member of the ferry's crew, but not all the passengers since tickets were bought anonymously and so couldn't be traced.

"The man in the *kiosk* thought he had noticed a person."

Claesson wiped his neck with his hand. No one here would suggest opening the window as it would probably make no difference.

A driver's license photo of a slightly older man appeared. His name was Ergün Bilgin and he was standing behind the counter of the little onboard *kiosk*, Karaoğlu told them. He'd seen how all the passengers had crowded into the front in order to get off first. He'd also noted a man of Scandinavian, American, or German appearance who'd been standing right at the back holding a dark cloth bag. Bilgin could also, with a certain tentativeness, venture that the man had come from the same direction in which the body was found, from the port side, just before he disembarked. From the left-hand side, that is, if they got off at the front.

"Could he give a description?"

Karaoğlu read aloud. Just over five-foot-ten, slim, young middle age perhaps, wearing a long-sleeved top with wide blue and green stripes and a collar. He also had on a cap with some kind of red logo, or so he thought.

"We questioned Ilyas Bank again, the man who found Olsson, and he also thought he had seen this man and had an idea that he was wearing a white cap with red writing on it."

"Yes, well," said Karaoğlu with a shrug. "It is a shot in the dark… But it is a shot nonetheless."

Merve Turpan returned and turned to Karaoğlu, who signaled to her with a nod.

She started writing energetically on the computer again. She radiated freshness and health, and reminded Claesson a little of his first love, even though she'd been blonde and blue-eyed. But this wholesomeness was the same and the softly rounded contours, even though Merve would still be considered slender. It was a figure that could easily become rounded if one wasn't careful. "She plumped out with age," as his father would always say of women who didn't manage to keep their hands off the pastry tray. Men, on the other hand, "acquired a certain gravitas with age."

Merve Turpan clearly had an astute mind, you could tell that at once. There was something about her bearing and the expression in her eyes. "A sparkling intellect," as his dad might well have called it. Not on one single point did she fit Claesson's image of a Turkish woman as being a subservient housewife whose main purpose in life was to have babies and look after home and husband. Instead, she seemed to be an urbane and highly educated woman, probably well on the way up the career ladder. Like Louise Jasinski back in Oskarshamn. What's more, Turpan's English was the best in their little group. Her entire being, from her posture to her way of speaking, bore witness to vigorous self-esteem.

She flashed up an amateurish photograph that could have been taken with a simple digital camera.

And it had been. One of the ferry's crew had taken it to test his new cell phone. The buildings had looked so nice, he'd said.

In the photograph could be seen one of the beautiful villas that their Turkish colleagues had mentioned before. This yali was several stories high and had columns, mullion windows, and sumptuous embellishments. It lay right at the water's edge beside a villa in the same style but decorated differently. In the next photograph, the house could just be made out in the background. In the foreground was a quay bathed in sunlight. The heat was almost tangible.

A total of five people were standing dotted around the quay, each seemingly having nothing to do with the other. They were all facing the water, clearly waiting for the ferry to dock so that they could climb aboard.

One of them was Carl-Ivar Olsson. It was undoubtedly him, standing on the far left. He was holding a soft bag made of some dark material, canvas or leather, it was impossible to say. His left arm and shoulder were cut off by the border of the photo.

"A typical carpet bag," Karaoğlu informed them.

"In that case it contains a very small carpet," said Mustafa Özen, speaking up for the first time. "The bag doesn't look full," he explained.

"One thing we do know," continued Karaoğlu, "is that that bag was nowhere to be seen when Olsson was found. The man who found him on the ferry saw no bag by his body. He might, of course, be lying, but I don't think so."

"What was carpet dealer Olsson doing in Yeniköy," Claesson said eventually. "Might there have been another carpet dealer there he'd been visiting?"

Karaoğlu gave a crafty look.

"Yes, there is a carpet dealer in Yeniköy. But he has never heard of someone called Carl-Ivar Olsson from Sweden. We have met him, you understand. He is quite a young man who has recently taken over the business from his father, who died of a heart attack six months ago. City life is stressful. Not good for the heart," Karaoğlu said, placing a hand against his chest.

Merve Turpan displayed a picture of the young carpet dealer, who looked around thirty, perhaps a little older. The young man who was assumed not to have anything to do with things.

She then turned the conversation toward the man who'd found Carl-Ivar Olsson's body.

"Ilyas Bank claims that he has no connections with Olsson or Sweden. Perhaps a relative there, but so do many Turks, in Sweden or Germany or some other country in Europe. But no one that Bank has close contact with. Anyway, there are two things that bother us. The one is that the bag is missing. The other is this…"

She clicked up the next picture, presumably taken by the same photographer. Olsson's left side was visible now, on the right of the picture. Carpet dealer Olsson in full-frontal, in other words.

They knew how to build up the drama here in Istanbul, thought Claesson. For on Olsson's left stood a woman.

They could've shown this photograph straight away, for Pete's sake! But he said nothing. "Who's she?" he asked instead.

"We don't know," said Merve Turpan.

They weren't standing shoulder to shoulder, and there was a little space between Olsson and the unknown woman, who was much younger than he was. She could, of course, be a total stranger, someone who didn't belong in the picture, anyone waiting to take the ferry. Or the classic lover. It was as if the air between them was vibrating, even though they were both looking directly ahead. Perhaps it was this, that they were so obviously making an effort not to look at each other.

The young woman's mouth was half open, as if she'd just said something. And the only one she could be talking to there where she stood was Olsson.

Unless she had a wireless hands-free earpiece concealed by the thick hair that hung down to her shoulders, but somehow that didn't seem likely.

But what had she just said to Olsson? What was her frame of mind? They both seemed a bit guarded. Or was that just a trick of the light?

Their job now was to find out who she was. Claesson felt his brain churning full speed, even though his eyes were stinging. He was so fired up that he'd probably have difficulty getting to sleep tonight.

He cleared his throat and pulled out the black and white photo that he'd taken from Olsson's shop in Oskarshamn. He'd had the foresight to make photocopies of it, which he now handed over to Karaoğlu and Merve Turpan. They studied them carefully.

"A very, very old rug," said Merve Turpan. "But I'm no rug expert."

Claesson gave a brief account of their meeting with carpet dealer Roland Karlgren in Kalmar, who'd given then the name of a carpet dealer in the Grand Bazaar. Karaoğlu asked Merve Turpan to make a note of the name. They decided that the Swedes should go there accompanied by a Turkish colleague. Merve wouldn't mind going with them, she said.

"In plain clothes," Karaoğlu pointed out. "There is no need for us to alarm a decent, honest carpet dealer. We will schedule this for tomorrow morning, before you go to the morgue, so that I can contact the coroner first."

Claesson had all the contact details for the Olsson family and promised to call them about the time for identification. The wife, the woman in the carpet shop, and the two children had all been in Sweden at the time of the murder, he impressed on them.

"They cannot possibly have murdered Olsson."

Their conversation turned to the hotel where Olsson had been staying with his wife before she flew home. It was called the Arkadia and was on the same side of the Golden Horn as they were now and that the ferry departed from.

"However, Carl-Ivar Olsson had checked out from the Arkadia on the same day his wife returned to Sweden," said Karaoğlu, giving the carpet dealer's name a very quaint pronunciation.

"Where did he go then?" wondered Karaoğlu, casting them a dramatic look. "Perhaps you can start at the Arkadia tomorrow?"

No rest, no peace, thought Claesson. Just roll up your sleeves and set to work. He felt a spasm of genuine enthusiasm. This was exciting! They promised to get their colleagues at home to check with Olsson's bank to see if he'd used the card to pay for a night spent at another hotel.

"If he actually stayed at a hotel, that is," said Claesson observing his Turkish colleagues to see how they took this. An insinuation of a lover was nothing out of the ordinary in Sweden. But here?

No one reacted. So the hotel ledger would be checked again. Who else was staying there at the same time?

"It would be easiest if you Swedes take care of this," Karaoğlu said. "You will find it easier to recognize the Scandinavian names. And you can take the opportunity to ask the wife tomorrow."

All four looked at each other, as if none of them really expected her to know where her husband had been.

And then they parted company.

Chapter 31

THE EVENING LIGHT SHONE ASKANCE through the kitchen window, blanketing the sink. Christoffer Daun tightened the faucet, which was dripping incessantly. Sounded like something clattering on a tin roof to his ears.

But the leak continued.

For far too long he'd been intending to ask someone to come and fix the washer. Annelie had nagged at him. Of course she had, but *of course* she could call someone herself!

Perhaps he'd put it off for the simple reason that the nearest plumber was Pär Rosenkvist.

Tina had placed herself in the middle of the outdated striped rag rug. The one that Annelie loved so much and that one of the local women had woven. It should, in other words, have been Annelie's flats that now walked on it. She belonged in the kitchen, not Tina. He tried to force Annelie out of his head. Watched Tina instead.

They were quite similar, Annelie and Tina. Very similar, even. The hair down to the throat, the soft cheeks, the well-defined behind. Graspable.

He was drawn to the same type, apparently, at least appearance-wise. But Tina was feistier in her movements. Accustomed to running through long hospital corridors. Efficient. Although he didn't know if he'd be able to put up with that for long. Sometimes you could have too much of a good thing – of the feminine energy that wrenched and tore at him and that wanted to draw him in. To mother him, flirt, and snuggle. And that had expectations of being eternally noticed.

Some of his female doctor colleagues snickered or laughed outright behind his back and said that he was spoiled. *They* didn't get that kind of backup from the nurses, they had to manage on their own without assistance and without a red carpet rolled out to parade their careers on. Who'd roll it out for them? they asked, rhetorically.

But honestly, was it even his problem? He thought them a gaggle of bitter old hens. It was simply a matter of pure envy. The worst was Fresia. He hadn't gotten anything for free, not he. On the contrary. He'd had it pretty heavy-going and gruff for long periods. He was worth all the attention he could get.

But then it pained him to be a cheating, lying bastard, even if it felt a little better to at least admit it to himself. Almost to the point of his actually enjoying being able to own up to his own faults and shortcomings. It was a kind of no-strings masochism.

Now he tried to get his eyes used to seeing Tina stand in the kitchen, but the truth was that the sexual tension between them in the car had dissipated, at least for the moment.

Tina bit her lip as if she, too, was thinking that she'd ended up in the wrong place.

But still she had no intention of leaving. She wasn't going to leave him now.

She even felt closer to him, strangely enough. Somehow got even more of him when she was in his house and part of his normal life. Saw the shelves of pretty porcelain, the tablecloth with its modern print design, the beautifully painted walls. She was stealing another woman's presence with her eyes, and she found that a turn-on. Why not? His wife wasn't her responsibility, she was his alone. She wasn't going to feel guilty; it hadn't even been her idea to accompany him in.

Christoffer was a doorway to a second, Pär-free life, she thought as she looked around. In the name of love. They loved each other more genuinely, she and Christoffer. She'd run all the arguments around her head a thousand times. Kneaded away until her mind was raw, and concluded that you only live once and that you should live that life to the fullest. And it was neither fair nor honest to live with the wrong man. With someone she neither respected nor loved. Together just out of habit and because they had two children together. But whom she was nonetheless fond of, in a weird way. This infernal dithering. Perhaps because, when it came down to it, things were so erratic with Christoffer.

She wasn't alone in her feelings for Christoffer, either, and that was another worry. There were always nurses strutting around him. A young, handsome doctor, neither tired nor worn out by long operations and late nights on duty.

The patients were also charmed by him, perhaps because he was so sensitive. A little melancholy at times, admittedly, but cute nevertheless, and he was phenomenal at listening to what she said without having his thoughts elsewhere, like Pär. He usually just sat with his eyes glued to the TV sports channel while trying to put food in his mouth. He never initiated conversation himself.

Once Christoffer touched her, when he caressed her with his warm hands, it was like getting an electric shock of bliss.

She'd never actually connected with Pär, she sometimes thought. But they'd been so young when they met. It was mostly that they'd just gotten used to each other. They'd boxed themselves in with children, home, family. They were loyal, but that wasn't the same thing as loving someone.

She wanted to take care of Christoffer and make life easier for him. It seemed as if Annelie didn't care. They'd drifted apart, he said. God, all the people who'd drifted apart! Christoffer said that she, Tina, understood him much better. That Annelie was really only interested in carpets.

But still he didn't leave her.

Tina had noticed that he was dragging his feet alright, and carrying on like this depressed her. This constant swinging between hope and despair. So she'd put her foot down. She'd realized that someone had to, and she was stronger, that was obvious. She'd told him that she didn't want to leave Pär and the kids. Not now, at least. That she wanted to wait.

So she'd said this to force a decision out of him. To make him see that he wasn't to go around thinking he could take her for granted. She also had her pride.

Christoffer excused himself and went to the bathroom.

Tina had found a scab on one of her forearms to pick at while she continued to look around. The light from the larger room opposite filtered in and spread itself over the hall carpet. It was richly colorful, one of those Oriental carpets that Annelie sold but that Tina actually found quite ugly. She preferred light, monotone, modern carpets.

She heard him flush and then he returned to the kitchen.

It was as if the air had cleared.

"Do you want coffee or tea?" he asked. "Or perhaps some wine?"

"A glass of wine would be nice."

"Red or white?"

"Red, if there is any."

He opened an old-style pantry door and took out a bottle and set out two glasses and poured. He gave her one, they clinked glasses and sipped, looking into each other's eyes.

"How about a nibble of something? Cheese and crackers?"

"The wine'll do just fine, thanks."

She was going to eat at home, but kept quiet about that. Dinner with Pär and the kids. Meat and beer and more wine for her.

Christoffer seemed to hesitate. Tina blinked while her eyes continued to drift. Finally, she tilted her head to one side in that inviting way of hers. She knew it would hit home.

He was still standing by the edge of the stainless steel sink, feeling the metal press harder and harder into his gluteal muscles, the Latin name for the buttocks popping into his head, giving a bit of distance and order, like at work.

Tina dropped her arm and took a couple of steps toward him to stand close to him but without touching. He sensed her breath at the same moment as she dropped her gaze. They stood like that for a while longer, dragging it out.

Then she bowed her head forwards and let her forehead rest against his chin and mouth. He stood reverently still, shut his eyes and gently parted his lips against her forehead. The tip of his tongue slipped out and played with her skin, and he could detect the not completely unexpected taste of salt and bitterness. His blood was pulsing hard. The cool distance that sometimes appears between two people, and on that rare occasion between him and Tina, evaporated at once.

She lifted her arm and, crooking it around his neck, pulled him close in to her and away from the sink. Her breasts pressed into him. She thrust her hips forward, pressing harder against his hips and groin as if she wanted to enter him, into his body, if that had been possible. With rhythmic motions she started to rub her pubic bone against his thigh. Her hair smelt of "a day at the hospital," he thought.

One of her hands was now playing inside his top, the tips of her fingers sliding along his spine up toward his neck. Hard and delicious, painfully pleasurable. He shut his eyes when her nails tore at his scalp while her other hand unbuttoned his jeans, pulled down the zip, and worked its way into his pants.

The telephone rang.

"What the... ?" he said thickly. "I'm gonna have to take it."

Did he really? It was nothing but an act of compulsion. The cordless phone sat in its black charger in the hall. Number withheld. He picked it up and stood with his back against the open kitchen door to avoid, if at all possible, bringing Tina into the conversation.

An unfamiliar man's voice wondered if he could come out and sign for the firewood he'd ordered.

Have we ordered some? he thought. Must've been Annelie.

"I'm just down the road," said the strange voice in the distinct Östergötland dialect of the neighboring county. "If you can come out we'll sort it all out. Just need to know where you want me to dump it... You want it near where you're gonna stack it, yeah?"

"Er, yes, sure. In the barn. We don't have a woodshed... I'll be right out."

He went into the kitchen and looked guiltily at Tina. His erection had subsided.

"Sit here and I'll be right back."

She nodded silently and sat down on one of the Ikea chairs they were using while waiting for the Windsor chairs to be painted. The day's newspaper lay in front of her on the kitchen table. She started leafing through it.

He walked outside. The air was crisp, but it was warm enough to go out in short sleeves.

He passed the tall lilac bushes marking the edge of his garden out by the courtyard. They'd be coming into flower soon. He tried to shake off his shame to keep it from showing. After all, he didn't know who'd be coming to unload the wood. The voice hadn't sounded like an old man's.

He couldn't hear the sound of a truck yet. He really didn't like having to wait under any circumstances, least of all ones like this.

He thought he heard steps and looked round. No, it was probably just the wind in the treetops.

Or did Tina follow him out? If so, that wasn't good. He peered toward the kitchen door in the gable end of the house, but it was concealed by the old outhouse and the chicken coop.

But she didn't appear and the footsteps died away. It must've been his imagination.

Christoffer never saw the man who stood pressed up behind the corner of the house and who slipped in through the kitchen door as soon as he was out of sight.

Tina looked up from her paper to find a man she'd never seen before looming over her. She hadn't even heard him come in.

"Where is it?" he hissed through tight lips. "I want it now!"

"What are you talking about?"

She rose from her chair.

"Don't fuck with me. The rug!"

"What rug?" she blurted, realizing as she stared at the stranger that he had the wrong person. He thought she was Annelie.

Her pulse shot up, the words lodged in her throat. There was something about his look that scared her. An aggression that you shouldn't mess with. She had to get out.

She tried to push past him and reach the kitchen door, but he was faster and, grabbing her arm, he yanked her back into the kitchen. It hurt so much she thought her arm would come loose.

"What do you want?" she screamed and hoped that Christoffer would hear her.

The man placed a hand over her mouth and held her in an iron grip. She couldn't even move, let alone call for help.

"Now I want you to tell me nice and calmly where I can find that valuable rug that you got hidden somewhere. Is that understood? And then I'll leave you and you'll forget all about this. If you scream again, you're dead." He removed his hand, probably so that she'd be able to answer.

She stared at him. He had her pushed up against the pantry door, and the handle was digging painfully into her back. Saying she hadn't got the foggiest idea what the hell he was talking about would just make things worse, that much she realized. He was crazy. A psycho. His eyes were hard and she was losing all sensation in her arms. And even if she'd been able to answer him, she couldn't have made a sound, paralyzed as she was with panic.

There was a sharp swish as his hand came so hard across her face that she thought her jaw had been dislocated. Blood spurted from her mouth.

"I ain't got all the time in the world! Now, out with it!"

"I don't know," she said weakly as, readying herself, she rammed her knee into his crotch, and hoped that he'd jack-knife forwards.

But he dodged. She saw his face redden and distort with rage.

"What the fuck are you playing at, bitch?" he growled, shoving her up against the pantry door with a hand squeezing her throat. He pressed her head back and tightened his grip.

She looked into his eyes, like burnished steel. Noticed his gloves. He was wearing black leather gloves. His body was so close to hers that she could smell him. Or rather the smell of sweat and too much aftershave. She was powerless. Where was Christoffer?

"I ain't letting you go till you tell me where it is! And don't fuck with me!"

She opened her mouth like a baby bird and tried to squeeze out of her throat that he had the wrong person, that she had nothing to do with rugs, that it had to be Annelie he wanted.

But it was too much, the words log-jammed and became a gurgle as he squeezed her throat tighter. He was not letting up. She wanted to vomit, and her body convulsed uncontrollably. He was pressing his thumbs into the soft spaces either side of her larynx, and it felt as if her head was going to come off.

"The fucking rug! Now! Hear me?"

Frothing mouth, an implacable wrath, she realized somewhere. There was a rushing in her ears and she saw red then black and gasped for air. She was finding it hard to stay upright. Couldn't answer him. Not even with a lie. Tried to pry his fingers away from her throat, but he wouldn't let go. He was squeezing harder, almost like he was enjoying it, and she saw a faint smile flicker across his lips. Then she saw nothing more, just felt how she slowly left the floor, not knowing if she was falling or flying.

Chapter 32

VERONIKA AND KLARA were singing in the car while Nora slept, freshly fed and fastened into the passenger seat. The sun stood relatively high even though it was evening. Her breasts were tender under her seatbelt. She sung, knowing that she wasn't much good at holding a tune. But Klara was happy and tra-la'd along cheerfully with her. Now *she* could hold a tune, their Klara, little though she was. How could she who sang so badly have such a nightingale for a child?

Veronika took the main route to Bråbo, it was quickest, and planned to turn down onto the narrow road to Applekulla, which was so pretty. So varied, with its fields, pastures, and forests and a winding road. Sheep and lambs and cows had been put out to pasture. The fields had been plowed in thick, glossy furrows. The spruces had been cut back here to let in more light, like in the old days, while the deciduous trees were left untouched. Fresh, delicate greenery on the treetops. They'd continued the tradition of trimming the trees here. The leafy twiglets were fodder for the animals, at least they were once upon a time. Veronika had learned all this from Else-Britt, or rather from Else-Britt's husband, Gösta.

The deciduous forest was Stone Age land, Gösta had said. Oak, elm, linden, beech, maple. Veronika tried to picture the different leaves, but her knowledge of the various species was a little shaky. She wanted to learn. As if nature divulged its secrets once you could name what you saw.

Anyway, the spruces came relatively late, roughly a thousand years ago, she now knew. This stately tree that so many associated with the county was just a newcomer, relatively speaking. Completely different plants and flowers populated the terrain where the spruce didn't spread, where the light reached all the way down. The leaves that then fell and rotted also provided extra nourishment.

Pastures and meadows. They sounded so beautiful and primal, but they were a lot of hard work.

The Swedish meadows, the ones that were left and maintained, were one of the most species-rich places in the world, Gösta said. A floral larder. The fields were still cut here, and the hay was allowed to lie and shed its seeds before it was raked together and dried into winter feed.

The old saying "the meadow is the mother of the field" came into her head. The hay of the meadows gave the cattle fodder for the winter so that they could survive to produce plenty of manure for the fields, which yielded rich harvests in return. One of nature's many cycles.

She approached Bråbo, the El Dorado of slant-pole fences. Nowhere else were there so many of this kind of traditional wooden enclosure. The delightfully graying stakes blended beautifully into the pastures and over the hills, dividing the landscape into patchworks of little fields.

She slowed down and swung into the village. People were out in their gardens. Some waved, others nodded, a few were preoccupied. She knew that Christoffer Daun lived around here and wondered which house it was.

Just as the thought popped into her mind, she saw him step out of a house. He came out through a door in the gable end, a classic kitchen entrance. She slowed down even more, and made ready to give him a wave. But he bent his steps toward the barn with his eyes on Applekulla.

He lived in an old well-proportioned wooden house, Falun red in color, naturally, and two stories tall. It was set back a little from the road, and behind it lay the valley, over which he must have an unrestricted view from the back of the house. She noticed at once that the corners were glowing white, just like the timbered veranda. Newly painted, nice and well-maintained. It looked idyllic, actually.

A luxuriant lilac bush stood a little way from the corner of the house. Oddly, someone was moving there behind it. A large, burly man stepped out and rounded the corner, perhaps to enter by the kitchen door? Christoffer probably had help looking after the property, maybe Poles, she thought. It would take a lot to maintain this rural idyll, time that was hard to scrape together when you worked long days.

A little further on she had to swerve to avoid a dark green Saab that stood carelessly parked on the bank of the ditch between two plots of land.

Then she turned left toward Applekulla.

Chapter 33

ANNELIE DAUN PEELED OFF the brown paper shades from the windows before shutting up for the night. She should have removed the shades earlier; they didn't look very nice. The sunlight had actually left the street hours ago, but she chalked up the oversight to her having been too busy.

Rushed off her feet, she thought contentedly.

She'd sold two prayer mats, first a densely woven Persian *kashan*, highly patterned and brightly colored – blue, red, and a little beige – and then a Turkish from Konya, which was lighter in yellow, brown, and a muted red.

For a while they were all there in the shop, four customers and her, and the mood was everything but funereal, even though all of the visitors had expressed their condolences.

Anyway, satisfied customers were an honor. It pleased her to see them leave the shop proud and happy and with rolled-up rugs under their arms.

The day had been a good one in another way, too.

Besides two sold rugs in one and the same day – that was no bad statistic – she now had a new mission in life. She'd worked it out herself. Her eagerness to get away had gradually turned into restlessness. Not long left!

She adjusted the carpets that were piled up in the corner and finished off by stroking her hand along the soft pile of a beautiful *bakhtiari* with its trees of life, flowers, and shrubs divided into fields. She couldn't help stroking carpets. Instead of stroking a dog, she thought. Or stroking Christoffer's hair.

She shook her head thoughtfully. Why does life have to be so complicated?

A red piece of paper flashed into her eyes. She let it flutter by, having promised herself not to lose her self-control. To say nothing. To act like she didn't know. What an effect that would have!

Business had been booming in the past few days, and she recovered a little of her flattened self-esteem because of it. On the other hand, it was frightening that death could be so good for trade. A murdered carpet dealer was the best thing to happen to the shop in a long time. It was a very depressing insight.

Another depressing thought was that she'd lost a rug.

She bit her lower lip. It was actually worrying, and she didn't want to think about it. Not now when everything was going so well.

The piece of paper with the name and phone number on it was still on the table, but she was so reluctant to call and confess what had happened that she hadn't done it.

What would the customer think? It was a colleague of Christoffer's, no less.

Rumors spread fast, and that worried her more given her new secret plan – that maybe she could try to succeed Carl-Ivar. If she could sort out parts of his stock somehow. Perhaps take out a salary?

The stolen item was an antique *sivas*, seriously threadbare, the pile of the prayer niche all rubbed away from all the foreheads that had been pressed against it toward Mecca. Who wanted it? But then when that heavily pregnant colleague of Christoffer's who seemed so pleasant brought in the rug for repair both she and Carl-Ivar had fallen for it. But how many more people could have known about it? In Oskarshamn, of all places? Or was someone just winding her up? Was it some prank?

It would have been if the repairer in Stockholm had taken it back, but it was beyond all reason to send a rug away after repair only to steal it again. He was also propriety itself, she knew that. She'd call him tomorrow. The customer would also have to wait until she felt ready to call and say what had happened.

The rug was not totally worthless, but wouldn't fetch much of a price on the open market. But a drug addict, say, who needed a quick fix wouldn't know that. But would you take a rug? Maybe you take what you can get your hands on.

She'd heard of the rug trick, of course. You mostly saw it in the cities, but mischief often spread like the plague over the country. She'd read about the gangs in the papers. They'd call and tell someone that they'd won a rug, and then drive to the person's house.

And while the prize was being shown to the baffled mark in his hallway, an accomplice would sneak in and snatch what he could: jewelry, money, whatever wasn't tied down and easily snatched. They usually targeted elderly or gullible people who hadn't the heart to drive the intruders away. Perhaps the victims thought that their memory had failed them, that they really had bought a raffle ticket and forgotten all about it. And owning up to a poor memory wasn't always the first thing an old person wanted to do.

She should call the police. But she couldn't quite bring herself to do that, either.

She turned the "closed" sign around, opened the door, and stepped out onto the stone step.

She had two hours, she noted. That'd be enough. She'd been invited over to Gabriella Eklund's at seven. Gabriella was her oldest and best friend, and lived on Mysingsö in a fancy new house with lots of glass in all directions, in particular toward the sea and Blå Jungfrun, the myth-shrouded island that protruded like a dome on the edge of the Oskarshamn archipelago.

Looking back at her friendship with Gabbi, she considered it one of life's little strokes of luck. She could have ended up with, or chosen, or however it was during the primary school years, a waste of a friend, straying here and drifting there. Out on the ragged edges of society. She'd been pretty vulnerable as a kid, and still was to some extent, living as she did with an indelible stamp of inferiority on her soul.

Gabbi was good, not the kind to drag others down into the shit with her. She could be a bit whiney at times, when Annelie would be the one doing the cheering up. But otherwise Gabbi was a happy soul who'd had something as uncommon, to Annelie's mind, as a harmonic childhood. Gabbi's parents had always been good to her. Birgitta and Carl-Ivar had also been kind. There'd been something laid-back about them, for the most part, even though there was nothing exactly laid-back about their children.

Possibly Johan, but certainly not Lotta, she thought, her lips pressed. Annelie had never really been able to tolerate her, not even before she got together with Magnus and then married him.

Gabbi was the only one of Annelie's friends who had some knowledge of her domestic circumstances. And Gabbi had kept quiet about things, and not told anyone. She in fact spoke very little about

Annelie's mother unless Annelie brought her up herself. Possibly asked how she was. Implying: Is she still alive?

That was probably why they were friends, thought Annelie, who was looking forward to the evening. Besides, Mysingsö was in the right direction, she thought, and stuck her hand into her thin jacket pocket to check if the key ring was really still there. Although she knew it was.

The keys she'd found by pure chance. Or perhaps, for once in her life, she'd just been lucky.

It was the opposite with the red paper ball that sometimes forced its way into her mind. The uphill struggle. Which actually wasn't new to her. She thought at times that she was injured. She'd put up with it as a child, and she could still put up with quite a lot. That's why she hadn't just taken off. Not yet. And because deep inside she was terrified.

Of what?

She knew. Of breaking up. She so dearly wanted things to go back to what they were, when Christoffer would blow away the hair from her sweating face as she straddled him and say that she was the best thing that had ever happened to him. She'd never been the best thing that had ever happened to anyone before.

She'd always been in the way, or clumsy or not quick enough. She would put up with almost anything to be the best that had ever happened to someone again. Like before, when she'd belonged to him and he to her for real and not just through some marriage certificate. Like two souls that were intimately close, each caring for the other. Devotion and tenderness. She'd rarely felt naked and alone then. They'd had each other. Mutual belonging was such a wonderful feeling, and once experienced, that yearning never went away.

It wasn't far. She took out her sunglasses, unlocked her little pea-green fiat with her remote key, threw her bag on the passenger seat, and backed out.

On the floor behind her was a bottle of red wine in its purple plastic bag that she was going to give Gabbi, sans bag, naturally. She'd learned the rules of decorum over the years.

It was some time ago that she'd started to suspect that Carl-Ivar had had an extra storeroom, or at least a place he went to now and then, and that wasn't in his house. He'd sometimes turn up at the shop with some precious articles that she was sure he didn't keep at home. She was more than familiar with Birgitta and Carl-Ivar's house, had been there thousands of times during her childhood and had never come across locked doors that concealed secret storerooms. The house wasn't that big. And anyway, most of the stuff was kept in the shop basement.

But not everything. Evidently!

As she made her way down toward Skeppsbron, she realized that Carl-Ivar must have tried to make sure that she was out of the way when extracting the key ring from the bottom of the camel bag.

The bag, or rather sack, had been his private hiding place and was probably safer than carrying the keys on him or keeping them at home. There wasn't much that escaped Birgitta. She was a methodical woman. Not assertively inquisitive but observant.

Annelie had never cornered Carl-Ivar to ask if he had a storeroom other than the one in the basement of the carpet shop. There'd been no reason to be pushy, and he'd never shown a willingness to talk about it.

The camel bag had hung collecting dust from the banister that led down to the basement for as long as Annelie had worked at the shop. It was striped and woven from coarse wool, almost horsehair, and decorated with tufts. Made to withstand sun, rain, and sandstorms. It had been draped there, seemingly empty and sunken, for ornamental purposes, she'd assumed, and to lend the shop a pleasant Oriental atmosphere: date palms, figs, succulent raisins, strong coffee, and hot tea. Along with the carpets on the floor and walls and the hookah and the little smoking table that Carl-Ivar had placed there after one of his many trips, you could be seduced into believing that you were, for a moment, in some far-away land.

But she'd caught him once, although without realizing it. Not then. But now she did.

She'd been out, as usual, to buy the buns for their coffee from Nilsson's, and realized that if she continued to do so, she'd soon be more rolling than walking. Cinnamon buns, sugared pastries, vanilla whirls, jam doughnuts. At least one a day – not the kind ready-packed in plastic bags either. Carl-Ivar considered that abominable when there was an excellent bakery just around the corner. Birgitta would've hit the roof had she known what he nibbled on during the day, she who was so careful about their diet.

That day the rain had started to pour, so she dashed, bag in hand, back to the carpet shop. She pulled open the oak door and whirled in like an autumn leaf. Carl-Ivar was on his way up from the basement, and giving a start, looked up at her in surprise and perhaps alarm.

A moment later everything was back to normal. They drank coffee and enjoyed their icing-coated vanilla whirls.

Of course it hadn't been her that had alarmed him. It was more like she'd caught him red-handed. But it wasn't until now that she realized doing what.

It was just when she'd sold the Turkish prayer mat from Konya and was unrolling some paper to pack it in that she happened to back up against the bag, knocking it onto the floor. The clinking sound it gave off betrayed the presence of something metal inside, but only faintly. She was probably the only one who heard it.

She let the bag lie where it was and once the customer had gone she picked it up and reached down into it with her arm. At the bottom she found a key ring holding three keys. Nothing else.

She'd then sat with the key ring in her hand, racking her brains. What were the keys for? The policemen who'd been there looking for reasons for Carl-Ivar's murder had apparently had as little mind as she did to look there.

She recognized one of the keys immediately. It didn't have a normal head, but was more rectangular, and such a key was all too familiar to her. She even had a similar one herself at home, on a hook inside the kitchen door. In case of emergencies. That Carl-Ivar had a duplicate wasn't strange at all.

But what about the other two? To an attic or a cellar? She didn't recognize them at all.

There was only one thing to do. Try them out!

She was approaching the roundabout by the railway station and could see the Gotland ferry terminal up to her left. She turned left at the station, which was as deserted as its platforms. The trains had stopped going several years ago, yet another sign that the town had decided to sink even further into obscurity. It was a little sad, she thought, continuing along Verkstadsgatan past the ferry terminal, crossing Grönlandsgatan, and driving into Gröndal, an old area of pretty wooden houses on tall stone plinths that nestled in a verdant lushness.

As she turned down Nitaregatan and finally into Filaregatan, the buildings started to change character. The old wharf lay right behind with its tall cranes and large, gloomy workshops with tin roofs. Once upon a time, it was mainly dockers and shipbuilders who lived here. Not any more.

Filaregatan was a short stump of a road. A light-blue inflatable paddling pool lay crumpled up and grimy on a lawn that hadn't yet come to life. Dark clouds suddenly piled up in the north, adding to her melancholy.

That's just the way it was. Gloom always smothered her when she came here. She had a love-hate thing with the place. Dilapidated, run down, gray, but home nonetheless. At least it had been. She could still feel the weird sense of security that greeted her whenever she'd step through the door. Walls that sheltered her from wind and rain, heat rising from burbling radiators.

If she'd only been able to drop the hysterical worry about the state her mother would be in when she came home from school. Or whether she'd have men back and refuse to let Annelie in while she did "all that" with them for a little loose change or a bottle of cheap vodka.

Sometimes her mother would have knocked together something that resembled dinner, fried sausage and macaroni and a lake of ketchup on the plate. They'd have a laugh then. But most of the time she didn't have the energy. Or the money. Not for food, anyway.

Annelie learned to boil eggs before she could read. She'd never been that interested in cooking later in life and throughout her school years had been grateful for school dinners, piling generous helpings onto her plate every day to the amazement of her friends. In fact she thought that anyone who complained about the food was quite frankly an idiot.

"Such poverty," she heard one of her teachers say once, making her want to die of shame out there in the corridor, even though she knew that the teacher was speaking from kindness.

She'd started to smell without realizing it. Whenever she thought about how she stank, and had done so for years, perhaps even as a baby, she'd blush inside. She reeked not only of cigarette smoke and kitchen odors, but of unwashed clothes that were seldom changed and that she'd even grown out of. Dirt or filth, it didn't matter what you called it. Not smelling nice as a child was unforgivable.

It was only in her late teens that she took control of her body and made sure to shower.

She wanted to avoid parking right outside the house. She noticed a space between the houses opposite and tucked her car in there in the hope that it would be less conspicuous.

The gray plastering had cracked and started to flake in places. It was so obvious to her now when she wasn't here so often. She stared down onto the asphalt as if she was looking for something as she approached the front door. It had been newly painted in brown, and sliced glossy and new through all the decrepitude, as if this little gesture of recalcitrance wanted to say that the building hadn't given up completely.

Six apartments joined by a stairwell. The smell wasn't as penetrating as when she grew up. Fewer cooking odors. Either oven fans were more efficient, or people were warming up fast food in their microwaves. The smell of cigarette smoke only began to dominate when she reached the second floor. She stepped carefully, creeping up the stairs and hoping that no one would appear and catch her. She could hear noise behind the familiar door where the name K Olsson was spelled out in white plastic letters on a blue nameplate. She drew up and held her breath for a few seconds as she waited for the noise to stop.

Her mother was drunk, as usual, she thought, and continued on up and past the next floor.

Then came the attic.

Up here it was always dry and warm, at least when the sun heated the roof tiles. She could already smell a kind of clean mustiness.

She didn't bother to turn the hall light on and stood in the dark as she inserted one key at a time. "Please, please," she prayed quietly when she only had one left, the key with the triangular head that resembled the one that fit the door of her mother's apartment and that she'd saved until last so as not to lose hope.

The key fit this door, too.

She turned it, pressed the handle, and nudged the door open with her shoulder. She stood just over the threshold to accustom her eyes while making sure that she was alone.

And then she turned on the light, which was just as yellow and dim as it had always been.

She started to creep along the storage compartments, each separated from the other by a metal grating. In her mother's compartment hung clothes in protective plastic wrappings. Was she really this neat and tidy after all? The boxes were coated in a visible layer of dust, and she could see her own figure skates dangling from a hook. So this is where they were! She'd missed them on one occasion, but hadn't wanted to go home to her mother's place to search for them as she wouldn't have been able to cope with having her in her face. So she bought a new pair, but they were hard and uncomfortable, as if her feet insisted on hating them.

A small gable window let in a meager glow of daylight. Some of the storage compartments were in a terrible state of chaos. The door to one of them stood open. On the floor were a stained mattress and a sleeping bag. A little cubbyhole partly hidden by large moving boxes. Her heart thumped. Someone was sleeping up here!

She spun around as if someone was standing behind her, watching her. Some empty beer cans and a squashed milk carton, plus a scattering of cigarette butts lay there, too. She bent down and picked up the carton, then walked over to the light and read the date. From last year. She gave a sigh of relief. The den had perhaps been abandoned.

The homeless lived dangerously, and he or she might not even be alive any more. Her own mother, who presumably was sitting chain-smoking two floors down, could have been one of them. But she'd survived. She had her own apartment, and quite a neat one, too, at the odd times when she was in good form and off the daily booze.

Annelie had never thought about how she got it together. Surely the welfare department wouldn't pay the rent year in year out? Sweden wasn't like that any longer. In certain respects, alcoholics, the unemployed, and the mentally ill had to manage as best they could without society's helping hand. The Salvation Army, welfare workers, the church. There was still benevolence around. And rich people who liked to donate. Charity. Non-profit organizations were proliferating. She herself had never forked out a krona for her mother's rent. She'd sometimes shoved a few hundreds into her mother's hands when she'd been completely broke and had pleaded and nagged with sufficient importunity to finally break Annelie's resolve.

For the rest, she'd had enough of her mother's manipulative ways. The entreating, syrup-sticky, maudlin tones: "Anneling, sweetie-pie, remember all that I've done for you. Don't be so ungrateful!" Most of the time Annelie responded by walking straight out the door.

Just as she unlocked the padlock to the storage compartment with one of the two smaller keys, she caught sight of the gray blanket. It was covering something in the far corner that looked like a large traveling chest. She held up the key ring.

Even before the heavy padlock clicked, she knew for certain who it was that had paid her mother's rent all these years.

CHAPTER 34

VERONIKA AND ELSE-BRITT EK stood by the white-painted enclosure fence. Klara was sitting dumb with delight on the pony's back while one of Else-Britt's sons led them slowly around.

The sky was turning purple over the treetops to the left, the evening light was mild but still ember warm. The tranquility made her heart trot along almost imperceptibly behind her ribcage.

Veronika brushed her breasts with her forearm. They were tender, but she was proud at their fullness. Although, she knew that they'd gently tire, become empty, and hang a little forlornly once she'd stopped breastfeeding.

Klara stared at her mom from under her riding hat. Veronika flashed her a broad smile. Her daughter barely managed to smile back, not having the simultaneous capacity to do a combination of such difficult things as remain in the saddle, return a smile, and enjoy the fun.

"Just look at you," called Veronika. She saw a splinter of pride shimmer in the corner of her daughter's eyes above her little round cheeks.

Else-Britt had invited them to sleep over. Veronika hadn't made up her mind, but they probably would. She wanted to remain here in the peace and quiet. To not leave. And anyway, there was nothing to hurry back home for.

Sirens wailed shrilly over the neighborhood.

Veronika and Else-Britt looked at each other with eyebrows raised.

And then they nodded.

"Well, there goes the company car," said Veronika.

"I think they're coming up from Bråbovägen," said Else-Britt.

"Where Christoffer Daun lives, I noticed. He was walking across his garden as I drove by."

Else-Britt nodded. She knew, of course.

"It was weird, but there was a man standing there behind a lilac bush. It was almost like he was hiding, but then he came out… A Pole helping him with the house probably," said Veronika.

"So you're sure it wasn't a woman?" asked Else-Britt.

Veronika shook her head.

"I've heard he's having an affair with Tina Rosenkvist," said Else-Britt. "She and her family don't live so many houses away. And Daun certainly knows how to get himself into a mess. He's probably the most unreliable man you could imagine being married to. But who are we to judge, eh?"

And no more was said. Nora started to whine in her stroller. It was feeding time.

CHAPTER 35

FRESIA GABRIELSSON WAS ON NIGHTS.

She chugged along the short corridor of the A&E unit and slumped down into her office chair. She liked to rest her legs. She wasn't exactly lightweight, and generally made sure not to stand when she didn't have to. The hours at the operating table were more than enough. The night ahead of her was long, and she was prepared for it in her supportive socks of pure white cotton.

It would probably have been best if she lost thirty pounds or so. At least. She thought these thoughts every single day. But thinking them didn't help in the slightest, of that she was all too aware.

Later, in some vague future when life was calmer, she'd do something about it. A conscious diet would be one trial too many as things looked now, what with her job and kids and a somewhat unengaged husband. Perhaps if she was slimmer she'd even manage to attract the occasional eye. A little glitter and glamour would've been nice, rather than just living with the feeling of being everyone's mom, or some sort of drawer to chuck odd socks in.

She picked up the phone. She could really have called from the desk that formed the heart of the unit, but she wanted to talk in private. One of the nurses had all but commanded her with a look from a superior height to use her own phone when she was on call. That irritated her.

But getting worked up just sucked energy. The nurse, who was called Gunnel, had a tendency to get strident when stressed, and didn't shy from barking out orders even though it wasn't her place to do so.

She had the piece of paper with Ronny Alexandersson's home number on it in her pocket, and dialed the number. It just so happened that she actually wanted Ronny there with her. Although on very different grounds than the purely medicinal. And in a way she understood that Gunnel was stressed, for she had good reason to.

Attempted strangulation!

Admittedly, it could have been worse, and after all, the patient was still alive.

But the hubbub around the central desk was caused by the fact that the victim was their own Rosie from ward six.

She heard Ronny panting down the line. He'd just come in through the door.

"I'll be there as soon as I can," he said, without a quibble or stalling for time.

Oh, how Fresia liked him! Happy was the woman who had him as a husband.

"There's no real hurry," she said. "The paramedics have just called. They said that she's breathing fine and there's nothing to worry about. More than anything, Tina's naturally very shaken. They said they'd be here in fifteen. They're driving from Bråbo but you know what it's like, it could take half an hour, perhaps longer. They're driving off-siren."

"But I'm coming right away really so I can get the job done and go back home to spend time with my family," he said.

His voice actually sounded a little happy, she thought, her lips curling in calm desire. Ronny often talked about his family, and did so with affection. A wife and four children that were more than just a backdrop to his medical career.

She returned to the emergency room to suture a fleshy gash in the forehead of a man who'd walked into a door, or so he claimed. She didn't give a fig what had happened, it still needed stitching.

She thought about her own emotionally tone-deaf technician at the nuclear plant. He was who he was, and things could've been much worse. He was good to have around. In some situations, anyway.

She drew some anesthetic from the glass bottle that the assistant nurse was holding upside-down for her.

Few things were as attractive as commitment and intimacy. Sigh.

She injected the one-percent Carbocain adrenalin solution into the gash and waited. The man on the stretcher said nothing under his green, sterile sheet, which the assistant nurse had placed over his face with its hole exposing the wounded area. He was putting on a brave face. He was probably more scared than he was prepared to let on.

"I'll head out. You'll manage fine on your own," said the assistant nurse in a commendatory tone.

Fresia stared at her, and before she had time to open her mouth the nurse was gone.

But her praise tasted bitter. Her assistant had just popped out for a smoke, of that she was certain. Grabbed the opportunity just because it was her, Fresia, mother of three and a doctor who was accustomed to getting things done. If she'd been Christoffer Daun, there's no way the assistant would've left! No way would she have walked out on the golden boy. Always the red carpet for him.

Fresia choked back her bitterness. It couldn't be much fun being in Christoffer Daun's shoes right now.... His sins coming back to bite him, perhaps?

Everyone at the clinic knew. Everyone who had eyes to see. Infidelity was rarely invisible, even if the love-struck fools involved were conceited enough to believe it.

Was it Christoffer or her husband that had attacked Rosie? This was a question that would be chewed over thoroughly until they knew the truth, of that she was certain.

Fresia placed the jaws of the needle driver around the bent needle and drew it from its package with the thread following it like a tail. She made the first stitch. The anesthetic had kicked in.

According to protocol, a forensic medical examination always took its time. That was the real reason she'd decided to call Ronny. And that it was Tina Rosenkvist, of course. They'd be collecting as much evidence from her body as they could, evidence that would then hopefully stand up in court.

Fresia had a year left before becoming a specialist, and this was the first time she'd had a case that would have such inevitable legal consequences. It would mean testifying in court to the nature and possible cause of the wounds, and that was nothing you subjected yourself to just like that.

Ronny was also one of the doctors who'd been selected and trained for writing certificates of medical evidence. In the past, all doctors had done it, but the National Board of Forensic Medicine had tightened up their competence requirements. Certificates were ideally to be written by a medico-legal expert, but the closest institute of forensic medicine was in Linköping and it went without saying that they couldn't handle every certificate from such a huge district.

The man under the sheet was still not reacting. She sewed on in silence. Placed single sutures, knotted and cut the thread herself. It was a neat job. The edges of the wound happened to be well-defined.

The door he'd walked into must have been sharp!

"Alright, you're done," she said, removing the green sheet.

The man smiled, relieved.

"You did a good job. Delicate lady's hands."

She glowed inside, and smiled broadly. She asked the man to lie where he was and went over to the counter.

"You can go in and dress it," she said to the assistant nurse as a kind of revenge for her desertion.

She then walked into the office and clicked up the right patient records on the computer to dictate into, turned on the microphone and let her mouth go as she stared out the window.

And then came the diagnosis code. This always put the brake on things just when you'd worked up some speed. She flipped through the quick reference guide and found "wound in forehead" and dictated it in. She also needed a supplementary diagnosis giving the cause of the wound. She thumbed backwards in the thicker directory toward W. Naturally there was no entry for "walked into a door," but she found "tripped up" and entered that, even though it was not quite accurate. And then it was the treatment code, which was "Revision of wound and suturing."

Then she rose and walked over to the counter again.

By now, the commotion had become almost tumultuous. She heard both Christoffer's and Rosie's name swish past and couldn't help giving herself a little squeeze of thrill, unforgivable though it was. She wasn't even ashamed of doing so. She could picture Christoffer Daun's ingratiating figure, forever flying after affirmation.

That man really did need a little guidance from a mature, sensible man like Ronny, no doubt about it, she thought. He'd had the perfect clinical supervisor.

"He's a real sweetie," she heard one of the women say with a grin. "Wants to be loved by everyone and he's got an almost morbid way of bonding with the patients."

"But only the women. He'll get what's coming to him sooner or later," said another. "Like that doctor in Skåne, the one who sexually exploited them."

"Don't be too sure, Daun knows where to draw the line, alright," said the secretary, suddenly appearing.
"But surely he's not the type to try to strangle someone? He's not that highly strung, is he?" asked the nurse.
"You never can tell with some people…" interjected Gunnel.
And no more was said.

At that moment both the ambulance and Ronny Alexandersson arrived, shortly followed by two police officers.
The gurney was rolled out unhurriedly and into one of the more spacious examination rooms. The patient wasn't in any danger.
Ronny had called the medico-legal expert in Linköping, who'd advised him what to think about. A&E stocked pre-prepared forensic examination boxes containing cotton swabs, measuring tape, a comb, wooden picks for whittling away with under nails and whatnot, and checklists for taking samples and swabs, and body templates on which to draw the wounds. The ones on her throat were immediately obvious.
Gunnel had already prepared the table and even had the camera ready for documenting the visible wounds. She really was organized, after all, thought Fresia, feeling generous.
"You might as well stay here with me," said Ronny with a nod at Fresia. "Four eyes see more than two."
One of the police officers held out some brown paper bags in which they were to place Tina's clothes for dispatch to technical analysis. They'd produced a white hospital gown for her to wear instead.
"Where have you got the guy who did this to her?" wondered Ronny.
"We're grillin' him down at the station," said the policeman, who was around thirty and spoke a broad local brogue.
That was all he said. Ronny nodded. The other officer was a short, blonde woman with a ponytail. The two officers were keen to talk to Tina after she'd been examined, and wondered if they could do it somewhere in the hospital.
"It's OK for you to stay here," said Gunnel. "You can have a cup of coffee while you're waiting."
They walked into the examination room. Tina didn't say much but looked relieved to see Ronny. She said that she didn't remember

much and cried when she said it. "It's so horrible not being able to remember! That things happen that you know nothing about!"

"You lose your memory just before you black out. I doubt you were out for very long," he said comfortingly and then said little more about it.

Retrograde amnesia, thought Fresia. A godsend sometimes, you had to admit.

Calmly and methodically, Ronny began the examination from top to bottom. Took hairs and placed them in a paper envelope, pressed with his fingertips over the scalp. He found a tender lump of roughly an inch's diameter on the left-hand side. The outer ear was uninjured. He dabbed cotton swabs over the skin of her face, over her cheeks and forehead, and then ran a swab over the inside of her cheek. He examined the eyes, lifted the eyelids.

"Can you write that she has petechia," he said to Fresia, who'd taken on the role of secretary. Tiny hemorrhages in the conjunctiva were a classic sign of strangulation or attempted strangulation. The veins were compressed and the blood clogged upwards.

Fresia took photographs, the camera acting as a shield between her and Rosie. Or rather, between her and the blood-red swellings and fingernail marks that Rosie had around her throat. Fresia made notes and took more pictures. Some of the marks would become more visible after a couple of days. They'd have to take a look at her again and get some fresh shots.

He scrutinized body part after body part. Arms, torso, legs. He scraped her nails with a wooden pick. Mostly with negative results. No signs of physical violence, therefore, other than on the head, throat, and arms, but that was bad enough.

Her pants hadn't been removed, not as far as Tina knew. Nor did she have any memory of a rape. She hardly remembered what the man had looked like, she repeated. If the man had been a stranger or not. Or if she'd gotten things mixed up. That it had been…

Christoffer Daun?

They arranged a meeting with a counselor, and the police wondered if Tina Rosenkvist could stay behind at the hospital overnight, mostly because they didn't want to send her home, just to be on the safe side.

"Husband?" wondered Ronny.

"We don't know yet. She wasn't found in their own house."

Ronny and Fresia nodded. This was a real mess. But it wasn't their concern.

CHAPTER 36

ANNELIE DAUN HELD HER WEIGHT against the door handle so that no one would hear the heavy fire door to the attic as it shut, and then glided quietly down the stairs. She wanted to get out quickly and jump into her car and drive off somewhere so that she could go through the contents burning away in her bag undisturbed. Immediately, if possible. Anyway, she didn't want to wait until after her evening with Gabbi.

She slammed the car door shut and backed out in a wide arc, threw the car into first, then squinted at the gentle sunset that was painting the asphalt gold as she drove away from the deserted street. But she'd be back.

Her mother and Carl-Ivar, well, well, well! she thought. The strong ties of sibling love. A common umbilical cord. Understanding, but hate too, could thrive in that shared soil. Her mother must've known, she realized. She'd been closer to her brother than Annelie had realized. As for herself, sibling love would be forever deprived her. She had neither brother nor sister, and so had no appreciation of what she was missing out on.

She then stopped thinking about her mother and herself, and her thoughts returned to the attic instead. A sequence of images scrolled past: her discovering the large chest, her pulling off the blanket and finding what she was after, and her realizing, even before her fingers had grabbed the rim of the lid and exposed the chest's contents, that what she was about to see would haunt her mind for days, weeks, perhaps longer.

So this was where he fetched his rugs and carpets from! Her flesh goose-pimpled. A broad grin crossed her face as she drove ahead in the sparse evening traffic.

But the gray file that lay on top was, on the other hand, a total surprise. It must have been there for a long time. The sides were of a gray marbled cardboard and were held together by a black rubber band that had lost its elasticity and lay curled over the card like a desiccated grass snake on a country road on a hot summer's day.

Did her mother know?

Obviously she knew that Carl-Ivar had a storage compartment in the attic, but maybe she just thought that he collected junk up there, window dressings and left-over carpets that he didn't want to throw out but that didn't go in his and Birgitta's well-ordered house.

She was struck by an image of the desirable items being unrolled. The desire to get her hands on them burned through her body. The eyes, the stomach, the heart all wanted the same thing: to own them. For their beauty – the harmonic colors and balanced patterns – but also for their economic value.

Which was not to be sniffed at, that much she knew.

She'd never had much money, but still enough to get by and she didn't ask for more than that. But things were different now. She'd at last set her mind on something in life. She wanted to be a carpet dealer and needed some start-up capital.

If Carl-Ivar had rented the storage in her mother's name, then the attic space was arguably her mother's.

If that was the case.

Annelie believed it was. The policemen who'd come to the shop to requisition the files hadn't asked about any extra storerooms. So they hadn't found any bank statements or receipts that suggested Carl-Ivar rented an attic space somewhere. Otherwise, that would have been the kind of thing that was written off as a business cost. But property that no one knew about couldn't, of course, be included in the estate.

This was her chance. She'd just have to interrogate her mother. One way out would be to include her in her plans. They could be in cahoots with each other and split the profits.

No sooner had she thought the idea than she rejected it. It would never work. She pictured her mother threatening to tell Birgitta, or the cousins, or the police, as soon as something got in her way and she didn't get what she wanted. And what her mother wanted could change from one moment to the next. She was as capricious as a Swedish summer.

Annelie had passed the Kristineberg tenements on her right, and then the houses. Then the residences dwindled away as the forest took over. On the left was the sea. She drove into the car park before the bridge over to Gunnarsö beach campsite and parked.

Now, she thought as she opened the bag to extract the gray-marbled file. Easy does it, she urged herself. She opened it slowly and reverentially. She had a strong hunch that it would bring her closer to the truth.

Inside were letters and photographs, all neatly organized. Carl-Ivar had archived them chronologically with the oldest letters at the back. The photographs were dated on their backs, and contained within three envelopes.

The file must be at least thirty years old. A treasure that had been kept locked away like a valuable pearl in its oyster shell, which she had now prized open. She wondered what Carl-Ivar would have said if he knew that she was to be the one to uncover his secret.

She was overcome by tenderness. She wanted to believe that he wouldn't have minded. Perhaps it was just her way of justifying her escapades to herself, but sooner or later someone would have exposed him. So why not her? He could have set fire to everything if he'd wanted to take all his secrets with him to the grave.

But he hadn't.

This was a big responsibility, she realized as she thumbed through the letters and opened the envelopes. It was all up to her now.

The languishing dusk that fell in through the windscreen was still bright enough for her to see without having to switch on the overhead light. It was a quarter to seven, and it would take her no more than just a couple of minutes to drive to Gabriella's. She didn't have loads of time, but enough to get a general picture. She held the letters and photographs by the corners, pinching them carefully between thumb and forefinger. She should have been wearing cotton gloves, she thought, like people who work with delicate material – or who perhaps didn't want to leave any traces of themselves behind.

Every letter was in English. She had a whole life in her hands. An unreal life at some strange place far away with another woman and another child. A girl.

The photographs were both color and monochrome, and most were taken in bright sunlight that gave sharp shadows and squinty eyes. Outdoor restaurants or cafés, palms and other exotic trees that indicated southern climates.

She picked out one of the photographs and looked at it more closely. It was a black-and-white outdoor shot, probably taken by an amateur, and only faintly sepia-tinted. Annelie's eyes flicked from Carl-Ivar to the woman beside him and back again at Carl-Ivar. Her heart melted to see him so young-looking. Memories of him from her childhood came flooding back.

She didn't possess any photo albums of her own that could help her remember. Her mother hadn't managed to put one together, either, but she did have one or two photographs that she kept in a grubby old envelope. Annelie rarely looked at them. Gabbi would let her flick through her well-filled family album, in which she made a sporadic appearance, and they could get all nostalgic together. But otherwise, photos of herself mostly depressed her. Therefore she'd never bought a camera. She didn't want to pin down time, and until now had never seen the good or point of it. Christoffer had a camera, of course, and took lots of photos, but she didn't look that often at those photos, either.

In this photo, Carl-Ivar was around thirty, she reckoned. His posture was less stiff, and he looked content. Or was it proud? He was slimmer and had thick hair, flaxen and combed back so that his forehead shone. He was wearing light pants and a white shirt with the sleeves rolled up, and on his feet were a pair of sandals of some ancient model that he'd always still worn in the summer. His forearms seemed heavily tanned.

As a child she'd found him funny and easy-going. Does everyone get so melancholy with age? Or was that her own childhood haunting her? That the difference between her own meager existence and his unfettered adult life was so sharp. Or was he only happy because of the woman at his side?

She took a closer look at her. She was short and slim, with dark, pinned-up hair. Her face was a soft oval and her eyebrows heavy and dark. Long earrings dangled at her earlobes, the kind that Birgitta would never dream of wearing. She looked more closely and thought they were of some delicate filigree design.

The woman was looking straight into the camera with friendly eyes, even if the mouth was serious and made it difficult to determine her frame of mind. A Mona Lisa smile.

But the two of them belonged together, enjoyed each other's company – there was no doubt about that. Even more warmth spread through her. She could feel a kind of lapping inside, like little waves slapping against her hull, as she browsed on. Oh, Carl-Ivar, she thought. You certainly seized life with both hands. And really got yourself into a pickle.

She felt envious and yet energized, not only because she'd revealed something hidden, but also because of the knowledge that Carl-Ivar had dared. And that he seemed both proud and happy with his other life. But there was cowardice there, too. He'd never had the courage to go the whole way, and had lived with the constant ambivalence.

Her mind spun as the twilight descended. She had to get going. She flipped through a little more quickly and noticed that the woman was in many of the photographs, and that she didn't change much over the years despite having changed her look by wearing her graying hair shorter.

And then there was the girl. First came the baby shots, then an increasingly mature woman who was not the spit of her mother, except for the dark hair. The years passed and the woman started to outgrow her mother. Did she look like Carl-Ivar? It was hard to tell.

Annelie tried to work out how old the girl could be with the help of the dates on the photographs, and figured she must be a few years younger than herself. She could even, not without a certain pleasure, see a likeness. The dimple in the chin that Carl-Ivar, her mother, and she had, but not the cousins. The family feature.

She skimmed a few letters and encountered affectionate words that were unfamiliar to her and that made her blush. But they were beautiful. "My beloved, magnificent Swede, like a…" Here was mentioned a plant or animal, probably, the name of which Annelie didn't recognize. A poetic language blossomed on the pages. Love like honey, as smooth as apricots or like balmy breezes and kisses that tasted of pine kernels and that had the sweetness of fresh grapes. The letters had been written by a woman with a different mode of expression than the more barren, Nordic style. It was romantic and beautiful. And so intimate. Long sentences, properly punctuated, light years from the choppy phrases of emails and lol-speak.

Annelie got a little teary-eyed.

The woman was called Tülüp, and the daughter Ayla.

But she had to close the file, which she placed back in the bag, not wanting it to lie in the dampness of the car. She started up and reversed a few feet, and then drove onto Amerikavägen and southwards toward Mysingsö.

As she passed by the renovated fisherman's cottages and houses that were built straight onto the gray granite, she realized that she'd just gotten two new relatives. An aunt by marriage and a real life cousin.

If things were as she assumed. What whetted her curiosity was how the letters from Carl-Ivar had been written. Had he been just as affectionately loving and open about his feelings as Tülüp?

The shadows had lengthened, and the trees stood lusciously against the darkened sea. Her dashboard clock told her that she wasn't going to be so many minutes late.

But what do I do now? she wondered.

Wait and see, was the obvious answer. She wasn't going to call Birgitta, at least. Not yet. She was fond of her, after all.

It was Carl-Ivar's lie, but the truth didn't only affect him. His weakness had controlled him. Perhaps he had unwittingly exploited the human ability of growing accustomed to most things. Birgitta to the blindness, and himself to the deceit.

She arrived and parked on the street, jumped out and walked past the bikes that crowded the garden path.

Bottle of wine in hand, she rang the bell.

Chapter 37

THE EVENING WAS MILD.

Claesson had just spoken to Louise Jasinski, who'd found out from the Swedish bank that Carl-Ivar had paid for their stay at the Arkadia with his Visa card. He'd checked out the same day as his wife returned home. He no longer needed a double room, presumably, and the Arkadia had no single rooms going just then, she told Claesson.

"Where the hell did he go then?" he said to Mustafa Özen once he'd hung up.

Özen shrugged. "Istanbul's a big city."

No more needed to be said.

"That guy, Lennart Ahl," continued Claesson, "who'd called his widow Birgitta, hasn't been tracked down yet. Maybe it was a bluff... Louise says hi, by the way."

They were standing outside the hotel waiting for Merve Turpan. They were going to have a bite to eat together. Unfortunately Fuat Karaoğlu was unable to join them, and had apologized repeatedly, but he had family reasons, he said; nothing strange about that, Claesson thought.

Shortly afterwards they heard a car door slam and saw Merve walking toward them. But not alone. A young man with a curly mop of hair that made him look happy accompanied her.

So she needs a chaperone when she meets the Swedish strangers, thought Claesson. Maybe he was her boyfriend. He noticed that Mustafa Özen had stiffened.

They walked a couple of blocks, no further, until they came to a car-free alley where they sat down at a round plastic table covered with a table cloth. They'd learned that the man's name was Cem and that he was a forensic technician. A chemist originally, actually, he told them. He'd been put on the case of the dead carpet dealer.

"A lot of blood," he said. "We think the knife is at the bottom of the sea. The cuts in his skin were so sharp that the coroner thinks that it was a very sharp knife. And a knife that completely destroyed his insides... You have heard the Wasp knife theory, yes?"

Claesson and Özen nodded. Özen had grown almost embarrassingly reserved, thought Claesson, and then told them about the call he'd just had. About the hotel that had been paid for with a Visa card from a Swedish bank.

"The question is where he went then."

"If we're lucky, he checked in at another hotel," said Claesson. "And if we're luckier, it won't be some dodgy backstreet dive but a hotel that keeps tabs on guests and registers, and that will want paying and to be rid of whatever personal effects he left behind. They'll get in touch sooner or later," he said reassuringly and refilled his beer glass.

They'd just eaten *meze*, which was a selection of small appetizers. There were many varieties to choose from. Özen had placed their orders, his too, which turned out to be currant *dolmas* filled with some kind of rice mixture, some cookie-like titbits made from ground beans and a garlic yogurt. It was really quite tasty. This they were to follow with broiled fish and a salad that consisted of chopped tomatoes, flat-leaf parsley, and onion.

"Delicious and very typical!" Özen explained in Swedish. "Usually with a little lemon juice squeezed over the salad and a few drops of oil."

Merve went to the ladies' room and Cem stepped a few paces away to enjoy a cigarette. "Can you cook?" Claesson took the opportunity to ask Özen.

"Well, yes, I can actually," he said without a hint of modesty.

"Then we've almost got a complete national cooking team down at the station. First there's Gotte, even if he is going to be quitting soon, and Lennie Ludvigsson, who wins one cooking competition after the other, and now you... and... well..."

He shrugged and looked down at the table but couldn't quite erase his smug expression. Özen noticed.

"You, too?"

"Veronika's not so keen on cooking so I've taken over. But I enjoy it," said Claesson with a delighted look.

Merve and Cem returned to their seats. Merve told them that Superintendent Fuat Karaoğlu's wife was seriously ill and he was devoting as much time as he could to looking after her and that's why he couldn't make it.

"I'm sorry to hear it," said Claesson. "I hope she gets better soon."

"That's unlikely, I'm afraid," said Merve. "She's been sick for a long time. There's something wrong with her entire body, she can hardly move."

Claesson downed a large swig of his cool beer, which was called Efes and which tasted good. He felt how the alcohol went straight to his head and made his face tighten out of sheer fatigue. He'd sleep like a log, that was for sure. Instead of lying there staring at the ceiling as he'd first thought. And with no kids whining and circling his bed.

He wondered how Veronika was. He didn't want a bad conscience.

"What do you think's going on?" asked Merve suddenly.

Özen said nothing. Claesson shrugged his shoulders.

"No idea. We can only guess. Valuable rugs, revenge or vengeance for something that we haven't yet figured out? Or was it simply the wrong person who got himself murdered? Istanbul's a big city… it's easy to get in someone's way… If we manage to solve this, then all well and good. All we can do is try," he said. "Anyway, it's nice to be here. *Skål*, as we say in Sweden!"

They raised their glasses. Merve was drinking water. There was a glint in Mustafa Özen's eyes – mainly when he looked at Merve, Claesson observed with a smile.

Her cell phone rang, and she answered it with her head bowed. Her voice was now tender, now cross. Her boyfriend? wondered Claesson.

She ended the call and looked up. "My mother," she said with an ironic smile. "She wanted to know if I was having a nice evening."

"And are you?" asked Claesson.

"Absolutely." She smiled at her Swedish guests and the atmosphere around the table lifted even more.

"So we'll pick you up tomorrow," she said when it was time to go their separate ways. "First stop, the Arkadia and then the Grand Bazaar and the carpet dealer there. OK?"

"Sure," said Claesson. "Am I right in thinking that we need to be at the coroner's at two o'clock for the identification? That's what I told the wife when I spoke to her, at least. We'll have to work out the transportation somehow."

"Give me her cell phone number and I'll do it," said Merve Turpan.

"Alright, but I'm not sure how much English she speaks," said Claesson.

"Call me, and I'll talk to the widow," said Özen, writing down his number and handing it over to Merve, who grinned even more broadly at him.

They decided to walk home, he and Özen. The dark night sky hovered above them.

It wasn't silent, but not far from it.

CHAPTER 38

JOHAN AND LOTTA, thought Annelie as she drove home from Gabbi's. How did they fit in with their father's death?

She pictured Johan's face. Things were less tricky with him; he was innocuous. Or was it just that he was conformable?

She hadn't hung around with Johan that much when she was growing up. She didn't know him so well. Not like Lotta. And she was made of tougher stuff, but even so not as *pompous* as at least Annelie's mother, Lotta's aunt, said she was. Lotta was more insecure, but it had taken Annelie many years to realize it. Pompous was otherwise the worst thing you could be in small-town Oskarshamn. How Lotta could have become both conceited and pompous with parents like hers....

Annelie thought about all the discussions she and Christoffer had had about this. It skipped a generation, he thought with his doctor's brain. What's more, Lotta had gotten worse when she'd made "a good catch" and moved to upper class Stockholm. It wasn't only her aunt who said that, thought Annelie, but herself and Christoffer, too.

Naturally, all Lotta wanted was to fit in. Who didn't? Annelie watched how she really struggled and adapted her taste in furniture and clothes and her ideas about schools for the kids because she thought that was the only way to be good enough. Going one's own way took strength. Or folly.

During the year that she and Christoffer had spent in Stockholm, they'd tried to have a meal together, the four of them, but it never really worked. Despite the fact that Christoffer came from an important family. Annelie knew why, and it had nothing to do with pride or background. Magnus knew, too, no doubt. She and Magnus never talked about it, of course. They could see it in each other's eyes, and let it go.

She sighed gently while the car radio played a serenade to the full moon. She was filled with unabashed satisfaction.

But enough was enough, she thought a moment later. The time had finally come when Magnus no longer burned in her breast. Not as much. Only a bit.

He had changed. Or was it she who had changed?

She'd watched Magnus, the eternal summertime boy, and seen how he'd followed in his parents' footsteps, placidly and securely at first, with an air of self-certainty. But then his posture had become more forced, ever since his parents took off abroad with money and securities and the taxman hot on their heels.

It wasn't Magnus's fault. But she suddenly glimpsed the once-veiled trait of unreliability. He was still witty and vain. And she still had a weakness for him, or perhaps it was more for the feeling of being in love than him.

Anyway, a long, tedious dinner it had been in Lotta and Magnus's fancy apartment during her and Christoffer's year in Stockholm. Their rooms were on Sibyllegatan, and had high ceilings and mullion windows framed by long, heavy curtains and gorgeous carpets on the floors. They were very exclusive, finely patterned and densely knotted. Big, too, and certainly not cheap. And all procured through Carl-Ivar, naturally.

He'd come in useful there, alright!

She felt a stab of pity for Carl-Ivar, thinking of him now like this. Kind Carl-Ivar, who'd done what he could to make everyone happy.

That evening she'd consistently avoided Magnus's eye.

The polite and slightly pale children went obediently to bed after having kissed their parents goodnight. Annelie had asked if she could read them a bedtime story, she needed to get away, but no, it would only disrupt their routine, said Lotta, so that was the end of that. They'd then eaten some sumptuous food, she could hardly recall what, the atmosphere was tense, and their culinary efforts thus in vain. They'd clinked glasses of vintage wine and said nothing but pleasantries to each other.

And then contact between them had petered out. Because, of course, all parties involved had made sure of it. Had she been younger, she would have fought to the bitter end. She remembered with a blush her eager attempts to make friends with Lotta when they were little, and even later as teenagers. How she'd looked up to Lotta, who was pretty and a year her senior, and who lived in very auspicious conditions like a lush plant thriving in a greenhouse.

Even when Lotta paired up with Magnus, Annelie had looked up to her, despite the physical nausea that the jealousy caused her. There were few people that she'd put so much energy into as Lotta. Except for her mother. Energy that she could have been invested in something else.

Now the whole family was in Istanbul to pay their last respects to Carl-Ivar. She just had to make do with placing a rose on his coffin at his funeral. Perhaps even give him one last bun from Nilsson's.

She smiled at the thought of placing a vanilla whirl on his coffin lid.

She shifted gears and drove up the final incline, slowed down and turned the steering wheel so the wheels could roll with habitual ease onto the drive.

The red Passat was there, but the house was dark. Christoffer was not waiting up for her and had no doubt gone to bed.

The door was locked. She dug her key out of her bag, stepped inside and thought how rare it was for them to lock the door when someone was in.

She hung up her bag on the rough wrought iron coat hook in the kitchen vestibule, draping her coat over it to hide its bulkiness. She walked into the kitchen, turned on the light, and froze.

Where had the kitchen rug gone?

The pine boards lay gray-varnished and bare. She frowned, anxiety squirming in her stomach as she wandered barefoot around the house. Christoffer wasn't at home, but his car was there. He had biked somewhere?

She got undressed, put her robe on and went into the bathroom to wash her face and dab a few blobs of face cream on her forehead and cheeks. As she did so, she heard the sound of an engine and a car rolling up the drive.

She walked out onto the landing and looked down. A police car was just dropping Christoffer off. What on earth had he been up to?

He walked in through the door just as she entered the kitchen. They met each other on the bare kitchen floor. His face was ashen.

"Annelie, there's something I have to tell you."

CHAPTER 39

IT WAS JUST PAST MIDNIGHT, and the night sky was speckled with stars.

Conny Larsson and Jessika Granlund were driving their patrol car at a snail's pace along Kyrkoallén down toward Södra Långgatan. They'd done a quick round of the cemetery after a person living in one of the apartments across the street called to report a blood-curdling scream coming from within, but there hadn't been a soul there. It was dark, of course, but they'd driven around and shone their spotlight over parts of the cemetery and up toward the park, but everywhere was just as deserted. The screamer was probably long gone.

Before they reached Slottsgatan they saw a swaying figure staggering up the hill on the other side of Södra Långgatan, occasionally leaning against the walls of houses for support.

"Stop," Larsson said to Granlund, and she pulled over to the pavement.

They were alone on the road without another vehicle in sight. The exceedingly unsteady pedestrian was clearly having the greatest difficulty making progress.

"I know him," said Conny Larsson.

"You do?"

Jessika Granlund sighed. She hadn't worked more than two months in Oskarshamn and hardly knew anyone. She wasn't from the area, but from Nybro. And she wasn't intending to stay here any longer than necessary. Not if nothing radical happened, whatever that could be. If she fell in love, that sort of thing. If…

She'd turned off the engine and was sitting waiting for orders from Larsson, with her eye on the heavily inebriated man as he struggled on. She felt sorry for him. And of course Conny knew who he was; everyone here knew everyone else, just like at home in Nybro. The man must have been a big shot of some kind, judging by his clothes. Sure, his coat was all creased and wrinkled, but he certainly wasn't dressed like a tramp.

"So who is he?" she said at last to keep some kind of conversation going. She was exhausted.

"I'm just sittin' here wonderin' if we should give him a hand…but…."

"But what?"

"Well, he lives just round the corner on Besvärsgatan, so he ain't got that far to go. He'll be alright."

"So do you want me to drive off?"

"Just give it a bit longer."

Jessika found it particularly pointless to do nothing but sit there watching. It would be better to drag him home, and get it over and done with.

Now the poor drunkard had come to a stop, supporting himself again with one hand against a wall, stooped forward. And then a wave seemed to surge through his body. He vomited. Copiously, too.

"Ah, hell," said Conny Larsson. "No way is he getting' into the car now… He's been at the pub in the A Petersson building, I bet. It's a long climb for someone so drunk. Wonder if he'll make it in to work tomorrow."

"He works?"

"Mm. A doctor, as a matter of fact."

"You're kidding me! It should be against the law for someone like him to have responsibility for others!"

"Yeah, but he's sober a lot of the time and they say he's pretty good. Name's Göran Bladh."

"But still!"

She was agitated. Her chubby face had completely knotted itself up. She lifted her hat and ran her fingers through her hair, which was cut about half an inch short over her entire head. Conny gave her a sideways glance and saw moons and stars and other studs in her earlobes. They were probably the most feminine thing about her, to his mind.

Bladh was off again, making it to the corner of Östra Torggatan, where he swung around and reeled out of sight of Larsson and Granlund.

Jessika Granlund started the car and drove off in the opposite direction, turning after a short distance onto the back end of Slottsgatan, as the one-way system dictated.

As they approached the police station, they saw Bladh lurching over the street ahead. He'd not even made it past the Post Hotel.

"Now he's just got to clear the local newspaper offices and he's pretty much home free," said Larsson.

"Really," said Jessika Granlund, still unconvinced that a person in Bladh's condition would have a hope of finding his way home, but then there was only one block to go.

Besvärsgatan was in front of the police station, behind the clinic.

"Well, he's givin' it a damn good go," grinned Larsson. "Alright. Now I could do with a bit of grub."

It was daybreak, and Nilla Söder wriggled out of her temporary accommodation, a sleeping bag in the basement of a block of apartments on Bäckgatan, feeling extremely rank and unrested. She ought to have been used to it by now, but she still found it unpleasant. As if her body refused to accustom itself to it.

She tugged at Andreas lying beside her and finally roused him.

The newspaper deliverer hadn't seen them, but then he wasn't normally bothered by them either. She and Andreas were like the ducks in the park, things you fed if you had the time and inclination or otherwise ignored. Though that was preferable to being shouted and screamed at or having dogs or the police set onto them.

She shoved her hand into her pocket and felt around. It was still there. Andreas knew nothing, and she wasn't that sure if she should tell him that she'd been given a whole hundred kronor note by some lady the day before. The lady must have been feeling guilty about something giving so much like that, but that didn't stop Nilla thanking her at once and taking it. Otherwise it was mostly a little loose change, a twenty at best.

She was longing for a shower and wished that she didn't have such human needs, as it would've made her life so much easier. The note was burning a hole in her pocket. She already had plans to go to the new swimming pool and pay the entry fee and then just stand under a hot shower for a very, very long time before heading into the sauna. There, she would sit contentedly for a few hours. Cleanse herself inside and out.

And then maybe she'd be able to start afresh. Go to the job center and the benefits office and ask who could help her "start over."

She missed Softie. Why did he have to go running out into the road? That woolly coat to bury her face in. So soft and warm. And those eyes, the eyes that said to her that she was the most important person in his little canine life.

Andreas said that Softie had fleas. She was deaf in that ear.

No, she'd be damned if she was going to share it with him, she decided. The money was hers.

They ambled slowly away to the harbor and up all the steps to Besväret, which lay on the cliff top. It was hard going. She was panting.

All the pretty houses were sleeping when they tramped past with backpacks and cases and plastic bags and all the other stuff they dragged about with them. She had to rest and catch her breath.

She looked askance at the idyll between breaths. She could hear the birds. The narrow cobblestone paved Besvärsgatan with its little wooden houses was the loveliest place in all of Oskarshamn, she thought. She would've liked to have lived here if she'd been born into a different life.

Weren't the lilacs coming into bloom?

"Shit, imagine living here," she couldn't help saying at last.

Andreas didn't even manage a grunt. They trudged off slowly toward Östra Torggatan.

When they were almost there, they came to a halt. Two legs were sticking out from behind a trash can.

"Who the fuck would go and lie down outside Shalom?" said Andreas.

They went over to inspect the human debris that lay spread-eagled on the cobblestones by their feet. Behind them was the café. The one that the Christians ran and that was called Shalom, but it was of course closed. It wasn't even four o'clock.

"Is he alive?" asked Nilla with repugnance in her voice and bent forwards. "He's all blue. Look."

Andreas squatted down, but instead of feeling for a pulse or determining if the body was warm or if it was breathing, he rummaged through his pockets.

"Someone's already gotten to him. Let's get out of here," he said.

Suddenly the man started to cough. They waited until he fell silent again. Andreas looked at the rolled-up rug that he was resting his head on. Then he grabbed hold of it and snatched it away so that the head landed heavily against the cobbles.

"Poor guy!" said Nilla while Andreas tried to wipe a patch of blood from off the back of the rug. The man had probably fallen over and hit himself during the night, as his hair looked matted with blood. "What do you want that for? Come on, let's put it back."

Andreas didn't answer. He put the rug under his arm and dragged Nilla with him off toward the park.

"This'll be perfect," he said when they'd passed the Post Hotel.

"For what?" Nilla said dubiously. Lugging around unnecessary stuff wasn't her thing. They had enough to carry as it was.

"Might think of something," he grinned. "You never heard of the rug trick?"

She hadn't.

He didn't unroll the rug until they'd walked some way into the park. He stared in disappointment at the warn nap.

"Though fuck knows if it'll work with a piece of shit like this. Just our fucking luck it's not in better shape… Though I guess that's why they threw the bastard out," he said with a shrug. "But, hey, it's worth a try."

The dashboard clock said 06:25. The police car crawled along. Conny Larsson yawned wide enough for a truck to pass through.

"Damn if it ain't been a slow night! Over soon, though, eh?"

He drummed his fingers against his thigh. Jessika Granlund said nothing. She was too tired to even open her mouth.

They'd just been out to the navy hut that someone had tried to torch. An observant neighbor had called to report some kids who were "up to no good," but the kids were of course nowhere to be seen when the police car eventually arrived.

They were driving along from Kråkerumsbacken. Lilla Torget Square was stone dead. Jessika drove at an even pace past the intersection with Besvärsgatan.

"Hey, look, is that a body lying there?" she said, braking. She backed up a few yards and turned into the street.

They climbed out. A pair of legs was sticking out from behind two large trash cans that stood at the edge of the garden opposite Café Shalom.

"Turn on a light!" said Conny when he saw who it was.

"We should've helped him get home," said Jessica in a whine.

"Well, he ain't dead, at least."

Jessika called an ambulance. Once it had driven off-siren to the hospital, a journey of less than ten minutes, they realized that it was time to inform his family.

Conny Larsson and Jessika Granlund had just rung Kajsa Bladh's doorbell. They weren't divorced, she and Göran, but lived apart, Kajsa Bladh informed them.

She called intensive care and was told that she was welcome there in an hour. They thought he'd had a heart attack and collapsed. Perhaps even a mild stroke.

"The nurse said there was quite a bit of ethyl in his blood, too," the wife told them. "I might as well be up front about it, it'll only come out, anyway, but he was a drinker. I was the one to move out. I couldn't take it, but…" tears welled up,"… but in my heart of hearts I thought he'd sort himself out. Unrealistic, I know, but… I love the man, in spite of everything."

"It's so tragic," she added in the next breath, "that he was just lying there."

Conny avoided Jessika's eyes. She'll screw up too one of these days, Miss Goody Fucking Two Shoes, he thought.

But they said nothing, neither Conny nor Jessika, but just remained sitting silently on the sofa like two pet cats. Until Conny gestured with his eyebrows. It was time to go.

And they said nothing on the way down the stairs, either.

Their shift was over.

CHAPTER 40

CLAES CLAESSON'S EYES shot open as he lay in his Istanbul hotel bed. He'd been jolted awake by a strange bellowing outside.

He turned on the bedside lamp. It was still only five o'clock, so he turned it off again and let his head sink back into the pillow. By which time he'd identified the noise as a human voice, reeling something off.

My God, he thought, is that what muezzins sound like?

He shut his eyes and after a while found it rather quaint. A wake-up call at dawn summoning the faithful to pray to Allah. It fitted in here, but he was glad not to have this particular alarm clock at home. Live and let live, as his father had once taught him. He turned over onto his other side, pressed one ear against the pillow, laid his arm over the other, and went back to sleep.

When his cell phone's alarm went off at half past six with its discreet metallic ringing, he was fairly well-rested. He sat up in his bed. The rain was clattering against roofs and gushing down drainpipes.

Great! He'd brought neither raincoat nor umbrella.

He stood in front of the bathroom mirror, and while his razor methodically scraped over his chin, he continued to mull theological questions. Where did mankind get its need for religion? This was no trifling subject to grapple with early in the morning with a semi-alert, recently surfaced brain, but his mind continued to churn away.

You had to differentiate between religion and tradition, many people said. He didn't agree. The agents of a faith got away with things too easily, regardless of confession, he thought. They relied on books that could hardly be considered recent. Some of their content was generally relevant, but much wasn't. More Stone Age, in fact. They ought to do what's right and make sure that tradition, to some extent at least, followed society's striving for democracy and equality. What was religion good for, anyway? A pale surrogate for the human longing for unconditional love, someone once said, he couldn't recall who, but it stuck in his mind because he thought there was something in it. The same fundamental love that a mother gives her child. Like a kind of infatuation, but eternal.

Gotte often talked of the need for security and belonging. "Don't forget we're social beings," he'd preach, and of course he was right. Much misery was caused by abused souls and deep loneliness. He and his colleagues saw the result of that in their day-to-day work.

It was still pouring outside. Claesson got dressed and went down to breakfast, where he met a somewhat pale Mustafa Özen.

"Sleep badly?"

"No, no," said Özen lamely as he dribbled golden honey over a piece of bread.

Claesson wolfed down some of the delicious yogurt, which was no doubt full of fat, but he couldn't be bothered to care.

"I tried to sum up yesterday's meeting and get it down on the computer," said Özen then. "Might as well do it now before we get muddled up. Or forget. And that took some time."

"Essay writing, in other words," said Claesson.

"You could say that," grinned Özen.

Literary skills in the force were a little hit and miss, Claesson knew that. Although what was in the reports was important and had to be able to stand up in court, many felt uncomfortable expressing themselves in writing. It wasn't because you were top of the class in Swedish that you applied to the academy. He didn't know about Özen, though. Some people had natural talent and would have no trouble writing thick books or scientific papers. Peter Berg was one of them. As was their technician Benny Grahn, who was an elegant writer and could usually throw something together, even with a little zest if the occasion called for it. He was the one who wrote the speeches when it was someone's birthday, and they always contained just the right amount of cruelty and were absolutely hilarious.

"You can read through it later," said Özen.

Claesson nodded. He had some feta, black olives, and a bun in front of him. And a cup of black coffee.

"Lucky they have coffee," he said.
A morning without coffee was a disappointment.

A while later they were jumping into the police car that had been driven to the front of the hotel. They only needed to trot a few steps in the downpour.

Merve Turpan was already inside. They were to go to the Arkadia Hotel. She had been assigned to join the Swedes on the case of the dead carpet dealer, with Fuat Karaoğlu's consent. There was no reason to sit through a morning meeting first, she said.

"Well, there's no point hanging around," said Claesson.

Merve was out of uniform, wearing trendy jeans and a brick-red top. The windshield wipers were working frenetically. The streets glistened, and people kept themselves indoors.

Outside the Arkadia stood a taxi with its trunk open, and a young man was packing in suitcases with one hand while holding an umbrella in the other. They dashed in through the foyer. There was a short line in front of the desk; they'd had the misfortune to arrive at check-out time. Merve stood at one end of the desk and caught the attention of a man in a suit. He looked more than a little piqued as he stood up and walked toward her. But Merve just smiled and showed him her badge and told him her business, at least that's what Claesson assumed she was doing. But the man looked no less vexed for that, even as he nodded and ushered her into the back offices. Claesson and Özen followed her.

They spoke for a while in Turkish.

"All the hotel guests are registered on the computer," Özen translated. "They promise to give us all the names."

"Ask if he can find out who was working at the desk when Olsson checked out. According to his wife, he must have done so after she left, but she took off pretty early in the morning by taxi to Atatürk airport."

Merve and Özen sprang into action. They made sure to get printouts of the hotel guest lists and a time when Carl-Ivar Olsson had checked out and left the hotel: half past ten. The man at the reception desk that day was the same man who was trying to work his way through all the guests checking out now.

Claesson was given some tea. He was charmed by the little tea glasses that stood on a small tray, each with a spoon and a lump of sugar. He'd be returning home a proper tea drinker.

At last the man at the counter was free. He looked at the photo of Mr. Olsson and shook his head.

No, he didn't recognize him. Claesson could understand that. Olsson had an undeniably nondescript appearance, at least for an elderly Swedish gentleman. Or northern European, for that matter. There were probably many like him who visited Istanbul – retirees who could afford such recreation.

They took the sheaf of paper containing the names of the hotel guests staying there at the time in question, and returned to the police car.

The wind picked up, scattering people into shops and restaurants. The wipers flicked even faster over the windscreen, the rubber squealing from the friction. The uniformed officer behind the wheel was the embodiment of composure. Özen began to skim through the lists.

"There are some Swedish names here. An entire group, it would seem, because they checked out together the day after Olsson. That's to say, the Saturday," he added in Swedish and looked at Claesson.

"The same day he was killed."

"Yes. They'd left the hotel by nine-fifteen."

"Then I wonder if they all flew home or on to another country. We'll ask Sweden to contact them and check with the airlines if they went home. Can you get on that?"

"Sure."

The Grand Bazaar stretched over several quarters, Claesson was informed by Merve, who had also discovered which of the myriad gateways they were to go in through. It was in the east.

"It's something of an experience to go to the Grand Bazaar if you've never been there before," she said. "It's got everything. Shops, cafés, restaurants, banks, post offices, a little police station, and even a mosque. But we don't have time for all that now. Not far from there is the Spice Bazaar, but we won't be going there, either."

Five minutes later, the car pulled up illegally in front of a medieval gateway, right in the middle of a crowd that was milling around in an indescribable chaos out on the rain-soaked street.

They jumped out and dashed for cover in the bazaar area. Özen had been there before, but Claesson hadn't and he was impressed.

The entire area was covered over, blue and white mosaics decorated the walls, and the shops stood wall to wall, like a colorful cavalcade of silk, wool, glass, and polished stones. An ancient shopping center indeed, and so much more pleasant than the monotonous developments that seemed to be popping up like mushrooms in the outskirts of most Swedish towns.

Merve took command, and led them along a street, turning into a narrower passageway and past a diminutive, curious-looking building, the "Oriental *Kiosk*," that lay in the middle of their path. A few paces further on they turned into an alleyway, exiting onto a small square under an open sky. This was Zincirli *Hani*, a famous square containing trading houses and a famous carpet dealership that had been operating there for years. The rain was striking the pavement with such force that it splashed upwards. Merve run-walked along the pink wall of a house, past a number of barred, green wooden doors to a large door further away that stood open. A sign above it announced that they'd arrived at Şişko Oman's and that here they could find TAPIS – KILIMS – CARPETS.

A proper carpet shop, in other words. And not just any old shop, realized Claesson once he was standing in the middle of the building with its open floor – carpet-covered, of course – and its walls clad with rugs. This was the fifth generation of carpet dealers to occupy the property, they learned from the newspaper cuttings taped up on a door inside. According to the carpet dealer in Kalmar, this was an extremely professional business.

A young, slightly astonished man greeted them when they'd burst in, rain dripping from their clothes. He'd bowed and immediately taken out his cell phone to call his father, or was it his uncle, who knew carpet dealer Olsson from Sweden very well.

While they were waiting, they sat themselves down on colorful cushions and drank tea, served, again, in tulip-shaped glasses. The friendly young man bowed again and said he was sorry to hear what had happened to carpet dealer Olsson. He knitted his heavy eyebrows and looked nothing short of disconsolate.

A distinguished gentleman with thick gray hair and bright eyes appeared. He was deeply moved to hear that carpet dealer Olsson had met his end. And in such a macabre way! He needed a few moments to recover himself. He found it particularly disturbing that it had happened in his own city of Istanbul, too.

"All I can say by way of consolation is that I know for certain that Olsson loved our city very much. But to die here…" He shook his head and looked even more miserable.

No more needs to be said, thought Claesson.

The man, like his younger relative, spoke a very easy-to-understand English.

Claesson drew a breath.

"When did you last meet Carl-Ivar Olsson?" he wondered.

"Let me see," said the man, stroking his beardless chin. He had a sharply chiseled face and was probably much older than he looked. He turned to the younger carpet dealer and said something in Turkish. Merve and Özen both listened, but all he was doing was asking for help with days and dates. They worked out that it had been two days before Carl-Ivar Olsson's tragic death that he'd visited his Turkish friend.

"A Thursday."

"A Thursday," repeated Claesson.

"That's right. A week ago to the day," said the carpet dealer.

"May I ask what you did?"

"We drank tea and chatted."

"About what?"

"About carpets, naturally," said the man, with a surprised look.

"So nothing in particular?" continued Claesson.

The man stared down at the busily patterned rug at his feet, slowly shaking his head.

"No, nothing in particular," he muttered.

"Can you help us with this?"

He took out the photocopy of the photograph of the shabby antique rug that they'd found in the carpet shop in Oskarshamn.

The man put on a pair of steel-rimmed glasses and the younger man moved closer to have a look. Merve Turpan said something in Turkish, and both men studied the photograph closely, but it was obvious from their body language that a quick glance would have sufficed.

"Yes, I can," said the older carpet dealer, and the other nodded. "This is a fragment of a…" and then said something that Claesson didn't understand.

The man resorted to Turkish.

"One of those that's smooth," said Mustafa Özen, searching for words while stroking his hand in the air as he looked around the shop for a suitable specimen. "Like that," he said, pointing at a carpet that was knotted rather than flat-woven.

"The rug is very old, fourteenth or fifteenth century, and you can see Kufic script along the border," continued the older of the two.

"Kufic?" wondered Claesson, sounding just as ignorant as he was. He knew the Swedish word *kuf*, but there was nothing *kufic* or oddball about this.

"It is a kind of Arabic script that was developed in Kufa a long time ago, at some time in the eighth century, I believe. Kufa is now a ruin in central Iraq by the famous Euphrates River."

"So that's where the rug comes from?"

"I think not. People have always traveled in our part of the world. The rug comes from the Anatolian Highlands."

"Central Turkey to us," added Özen.

Claesson knew that. Something had seeped in, after all.

"It was found in a mosque in a village in Cappadocia, Ayvali, if you want to know," continued the carpet dealer and Claesson and Özen exchanged glances. Now they were getting somewhere. It was the same provenance that they had been given by the young woman who had taken over the carpet shop in Oskarshamn.

"So you recognize this rug, then?" asked Claesson.

"Oh, yes, indeed," said the older man as the younger nodded.

"It was from me that Mr. Olsson had bought the rug on behalf of a very particular customer."

In the silence that followed you could have heard a pin drop, if it hadn't been for the thick carpets.

"I'm sorry, but do you happen to know where it is now?" asked Claesson.

"No, I have absolutely no idea, I'm afraid. Has it been mislaid?"

"We don't know."

"But Olsson collected it from us the next day. Unfortunately it was not me who handed it to him but a cousin of mine."

All these cousins, Claesson thought with a concealed sigh.

"Where can we find this cousin?"

"Oh, that is me," said the other man, the one who had welcomed them into the shop and who was much younger. "I assumed he would be flying home right away, but we never spoke of this. Expensive rugs like that are not things you want lying around a hotel room. They are much sought-after… Most people who buy an expensive carpet have their taxi drive past the shop on the way to the airport to pick it up."

"Was it large?"

"No bigger than fitted in a medium-sized carpet bag, which we supply our customers with. Since it was an old rug, we had folded it in a piece of washed-out cotton to protect the pile and to prevent sharp creases from forming. Olsson could take it on a plane as a carry-on," said the carpet dealer.

Well, whaddaya know?

Claesson's mind was a blank. He looked at Özen.

"Is there something I've forgotten," he asked in Swedish?

"I don't know, maybe you could ask them what the rug might be worth."

Right! So he asked. It was the older of the two, now with glasses in hand, who spoke.

"Well, it is certainly not the cheapest kind of rug. In my humble opinion I would say quite the opposite. It is the kind, I mean, that would fetch a higher price."

The man smiled crookedly and then gave a price in dollars that made Claesson and Özen reel. They looked at each other while they converted it into Swedish.

"One and a half million. More, even!"

CHAPTER 41

VERONIKA SAT WITH THE THURSDAY PAPER in her kitchen. At last! A cup of strong coffee.

Klara was at the Bumble Bee nursery and Nora was sleeping, newly fed and content, in her bassinet in the sitting room. The whole morning had been chaotic after a hectic night. She'd had to lower her voice to a muffled, collected tone as she got the kids ready and drove the short distance to the preschool. She tended to slip into a falsetto when tired or stressed and her voice would harden, which just made Klara cry, and it would take forever to comfort her again. And with another child in tow.

No, she'd just have to pull herself together.

She saw the article. Read that a woman had been assaulted in Bråbo at six o'clock yesterday evening, and had been taken to hospital with her injuries. The police were now hunting her attacker and were keen to hear from anyone who might have seen something.

Oh.

Should she give them a call? If Claes had been home, she'd have talked to him first to avoid making a fool of herself and wasting police time.

She stood up as she spoke to an operator who'd make sure that she'd be put through to the right person. A man answered. She said who she was and told him what she'd seen the day before. He asked her to wait. Another person came on the line. It was Louise Jasinski. She began with all the expressions of congratulations in the world that she could think of, Veronika could hear that.

"But listen," she then said. "It'd be good if you came down to the station so that we can get your statement officially in writing."

"Please, do I have to? I'm alone here with two kids."

"I know."

"One of them's asleep and the other's got to be picked up at eleven. Can't someone come here and take it?"

There was silence. She could tell that Louise was deliberating with herself.

"Of course we can pick you up. But…"

"No," sighed Veronika. "I realize it'll be difficult for you. And I guess you don't have child seats for an infant and another little one. Either you see me now at once or I'll come down this afternoon, in which case you'll have to put up with my having two children in tow."

Half an hour later, she was sitting in the police station in front of a man called Martin Lerde, and who was a little on edge, she being who she was. The boss's wife, with kids and all.

She was a good interviewee, she thought smugly. She'd seen Christoffer Daun out in the yard, she could attest to that, she wasn't mistaken, she recognized him easily; after all, he was a colleague. And it sounded very convincing.

However, she felt less convincing when she was asked to talk about the man who'd crept behind the lilac bush and who she thought was someone Christoffer had helping him. What could she say about him? Not much. He moved more like a forty-year-old than a seventy-year-old. Average height, neither fat nor thin. Brown hair, probably. That was about it.

And then there was the car. A dark green Saab.

"Are you sure about that?"

Nora whined. Veronika picked her up from out of the infant carrier she'd brought her in with.

"Yes," she finally answered.

Her parents drove a similar car, though of an older model.

Nora started screaming at the top of her lungs. The idea of sitting there breast-feeding her under this young whippersnapper's nose was unthinkable.

"Can I go somewhere private?"

"Er, yes, of course. I think we're done. I'll be in touch if need be."

"Feel free."

She stood up with Nora in her arms. Where could she sit? Preferably not on the couch out in the corridor in front of everyone. In Claes's office, perhaps?

She passed Louise's office.

"Of course you can sit in there!"

She didn't sit at his desk but on the upholstered visitor's chair with armrests facing it. Her body relaxed once she'd put Nora to her breast. The door was closed. She could hear footsteps in the corridor and the odd car passing by outside. Otherwise it was peaceful.

She looked around while Nora drank her fill. Claes's presence was palpable, even though he wasn't actually there, she thought. Claes, far away, but here nonetheless. She got a thrill out of that. She missed him, but was with him still.

She'd been here before, but had just popped in. Now she had time to take in his life here from the visitor's perspective. It was a spacious room with windows along the entire north wall. Well-stocked bookshelves and cupboards of various ages. It was obvious that some had been fitted later, a little ad hoc, as his need had increased.

She thought how nice it was to be married to a man she could be proud of. He had a solid reputation, mostly on account of his stability and integrity. And that was good. Imagine living with someone who was generally considered a blockhead or a grump or a whiner! But there were, of course, people who did that.

She then noticed that it said M & MS on the spine of a binder.

M & MS?

Murder and Manslaughter, of course. She smiled.

Tina Rosenkvist had been given a private room and felt no shame for that, since there were many empty beds around. She wasn't sick "for real" and didn't demand much of the staff. She'd showered and put on a new nightshirt. Her mother would soon arrive with some clean clothes; the ones she'd been wearing the day before had been taken by the police and sent away to be analyzed for DNA from the so-called perpetrator. Hairs, fibers, saliva, and all that. She hadn't been raped after all.

Dear old Sofa came in with a tray of sandwiches and tea and a stainless steel jug containing juice and ice.

"How nice of you," said Tina, curling her lips into a vague smile. It meant she didn't have to show herself with her swollen throat in the lounge.

"I reckoned a little extra service for one of our own was in order," said Sofa.

A shortcut to treatment was really the only perk they had, they liked to joke. As long as you worked, you could ask the doctors to write prescriptions or arrange referrals to the doctor you wanted to see. Things weren't so easy for other people though. Like retirees. She remembered how embarrassing it had been when an elderly man had had to lie in the corridor for hours in agony as they didn't have a bed for him. He'd had a hip fracture, hadn't he? God, the time it took to get him off to radiology!

And then his wife had shown up. She said nothing, but they recognized her. Turned out the man had been a doctor at the clinic. In fact, if it hadn't been for him, the clinic wouldn't be what it was today. But what good did that do him now? Now that he couldn't speak up for himself.

Sofa pulled up the blinds and opened the window vent. Tina squinted and shaded her eyes with a hand.

"Oh, sorry, was that too bright?" asked Sofa.

"No, I'll be alright."

Mercifully, Sofa asked no more. She didn't even seem curious, nothing in her body language said that she was hungry to wheedle out from her something about what had happened.

"Let me know if there's something you need," she said and walked out.

Once Sofa had left her alone and she'd eaten breakfast on the edge of her bed, she sat down in the armchair with a two-year-old gossip magazine and let her eyes flit over a double-page spread showing the royal family in their evening wear. She hardly took in anything of what she was looking at. Their lives seemed so sparkly, smiling, and superficial in comparison with her own situation, but of course that wasn't really the case. Not always, anyway: even the royal family had their problems. No one was spared, Birgitta Olsson liked to say, without sounding bitter for all that.

I wonder how Birgitta's feeling, for that matter, poor thing.

But her interest in Birgitta soon waned. She didn't have the energy to think about anyone else. She had enough on her plate as it was.

A police officer had asked her a whole load of questions. He'd sat there in the armchair yesterday evening, talking kindly. He didn't seem to be in any hurry, and so he was soon done. Things always went more quickly when you weren't stressed and could work calmly and methodically. She recognized it from her own work; if you get stressed you always screw up, and you have a hell of a job getting the needles in and the drip counters get all in a mess and the patients keep asking if everything's OK until they drive you insane!

The police didn't say a word about what had happened to Christoffer They'd be questioning him too, naturally, she took that for granted. The officer was just wondering what she was doing in his house, and she told them how it was, that Christoffer had given her a lift home, that they were workmates, and that they'd then sat down to have a chat

"So you just talked?"

What did he think? She was offended and slightly scared of all the rumors that would start flying.

"Yes, actually. And a glass of wine. But I never got around to drinking it."

The police had obviously seen the glass. Maybe even taken it to look for traces of saliva. They'd discover that they came from her and Christoffer.

Christoffer…

Her heart pounded and spread a euphoric warmth through her body when she thought about him. She closed her eyelids and leaned her head back against the armchair's headrest and let the sensation settle in her.

She tingled from head to toe. Christoffer held his arms around her and rocked her while hugging her almost to the point of pain. "Baby, you've got no idea how much I love you," he whispered in her ear. "I promise to take care of you, my love. I will protect you from everything. What's happened is merely a sign that we belong together."

Damn Christoffer for not seeing that they were twin souls! For not being braver and daring to let himself go, and not realizing what was important in life and getting around to leaving his wife. A stinging, bitter sensation took root in her guts.

But if he did insist on being a spineless coward…

She got up and poured herself some of the light red juice. She felt only a slight tenderness in her throat as she drank. But the back of her eyes stung. Burned because Christoffer didn't want her most. And because there had to be something else mysterious about him too, bearing in mind what happened yesterday.

What *were* they up to? That maniac had been shouting about a rug. It must have had something to do with his wife's job.

Tina had an anxiety attack, and was gripped by a sheer torment that sent ants crawling over her body when she thought about it. But if Christoffer really was up to no good, it was probably just as well he didn't want her, wasn't it?

The defiance swelled within her.

He'd get no begging from her, if that's what he wanted.

She wiped her mouth with the back of her hand. The policeman had tried to coax out of her who it was that had attacked her in the kitchen. She couldn't remember, she said. He'd asked her if she could remember his voice. The ears could sometimes be sharper than the eyes, he'd said. Yes, she did…maybe, she'd replied.

He didn't wish to put words in her mouth, of course, but was naturally wanting to find out if it was a voice she recognized.

And it wasn't.

But she didn't tell him. She needed more time to think, she said.

"If you say so," the policeman had said, regarding her. "But people often remember best when they don't have time to reflect."

Maybe the policeman could tell that she was lying when she refused to say that it hadn't been Christoffer. Noticed that she wanted the possibility to hang in the air for a while? No way was she going to let Christoffer off that easily. Not now that he didn't want her.

The door opened to reveal Pär standing there holding a shopping bag. Her stomach turned to ice. Her mother was supposed to be coming to fetch her with a change of clothes, that had been agreed.

"Hi," he said, avoiding her eye. "Here."

He held out the bag with the clothes in it. She took it and opened it.

"Thanks," she mumbled and started to sort out a pair of underwear, a bra, a pair of jeans that were actually too tight, and a top that was too warm, but he'd done as best he could, no doubt.

She wondered where the kids were. They were with his mom, he said, but they could pick them up later.

Tina didn't like Pär's mother, but this wasn't the time or place to argue about that. At least the woman didn't harm the kids, she thought, even though she lacked patience and easily grew short-tempered when they were with her.

She stood there with the bag in her hand and felt an instinctive reluctance to undress there in the room in front of him. It was odd, but the thought embarrassed her. And to think that they'd been married and shared a bedroom for so long! Without another word, she slipped into the bathroom to get changed.

She then waved goodbye to Sofa in the corridor and left the ward. She and Pär took the elevator down in silence and continued to ignore each other as they walked out to the car. A fluffy but ominous iron-gray cloud blocked the sun just as they were climbing into the Volvo.

He turned the stereo on. She couldn't really cope with having something thundering in her ears, but she put up with it. It was better than talking.

When they turned off toward Bråbo and were almost home, that was when her heart started to thump. She pressed a hand against her chest and swallowed.

"What's wrong?" he asked.

"It's nothing," she said, swallowing a second time. She removed her hand.

There were no doubt many eyes watching them as they drove home through the village. She thought that the house looked cold, which was unusual. After all, she'd spent hours in the garden planting petunias of different shades in large pots and the flowerbeds were bursting with color. The kids' toys lay strewn about the lawn.

Pär yanked open the mailbox and retrieved the newspaper. What, hadn't he collected it yet?

She wondered if there was anything in it and trembled inside.

He unlocked the front door and held it open for her. She hung her coat up, feeling like a stranger in her own home.

She blew her nose. When she tossed the tissue into the trash can under the sink, she noticed that Pär had placed an empty vodka bottle there. He'd been drinking that night.

There were flowers on the table. He'd already set out some cups and was now putting on some coffee, strangely enough, for that had always been her thing. The air was fragile, as if the world could fall apart at any moment.

They seated themselves opposite each other and then it came.

"What were you doing at that Daun's place?" Pär said through clenched jaws.

She said nothing.

"Explain yourself, for fuck's sake. Jesus, the whole fucking village knows!"

Still she said nothing. He got up and walked around the table and, grabbing her top, wrenched her up onto her feet.

The blows came raining down. The cheeks, the head, teeth crunching, the chest, the head again. She tried to get away, but he came after her, knocked her down, took hold of a leg and dragged her into their walk-in closet.

"Explain yourself, you fucking cunt!" he roared and started kicking her, making the clothes tumble down from their hangers. He forced apart her legs and kicked her hard in the crotch, wrenched off her jeans despite her attempts to lash out, tore off her underwear. And then, picking up one of her pointed high-heeled shoes, he rammed the toe into her vagina. She squirmed and screamed and he pushed and pushed until most of the shoe was inside her. She could feel something rupturing inside. She tried to grasp hold of the shoe to pull it out, but he twisted her arms until something must have snapped. He went for her head again.

When his rage had subsided he locked the closet door.

"Jesus fuck, you've only got yourself to blame!" he screamed at the door.

And then he went into the kitchen and washed up the coffee cups.

CHAPTER 42

IT HAD STOPPED RAINING. The black clouds had blown away in an almost storm-like wind that then suddenly and quickly subsided. The sun was starting to break through, and at once the temperature rose. Classic coastal weather, thought Claesson. Like in Oskarshamn, though that's as far as comparisons went.

Merve had found a "hole in the wall" kind of restaurant, a simple eatery, in other words. This sort of place wasn't, on the other hand, hard to find in Istanbul. As they stood by the counter making their selections and Claesson pointed at the stainless steel tubs of steaming dishes, he couldn't help but think about what Janne Lundin would have said: Where there are locals, there's no food poisoning.

And that's where they were now. But why would chefs slob around their kitchens "just" because they had tourists as guests? That had to be a fabrication.

They were each handed a plate of rice, chicken, and different-colored peppers cooked in a delicious stock, and went to sit down at a wobbly plastic table out on the pavement. They were hungry. Cars blared their horns and people slid around them in one big chaotic muddle. The Grand Bazaar was just a block away, and it was the same atmosphere here, with eager salesmen calling out their wares. On one side of the café was a little supermarket, on the other a trinket shop and then some food stores. Claesson saw one of the carpet dealers smiling broadly to a tall, robust woman with short, ash-blonde hair.

"Where are you from?" he called.

"Sweden," she tossed out with a smile.

That doesn't surprise me, thought Claesson. That kind of linen-wear could only be found in Sweden.

"Ah! Markaryd and Gnosjö!" called the carpet dealer happily after her as she walked past without stopping.

If you've seen Markaryd and Gnosjö, you've seen Sweden, thought Claesson.

At the same moment, he noted that Mustafa Özen and Merve had held each other's gazes for that little bit too long. And it wasn't the first time.

Claesson kicked Özen's shin.

"Don't forget you're a Swedish cop and that you're coming home with me," he said thickly in Swedish.

Özen grinned embarrassedly back. Merve countered with something in Turkish to Özen, who replied in a velvety voice in their shared language and shook his head. Merve smiled, tilted her head to one side, and glittered so intensely at Claesson that it felt as if his head was about to explode.

"What was that you just said?" he asked in Swedish, wiping his mouth with the tiny paper napkin.

"I just told her that you think she's hot," smiled Özen.

Love is in the air, sung Claesson to himself.

They were to go on to the coroner, who had Carl-Ivar Olsson's corpse in cold storage. They'd managed after a little hard work to coordinate things with his widow and two children. Claesson hadn't met any of them, which was an oversight that he intended to rectify. The family were here to identify Carl-Ivar Olsson's body.

Merve stepped into the traffic and waved down a yellow taxi.

The forensic pathology building was adjacent to a large hospital. They drove through narrow, winding streets and alleys, and then onto a busy main road, where car horns seemed to be the most popularly used signaling system.

The taxi driver had his seatbelt pulled over his shoulder for appearances' sake, but hadn't done it up. Claesson remembered back to the seventies when seatbelts became compulsory in Sweden, and how many drivers, usually men, did the same thing in the belief that a skilled driver, in principal, was immortal.

It was exaggeratedly quiet in the back seat. Claesson turned. Merve and Özen were sitting like two opposite poles in a magnetic field. Claesson could sense how they were making every effort to look normal while staring absently ahead.

Do they think I'm totally stupid? he thought as he watched a poor emaciated man try to dodge the traffic with his overburdened wooden cart.

At the same time, he could feel that chilly sensation of exclusion and perhaps a little jealousy wash over him as the third wheel. Get a grip, man! he told himself, and the moment the feeling had been rationalized, it evaporated. He'd made it in life. Not only was he married with kids, he was also a man who liked being married with kids.

The car slowed down and passed through a pair of iron gates, coming to a stop shortly afterwards by an almost cubic building standing beside a larger hospital complex. Another taxi had stopped just ahead of them. Three people were getting out of it – no, four, he saw. The family.

Merve Turpan's cell phone rang, and after a glance at the display she switched it off. Was it her mother? Claesson wondered. She'd called now and then and Merve had made excuses, saying that her mother was a woman with an inexhaustible capacity to fuss her daughter.

Merve led them inside and walked over to a plump woman in a green hospital gown. Her pants were stretched tight over her bottom, and her wide blouse also seemed fit to burst. It was the coroner. She disappeared behind a door of milky glass, leaving the Olsson family there treading water.

Claesson greeted them in turn. The wife, Birgitta Olsson, was a prim and relatively well-preserved woman. She looked pleasant, but her face, for obvious reasons, was slack. The daughter, Lotta Öberg, was staring at the floor, constantly and nervously licking her lips. The son, Johan, greeted him with a firm handshake, and the son-in-law, whatever his name was, made absolutely no impression at all.

"I'm very grateful that you've come all the way here to find out what happened to Carl-Ivar," his widow said in a muted voice.

"We're doing what we can," said Claesson. "It would be helpful if I could ask you a few questions afterwards… I mean once you've been inside and…"

The green-clad coroner returned with an assistant, a much younger man with a hairy chest, who led them into a small room with cool, bare walls, where the body they believed to be Carl-Ivar Olsson's lay covered in a white sheet up to his chin.

Birgitta Olsson broke down at once. So this was her husband, Claesson said silently to himself. An ordinary man of typical Swedish model.

Everyone wept, except for the son-in-law, who, with tight-lipped gravity, laid an arm around the shoulder of his wife, a slim woman with thick, flaxen hair cut short in a way that made her look sporty and youthful. Stones twinkled in her earlobes.

The three police officers left the room so that the family could pay their last respects in peace and quiet. Merve pulled out her phone and ordered two police cars to come and take them and the grieving family to the station.

They lingered in the corridor for a while without saying a great deal to each other. The family came dribbling out one by one and had to sit and wait in a visitors' room that was not of this world and as small and as hot as a sauna.

Then the police cars arrived.

When they arrived at the station, Fuat Karaoğlu came out to meet them.

"How is it coming on?" he asked.

"Fine," answered Claesson, meaning it. By "fine," he didn't mean that they were close to a solution, but that things were rolling along as normal, pretty much. Although in Turkey instead of Sweden.

"And you are pleased with DI Turpan?" Karaoğlu asked.

Claesson couldn't work out if his eyes were glistening with mockery or affection.

"Very much so," said Claesson, stressing the very.

"I mean it," Karaoğlu said contentedly. "She is one of the best," he continued, tapping a finger against his skull.

He then said a few pleasantries and apologized once more for not being able to take more active part in the investigation. And Claesson, for his part, said a few polite words about how grateful he was for the help that the Oskarshamn police had received, and not the least for this collaboration, which had let them so generously into the investigation that it would be easier to continue it when they returned to Sweden. Contact with Turkey was particularly well established, he said.

"Talking of the investigation, can you say when the body can be transported to Sweden?"

"As far as we are concerned, you may take it to Sweden whenever you wish. The forensic examination has been completed."

"Thank you. I'll let the family know."

It was time to question the Olssons. Claesson's head was tired and stuffy, but what the hell. The quicker they got things done, the sooner he'd be home.

They began with Birgitta Olsson. Claesson asked Özen to sit in with him, but as they were to conduct the interviews in Swedish, Merve Turpan didn't have to be present. They intended to go through what was said with her later. Or rather Özen promised to do so.

Birgitta Olsson agreed to their conversation being taped. So Özen took out the little Dictaphone that he had brought down from Oskarshamn. He also had a notepad in front of him, just in case. He was organized, and that was good. It wasn't smart to depend on gadgets exclusively.

They'd been given Merve Turpan's office. It was warm but not insufferably hot inside; it had rained all afternoon and the air had been washed clean. Claesson didn't bother to turn on the desk fan.

He told the widow straight off that she was perfectly entitled to take the body home whenever she could arrange to do so.

"What if he'd preferred to have been laid to rest in Turkish soil?" she said spontaneously with a thick voice.

Claesson waited a few seconds.

"What makes you think that?"

She shrugged. "I don't know, I've always had a feeling that he loved it here."

"So he never expressed any special desire to be buried in Turkey?"

"Not at all. It's just me being so impressionable, now that we're here… and because he died here. But I want to take him home… of course I do."

She shook her head as if shaking off the worries. The ones that she actually couldn't escape from.

Claesson asked her to tell him in her own words what had gone through her head when she first heard the news of his death. If she'd suspected something when she left him the day before in Istanbul, and naturally she hadn't. Carl-Ivar's death came like a thunderbolt out of the blue.

"It's so terrible to think about that I get the shudders all the time," she said softly between closed lips, as if she was trying hard to force back an urge to throw up.

"Your husband had a long life as a carpet dealer," he then said, which was possibly a little too emotional, as Birgitta Olsson started to wail so tearfully that he had to stop and wait for her to blow her nose. "I wonder if you know anything about your husband's dealings in the carpet business," he continued.

"Nothing at all, actually. I've never been that interested in carpets, even though the odd one has come my way over the years," she said with a sad smile. "I'm a nurse, as you know. But Carl-Ivar's assistant, or whatever we can call her… knows for sure. Annelie Daun's her name, but maybe you've already spoken to her. She's his niece."

She looked up. Claesson said nothing, wondering if the wife was deliberately or unconsciously trying to shift the focus from herself.

"So you know nothing about a rug of the more exclusive kind that your husband had undertaken to arrange for a very fastidious customer in Sweden?" he asked.

She twisted the paper hanky in her hands.

"No. Who's saying he did? Annelie?"

Claesson didn't have to answer, he knew that. But he chose his own way.

"We've met one of your husband's carpet contacts here in Istanbul. A very professional dealer."

"I see," she said, sounding like she was listening with half an ear. "And so who was the customer… the man who wanted the rug?"

She looked up at him. Her eyes were light blue, like frozen ice.

"I'm afraid we don't know. Do you?"

"No," she said with an earnest shake of her head.

"Have you any idea where the rug might be?"

"No. But I went home before Carl-Ivar, so I've no idea what he did afterwards. One might wonder… given what happened to him."

"According to the Turkish dealer, people who buy expensive carpets leave them in the shop and then pick them up in a taxi on their way to the airport so that they don't have to leave them lying round a hotel where they can easily get stolen. But perhaps you already know that."

She nodded silently.

"We know that Carl-Ivar picked up this carpet around the time of your flight home. The evening before, actually. What do you know about that?"

"Nothing," she said without a pause, and shook her head again. "I went from the hotel to the airport, and Carl-Ivar carried my bags down and waved me off, but a rug, no. Have you asked at the hotel if it's lying around there somewhere? Or if someone's taken it? Hotel thefts are very common."

Claesson didn't answer. He placed the photograph of the rug in front of her, and she studied it carefully.

"I've never seen a rug like that before."

"What did you do the evening before you left for home?"

She stared at the wall.

"We went out for a meal. Then Carl-Ivar said he had to go and do something so I went home and went to bed. I lay reading for a while and was asleep by the time he got back."

"Did you notice if he came back with a bag?"

"No. I said I was sleeping."

"What about in the morning? Did you notice a bag then?"

"What's it supposed to look like, this bag?" she said, and seemed pleased with herself for thinking of the question.

"Don't you know what the bags you take rugs home in look like?"

She looked embarrassed.

"Yes, dark canvas. Soft bags that can handle being stuffed."

"And you didn't see a bag like that?"

"No. But then he could've put it somewhere where I couldn't see it. In a closet, maybe. I had enough to do to with my packing and everything."

"Did you have breakfast together that morning, you and your husband?"

"I guess so."

"Guess?"

"Yes, we did. But it was a quick breakfast. I had a taxi waiting, didn't I?"

We'll have to check up on that, thought Claesson. If they could get hold of a witness that could say that they'd had breakfast together or if her husband was watching over a bag.

"Do you know if your husband had other contacts here in Turkey than the carpet dealer in the Grand Bazaar?"

"He knew several dealers, one who lives a little outside the city, but I don't know his name, and someone in another city, but I don't know them that well."

"No one else other than dealers?"

Claesson and Özen avoided each other's eye. Then Claesson took the photograph of the Yeniköy quayside that one of the crew had taken. Carl-Ivar was standing fully visible in light summer trousers, a light blue shirt and an open, lightweight poplin jacket. He was holding what looked like a soft, dark bag.

"Oh, is it that the bag you mean?" she said. "No, I haven't seen one. Not on this trip. He used to come home with ones like that, though."

"OK," said Claesson. "But if you look at the woman standing next to him?"

She bent her head over the photo and Claesson could see that she started to blush – her throat and face were turning a deep red. It was always such a giveaway.

"Who is she?" she asked.

"That's what we're wondering."

"I've never seen her before," said Birgitta Olsson. She looked Claesson straight in the eye. "But she could be anyone just standing there waiting for the ferry."

She suddenly sounded tired and flat.

They stretched their legs and had some tea brought into the office.

The son, Johan Olsson, was called in, but had nothing much to bring to the investigation. He'd hardly even known that his father had been in Istanbul. He lived his own life, but described his relationship with both parents as good.

"But we all do our own thing," he said.

The daughter, Lotta Öberg, knew just as little about what her father had been up to, she claimed. She had a job and two kids and lived in Stockholm, a hectic life, it seemed. She knew that her parents had been in Istanbul and that her mother had left for home some days before her father, as was the plan, since mother and daughter had spoken to each other on the phone.

"How often do you do that?"

"Often enough… Maybe every other day, it varies."

As usual, thought Claesson. Mother and daughter keeping the social wheels turning. He thought about Veronika and Cecilia, who called each other frequently.

But that wasn't how he was going to do things, he'd promised himself. He was going to have his own channels open to his girls! And what's more, he was the only one in his family who saw to their own senile mother, but then that was because she lived in Oskarshamn. He'd have to go and see her to tell her about Nora, and resolved to do so as soon as he got home. Even if she never took in what he said. He'd hold her by the arm, or perhaps even by the hand, to help her gather her wits. Say: "Mom, it's Claes. You've got a new grandchild. It's a little girl and her name's Nora." He had no idea what would sink in, but he wanted to tell her anyway. For his own sake, perhaps.

The son-in-law Magnus Öberg was even briefer, curt even, in his answers. He hadn't even been at home in Stockholm when Carl-Ivar was found dead on the Bosporus ferry. He was away on business in Germany, as his wife had previously testified.

"Is that so?" said Claesson. "So there's not much you can help us with then, is there," he said, dismissing him with a nod.

But just as the man stood up to leave the office, Claesson cleared his throat.

"You know, I was just wondering where in Germany you were."

Magnus Öberg looked confused.

"Here and there, Lübeck and Munich among other places," he said. "Does it matter?"

"We're just a little pedantic in circumstances like this, but if you could somehow confirm that you were at these places in Germany, and state whom you met and when, and report to the police station in Oskarshamn, we'd be very grateful."

If he stiffened or not it was hard to tell. Perhaps he'd turned pale thinking of all the hard work that would entail.

"Er, of course. No problem. What kind of things are you after?"

"Any airplane tickets…"

"But I drove down."

"OK, so the names of people you met, and…"

"I understand. I'll sort out what you need when I return home."

"Good," said Claesson. "We'll be checking this, of course, with your employer. Purely routine," he said in the same neutral tone.

"That'll be easy," said Magnus Öberg, looking a little more confident. "I work for myself."

CHAPTER 43

"I GUESS WE'RE PRETTY MUCH done here," said Claesson, straightening his back.

It was past six o'clock. He was tired. His longing for home really ached now that he had the time to think about it.

Mustafa Özen nodded. Claesson noticed how he tried hard not to look disappointed, although his head drooped like a miserable dog's.

Özen had put on a smart t-shirt today, too. Not quite the same relaxed style back home in Oskarshamn, but then so what? thought Claesson.

"It'd be nice, of course, to see more of the city, but that's not why we're here," he continued in a neutral tone.

"Otherwise, a trip along the Bosporus wouldn't have been such a bad idea," he continued dreamily just to torture poor love-struck Özen, whose eyes suddenly brightened. They'd talked earlier about following in Olsson's footsteps, but things don't always turn out as you'd like. You had to be flexible – a prestige word for modern people.

"Don't we have to take that trip?" said Özen. "Don't we have to do it for the sake of the investigation? We can't just go home without seeing the scene of the crime for ourselves, can we?"

He was eager. Wagging his tail like a puppy.

"But it probably wouldn't give us anything. The Istanbul people have already done the necessary work. And thoroughly, to boot," said Claesson.

Özen's eyes immediately went dead.

"They might even be offended if we go tramping around there. As if the job they'd done wasn't good enough."

Özen was by now really glum.

"Do you think you can check tomorrow's flights?"

"Sure," said Özen dully, and slunk away to look for Merve to ask if he could borrow her computer. Claesson prepared himself for a long wait.

He went out into the corridor to listen to the buzz and din of the city outside the open window.

A while later, Özen returned with a suggested itinerary.

Departure 8:50 a.m. from Atatürk airport. Up at the crack of dawn, in other words. They'd get home nice and early.

"Let me know when it's all booked," said Claesson, waving away Özen and Merve, who were both looking equally glum.

Just then, a skinny police officer in a light-blue uniform shirt appeared holding a piece of paper. After a moment's hesitation, he finally decided to address Özen in Turkish.

"Well, what do you know!" said Özen. "They've found Olsson's passport."

"Where?"

"A hotel's reported it, as far as I can tell."

Claesson stood silently staring at the floor. He'd have to brush his disappointment under the carpet. He might not be taking the morning flight, after all.

"OK, then," he said when he'd pulled himself together sufficiently. "I suppose we'd better go there."

"It's on the other side of the Golden Horn," said Merve.

"So what do we do now?" wondered Özen, all at a loss.

"About what?"

"About the tickets."

"Pah. Cancel them," said Claesson.

Özen nodded contentedly and flashed a toothy grin.

They crowded into a police car to go to the hotel that had been sitting on the passport. It wasn't one of the larger or more famous ones, said Merve, who was accompanying them.

This was turning out well, after all, thought Claesson. If they could get this over and done with by this evening he could take a later plane tomorrow. Things would work themselves out.

They were heading for the Galata Bridge to cross over to Beyoğlu. The Golden Horn was heaving with large, dull-green waves. The wind had picked up but the sky was still clear, even if the sun was setting.

Merve and the officer behind the wheel were unsure where the street they needed lay. The car trundled down yet another narrow alley, creeping forwards as they tried to read the signs.

"By the way, we're not far from one of the more famous hotels, the Pera Palas," said Merve. "It was built during the age of the Orient Express and is fantastic. A bit run down, but they're renovating like mad and will be ready soon. It's got an Agatha Christie suite that you can see if you like. They say she sat there writing. Atatürk also stayed there."

Claesson nodded.

"Some people make a lot of money from murder," she grinned. "Maybe we should settle for that instead of investigating real ones. It doesn't pay as well."

"Well, all you need to do is know how to write," said Claesson. "People have always been fascinated by cold-blooded murder, disasters, and crazy people. They can't seem to get enough."

"No," said Özen. "And neither can we."

The police car pulled up. The hotel was called the Galata New Hotel and was about as new as it was large. They stepped out. By now the air was cool and refreshing.

The little hotel foyer was empty. They walked over to the dark-stained counter and ringed the bell. They could hear a voice somewhere in the background, as if someone was talking on the phone.

The foyer was the hotel's public face. It gave a good impression, thought Claesson. It was the kind of hotel that he liked to stay at himself. He didn't feel comfortable in the grandiose and luxurious ones; they just made him feel dim-witted and lost.

He walked round. There was a little table in a corner with a desktop computer on it for the hotel guests to surf on. The service was free, a sign in English announced. He opened a door straight ahead of him an inch and peeked into a glazed conservatory that served as a breakfast room and that lay facing a small courtyard, which also looked pleasant. He shut the door, looked around the vestibule again, and noted that the rugs in it were quite beautiful. His knowledge of carpets was extremely rudimentary, but he found himself inspecting them rather than just stepping on them nonetheless. He was able to conclude without blinking that two of the rugs were knotted, no doubt in classical Turkish patterns, and that the third, the smallest, was a woven so-called *kelim*. Its colors were bright, with a lot of red. He liked it the best.

The telephone voice from within the hotel had gone quiet and a woman appeared behind the counter and said something in Turkish.

"How can I help you?" she asked in English.

She was in her sixties and looked charming. Her hair was thick and earlobe length in that cold, gray color that many dark-haired people go. She was wearing black pants and a warm red, long-sleeved top that went right up to her throat.

While Merve told her who they were, the woman pulled her sleeves up with nails the color of blood. Gold bangles decorated with large charms clanked around both wrists. Merve asked her to speak English, if that wasn't too awkward for her. It wasn't.

She was the one who'd called the police, she told them. She turned around and took out a plastic bag from a cabinet behind the counter. Its contents consisted of Carl-Ivar Olsson's passport and a key ring. But no cell phone.

"We did not empty Mr. Olsson's room until yesterday. He was meant to check out the day before. We did not know here he had gone, but we let it go for one day. Maybe he will show up, we thought. We were not full, so it did not matter."

Her smile had faded, and her brown eyes were studying them seriously. Claesson thought that she sounded more acquainted with her guest than one might normally expect.

"Usually, we give the passport back after the first night, but this time we did not do it," she continued. "Mr. Olsson did not leave his room key with reception… with me, that is, or with my brother. He took the key with him and he came and went as he pleased. He usually does this… He would of course be given his passport back when he checked out."

Her eyes drifted again from Özen to Merve before finally landing on Claesson.

"Something serious has happened, I understand," she said quietly at last.

"Yes. Mr. Olsson is dead. Murdered," said Claesson, without going into the difference between murder and manslaughter, and that it was impossible for them to say how they would treat the case.

"Oh!" she ejaculated, pressing a hand, fingers splayed, to her breast. Her pupils seemed to shrink.

"That is terrible." She collected herself. "We have his luggage here behind the counter," she said. "We tidied them all away so that we could clean the room. But maybe that was stupid? We waited for twenty-four hours and thought that he was delayed… It happens. We tried to reach him on his cell phone, but he did not answer. We left a message."

"So Olsson stayed here before?" asked Claesson.

"Oh, yes. Many times."

"How many times, roughly."

She turned her torso and stared at the end wall while counting.

"I cannot say, but he stayed here once a year even during the time when my parents ran the hotel. They are dead, I am afraid, so I cannot ask them. It was over twenty years ago when they passed the hotel on to me and my brother, and Mr. Olsson always came for all these years. Sometimes more than once a year. He almost became a friend of the family."

"Did he stay on his own?"

"Oh, yes. He was always here on his own."

"He never had his wife with him?"

"I did not know, he was married? That is not the kind of question we ask our guests."

"Do you have any idea what he did when he was here?" asked Claesson.

"We never inquire what our guests do," she said proudly. "Mr. Olsson always paid and was a good guest, and that is all that counts. He would often pay for his whole stay upon checking in, even."

"How did he pay?"

"With a card, I presume. I can check."

"And how long did he intend to stay this time?"

She turned toward the computer, tapped some keys.

"A week."

Claesson nodded. His wife said that he was going to be staying four days longer than her. Had he been planning to call and say that something had come up so he could stretch out his visit?

He turned to Özen and asked him in Swedish to make a note that they'd have to ask the wife if this was something he used to do a lot.

They were shown his room, which was now ready for the next guest. A nice room, Claesson thought. A tiny writing desk and a robust, dark wood bedside table, burgundy curtains, and a TV mounted on the wall at the end of the bed, which was wide and covered with a shiny bedspread decorated with tulips. There were also discreet tulips on the walls. There were a lot of tulips in Turkey in general, as this was the tulip's country of origin, he'd learned. He'd seen them flowering freshly and abundantly in parks and on the banks of ditches. In fact, the entire road from the airport was lined with tall tulips of different colors.

But the room wasn't exactly a goldmine for a forensic team. No other guest had stayed in the room since Olsson, and that was all well and good. But the cleaner had done a thorough job and the sheets had been taken to the laundry along with the towels.

They went through his suitcase.

"There's something fishy here," said Claesson, once he'd looked through the contents. "There's no toiletry bag."

Merve went out to her colleague in the car and asked him to cordon off the room anyway. The elegant woman who called herself hotel director had little choice but to consent. Merve would make sure that they'd send a forensic technician, she promised Claesson. He asked her to go through the guest list as well.

"And look for what?"

He shrugged.

"Anything. If you find someone from Sweden, or Scandinavia, it'd be good. Or perhaps a German."

"A German?" asked Özen. "Why a German?"

"I don't know. It just came out, but I guess it's wrong," said Claesson with a smile at Merve, who was writing away in her notebook. She had charisma, he thought. Her ears stuck out slightly. They looked appealing and were emphasized by the way she wore her thick black hair in a ponytail.

But what *had* Olsson been up to during his solitary days in Istanbul? Looking at carpets?

Nah, thought Claesson.

The photo of the quayside in Yeniköy, with all those sumptuous villas reflected in the rippling waters, was burned on his retina. The photo that one of the crew had taken to test out his new phone camera. The photo in which Olsson seemed to be standing waiting for the ferry. With a woman by his side.

She could be any old passenger awaiting the ferry, too. But she could, on the other hand, be someone completely different.

CHAPTER 44

VERONIKA POPPED HER BREAST back into her bra and burped Nora over her shoulder. A wet splodge of excess breast milk landed on her top. She laid her baby daughter in the bassinet and went upstairs to get changed.

She checked the time. She'd have to hurry to the preschool.

As she arrived and was about to go in to pick up Klara, her cell phone rang. It was Cecilia.

"Hi," she said. "Can I call you back in minute? I'm just about to pick up Klara."

She hung up before Cecilia had time to open her mouth. It worried her, but only afterwards.

Was it something important? After all, it had sounded like it, hadn't it?

As soon as she'd enticed Klara away from her friends, who were about to sit down to eat, and they were outside the Bumble Bee preschool, she dialed Cecilia back. Veronika pushed the stroller with one hand while Klara walked sulkily alongside. Cecilia didn't answer.

They crossed Kolbergavägen and went into Coop supermarket. Klara had forgotten all about the preschool by now, and cheerily helped Veronika with the groceries. She enjoyed it and loved to do the big weekly shopping with Claes. Veronika just took some milk and bread for lunch, as she couldn't be bothered to carry home any more than that. Just didn't feel like it. She hoped that Claes would call and say that he was on his way home.

She tried giving Cecilia a call again when they left the shop. No reply. They walked home. Klara was whining a bit, she was hungry, but Nora was asleep. That kid was incredible.

Veronika couldn't get Cecilia out of her mind. Tried calling again. She had to get hold of her. What had she wanted?

Veronika knew that she easily got distressed when she couldn't reach her daughter. The indescribable anxiety when she couldn't get hold of Cecilia that time came flooding back. Then she was lying unconscious and injured and no one knew where she was. Experiences like that left you marked for life. On the other hand, Cecilia usually just called for a chat. Relax, she told herself.

She set out bowls of milk. Klara climbed up into her highchair by herself, and taking hold of the box, poured some muesli into her bowl. Veronika was too slow, and Klara gave herself far too much, which had probably been her intention. She smiled at Klara who had merrily started to pick the raisins and nuts out with her fingers.

"Have some of the milk too, sweetheart," she said, stroking her soft hair. Klara looked at her innocently, and continued to stubbornly pick out the bits she liked best.

Veronika picked up her phone again and pressed in Cecilia's number.

This time she answered.

CHAPTER 45

IT WAS FRIDAY MORNING in Istanbul and a cooler wind was slipping in though the crack in the window at the police station. It looked like it was going to be a hot day, but at this time of year you never could tell, Merve Turpan had just said. It was still only May, and the sunshine could easily be banished by rain and colder winds. In July and August, on the other hand, it got really hot, she said. Or, by Swedish standards, as hot as hell, thought Claesson. Though here in Istanbul there was at least some reprieve from the heat, as the city lay with the sea in all directions.

Claesson had slept heavily that night, even through the call to prayer. He'd left Özen and Merve yesterday evening, saying they were off somewhere, he hadn't paid much attention to where – they were adults after all – while he went back to the hotel to get some sleep. They'd have to get up early tomorrow to catch the flight home – this Claesson had decided as he ate breakfast alone: coffee, yogurt, bread, feta cheese, olives, tomatoes, and cucumber. But he hadn't yet imparted this information to his colleague. Though Özen knew, alright. It would soon be the end of his halcyon days. Of the chirping and Turkish delight.

Özen was nowhere to be seen in the breakfast room, but surely the lad had the sense to turn up at the police station in time, he thought. Otherwise he was prepared to give him a wake-up call.

But Özen appeared, shortly followed by Merve, but with enough of an interval to make it seem like they'd arrived at the station from different directions. He doubted they'd had much sleep, but they were glowing nonetheless, noted Claesson as his eyes scanned their sallow faces.

He smiled at them just as Superintendent Fuat Karaoğlu stepped through the door, announcing that he intended to take part in the day's morning meeting. He'd heard the Swedes were due home the next day; Claesson had called him to say that he figured they could continue their collaboration from Sweden.

Özen looked like someone had just punched him in the face. He'd just have to take it on the chin.

"Our collaboration will continue. You have many threads to pull together at home in..." and then something came out of Karaoğlu's mouth that was meant to sound like Oskarshamn. "You have, you know, your Turkish contact man," he said with a friendly nod to Özen. "That makes things much easier. The trial, if one is ever called that is... I mean, if we ever find a suspect for the manslaughter, or murder, or whatever you will treat the case as, will take place here in Istanbul. That is something I will look forward to. Turkish law will apply," he said, and Claesson nodded.

Crimes are always atoned for in the country where they are committed and tried in accordance with the local laws, which no doubt had made many people regret their attempt to smuggle drugs or guns into foreign countries with legislation that did not really correspond to the Swedish one.

"But certainly our prisons are already full... What is it like in your country?" wondered Karaoğlu.

Claesson had to admit that it was the same in Sweden. Overcrowded prisons.

Luckily, the discussion didn't move on to more or less humane prisons. Claesson was of the decided opinion that there was a critical difference between the treatment of offenders, as it was so politely called, in Turkey and Sweden. But he could be wrong.

His musings were interrupted by the arrival of the forensic technician, who was called Cem something, a surname that had failed to stick in Claesson's mind. He gave them a quick rundown on the evidence, or rather lack of really clear evidence, that they'd found. The shoeprint they'd discovered on the floor next to the body came from a very common kind of sports shoe of an international make of Taiwanese manufacture. A kind of shoe that you could buy both in Turkey and in Sweden, in other words. And anyway, they'd only been able to make out half the tread pattern. It was probably a men's size 10 ½.

"Is that a common shoe size in Sweden?"

Claesson and Özen looked at each other.

"I wear a 10," said Claesson. "I'm of average Swedish height. There are many men in Sweden who are taller than me, but shorter too. I'd say that 10 ½ is pretty common."

"We believe that the killer had pulled the knife blade out and disappeared before the blood had really started to pump copiously out of the wound and run down onto the floor," continued Cem.

Claesson thought that it must have been a bloodbath. He pictured in his mind again Olsson sitting there dozing in peace and quiet out by the railing while being stroked by the warm breeze. It had been afternoon, and perhaps Olsson had been taking a nap, much as he himself liked to do given half a chance. To just lean back his office chair, feet up on an open drawer, and drift away for five, maybe fifteen minutes, no more. The killer who crept up on the snoozing Olsson in his size 10 ½ stuck his knife in him so quickly that the carpet dealer had hardly had time to blink. Snatched the bag that Olsson was seen holding on the quay in Yeniköy, withdrew the knife, tossed it into the sea and walked nonchalantly and coolly away.

A professional, he thought.

"A man with ice in his stomach," he said, translating the Swedish expression aloud into English.

Judging by the strange looks on Karaoğlu's and Merve's faces, he realized that it was not one that people here used. He rephrased himself.

"The killer had to be a very cool and composed," he said.

"They usually are," said Karaoğlu. "People with no barriers."

Cem left them and they reviewed the previous day's events. They began with the Arkadia Hotel, where the Olssons had been staying. They hadn't yet gone through the lists of all the guests who were staying there at the same time, but Merve and Özen would try to do so later.

Then they briefed him on their visit to the Galata New Hotel.

"A breakthrough in the investigation," said Karaoğlu, and the others nodded and the temperature rose a few degrees.

"I've already sent off the Swedish names from the hotel, ten all told, to Oskarshamn to have a check run on them. Did it last night," said Özen.

Good boy, thought Claesson. Efficient.

"Maybe we'll have time to check out the hotels near the Galata today?" suggested Özen.

And maybe there'd be time to take a quick tour of the Blue Mosque, if nothing else, thought Claesson. Or Hagia Sofia. Or to go down to Eminönü to breathe some sea air and watch the ferries.

Then he gave Karaoğlu an account of their visit to the carpet dealer in the Grand Bazaar – a pleasant experience, he felt – to have the existence of the valuable rug confirmed. Olsson had picked it up the day before his wife had left for home, but she had no idea what kind of rug it was. He summed up his interview with her from the day before.

"Nor had she seen any suspect rug packed away in a classic carpet bag, she claimed," said Claesson.

"Did you feel as if she was telling the truth?" Karaoğlu asked.

"Hard to say," said Claesson. "It seems to fit. Olsson was holding a bag like that in the photo from the quay in Yeniköy, and that was the day after his wife had left. It's possible that she never came anywhere near it. Maybe Olsson had hidden it in a cupboard in the hotel over night and took it with him when he moved to the Galata New Hotel. But it's not there amongst his remaining personal effects… Er, yes, one thing we noted there was that his suitcase was still there, his clothes and some paperbacks. But no toiletry bag."

Karaoğlu nodded.

"Maybe he had stayed over in Yeniköy," he said.

"Who knows," said Claesson with a shrug. "As you know, we sat here and talked to the family after the identification, but nothing in particular emerged other than that his wife had no idea who the woman in the photo was. But I thought she reacted anyway."

"Really?"

"She stiffened. Blushed," said Claesson, drawing his hand over his own face.

Karaoğlu nodded again to show he understood.

"Someone her husband knew… a woman, young too. Can't have been much fun for his wife to see," he said.

But still the possibility that it was a total stranger who had nothing whatsoever to do with Olsson was just as great, if not greater, thought Claesson.

"And what do you believe about the rug?" asked Karaoğlu. "Who paid for it?"

"We're looking through Olsson's bank accounts in Sweden," said Claesson. "We're talking a lot of money. The carpet dealer in the

Grand Bazaar had had the money deposited into his company account, he said, and that can be checked."

"We will get onto it," said Karaoğlu.

"Neither his assistant in the carpet shop back in Oskarshamn nor the dealer in the Grand Bazaar had any idea who'd ordered the rug from Olsson," Claesson continued. "It wasn't something you asked, apparently. There's a certain degree of discretion when it comes to carpets."

"He cannot have bought it for himself?" wondered Karaoğlu.

Claesson and Özen looked at each other.

"Maybe he is a genuine carpet collector," continued Karaoğlu. "They would do almost anything... exactly like all compulsive collectors. If they have money they can pay out a fortune."

"But we haven't got that feeling from Sweden," said Claesson. "Not that Olsson was a collector in that sense, or that he was a rich man... But people have a lot of secrets. Olsson had a stockroom in his shop, of course, and it's possible that he amassed a fortune there in carpets without anyone knowing, not even the woman who works there... Perfect if you want to keep thieves away. We'll have to ask someone to go and check out what the carpets there are worth."

He stroked his neck with his hand, as he liked to do when thinking.

"I'm sure we can find someone from Stockholm or somewhere who can value his stock."

He thought of *The Antiques Roadshow*. One of the men on that tv show was no doubt a carpet expert.

They separated and decided to meet up again at a quarter to three.

Claesson asked Özen and Merve if they could take it upon themselves to check the hotels again to get more information on the guests. Maybe even get around to cross-checking with Sweden. He couldn't have given them a better present. To work together. To be left to themselves. To be free of the boss.

They'll sit languishing over a cup of tea or a plate of *kofta*. If they even gave themselves time to eat, that is. If the widow had still been in town, he could have had another chat with her – he felt there was a need for it – but she wasn't. She'd left for Sweden earlier that day.

That left only one thing to do. To go sightseeing.

Why not mix business and pleasure?

He walked through the crowded quarter down to the sea, forcing his way randomly through the swarm of people that moved like some viscous semi-solid. People were selling things on either side of the street – underwear, towels, bedclothes, leather belts, bags, plastic, synthetic or leather shoes, none of which looked comfortable. In between were cafes. They smelled good, and he started to feel hungry, but dared not buy anything. He thought about his stomach. It'd be aggravating if he got sick on his last day.

He arrived at an open place and a huge mosque. A garden dotted with pleasant-looking restaurants was on the other side. But he was too restless to sit down, and continued down to the wide quayside close to the abutment of the Galata Bridge. The crowd was, impossibly, even thicker there: it was apparently where everyone passed by or met up.

Trolleys squealed in the background. The odd boat whistle sounded. The ferries lay densely packed, each with its own destination in one of the myriad directions in this kingdom of the sea. He liked what he saw. He liked it very much indeed.

He took out his cell phone and called Özen to ask him to find out where the ferries that went up toward the Bosporus were berthed. He could hear him consult Merve.

"You're to go to berth number three. Are you thinking of taking a ride up there?"

Özen breathed down the line. He'd probably have loved to have gone with him.

"Yes. If there's one that goes at a reasonable time."

"But you won't have time to go all the way there and back."

"I know. I was thinking of just going as far as Yeniköy."

He heard Özen talk to Merve again.

"OK. You can take a taxi from there, or go by *dolmus*."

"OK, and what's that?"

"A kind of shared taxi with fixed prices. Minibuses, often white. You'll find them. The buses don't leave until they're full, otherwise they pick people up on the way. It can be quite an experience if you've got time. If you have, go to Taksim and take a taxi from there. Anyway taxis are cheap."

"Good, thanks."

"Merve says that you get cakes, sweets, and stuff like that on board, but no food. Just so you know."

He turned toward berth number three, forcing his way through the crowd and almost tripping over a man grilling fish. Unable to contain himself any longer, he bought a hot, freshly grilled fish stuffed into white bread, and a Coke. He ate and drank as he pressed on. It tasted good.

Young boys tried to entice him onto diverse ferry trips that he wasn't interested in. Asking people as he went, he eventually came to a ticket booth. The ferry was leaviyng in ten minutes. He was in luck.

As he boarded he saw the name of the ferry. Thought he recognized it. Could he really be this lucky?

He swallowed the last of the fish burger, or whatever it was called, pulled out his phone again and called Özen, who asked Merve for the name of the ferry on which Olsson had spent his last luckless moments on earth.

"*Tirowor*, she says."

"Thanks!"

Bingo.

He'd been given a brochure with his ticket, and learned from the English translation that the ferry made three trips a day during peak season. Yeniköy lay in the section that was called Central Bosporus. The ferry made six stops in all, but instead of going right up to the Black Sea, it turned around and chugged back the way it came. Yeniköy was the third stop from Istanbul and was on the European side. But the boat zigzagged between the shores along the narrow strait.

Had Olsson also taken the ferry to Yeniköy, and not just from it? Or had he gone the whole journey, remaining on the ferry as it returned? He could, of course, have disembarked on the way up and taken a later ferry back. The rules allowed one stop off; if you wanted to do more, you had to buy a new ticket. Karaoğlu had said they'd questioned the crew on the other ferries, too, but were none the wiser about how Olsson had traveled. No more than just the photo from the quay in Yeniköy and the testimonies of the tea-seller and the guy in the *kiosk*.

The ferry put out, its engine throbbing. The bow plowed the water so that it frothed.

The boat was far from packed with tourists, although there was quite a crowd on board, and quite a line had formed by the onboard *kiosk*. Claesson had already recognized the man behind the counter. He looked exactly like he did in the photos that Karaoğlu and Merve had projected onto the screen at the police station that first night in Istanbul.

He couldn't recall his name. It was something beginning with E. But he didn't call Özen to ask. The man looked friendly. Good-natured, with a tanned, glossy crown and hair that curled by his ears.

When it was his turn in line, Claesson pointed at the ice cream sign. The man could have been in his forties and was lacking some molars, although his front teeth were big and strong-looking, as were the canines, which, incidentally, are the last to go. He'd learned that from the forensics expert. The man nodded in comprehension, opened the freezer, and fished out an ice cream pop wrapped in shiny paper.

Ergün.

The name came to Claesson as soon as he'd turned his back on him. Ergün, with a surname beginning with B, that was it! But he had no use for the name. He wasn't going to address him. He didn't have the authority. Or the inclination. He was enjoying being an observer.

Claesson strolled around as he ate, praying to himself that his stomach could take it. Eggs and cream, common bacterial substrates.

He stood by the rail watching the entire city show itself in all its glory before disappearing. A magnificent view. There were rudimentary wooden benches to sit on if you could take the outside air. He examined the long bench toward the stern. Lashed down at its far end were the lifeboats, probably of rubber but protected by a hard shell that you could lean against. There was a free space there. In Olsson's place, in other words.

He squeezed past some Germans that were sitting there, unaware that they were at a murder scene. But Claesson knew, and he confirmed it solemnly to himself in a way that he rarely did. Although he was jaded by now, he needed to do this maneuver, probably to heighten his awareness and intensify his sense of presence, since he had not been here before. Not been first on the scene as he usually was, but had had to make do with photos and his own powers of imagination – his fantasy, if you will.

The smell of the sea and the diesel engines reached him when he sank down onto the bench. A splash of spray landed on his cheek and he wiped it away as he leaned against the wall of the after-saloon, realizing that when Olsson had sat here he had had a view of the Marmara Sea instead, since the ferry was heading into Istanbul rather than away from it. The incongruous thing was that none of the tourists on board had any idea about what had happened less than a week previously. All traces were gone. People were smiling with the wind in their hair.

The first stop was on the European side and was called Paşa. Buildings flowed uninterruptedly into each other as Istanbul sprawled into its various suburbs. Next to Paşa was a village called Beşiktaş, he read on the map, a name he actually recognized. Beşiktaş was one of Turkey's better football teams, and played in black and white striped jerseys.

They continued on under the Bosporus Bridge, which linked the European and the Asian sides of Istanbul. A shoe-shiner had come on board and was offering his services, but Claesson's sports shoes were suited for neither polish nor buffer. Magnificent buildings could be seen on either side of the Bosporus: palaces, mosques, forts, towers. There was nothing for it but to gape.

A man bearing a round tray came up to him, squeezing himself between the rail and the bench Claesson was sitting on.

"Tea?"

Claesson looked at him and nodded, and dug into his pants pocket for a lira. He was a young man, barely twenty. Black, neatly cut hair, slightly sad brown eyes. His face was pale; he clearly hadn't seen much of the sun recently, thought Claesson. Or perhaps he'd been sleeping badly? Bad conscience? The young tea-seller was called Ilyas Bank, Claesson told himself. It was a name he remembered.

One week ago tomorrow, the man who had just received the lira note and who was now handing him his tea had just had the surprise of his life. Here, on this very seat, thought Claesson, he found a dead man. Or half dead, with a body still warm and blood pumping copiously out of his gut.

Claesson watched Ilyas Bank as he returned seemingly indifferently to the after-saloon with his tray.

As they approached Yeniköy, it struck him that Olsson might simply have taken the ferry because he enjoyed the boat ride, nothing more. It was pleasant and soothing. He could see the city spread itself out, all the beautiful buildings.

All the beautiful *yalis*, he thought. "They are very, very beautiful," as Merve Turpan would have said.

They really were quite beautiful, these tall, ornate nineteenth-century wood-built, multi-story villas. They stood there huddled together, reflected in the sea, with windows and verandas overlooking the waters of the Bosporus.

The quay was bathed in sunlight, and the heat smote him, but no pretty Turkish woman came to greet him as he disembarked.

By three o'clock, they were all assembled once again at the police station, and a fairly weary troop they made. The plane would be leaving inexorably for home the next day. The morning flight. Claesson reminded Özen of this in Swedish.

"And we're not rescheduling again, OK?"

Karaoğlu wasn't present, but had conveyed via Merve his wish to invite them all to try some Ottoman fare that evening at a restaurant that Karaoğlu himself particularly liked.

"Unfortunately they don't serve alcohol, just so you know," said Merve with a look that anticipated their disappointment. "During the Ottoman era, most people here were Muslims, and Muslims don't drink. At least not the devout ones."

"That doesn't matter in the slightest," said Claesson, and asked her to thank Karaoğlu for the invitation.

Mohammed knew what he was doing. If you're going to keep a large, unruly population in check, you couldn't allow them to get drunk.

Merve left them, so Özen and Claesson could return to speaking Swedish.

"We can start with the hotel that Olsson was staying at when he died…the Galata New Hotel," said Özen. "There were fewer than ten other Swedes there at the time of the murder, but it's unlikely they've got anything to do with it."

He placed another sheet of paper in front of Claesson listing the names and birthdates of the guests and details of where they lived.

"Have you managed to get all this from Sweden?"

"Yep!" said Özen, not without a modicum of pride.

Claesson skimmed through the list. Every one of them was born between 1937 and 1955.

"They stayed one night and were in a group that was then going on to Uzbekistan, or so the owner thought. And she was right," said Özen. "I've spoken to the tour operator. The hotel owner, that older woman we met, gave me the number of the travel agency." He thumbed through his papers and pulled out a new sheet. "This is it, and it's in Stockholm, as you can see. I started by going onto the net to check it out. They arrange tour packages for small groups to special places around the world. It really made me want to travel! They're doing the Silk Road from Istanbul to Beijing, they said at the Stockholm office, and they'll be away for a month. A long trip by train and bus and sometimes plane over Central Asia and the whole of China, and they won't be home for another three weeks from today."

"And you don't think that any of them got round to committing a murder on the way?" said Claesson.

Özen shook his head.

"I asked Stockholm to contact the Swedish guide, which they did, and apparently they're somewhere in China now. I spoke to the guide and she said that of course the group didn't all stick together the whole time in Istanbul, these kinds of trip attract typical individualists, but there was no way, she said, that one of them would have had time to hop on a ferry through the Bosporus."

"Then let's put them to one side for the time being," said Claesson. "They'll probably be casting suspicious looks at each other for the rest of their trip," he added mirthfully.

"At the other hotel, opposite the Galata, there were two Swedish guests staying at the time of Olsson's visit and death," continued Özen, handing Claesson yet another sheet of paper.

"Karl Öberg and Bengt-Ove Nordin," Claesson read aloud. "Have you gotten around to checking them out?"

"No. We'll have to do it when we come home."

It was as if they'd both run out of steam.

"Let's call it a day," said Claesson. "This is as far as we can get. We'll keep in touch with Istanbul… I'll leave that to you," he said with a grin at Özen, who was staring at the table.

They returned to their hotel to stretch out for a while. Claesson was grateful for the jacket he'd brought. It had smoothed itself out on a hanger and would be perfect for their farewell dinner that evening.

One thing was sure, he thought before dropping off. This was a place he'd be coming back to.

Chapter 46

IT WAS APPROACHING FOUR P.M. on this slow day, and Martin Lerde was sitting in the Oskarshamn police station with a man in front of him who was claiming that his wife was missing. He'd have preferred to have gone home. It was Friday. Beer and something nice to eat in solitude, some movies and then sleeping late in the morning. Not bad! Even though it could've been better. A soft body to cozy up to on the sofa. . . .

Martin had already had two jokers today on the line, people with totally absurd stories. One of them was about a green fluorescent glow from a man who then disappeared in a puff of smoke, like Christ ascending to heaven. When the caller heard that Lerde was a mite skeptical about the story's veracity, he elaborated with dangerous light rays from outer space that he had to warn everyone in Oskarshamn about. If not the entire nation.

The other caller went on in great detail about a neighbor who was spraying an odorless gas through his keyhole. Last week, there was one who'd seen snakes crawl up out of his toilet bowl. It must be horrible to live with delusions like these, thought Lerde. Nonetheless, he'd reckoned he was done for the day.

But now there was this missing wife. That was a little more tangible. Simpler to deal with, to be honest. At least there was an investigative procedure for missing persons.

His wife had never just taken off like that before, protested the husband.

It didn't help matters that Martin Lerde was finding it difficult to keep his mind as active as it should be. His ambition was always to be a cut above everyone else, but he'd had far too little sleep for that recently.

His girl didn't want him, and Lerde felt he could sympathize with the concerned husband's emotional frame of mind, at least at first. His life was simply slip-sliding away, although this interpretation he kept to himself. He knew the signs. The greasy countenance, the lusterless hair, the stooped shoulders. Not even his pumped-up biceps helped.

There was, however, something about the man's manner that irritated Martin Lerde. And since he was tired, it got on his nerves even more. The officious tone and the offensive body language, combined with the man's inflated humility. Or feigned humility, more like. The wad of *snus* under his upper lip looked as if it had melded with his body in despair.

It wasn't that Martin was a moralist, but he didn't think it appropriate for a man to sit there with a bulbous swelling under his nose when his wife, who'd given him two kids, had just run off. Not if he really loved her. She should be worth more, he thought, and listened with half an ear to how the man had awakened that morning, Friday that is, at a quarter past eight to be exact, and found the other side of the bed empty. He couldn't find her anywhere. He'd looked in the garden and searched the garage and woodshed. She wasn't even anywhere in Bråbo, he claimed. Nor in Kulltorp, Bjälebo, or Saxtorp, either. Nor in Applekulla, but there were only a handful of farms there so he'd driven right through. He'd even driven to Krokshult to look for her.

"I've not been able to do anything worthwhile all day," he moaned.

Apparently, looking for a missing wife was something the man didn't consider "worthwhile," Lerde thought disdainfully.

"Did you knock on people's doors and asked them if they'd seen her, or how did you go about looking for her?" he wondered.

"Nah, I mostly just drove around, you know? Should I have done that? Knocked on doors, I mean? Isn't that the job of the police?"

"And the kids?"

"They're with my mother. We'd planned a cozy evening together, the missus and me, yesterday. And so then I asked them to say with Mom while I went around in the car looking… This is such a goddam embarrassment!"

"So did you have… a nice, cozy evening?"

The man's face got stuck in neutral for a moment. Lerde registered that and placed it in a pigeonhole in his well-furnished brain.

"Sure we did. But that was last night. It was this morning, wasn't it, when I couldn't find her."

"No fight?"

"Nah. What would we have fought about?"

Martin gave a little shrug.

"People do. And it was this morning when you discovered her missing?"

"Yeah."

"What time was it you said you discovered it?"

"Around nine, I'd reckon."

He'd just said a quarter past eight, thought Lerde.

"Reckon? What, didn't you check the time?"

The man grew befuddled.

"Er, I usually wake up earlier. Around six. I start work early, you see, around seven, but I'd told the boys that I'd be home a little later."

"So, what, you'd taken half the day off?"

"Yeah. I'm self-employed, see… I've got a lot of work going, plumbing, pipes, and stuff…"

"You said you'd taken time off. What were you going to do?"

"Er, it was really just so that we'd get a bit of time to ourselves, the missus and me."

"On a Friday afternoon?"

"Yeah, and?"

"So on the Thursday you were working as normal."

"Yeah… No, not really."

"No?"

"I picked the missus up a little earlier."

"Where does she work?"

"At the hospital."

"So you picked her up there, then?"

"Yeah."

"Have you checked there? Asked anyone if they've seen her?"

The man who'd given his name as Pär – with a pretentious ä rather than the usual e – suddenly fell silent.

"Would you like me to repeat the question?" wondered Martin Lerde.

"No! I haven't asked there," he said irritably.

That stung, thought Martin sitting up, suddenly smelling one hell of a rat.

He glanced at the name of the missing wife again. Tina Rosenkvist. And he noted again that they lived in Bråbo.

Hadn't something happened there just the other day?

Uh-oh.

CHAPTER 47

BIRGITTA WAS SITTING in the funeral director's office. He was a polite, gentle man whom she knew a little from before. One of his daughters had gone to the same school as Lotta, but that was not something they took up now. She'd called him as soon as the office opened. Sure, he could see her, despite its being a Saturday. No problem.

Johan was with her. Lotta had such a backlog of work to do in Stockholm that it would've been difficult for her to join them. Birgitta didn't have the heart to say that it really didn't matter. In actual fact, she'd have preferred to sit there alone and decide everything herself without having to take the children and their various opinions into account. Although it was mostly Lotta who gave them.

In some peculiar way she got closer to Carl-Ivar when she wasn't surrounded by people, she thought as she sat there on her upholstered chair. She longed to be left in peace. To be alone.

Brochures in which funeral assistance was couched in words like *empathy* and *dignity* lay in small piles at one end of the table.

She felt, strangely enough, strong. Or was she just numb and refusing to connect with her feelings? She didn't think she needed that much support right now.

The funeral was set for a Friday, a mere fortnight away, which the man in the dark gray suit considered reasonable. That would be three weeks after they'd found Carl-Ivar dead in Istanbul. His funeral was to be held in the chapel in the Western Cemetery, and followed by coffee in the Parish Hall by the Old Churchyard.

Johan didn't say much, just hemmed and hawed mostly. But when they got to the choice of coffin, a folder showing the different models available having been placed in front of them, he cleared his throat and placed his index finger on a plain yet elegant design. But it was one of the cheaper kinds made of fiberboard rather than solid wood.

Oh, dear, thought Birgitta, what will people think?

"But why *that* one?" she asked in a whisper so the funeral director wouldn't hear.

"I'll leave you two alone to browse in your own time," he said considerately and left the room.

"It's only going to be incinerated anyway," said Johan. "Dad would think it too much to have one of these," he said, turning pages to get to the solid wood coffins.

The younger generation had a completely different take on life, she thought. And maybe that was a good thing. She could also tell that Johan wasn't suffering any bad conscience toward Carl-Ivar. Nor any kind of ambivalence that needed compensating for with an extravagant funeral. Johan and his father had always got on well together.

That his body was to be cremated was beyond all discussion. It was one of the few things that Carl-Ivar had actually expressed any desire about. "When I die, I want to be cremated, and that's that!" They could both hear his voice.

It finally came round to the obituary. Perhaps his death should have been announced earlier, but the very idea was distressing; and anyway, there had been so much uncertainty.

Burying someone who'd been stabbed to death was a very different thing to interring a husband who'd died of disease or old age.

The funeral director told them that it was by no means too late to publish an obituary. It was actually quite common for it to take time. But he said nothing about what all three in the room already knew: that most people were aware of what had happened anyway, with or without an announcement in the paper. You just had to open the newspaper. The murder had become something of a serial.

And that's exactly why an obituary is even more important, thought Birgitta determinedly. Simply because it would make the loss of Carl-Ivar more serious and tangible. It would give him redress, somehow, for all the speculations being made, above all, by the tabloid press. There was much more to it than just violent murder, blood, flashing knife blades, and mysterious circumstances in a far-away land. Than things that teased the imagination, but did nothing to call to mind the reliable, and in a way scarcely exciting person that Carl-Ivar had been. He really had been a typical, run-of-the-mill "Svensson," even though he was an Olsson, and she'd been satisfied with that.

She broke her reverie when an unpleasant chill passed through her. It wasn't quite true, she thought, but no one need know.

She started to browse listlessly through all the symbols that were available nowadays for decorating obituaries.

"What do you think?" she said turning to Johan, who shrugged.

"A carpet, maybe," he said at last, and she couldn't tell if he was pulling her leg or not.

But the undertaker took him seriously, he'd heard worse, and bent over the pages of the file to help them look – by which time she was already imagining an Oriental carpet hovering in the air with its fringes wafting out in both directions.

She smiled. On a carpet like that Carl-Ivar could fly wherever he wanted, she thought. Perhaps even all the way up to heaven for some well-deserved peace. Oh yes, she'd comprehended more than he'd realized…

But there was no carpet.

"I am terribly sorry," said the funeral director. "Maybe I can see to it that the newspapers arrange one for you."

But Birgitta and Johan thought it was just too much trouble. They finally chose a simple filled cross.

"Everyone recognizes that," she said. "Clear and *dignified.*"

On the car ride home with half an almond ring in a pastry bag beside her, she began to wonder what to do with the carpet shop. And no less urgently: what she would do with Annelie. She liked the girl and the shop *was* doing well at the moment. Disasters created publicity.

She hadn't spoken to Annelie since coming home from Istanbul. She couldn't really bring herself to do it yet. She could wait before making up her mind, at least until after the estate inventory deeds had been drawn up. The children had to have their say. She wondered how she'd make ends meet now. It had been Carl-Ivar who'd looked after all that, and a widow's and nurse's pension didn't stretch that far. But now at least she had the consolation of a backup. Thank God for the black cloth bag… She smiled to herself, and couldn't help seeing it as compensation, of sorts, for all of Carl-Ivar's escapades down there in Turkey.

As she drew up into the driveway, the rain stopped. She picked up the bag from the pastry shop, slammed the car door shut, and entered the house. She'd hardly had time to hang up her thin summer jacket before there was a knock at the door. Not a ring. She knew who it was, opened, and sure enough there he was. Sven had turned up once before that past week, since Carl-Ivar had been found dead.

And he now, of course, had his eye out for her.

She let him in and didn't ask after Agneta, or Nettan, as he called his wife. She was at work, Birgitta assumed, who didn't want her neighbor's wife in the house even by name. Not if it wasn't necessary. How Sven spent his days of retirement was up to him.

"Can I get you some coffee?"

Yes, he'd love some, he said. She went into the kitchen and filled the filter. He placed his hands on the kitchen table, leaned forwards, and squinted out through the window. A large Volvo was passing, he announced.

"A Cross Country, not cheap," he said.

She wasn't listening. She cut up the almond ring.

"You know what's happened to them, right?" he asked then.

"Who?"

"The neighbors, the ones doing the total renovation down by the water. He died when you were in Istanbul. Too."

She stopped what she was doing and turned to him. There was something not right about this, she could feel it.

"It was extraordinary, but he had a heart attack as he was sitting on his lawn mower. I suppose he couldn't get off, and if he screamed, his wife certainly didn't hear him," Sven continued.

She stared at him.

"He was so young. No more than, what, forty? But he didn't look after himself, I suppose. He was over-stressed... You have to make choices in life, you know."

He looked at her.

"What's the matter? Did I say something wrong?"

She opened her mouth, but shut it again. Was she psychic, on top of everything else? She swallowed.

"How awful," she said lamely instead but with no intention of asking if he'd driven it into the neighbor's pool. Sven would think she was out of her mind. And if he *had*, he would have said so. Incidents like that quickly spread.

She hurriedly set the cups out in the living room, which looked out onto the back of the garden and was more private.

The phone rang. A man's voice told her that she'd won a rug. Her ears pricked up. Didn't he sound a little incoherent?

"Won? What do you mean?" She hadn't entered a lottery or anything, but on the other hand her head had been in such a muddle recently that she had little idea of what she had and hadn't done. And a rug? "I've got enough rugs," she replied.

But he insisted, and said he'd soon be popping by to show her some items for her to choose from.

Oh, for Heaven's sake, she thought. "Go on then," she said to get rid of him, and hung up.

"Who was that?" asked Sven.

"Pah, it was nobody." She couldn't be bothered to give an account of the call; even more so to reveal her own helplessness. The fact that she wasn't woman enough to stand up to any old person – be it her male neighbors or rug salesmen.

The almond ring was lying cut up in thin slices, glistening invitingly in the breadbasket. She didn't usually eat such unhealthy things, but right now it was as if everything had fallen apart, and suddenly her mastery of both temptation and bodily functions no longer gave her the same satisfaction. Compared to Carl-Ivar, she'd been a paragon of health and fitness. They'd competed with each other more than she'd been willing to realize. He, *the special one*, with a profound knowledge and feeling for quality and style. She, *the able one*, practical and healthy.

But what did all that matter now? She bathed silently in the calm that Sven was radiating across the coffee table. She could feel his warmth even without touching him.

Just as she was about to take a slice of almond ring the doorbell rang. She excused herself and asked Sven to wait on the sofa while she went to answer it. On the doorstep stood a man with a rolled-up rug under his arm. He entered without invitation, and a woman slipped in behind him. Something matted, registered Birgitta, without really seeing who she was.

And then everything happened very quickly. The man, clearly – to put it bluntly – one of the great unwashed, rolled out the rug and held it out in front of him.

A moth-eaten old prayer rug! What was going on?

The woman, whom she'd merely glimpsed, had disappeared into the house.

"Sven," she called. "Get into the bedroom!"

The man with the rug hesitated then dropped his arms, though without letting go of the edge of the rug. It was then she noticed that he was lacking a finger on his right hand and she was distracted.

The woman jumped into the hall like a flea. She skidded to a halt, however, and stared at Birgitta Olsson.

"Nilla?" Birgitta exclaimed and surprised herself that she'd remembered the name of the patient she'd tended to a few days ago.

Quicker than a cat from a tub they were out again, the man without a finger and her patient Nilla.

Birgitta rushed after them, but Sven, the coward, didn't want to show his face. She ran down the street, as agile and light-footed as a hind, but the thieves were quicker, sprinting away with hair and clothes flapping behind them. Birgitta watched the rug roll disappear round the corner down on Strandvägen and gave up the chase.

She walked back, slowly so as to catch her breath. And to let her anger subside.

Sven was standing in the hall.

"You have to call the police," he said.

"And say what? They won't believe me."

"Nonsense."

But the call had already been registered by the police, who were keeping tabs on all incoming and outgoing telephone traffic – with her consent, of course. Part of their efforts to find Carl-Ivar's killer.

When Sven returned home an hour or so later, she wondered if he would tell Agneta what had happened.

Probably not. For that would mean revealing his occasional secret visits. Otherwise what had happened was quite a story!

Nilla's haggard face dropped into her mind later as she sat in front of the old TV in Johan's room watching the early news followed by the local news. She wanted to see if more people had fallen victim to the trickster with the rug.

She'd left the main TV in the sitting room standing like a black, highly polished altar. Carl-Ivar was the only one who could get the thing to work. Expensive, recordable with three remotes that were to be used in a *special* order, otherwise nothing would happen. This special order Carl-Ivar had never noted down. She'd just have to call in somebody, perhaps Johan would take pity on her. But otherwise the old one was fine. Good enough for her, anyway.

She pulled the angora blanket tighter round herself. There was nothing on the news about rug hustlers. Damn drugs, she thought in her next breath. They steal everything, all common sense, and leave the body an empty shell.

Anyway, who *was* that guy? Her memory worked. She recalled the image of the boy she'd once nursed. That was a long time ago. Bruised and with a hunted look, he'd tried to settle down in the far too large hospital bed. Adjusting his arms and legs, trying to find the least tender part of his battered torso. Was he four or five? Then, that time?

She remembered that she'd relieved the assistant nurse who was sitting on the edge of the bed. The lamp was shielded, the nightfall gray. The boy jerked now and then and tossed his head from side to side on his pillow, perhaps in the throes of a nightmare. They'd given him a painkiller, junior aspirin probably, since that was what they mostly used back then. It wasn't much, but sometimes they had an unwarranted fear of powerful analgesics and just let the little children suffer instead.

Finally he settled, his bandaged hand lying as white as snow on the pillow by his head. He was missing a finger. A pair of pincers had done their job. How could he, this man who was meant to be his father?

She'd stroked his forehead and bent down to give him a peck on the cheek. She couldn't help herself.

No one saw what she'd done, that she'd kissed a sleeping child who wasn't hers. It wouldn't have been considered appropriate. But even then she knew that the image of this little patient would stay with her for many years. Perhaps forever.

He was grown up now. The kiss she'd given him had, of course, been in vain. Life hadn't been kind to him.

She breathed deeply. It just wasn't fair!

But who said things had to be fair?

CHAPTER 48

CECILIA WAS SPEAKING UNCHARACTERISTICALLY quickly. There was a distinct zip in her voice.

Wasn't her daughter sounding like her old self? That healthy, happy babble, a sound that she'd almost forgotten. How she'd missed it, she realized now. Veronika could feel the corners of her mouth tingle and twitch, her glee rise.

She'd seen it thousands of times in her daily work at the hospital. How diseases and afflictions didn't turn people into victims but fired their fighting spirit or humility over what they had left. A new spark of life. A struggle, but still. And not uncommonly in those that seemed the least likely to possess the resources.

She was wearing her earpiece, and had the telephone in her pocket so that she could hang the washing in the basement while she talked. Nora was sleeping in her bassinet upstairs, and Klara was sitting on the old, washed-out rag rug that lay like an intestine on the concrete floor of the laundry room, sorting out clothespins.

Cecilia had gone a couple of times to the Gerda Gym, and it had changed her life, she was saying. A physical therapist had helped her, and he was very nice, and now she'd started doing weights.

"You know, Mom, the physical therapist thought that I'd manage the normal sessions, but not the fastest… with all the jumping and sudden changes of position and so on. Maybe I should wait a bit, he said. So that I didn't get all discouraged for not keeping up. And I'm so out of shape. Well, unfit, at least. So I'm on weights for now, and there's so much to look at!"

Cecilia gave a giggle. Perhaps a tiny bit too loud, Veronika felt, but immediately brushed the thought away. Her daughter could still forget to moderate herself, and her intonation was slightly stiffer. But only very slightly, if you compared with what it was like before. Veronika wasn't sure that other people even noticed.

Today was, miraculously, much better. This wasn't a gradual change but a quantum leap!

"You don't say," she said affectionately.

Her daughter meant guys, she thought, and had to stop herself before she asked too much. It would be so great if Cecilia built up enough self-confidence to find a friend.

This fear that her children would end up alone without someone to share their lives with… Before the accident there hadn't been the slightest trace of a thought in that direction. Cecilia's circle of friends had always been large and closely knit. But then. The threads by which she held on to the outside world grew tenuous after the skull injury. Perhaps things would get better now.

They hung up. Veronika and Klara emerged from the basement, and her daughter skipped off into the sitting room to the hideout that she'd built with Veronika's help out of sofa cushions and an old blanket. Veronika walked into the kitchen and stood by the window.

It was late afternoon, a time when lethargy slowly creeps through the body. She didn't dare sit down out of fear that she might fall asleep. Her eyelids chafed, her arms and legs were heavy.

A few hours in an upright position, she thought, and then she'd try to put Klara down.

Claes had called, he was on his way home. She was already feeling the relief of being able to dump the kids onto him. He, who'd been out on an adventure in a strange and exciting country, while she'd been cooped up around here at home, tied down both day and night.

Bitter thoughts and envy puckered her mouth. She noticed it herself. Let them. And even enjoy it.

She felt very, very sorry for herself.

She should have gone shopping, she realized then. Like a good, considerate housewife. Some steaks, cheese, and new potatoes to welcome him home with, but she'd been so occupied with the kids that the idea of going to the store just seemed too much for her to cope with.

Anyway, they wouldn't starve. Nor have to sit eating sandwiches. She'd opened the fridge and seen two packs of bacon. They had tagliatelle, and a nice chunk of parmesan, too, so they'd be fine.

At that moment she saw a taxi pull up by the gate and Claes step out. The pink peony buds in the flower bed were heavy balls; some had even bloomed, but he probably didn't notice.

There's my husband, she thought, and the fire burned in her breast. My husband, who makes me strong and happy.

She walked into the hall to greet him. He stepped inside, and she buried her nose in his chest while he placed an arm around her neck.

"Oh, it's so nice to have you home."

Klara ran between their legs.

They'd finished dinner: pasta with bacon bits and grated parmesan that Claes had thrown together with Klara as his eager assistant.

Veronika was sitting at the table nursing Nora. The light outside the kitchen window was still bright, as it could be only at this time of year.

Claes got up to clear the table.

"I'll do that later. You go up and read to Klara," she said.

The two of them disappeared upstairs, Klara skipping ahead with her father close behind. Veronika heard them going into the bathroom to clean their teeth, heard Claes answering Klara's many questions and joking with her.

She'd just placed Nora in the bassinet and stacked the plates in the dishwasher when there was a knock at the door. She opened it and found a man standing there. He looked wild and slovenly.

"Yeah, right, I'm here about the rug madam was going to get to choose."

How absurd, she thought. Choosing a rug? And what was all that with "madam"? No one ever called her that. Not these days.

She remembered now that some joker had called her during the day and babbled on about how she'd won a rug and that he'd come by, and that she'd said, quite firmly, that she wasn't going to be in. She'd thought then that the misunderstanding had thus been cleared up.

But now he was standing there with a rolled-up rug under his arm. Strangely, there was something familiar about it. Even though it was rolled up. Her clinical mind also told her that the man wasn't a member of the town's more honest, law-abiding citizenry. Undoubtedly a substance abuser of some kind. Probably narcotics. Though maybe he was a mental patient on poorly dosed medication.

"Will madam not let me in so that I can show her this beautiful treasure?"

Veronika was grasping the door handle tightly. She had absolutely no intention of letting this man in. But she dearly wanted to look at the rug.

"Can't you show it to me out here?"

A woman somewhere in her twenties, so ravaged-looking that it was hard to really tell her age, appeared as if from nowhere. She'd been lurking around the corner of the house, Veronika guessed. The woman's legs were sticks clad in tight, black jeans under a far-too-wide parka. Her hair was dead straight and hung down to her shoulders. It had not been washed today, that was for sure. Probably not yesterday, either.

"It would be best to go indoors, you understand, madam. This is my assistant," he persisted, but started to get nervous and jittery and kept twisting his head in all directions as if he was afraid of being spotted.

Veronika heard the stairs behind her creak.

And then Claes was standing in the doorway.

"What's all this then?"

His voice was authoritative. Before the man had time to turn and run off, Claes had an iron grip on his arm. The woman took off up the garden path with the gravel spraying behind her.

Claes shoved the man roughly into the hall. Klara had appeared at the bottom of the stairs and was standing there holding the banister rods with whitening fingers.

"Shut the door and lock it," he commanded Veronika as he tried to manhandle his captive onto the floor.

His opponent seemed just a milksop in an unhealthy body, thought Veronika.

"Mommy…" whined Klara.

Veronika picked her up and went to fetch Nora, who was still asleep in the kitchen, and took both children into the sitting room.

She heard Claes speak in a voice she'd never heard before. Not loud, but brusque and firm.

"Call the police," he roared from the hall to Veronika, who picked up the phone from off the coffee table.

"What number?" she called.

"The emergency number," he yelled, and she bit her lower lip. How stupid could she be?

She found herself at the emergency switchboard, and heard a woman's voice, calm and clear.

Suddenly she too grew cucumber cool, and was informative yet brief. What had happened, the intruder was still there, address, town, hurry.

Yes, of course, they'd send a car right over.

Just as she hung up she heard a sudden crash out in the hall, and she caught up her worried daughter and sat her on her lap. She wondered what was going on out there.

"And where have you gotten this rug from?" she heard Claes say.

"Er, I got it from my mom."

"Like hell. I know you're lying."

Veronika snatched up a comic from the coffee table and started to read an episode to Klara. But it was no use, the daughter had her entire anxious attention directed at the hall and the kitchen.

"Is Daddy angry?" asked Klara with childishly forced heartiness.

Yeah, guess you could say that. Veronika stroked Klara's hair reassuringly. Held her in her arms. "Ssh, it's alright. Daddy's just making sure that someone comes and takes away that man."

"Why? Is he naughty?"

"Yes, he's being naughty."

"But not dangerous," said Klara firmly.

"No, not dangerous. It'll be just fine, you'll see."

The patrol car arrived and two uniformed police officers were suddenly filling the entire hall. They knew the hustler, of course. Andreas Gustavsson was his name.

"Boy, did you ever choose the wrong house," joked Lennie Ludvigsson, a large, flame-haired man whose main interest in life, Veronika knew, was cooking. You could tell that by his build, too.

"Come on, Andreas," said the other officer, who was called Conny Larsson, a northerner whom Veronika had sat next to at a dinner party once. He sounded paternal and took the man by the arm. "It won't do you no good resistin', you know that… And we might as well take your rug thing, too," Veronika heard him say. "Nora, Andreas, couldn't you have found one in better shape?" he joked.

"The rug is to be returned to me," said Claes. "It's ours."

An almost silent whistle could be heard through the house.

"OK… so you're into old rugs then, eh?" joked Conny Larsson indifferently.

And then they left.

Chapter 49

CLAES CLIMBED OUT of the warm bed into air that was stuffy despite the window having been open all night. He needed to go to the bathroom. The time was a few minutes to seven, he noticed.

He and Mustafa Özen had decided that they'd get some separate rest over the weekend. They had many impressions to digest after their whistle-stop trip. On Monday they'd be reporting back at the regular morning briefing on their experiences in Istanbul.

And then they'd see which threads they would start pulling.

He returned to the bedroom, and stood looking down at all the sleeping bodies in the wide double bed. Looked at Veronika, eyes shut like someone unconscious, her forehead relaxed and her back toward the center as if she were asking to be left in peace for just a few moments more. At Klara in her nightie with the red-hearts on it, with a sweat-glistening forehead and chubby legs on his half of the bed – she'd been kicking him during the night – and her head pressed against the small of Veronika's back. And then at little Nora who, miraculously, had claimed her place in the family and was sleeping sweetly above her big sister's head, behind her mother, without blanket or anything covering her tiny body. He felt her legs. They were warm.

He went downstairs to make some coffee. The apple tree had shed its blossoms, which lay swirling on the ground. The world just couldn't get better than this, he thought, and set the butter, bread, and cheese on the table. He then took out a delicate rose-patterned cup and saucer – a family heirloom that he thought coffee tasted the very best in – and plonked a more robust honey-yellow mug onto the table in Veronika's place. He'd take the opportunity to take paternal leave for the entire day, he thought a mite ironically. His off-duty time had shrunk.

He made two open-face sandwiches, sat down, poured a cup of the hot, strong coffee, and reached for the week's harvest of old newspapers. He started with the latest, from yesterday. A woman from Bråbygden had gone missing, he read. Is that so? Well, he'd find out more tomorrow. And Veronika had been called in as a witness to an assault around there. She'd told him about it yesterday. She'd not seen the victim, whom she actually knew – a nurse from the clinic – but she'd spotted a possible suspect. Whatever that might lead to…

He browsed on. After a while, Veronika came down.

"Is Klara still asleep?" he asked.

She nodded and yawned widely.

"Nora, too. I put her in her bassinet so that Klara wouldn't accidentally kick her out of bed."

Nora had changed, Claes had seen that straight away. Her contours were more even, more filled out. A week made a big difference to a little baby. But she was still recognizable. Although she'd complained when he picked her up. She'd been wallowing in her mother's smell, had become imprinted. But he'd have to assert his rank. Reclaim it. Accustom the little one to himself, too.

Veronika inhaled deeply, staring in a state of morning torpor at the table.

"God, it's so nice to have you home!" she said, and lifted her eyes to his face.

He smiled easily. How he loved all this!

"Coffee?"

She nodded, sitting there in her oversized t-shirt bearing the words "One better!" He filled her mug and poured himself more, too.

He looked down at his cup, which he had always washed up by hand. It came from his grandmother. A bourgeois home, hers had been, with silver cutlery and hand-painted china. It had almost been laughable when his mother, when she was still of sound mind that is, had insisted that he should inherit the coffee service. It suited a chief inspector, she said. He still didn't know if she'd meant it seriously or not. None of his siblings had been interested, so he lugged the box home and stacked the delicate cups and saucers in his bachelor apartment. The set came from an esteemed Swedish porcelain factory and was representative of its time. Embroidered tablecloth, the *de rigueur* assortment of seven delicacies and a cake elevated above them on a dish standing atop a foot of pressed glass.

The clock was ticking toward eleven. Countdown.

Claesson really *detested* visiting his mother. Detested was such a strong and almost indecent word that he'd never let it actually cross his lips. It pained him, actually, to think in those terms.

He hadn't even divulged his less than respectable feelings to Veronika, but he figured she realized how that land lay, anyway.

His mother was a thin woman who'd always taken care of her appearance, from the well-maintained coiffure to her choice of garments and jewelry. He couldn't remember her ever wearing any brighter colors than powder blue and soft pink. Most of her clothes were gray, white or naturally toned, and always discreet, unfussy and of proper quality. During his childhood, she always wore a necklace of graduated, rose-tinted pearls, be it with sweaters or blouses.

Klara wanted to come, too. He placed the two children almost ritually into the car, buckled them up, and drove to the Gullregnet nursing home, parked, helped Klara out of the car, and then lifted Nora in her infant carrier. She was newly fed and sleeping soundly.

He walked in and was greeted by one of the staff, a caregiver or assistant or helper or whatever she was called, in a striped apron with flouncy shoulder wings. The middle-aged woman bent over and baby-talked to Nora, Klara watching from her under heavy brows.

"Ester has had a nice, restful day," she informed them.

He nodded, and took the children into his mother's room. The familiar shroud of light depression descended on him as it always did.

She was sitting in an easy chair, asleep. Klara stared rigidly at her grandmother with an air of distaste. Claesson pulled over a chair and sat down beside his sleeping mother. The head with its curly gray hair, like that of a docile, open-pasture sheep, hung forward. He laid his hand on her spindly forearm and she gave a jolt, but then fell back into her slumber.

"Mom," he said, quite loudly.

She lifted her head and stared at him in newly awakened confusion.

"Heavens above, how you frightened me!" she said. "Is that you, Ulf?"

Almost right, he thought. His little brother. Not bad!

"No, it's me, Claes."

"Oh my word, what brings you here?"

"Mom, look, I've brought Klara with me," he said, and laid an arm around his daughter. "She's your granddaughter."

"Really? Where's she from?"

"You've met Klara before. She's my daughter. Do you remember?"

His mother stared into space.

"No, I can't say I do."

"And this little girl's called Nora. She's just been born and she's also your granddaughter."

He held up the child seat and was about to tell her that the girl was also called CB, but decided it would be pointless.

His mother bent to look at the girl, who happened to stir just then and open her eyes carefully to have a proper look around.

Her grandmother looked at her. In wonder, possibly.

"Whose baby is that?" she asked.

"She's mine, too," he said, swollen with pride, even if his mother was incapable of sharing his joy.

"You don't say?" she said wearily, and sank back into her high-backed, upholstered throne.

He drove home with his two daughters. CB whined incessantly. It was feeding time.

"Do you want to come shopping later," he asked Klara in the back seat.

"Yes!" she cheered.

She loved doing the weekly shopping. It was an unexpected pleasure, but a pleasure it was.

He drove home and relieved himself of his inconsolable daughter, and then took off with Klara to the supermarket.

A few hours later he was back unpacking the car and carrying inside a sleeping Klara – she'd been up late the night before. As he hoisted the shopping bags onto the kitchen counter, he saw what was printed on the bags in red letters on white: ICA.

Could it be so simple? he thought as he started stacking the goods in the fridge. Worth a try, at least.

It was half past three when he finally got down to calling Mustafa Özen, who picked up almost immediately. Claesson reeled off a brief apology for not having called him over the weekend.

"Have you seen if ICA has been handing out white caps with a red logo?"

Özen was quiet for a moment.

"I don't actually know… but we can probably find out. I'll do it today."

"That's if you've got nothing else to do," said Claesson in a tone that said that he'd like Özen to get onto it straight away.

"I can send a picture of the cap to Merve, and she can check with the witnesses on the boat to see if they recognize it," said Özen, and Claesson couldn't miss how eager he sounded at the prospect of getting in touch with Istanbul.

"Do that! By the way, are you at home?"

"Nope. At work, actually. I've got a bunch of reports to write, you could say. And some other stuff to do to. So, no, I'd nothing else to do."

What it was like to be young! Claesson recalled. Let's see if the guy can write, too!

"Let me know if you find anything," he said.

When he was lying a few hours later on the sofa with CB on his chest watching the evening news, his phone went off out in his jacket pocket. Veronica was bathing Klara, who'd got jam rubbed into her hair. He'd served his ladies a dish no more dramatic than bacon pancakes. Klara loved them, he loved them, and Veronika thought they were pretty good, too.

He let the phone ring. But once Veronika had come back down with a bathed and clean-smelling Klara, he asked her to take Nora and went to fetch his phone. It had been Özen.

He shouldn't really be disturbing his Sunday evening, he realized as he called his younger colleague.

Özen picked up.

"I've checked out Karl Öberg and Bengt-Ove Nordin, who were staying at the hotel opposite the Galata," he said. "Neither of them is on our records. But what I'm not sure about is whether that Öberg really does call himself Karl. According to the civil records he was baptized Karl-Magnus, but then again that's quite a mouthful."

"So he might have removed the Karl…" said Claesson.

"Maybe?"

"Magnus Öberg. In which case we have a face," said Claesson. "Good! Then all we have to do is find a way to run a check on him. I bet it's that valuable rug… Is the son-in-law struggling financially?"

"Don't know."

He could hear that Özen wanted him to know that there were limits to what he could reasonably have achieved.

"But I've got a whole list of telephone numbers here. All the calls made to and from Olsson's home and to his shop over the past months. Our guys have compiled a whole bunch of calls and numbers while we were away, it's tiring to go through them all, but the cell phone number that Öberg or his firm is listed as the subscriber to, isn't there."

"But what *is* there?"

"His home number. Someone has made calls from his landline in Stockholm to Olsson's home, both when he was alive and now after his death and to the carpet shop and a whole load of other places. To Annelie Daun's cell phone, too, in fact."

"That could just be the mother and daughter talking to each other. It'll be hard to prove anything," said Claesson. "Any texting?"

"No."

"Do you remember that Magnus Öberg said, there at the coroner's in Istanbul, that he'd been on business in Germany when the carpet dealer was killed?"

"Yes, I remember that."

"He seemed a bit shifty even then. He was meant to give us some sort of proof that he really had been in Germany, but he hasn't done so yet… But then that was just a few days ago, and we haven't got round to pressing him for it. The question is whether we should take a trip to Stockholm," Claesson said, thinking aloud. "Or perhaps wait until after the funeral? But that could be a long time coming. We can check with his widow when it'll be."

"But," said Özen then. "I have a photo here that I'd like you to look at, as my superior, before I send it to Istanbul."

"What photo? Can't it wait till tomorrow?"

"Sure, of course, but…"

Claesson realized that he had no choice but to leave the warmth of home and family bliss, however reluctantly.

"I won't be long," he said ashamedly to Veronika before shutting the door behind him.

He took the car, parked it in the police station's underground lot, and climbed the stairs. The CID department was quiet and deserted, with the exception of one of the smaller rooms at the back, where the lamp of diligence glowed.

Mustafa Özen had in all haste taken a desk for himself in Claesson's department, having borrowed Erika Ljung's office, which was empty during her leave of absence while she served down south in Malmö. It was tough there, as far as Claesson understood, but he still figured she wouldn't be returning. She had her roots in one of Malmö's immigrant districts, just like Özen, and no immediate ties with Oskarshamn or the rest of Småland County.

He placed himself in the doorway.

"Check this out," said Özen, holding out a photograph.

It was an enlarged and manipulated passport photograph showing a dark-haired young man in a white cap with ICA printed on it in large red letters.

Claesson raised his eyebrows and looked at Özen, who seemed to be wagging his tail and waiting for a rewarding tickle behind the ear.

And that's just what he got.

"Great! You can work that photo editing software?" asked Claesson.

"Well, one does one's best!"

Claesson nodded as he continued to gaze at the picture.

"Where did you get the cap from?"

"Called ICA. They're open on Sundays. And then I just strolled on over there to pick one up. It's part of some promotional campaign that's been going on for a while. It's a golf cap, don't you know!" he said, jamming the white cap that lay on his desk over his head.

"You play golf?"

"Nah. But I can imagine that the PR guys have thought along those lines. The new ICA man!"

Claesson had no idea what the PR guys had been thinking.

"Of course you must send the picture to Merve. Now, this instant! It means she'll be able to talk to the two guys from the ferry tomorrow, hopefully."

"That's what I thought," said Özen, smiling broadly with his eyes lowered so as not to expose his vulnerability. Merve and Özen.

I think I'll keep mum about this, Claesson decided to himself. Love is a fragile thing.

CHAPTER 50

IT WAS MONDAY MORNING. Claesson hung up his coat in his office and turned on his computer, which would take a while to run all its security software. While he was waiting, his eyes landed on the pile of papers that lay in front of him, the product of Özen's industry. He flipped through them. Most of what they'd done in Istanbul had been recorded, and partly translated into Swedish, at least the Turkish bits. He looked more closely at the text. It was well written.

Out in the corridor, he bumped into a very hollow-eyed Mustafa Özen.

"Before I forget, you write good reports," said Claesson.

Özen smiled shyly.

"Thanks."

"Did you send the photo off to Merve?"

"Yep."

"Good."

They took the stairs down to the morning briefing. Fifteen people or so were gathered in the basement room.

"Hello! Welcome home! How were the Turks?"

"Like us, pretty much," Claesson answered Janne Lundin, and felt the immediate presence of Fuat Karaoğlu and Merve. "It's always inspiring to see something new."

The large TV screens were on. The different police districts in the Kalmar-Oskarshamn area were reporting on what had happened over the past 24 hours. The reports were efficient, and everyone sat watching and listening in silence.

Then it was Oskarshamn's turn. Peter Berg reported on a break-in at a *kiosk*. For the umpteenth time in a row, everyone thought, it being a popular target for thieves. It was a mystery how the owner could stand it. Then came a report on a missing woman from Bråbo, and another on a confiscated rug.

They looked at each other in the long, narrow room. A rug! Why was Berg reporting on such a trifle as this?

"And an ugly old bugger it is, too," said Conny Larsson, not on screen though, but afterwards, fully aware of the identity of the rug's rightful owner. "Andreas Gustavsson went and stole it believin' it was worth somethin'."

"So whose rug is it?" wondered Janne Lundin.

Claes had no option but to admit it was his.

"But how in God's name did Gustavsson get hold of it? What, is it a flying carpet?" joked Lundin.

Spirits were high and the atmosphere pleasant.

"Gustavsson claims he found it on Besvärsgatan," said Conny Larsson in his kindly northern dialect. "By a couple of trash bins, but Lord knows who'd dumped it there. Gustavsson had read about that rug trick that some low-lifes had been runnin' in Stockholm…" He went into what the trick consisted of. "Gustavsson reckoned he'd give it a go with his *assistant*, as he calls Nilla Söder. You know, that junkie girl whose old lady worked the streets down by the harbor, though she's dead now… her ma, that is."

"Where's the rug now," Jasinski butted in.

"Benny's taken it to forensics. It might've had blood on it," said Conny Larsson.

"Blood? Gustavsson's not usually violent, is he? Just mouthy and thieves like a magpie… like most druggies," said Jasinski.

"Yeah, but there was still blood on the back," Conny Larsson insisted.

"That's correct," said Benny Grahn. "I'll be takin' a right close look at it. That unconscious guy you picked up and drove to the emergency room last Saturday mornin' was lyin' beside it, like. There'll be DNA that'll go to Linköping for analysis."

"Well, looks like you won't be seein' that rug again for a while," said Conny Larsson to Claesson. "It'll lie nicely in storage there. But rest assured. Johanna will be hovering over it like a hawk, she will, so you won't be losin' it again," he grinned.

Johanna Huaryd was a civilian employed to manage the different storerooms of confiscated and commandeered items.

Claesson realized that things had been going on while he'd been away.

What unconscious guy to the emergency room?

But he let it go. He had his own case to work on.

And then Martin Lerde gave some further details of the missing woman, one Tina Rosenkvist, resident of Bråbo. Said that the husband had reported her missing at around six on the Friday evening.

Claesson listened with half an ear at first until he heard that the victim had been taken to hospital after having been seriously assaulted by an unknown man because of a rug.

"We might well be treating the case as attempted murder," said Lerde.

Another rug? All that rug business seemed to have caught on in town recently.

"It happened last Wednesday at around six p.m., at the home of a man who works at the same place as her, at the hospital," said Peter Berg taking over, as he was the one who'd been dispatched to the scene. "This man had given her a lift back to his place, in Bråbo. You could say they're almost neighbors, there's just a few houses between them. What actually took place there in the kitchen we don't really know, we've heard different stories, but they'd poured themselves some wine at least… According to the woman, it was someone who'd come in from the outside and tried to strangle her to make her tell him where some rug was. Who this *someone* is, we don't know. She doesn't remember so much. We questioned her at the hospital that evening, she was in overnight… I'll get to that later."

He inhaled and looked at his papers before continuing.

"So if it was the man whom she was visiting and in whose kitchen she was sitting sipping wine who assaulted her, we don't know… but it seems unlikely. We've released him for the time being. He says that he was outside, that someone had called about a delivery of firewood that he was to sign for and that he went outside to wait for it. He claims that he wasn't even aware that they'd ordered any wood, but figured his wife must've ordered it.

"It sounds to me as if he'd got lured out… So, in other words, it could be an as-yet-unknown assailant who attacked her. The victim was unsure about it herself, she said. Her memory was shaky. She'd blacked out, you see, and I guess what had happened just before the attack just vanished from her memory. Or maybe she's repressing it." Berg shrugged. "It was a nasty experience, and she could've died. Well… and now she's gone missing."

He surveyed the assembled officers, who were sitting still and attentive.

"We have a witness who was driving past and who can confirm that the owner of the house really was standing in the stable yard waiting, possibly for the delivery of firewood that never came. But if it was before or after the attack, we of course can't tell. The witness also saw a man pass quickly around the corner of the house," he continued. "And a car that we can probably tie to him… a dark green Saab, but we've got no registration number or anything. Er, and the witness is someone we all know… Veronika Lundborg."

Peter Berg's flicked a glance at Claesson, who nodded in acknowledgement that he knew of these events, even though Veronika only figured on the periphery.

"Might it have been your rug that the assailant was after?" Berg said to him, smiling kindly.

"Mine's not the only rug in the world," Claesson said. "Carl-Ivar Olsson had something going on with a fragment worth at least one and a half mill. Not the eight-figure jobs that the Economic Crime Authority has to deal with, but a hefty sum nonetheless."

"Who the hell would buy a rug for that kind of money?" Janne Lundin broke in.

"There's a lot we don't understand," answered Claesson. "But I want to hear the rest."

"So the woman, Tina Rosenkvist, blacked out on her neighbor's kitchen floor and was rushed by ambulance to the hospital, where she was kept in overnight, until Thursday, that is. She had strangulation marks on her throat, but felt fine, considering. And then her husband apparently came to fetch her from the ward the next day, and that was *not* according to the agreed procedure. We'd agreed that she was to go to the women's refuge for some counseling. The victim, the doctor, the nurse, and I decided that together. But you know how it is. People end up doing what they want to do, anyway, and so we'll have to sort out all this mess later…" Peter Berg said, taking a deep breath. "Anyway, it seems her husband just strolled right into the ward the next day, on the Thursday, I mean."

"I guess the duty staff had been relieved by then," said Jasinski dryly.

"No doubt. Change-of-shift reporting is a well-known problem. They knew the husband on the ward, the woman usually works there.

And you can imagine the frame of mind he was in… Wife found in another man's house… unconscious, almost dead."

Berg looked out over the room once more.

"What was going through his head is hard to know, but he can't have been a happy camper. And he shouldn't have been allowed to pick her up alone… This is hopeless. You know, however hard you try, things always go to hell."

Thus was his final point.

Martin Lerde took over: "Anyway, the husband swears that he didn't hurt a hair of his wife's head. That he never turns violent, period. She just took off at some early hour that Friday morning before he woke up."

Lerde continued to describe how they'd dispatched a description of the wife to all the other local police districts. "Well, as you heard during the briefing – we just have to keep our eyes open."

Benny Grahn had been in Bråbo with two technicians, combing the home of the missing woman.

"Second time in the same week we were in the area, searchin' for physical evidence. *Lex dublicata*, or whatever it's called… that things always come in pairs… well, anyway, there's something shady goin' on here," said Grahn. "You can smell the cleanin' fluid in parts of the house from miles off, like. Most suspect is one of the wardrobes… but it's also in the hall an' kitchen. Scrubbed clean, they are. The husband says that the wife, the missin' woman that is, had given the house a thorough goin' over the days before this happened. A spring cleanin', like. I didn't think that young families did stuff like that any more. We haven't had time to go through the car yet."

Louise Jasinski nodded at Roger Lindström, nicknamed Roggy, who was in charge of the canine unit. He addressed the room.

"Well, we've covered a large area of about two miles radius in all directions."

And that was it. Rogge was more for a worker than a talker, as everyone knew.

"And?" said Jasinski.

"We haven't found her. It's as if she's disappeared into thin air. Either that or he's buried her deep down."

That was all they could get from him. Claes liked Roggy. Tough and a little prickly, like a juniper bush. A typical good person.

"There are many more people left to question," said Martin Lerde, taking the conch back. "Neighbors normally see and hear things, but in this case they seem not to have noticed anything. We'll continue to work on it."

"That male colleague who she was with when the attempted strangulation took place… ?" wondered Claesson.

"Has an alibi. First off, his own wife in the morning, who works, incidentally, in a carpet shop, and who was probably that psycho's intended target. But she can't make head nor tail of it, she says, and knows nothing about any rug. All she knew was that her husband had had a so-called 'friend' over to visit… she picked that up pretty quickly. She doesn't seem that bright. Annelie Daun's her name. Anyway, we've given her a security phone and an alarm pendant to wear. We haven't yet reached the point where we judge her personal safety to be so at risk that she needs police protection or to be placed in a secure apartment."

Claesson and Özen looked at each other.

"Carpets here, rugs there, could there be a link between them all?" wondered Louise Jasinski, raising her eyebrows.

"I don't know, but I want all the reports on my desk ASAP," said Claesson, struck by a sense that the right hand had absolutely no idea what the left was doing. At the station, that is, this time.

Berg, Lerde, and Grahn nodded obligingly.

"Are Annelie Daun and her husband giving each other alibis somehow for the time of Tina Rosenkvist's disappearance?" he asked.

"They are," said Peter Berg. "But we'll have to see… we're not done with them yet."

"Now we want to hear about Istanbul!" interjected Louise Jasinski.

It was as if Claesson and Özen had both run out of oomph. They wanted to work, not talk. But Claesson gave a dutiful account of what they'd found out.

"So how do they operate?" wondered Conny Larsson.

"Like us, pretty much," said Claesson. "It's actually quite interesting how you can step into some place far away from your own domains and still feel at home. Anyway, we've got a lot to get to grips with here at home. We'll have to see if it gives us anything. We'll probably need a car today. Is it OK to take an unmarked one from the pool?"

Jasinski nodded.

"Where are you going?"

"Maybe to Stockholm. We'll see."

CHAPTER 51

CLAESSON AND ÖZEN took a morning break with the others in the lunchroom. Claesson coffee, Özen tea.

They then went up to Claesson's office, and he closed the window that he'd left open slightly to clear the room of an entire week's stuffiness.

"What's our best tactic now, do you reckon?" said Claesson. "Shall we go to Stockholm on the off chance and put the squeeze on that Öberg guy, or…"

"Yeah, dunno," said Özen, irresolutely. "What about the carpet shop girl?"

"Good idea! We'll go there first."

Claesson checked the time. Soon half past ten.

"If we're lucky she opens up at ten."

His jacket was too thin, he felt, as they stepped onto Slottsgatan. As they crossed Lilla Torget Square he saw some young women, still teenagers he guessed, shivering as they walked in the opposite direction. They had on tight jeans that ended above the ankles and no socks with their flat ballerina shoes. He assumed they were refusing to accept that the late spring and imminent summer had taken a pause. Like in the old nursery rhyme about the hepatica that stands alone in the grass, curtseys and says, "It's spring at last!"

They arrived and climbed the few steps on the corner and opened the door. The woman called Annelie Daun gave a little jump. They didn't need to ask if they'd startled her.

He introduced himself and Mustafa Özen in a calm and collected manner. She nodded and said that she remembered them both very well from the first time they came into the shop. She smiled stiffly, on her guard.

"The thing is that my wife brought in a rug for repair here. Her name's Veronika Lundborg," he began.

Annelie Daun launched immediately into an apology. "I… I'm really sorry," she stammered, "but there's been a hang-up at the repairer's in Stockholm. He's not finished with it yet, I'm afraid!"

She clearly didn't know what had happened. Claes waited a moment, giving her a chance to change her mind, to stop lying. He could see her face quickly changing color from a rather becoming pre-summer tan to a pinkish red, which spread far down her throat, clashing horribly with her light green top with its plunging neckline.

"The rug's currently at the police station," he said at last, and studied her reaction.

Her eyes widened, she swallowed and then her eyes began to flit about violently, unsure of where to attach themselves. On a *loribaft*, *mahal*, *ingelas*, *kashan*, or whatever these rugs and carpets might be called. She'd stuck small labels to them declaring their names and provenances, he noted. She was making improvements. She clearly had plans for the place.

"Come on, the truth now," he said at last.

"God, I've been so stupid…"

She sank down onto the chair behind the desk and, placing her elbows on the cherry-wood top, hid her face in her hands. She remained sitting like that for some time.

Özen hung around by the door while Claesson went to sit on the probably antique armchair with its upholstered seat – an interesting weave decorated with tigers, lions and other felines – which was standing by the wall next to one of the windows.

Annelie Daun began to collect herself, and slowly lifted her head.

"It was probably a man who took the rug," she said finally. "I think so, but I didn't dare go to the police… and that was stupid, I realize that now… The truth always comes out eventually. But I thought it might come back. The rug, I mean. I was afraid that the shop would get a bad reputation, now that Carl-Ivar's been murdered and everything! That's bad enough… Although we have been quite busy since then."

Claesson looked at her inquiringly.

"Business has actually been unusually good." She shrugged. "Maybe because people are curious."

He asked her to account for what happened when the rug disappeared. And she told him how the rug was there rolled up in its plastic wrapping when the door had been opened, but she didn't make it up from the basement in time, and when she did the rug was nowhere to be seen!

She told him also that a man had turned up a few days earlier asking after Carl-Ivar, and that she'd seen the same man walking along the pavement when she was going to the post office to pick up Claes and Veronika's rug.

"A lovely Anatolian prayer mat," she added and smiled. "You must get it back, of course!"

He nodded. The boys back at the station should hear this. An expert opinion. Their rug was *lovely*. So there!

"Maybe the man followed me when I went to the post office to pick it up," she said, developing her line, and Claesson could tell she'd thought it through.

She excused herself, snuffled, and, needing to blow her nose, dashed downstairs to the bathroom.

But it was the wrong rug he'd grabbed, thought Claesson. So he dumped it in a dumpster that happened to belong to a house with a side entrance from Besvärsgatan. No one in the house had thrown away a rug, his colleagues had already ascertained that.

Had it been the nearest dumpster? Did the man live around there, or did he just happen to be walking past? There weren't that many apartments in this particular quarter in the heart of town, mostly shops, he thought. Unless the man lived in one of the idyllic houses in Besväret, of course.

They should do some door-knocking, he and Özen. But he balked at the thought. The time was long gone when he did that kind of groundwork. Time consuming, it was. But it wasn't without its merits. Systematic work always paid off, he knew that in his guts. Maybe he could put Özen onto it, he thought, or ask Louise to give him a few more officers.

When Annelie Daun returned, he asked her to describe the man while he took notes. About thirty-five, ordinary, a rather long body, short-legged in other words, bow-legged too, nice-looking, had a pleasant manner, perhaps there was something of the salesman about him, she said.

Claesson sighed quietly to himself. How many people didn't match this description?

"He sounded as if he came from further north, from Norrköping," she said then.

That fleshed things out a bit.

"He obviously took the wrong rug. Which one do you think he was after?" he asked, and fixed his hopefully penetrating blue eyes on her equally blue ones.

Annelie Daun sat down again, and jammed her hands between her knees.

"I haven't got a clue, to be honest."

"The carpet dealer in Istanbul said that Olsson had bought a fine antique from him, the one that we found the photo of here in the shop the first day we came. A shabby old thing. Remember it?"

"Yes, I think so."

Claesson took out the photocopy and showed her and she nodded in recognition.

"Oh, that one, yes, of course."

"Do you think that the man who took… er… my rug was really after this one?"

"But how should I know that? If he was, he must have expected someone to have brought it here from Istanbul. And it's not here, I promise you… Carl-Ivar himself was probably going to take it home to his place, but he… Or…"

She fell silent.

"Or?" prompted Claesson.

"Someone else maybe, but I haven't seen the rug here… No one's brought it here, so it must've gone missing en route. Maybe it was stolen in Istanbul?"

"But who would've been able to bring it back to Sweden apart from Carl-Ivar Olsson himself?"

"Someone else who'd been in Istanbul, I guess. It's not my job to answer this question, but maybe Birgitta brought it in, what do I know?" she said with a shrug.

"Can you tell us about it? We've not seen it, you see."

"Me, neither, but… I know at least that it's a fragment that had been found in an old mosque in Turkey, in Cappadocia. Well, what can I tell you? You can bet it's got a lot of blue and red in it. The old folk art of the Near East and Central Asia used a lot of blues and reds, and still does to some extent. The colors symbolize Heaven and Earth, among other things. To the nomadic people, who still live with the old worldview, you know, the Earth is a mid-level between the heavens above and a number of worlds below. A cosmic axis mundi, if you like. Or a world tree that unites Heaven and Earth, and you can see that in the patterning."

She fell silent, and looked anxiously at Claesson. You learn something new every day, he thought, but clearly wasn't conveying.

"This is irrelevant, I realize," she said self-consciously. "But I don't know what this particular fragment looked like in real life. I've only ever seen a black-and-white photo of it. But… anyway, there was a collector that Carl-Ivar had promised to procure the rug for."

"And what's the name of this collector?"

"I don't actually know." The silence hovered for a moment. "It's true, honestly, I'd give you the name if I knew it… But in a way it's been nice not knowing everything that Carl-Ivar was up to."

"Like what, for example?"

"Oh, nothing in particular."

It looked like she was regretting her candidness.

"Look, I was just an assistant… Carl-Ivar was always good to me. I helped out. That's all."

"Can you tell us who else has come to the shop since Olsson's death?"

"Customers, of course! I don't know their names… but most have paid by card so you can find out…"

He nodded.

"No one else? No lady friend or a friend of yours or Carl-Ivar's?"

"Nope."

She stared down at the table.

"No one else from the Olsson family?"

"Nope."

"Not his wife?"

"No. We haven't actually had time to meet since she returned from Istanbul. But there'll be the funeral… and we'll have to discuss what's to become of the business."

He nodded encouragingly.

"I'd love to keep the carpet business going, but maybe it won't be possible. You need capital to do that, to buy up the company with…" she said, and then bit her lip as if she'd suddenly caught herself letting a cat out of a bag.

Claesson made no comment.

"I'll repeat the question: Has no one else been here? Think back!" he said, as he sat leaning easily against the back the chair with one jeaned leg crossed over the other.

He kept his gaze on her. He was aware that he gave a stable impression, calming possibly – maybe deceptively calming. He also knew that the stillness that surrounded him could also make people feel unsure of themselves. Or so secure that they ended up saying more than they'd intended.

"No," she repeated finally with a shake of her head. "No one else."

She's lying, he thought. Her throat, which had paled, was now recovering its heavy blush.

But who was she protecting?

Claesson and Özen had a quick discussion as they crossed the square, battling the biting wind.

Should they take off for Stockholm now and have things out with Öberg face to face, or follow up the lead of Claesson's rug and try to find out who'd stolen it and then dumped it by a fatally sick man crawling along the cobblestones only a few yards from his own home?

That story they'd heard over the morning coffee. Conny Larsson had been looking properly guilty. The new girl, Jessika Granlund, a cropped-haired masculine thing, had had the sense, at least, not to dump her colleague in the shit. You can get a bit lazy over the years, and Claesson supposed that that was what had happened to Larsson.

They agreed to dig around their own patch and stay in Oskarshamn. To be quite honest, both were a bit tired of all the travel. Physically. Özen was to go knocking on doors around Lilla Torget Square, while Claesson intended to investigate things in his own little way.

They parted a short distance along Östra Torggatan. Özen walked back toward Kråkerumsbacken to attack the residents in the houses there. Claesson remained standing for a while, looking up at the facades. At the apartments above the shops. He had the pedestrianiszed Flanaden in one direction and the cobblestoned Besvärsgatan down toward the harbor in the other, with the Shalom Café at its head.

He went that way.

Shalom was a Christian mission that he actually knew little about. He knew that they had a boat that they sailed along the east coast in, preaching and teaching or whatever it was they did. And they had a conference center not that far from where he himself lived.

After Shalom, the idyllic detached wooden houses stretched down Besvärsgatan. Opposite the café on a corner plot, where there was once a parking lot, stood a modern, larger house of rather unsubtle design, to put it politely, its front garden facing Torggatan.

The house's two dark gray trash cans, on the other hand, stood at the edge of the plot on Besvärsgatan, opposite Shalom. He walked over to them, and lifted the lids. They were just the same as his trash can at home. Nothing unusual there.

So this is where the rug had been taken by Andreas Gustavsson. It had been lying under the unconscious radiologist's body on the cobblestones. The doctor was still alive, but in intensive care, he'd been told. Gustavsson had sworn that neither he nor his woman, the so-called assistant Nilla Söder, had touched the body.

Claesson knew, of course, all too well who Andreas Gustavsson was – a notorious druggie who lived in a state of general degradation. Many had tried to save him over the years, for he was the kind of person who, despite his miserable life, easily evoked maternal feelings in others. Perhaps because the man had something gentle and unassertive about him, especially during the times when he wasn't high. He'd lost a finger. Rumor had it that his malicious father had clipped it off with a pair of pincers when he was little, but whether this was true or not, he didn't know. He shuddered when he thought of such out-and-out cruelty. Especially now, when he had his own children. To cut off one of Klara's little fingers! Utterly unthinkable!

Andreas Gustavsson had never had a guardian angel. These days, he looked scruffy and few people took him seriously. He was mostly considered a bit of a jerk. But he was neither dangerous nor serious in his delinquency. Not in Claesson's opinion or anyone else's at the station. A petty thief, quite simply.

Claesson found himself only a block from the police station. He stared at the café door. It was more time for lunch than just a coffee, but making up his mind to check, just in case, he walked up to the door and opened it.

Standing behind the counter was a dumpy woman in her fifties sporting a floral apron and transferring freshly baked cinnamon buns from an oven tray to a footed glass dish. The same kind that his mother always brought out during special coffee mornings with the rose-patterned china.

He shouldn't, but he couldn't help it. Suddenly, he found himself sitting at a round table covered by a checkered cloth, with an oven-warm bun on a side plate and a cup of steaming hot coffee in front of him. Standard Swedish coffee, too. Not Turkish coffee, or latte or espresso or cappuccino. Fresh Swedish coffee was the best in the world.

They were alone. The woman with the flowery apron continued to busy herself with her buns, until he told her who he was – at which time she put down her tongs and straightened her back. But she soon relaxed and talked about the weather; it had started to hail outside.

"In May, too, well I never!" she said, shaking her head. "I hope it turns! Imagine if we had a summer like last year's! We deserve it!" she said and smiled charmingly.

She brushed away a grain of pearl sugar that had attached itself to her pant leg.

"You see, I'm looking for a man," he said, and she looked curiously at him. "He's not a dangerous man," he reassured her, "but you might be able to help me."

He described the man from the carpet shop. Average height, bow-legged. Those were the most characteristic features that he'd gleaned from Annelie Daun. And they weren't much.

"Maybe you've seen him out here on the street. He's probably not from around here, his dialect is more from the next county. Norrköping or Linköping or Mjölby… ? Maybe he's come in for a coffee? Possibly with a rug under his arm."

"A rolled-up rug?" she said, her mouth twitching.

"Yes."

"A big or small one?"

"Not so big."

He demonstrated with his hands.

"Let me have a think," she said.

"I wonder where he's staying in that case," Claesson said a little off-handedly and went to get a refill at the counter.

"I would say I recognize most people who live round here, the ones that pass by," she said, stroking her hands over her apron as if to smooth it out despite it already being stretched taut over her round tummy.

He nodded and sipped his coffee.

"And I must say I haven't seen anyone walk past with a rug, that's the kind of thing one remembers. But he might be staying in a hotel," she suggested. "Which makes things more difficult for you, I should think."

He noticed that he'd got her going. She liked being helpful.

"There's the Post Hotel on the main square, although its guests probably don't walk past here on Besvärsgatan, they'd go along Östra Torggatan instead," she said.

Claesson nodded.

"But those staying at the Marine Hotel down in the harbor usually take this route through Besväret and down the steps... the ones not driving, that is."

He nodded again, declined another refill and, after handing her his card in case she thought of anything else, left the café.

The wind was almost ripping the jacket off his back, but at least it had stopped hailing. The solid white grains dotted the cobblestones. They'd soon melt.

He descended the hillside to Skeppsbron and continued along to the Marine Hotel, which was nicely situated with a wide and unrestricted view of the harbor.

He stepped in out of the cold and introduced himself, asking if it was possible for him to see who'd been staying there the days around the rug's disappearance. Although without actually mentioning the rug, of course.

Eventually he was given a printout after the rather hesitant receptionist had called her boss to get approval to hand over the names.

He tried the description of the man on her, but she just shook her head. Not even the man's distinct dialect was anything that had stuck in her ears. However, a man coming in carrying a rolled-up rug under his arm she would've remembered, she said, but she'd come across no one like that among her guests.

Once outside, he looked out over the harbor. Since it was low-lying with the town high up on a hill, it was a rather dreary place. The harbor and the town center were like two completely separate and totally unrelated entities. The shops and houses, which were barely visible from the harbor, lent no color at all to it, and if you came by ferry from Gotland and disembarked in Oskarshamn, you missed the heart of the town altogether.

But that was the case everywhere, these days. Roads were laid around towns, not through them, he thought then, and walked quickly back to the police station.

He hung up his jacket in his room and went in to see Özen, who happened to be at his desk, to ask if he could take a moment to look through the guest list from the Marine Hotel.

Özen nodded efficiently, took the paper without a word, and turned to his computer.

"We'll have to check the Post Hotel, too. Did you find anything, by the way?" he asked Özen.

"Nope."

Before Claesson left, Özen handed him a bunch of papers. Claesson saw that they were more reports from Istanbul.

"Thanks," he said.

Just as he turned to go and collect his things so he could leave early – he was, after all, meant to be on parental leave – he heard Özen's phone ring and Özen answering it in Turkish.

He needed something to eat. The cinnamon bun was still sitting heavily in his stomach. He went to fetch more than a week's mail from his box, threw the pile onto his desk, and decided not to take up his letter opener until the next morning.

He was just putting on his jacket when Özen suddenly appeared in the doorway.

"Yes?"

"That was Merve."

"And?"

"One of the witnesses from the ferry has disappeared."

Claesson furrowed his brow.

"The tea-seller wasn't there today. He's run off."

This was something to ponder over. Claesson backed up to the desk and sat down.

"Tell me more."

He could see the young tea-seller, whose name was Ilyas Bank, clearly in front of him.

"Merve was on the ferry to show them the photo of Öberg wearing an ICA cap. But then the older man who works in the onboard *kiosk*, Ergün Bilgin's his name," said Özen, who found it easier to memorize the Turkish names, "he thought that the man in the photo, Magnus Öberg in his ICA cap that is, could well have been the person he'd seen on the boat and who'd got off last, and who might've been carrying a soft bag… and this is a breakthrough in our investigation."

"Hmm," nodded Claesson. "But it's got to stand up in court, too. This'll be too easy to just sweep aside. Live confrontation is better. Never mind, continue."

"What's strange is that the younger man who sells tea hasn't been there all day," continued Özen. "Nor has he got in touch. This is the first time it's happened. Sure, he's been late, maybe missed the ferry, but he's never been gone a whole day."

"Maybe he's sick?"

"That's what Ergün Bilgin thought. He's called his cell phone, and so has Merve, but he's not picking up."

"OK."

"Bilgin actually said he thought he'd left the country. He's apparently been going on about going abroad for a long time."

"Where? Doesn't he need a visa to travel to most countries?"

"Ergün Bilgin guessed that he went to Germany or Sweden, or possibly the USA."

Claesson stiffened.

"But that's not cheap."

"Hmm."

"Wasn't he told by Merve not to leave Istanbul?"

"He was."

Claesson ran his hand over his neck. He checked the time. It was coming up to three. That meant almost four o'clock in Istanbul.

"Very well. We'll have to get Interpol to put a warrant out for him, if we're going to get this sorted out," he said, and taking off his jacket again with a slight air of despondency, stood up and hung it back on the hook. "Leave it to me," he said quietly. "There are certain formalities. It'd be better if you contacted all the airlines that fly between Istanbul and Sweden or Copenhagen today, and perhaps tomorrow. You can start with that and we'll just have to take the other countries later. Ask if an Ilyas Bank has booked a ticket."

Özen looked at his watch.

"Maybe the plane's already landed," he pointed out.

"I know that."

Claesson was finding it hard to conceal his irritation. He wanted to go home.

"I'll try to contact the Swedish Consulate General in Istanbul and find out if they've issued a visa to an Ilyas Bank."

Özen nodded, but without listening.

"There's more than one airline that flies to Turkey you know, and to Istanbul in particular," he said instead, raising Claesson's hackles even more.

Claesson gave him a lingering look. He could feel that they'd been hanging around each other for quite a time now. That they really could've done with a break from the case of the dead Carl-Ivar Olsson, and from each other.

But he had no choice other than to sigh deeply.

"I'll start with Turkish Airlines, they're the biggest in Turkey," said Özen sort of to himself, but in a drawn-out way that conveyed his total disinclination to do so.

Well, forget it then, I'll do it myself, Claesson found himself on the point of retorting.

"Do that. Sounds like a good place to start," he said instead in a tone he might have reserved for a small child. Had Özen suddenly lost all the autonomy that he'd shown so much of to date?

Özen slunk away, muttering something about how the offices would all be closing soon anyway.

But he was tired, Claesson realized. The man hadn't had much sleep recently. Madly in love. And ambitious.

Özen saw, of course, his chance to remain in the department. He'd been hand-picked for this very case. But Claesson guessed he wanted more.

We'll cross that bridge when we come to it, thought Claesson as he lifted the receiver to call home.

"I'll be late," he said.

There was no other way of saying it. No beating about the bush. Although he could have added an *I'm afraid.*

As he passed by Mustafa Özen's room an hour or so later to tell him he was going home, he heard him sitting talking in Turkish on the phone.

Is he sitting there flirting with Merve right in the middle of everything? he thought huffily. They certainly weren't hanging about.

But his voice was quite formal, he then realized, even if Özen seemed angry.

"Fucking bitch," he heard him say as he slammed the receiver down.

One thing was for sure, the "fucking bitch" wasn't Merve Turpan.

"They're so up themselves with their formalities… so fucking inflexible and slow!" he spit out.

Claesson waited.

"The airlines! Like a fool I started with the Swedish office, but they had half-day closing or whatever it was. Anyway, they were closed. So I called Turkey," he said, giving Claesson a black look. "'We can't just pass on the details of our passengers to any old Tom, Dick, or Harry'," he mimicked. "And of course they can't. But then I'm not any old Tom, Dick, or Harry, which I tried to get into their thick skulls."

"Ask Merve to get on it," said Claesson smiling kindly. "Ask her or Fuat Karaoğlu to call Turkish Airlines. They'll have better luck, I'm sure."

While Claesson trudged home, it occurred to him that they'd forgotten to cancel the car. But what the hell, he thought, no one else had asked to borrow it.

His guilty conscience made him dread that Veronika would make him feel worse by being in a foul mood. But his main struggle was with his own latent depression. He really didn't want this. He wanted to be at home. Ten days, as planned.

But now things were as they were.

And Veronika wasn't in a foul mood. He'd psyched himself up for it unnecessarily. She was hardly awake.

He found her crashed out on the living room sofa, and it was only a quarter past six. The TV was on. Klara was sitting quietly and obediently, watching kids' shows. Nora was sleeping.

He sat down, or rather squeezed himself next to her floppy body. She opened her eyes, and looked around, still thick with sleep.

"Oh, my God. I guess I dropped off."

She lifted her head to see where Klara was.

"Lucky for us we've got well-behaved kids…"

"Mmm," he said and felt his irritation dissipate. "Have you had dinner?"

"No, I haven't actually."

"I'll get something going."

He went into the kitchen. They had some new potatoes. These delicious delicacies, the kings of the potato family. Boiled potatoes it would have to be today, and a piece of salmon, which he threw into the oven. They had some lemons at home, too. And with it he made a yogurt sauce and a green salad with cocktail tomatoes. Expensive, but tasty. The juicy Swedish ones would soon be in the shops. During the winter he didn't bother with cucumber and tomatoes that had been shipped half way around the world. Pepper was OK, but the rest just tasted of water.

He found it quite convenient to stand there puttering around among the pots. His work day seeped away from his body, out through the pores and in his breath, emptying his skull.

His cell phone rang.

"Ilyas Bank is arriving in Copenhagen with Turkish Airlines at 11:15 tomorrow morning," said Özen.

"What the… ?"

Things were heating up.

"His plane took off at nine from Atatürk airport," said Özen.

A little over a two-hour flight, thought Claesson. No, three, with the hour's difference. They'd have to have their wits about them now. Bank was already wanted by Interpol. But things would have to run smoothly tomorrow. No screw-ups.

"What do you say we go to pick him up? The Danish police make the formal arrest, we'll contact them. I reckon they can apprehend him at the gate. But then I'll want him here at once. You and someone else will do."

"OK."

"This is no hooligan we're dealing with here. You drive to Kastrup and get him. It doesn't have to be a marked car. I'll ring Louise and ask her to find someone to back you up. You'll have to leave early. It takes at least three and a half hours, count on four. Drive via Växjö, it's quicker. And then it's just over the Öresund bridge."

The salmon had started to color in the oven just as he was finishing his call to Louise Jasinski. She rarely grumbled these days. She'd make the necessary arrangements and then call Özen.

It was a good-humored Claesson who called out that dinner was ready.

The rest of the evening was spent getting the kids to bed. He took Klara, and Veronika, who had the breasts, took charge of Nora.

He'd already made up his mind to have a chat with the widow in the morning, and was thinking about confronting the young surgeon

Christoffer Daun man-to-man. He didn't know what he should expect to get out of it, but there was something about the missing rug and the woman he was probably having an affair with. The woman who was now also missing.

Veronika might be able to give him some pointers. She knew Daun, after all. But not too many. Prejudice always colored one's impression.

CHAPTER 52

AT LAST HE WAS in the air!

It had been a fretful period. His stomach couldn't take any more, and heaved at the slightest morsel, even though he wasn't actually vomiting any more.

But it'd soon be over now. He was high up in the clouds, literally. Ilyas Bank looked out through the little window at an infinitely blue sky, with fluffy white cloud formations forming a wall-to-wall carpet below.

The police hadn't gotten in touch. He supposed they'd forgotten all about him and Ergün, but that was probably because they hadn't nailed a suspect yet, as Ergün had said. And he always knew best, right? It hadn't been that long ago they'd found the dead man, and investigations take time. We'll just have to wait and see, he'd said.

It was nice to be free of Ergün and his know-it-all attitude. Although he was a good guy, too, Ilyas reminded himself. He'd helped him out like a real big brother. The thought of Ergün pricked at his conscience. Wonder what he's thinking now?

But it was liberating not to have to put up with his going on and on about where he got the money from. And yet he'd not said a word about it himself, just that he was going on a trip – but that was enough to set Ergün off, he who had kids to feed and who was always broke and who, naturally, felt that life was slipping away from him. But such was Allah's will!

He'd managed to evade his questions deftly, he thought proudly. Had said that his parents had helped him out and that his relatives in Sweden had contributed something as well.

Ergün had just stared at him silently. Ilyas realized that he'd be found out sooner or later, so it was just as well that he wasn't still on the boat. Lying was hard work. You had to remember what you said the whole time.

Ergün had tried to get hold of him yesterday. He'd seen it on his cell phone display but just let it ring. He'd been totally tied up on Monday, sorting everything out for his journey.

First, he'd picked up his visa at the Swedish Consulate General on İstiklal Caddesi, and then bought a few things in the shops in Beyoğlu while he was there: new jeans, a cool pair of sneakers, some tops, one a bit warmer than the others. His preparations took the whole day. He bought a new bag, too, a good quality one. He didn't want to arrive at his cousins' place in Sweden with any old piece of shit.

So he hadn't had time to go to work yesterday. Or rather, he'd blown it off.

The plane had reached cruising height. The refreshments cart had rattled past, and he'd taken an apple juice, but realized that it was too sharp for his stomach and so he put the glass down. All he needed was a bite to eat and it would settle. The menu offered a chicken or vegetarian pasta dish. He intended to take the chicken.

And then try to get some sleep.

Once the plane had landed in Copenhagen and he was on his way to the gate, he saw a group of policemen standing at the narrowest point of the passage. At least four of them. Two female, both tall, slim, and blonde. He'd heard, of course, that Scandinavia was full of hot chicks, but that offered him little joy at this juncture. His stomach turned over the moment he saw them and he felt the sudden urge to empty his bowels. He'd just have to clench and resist.

He talked reassuringly to himself. He had everything in order. Passport and four-week visa. There was no cause for alarm.

Ergün had said that he could count himself lucky, not even Turks who had a relative on their deathbed in Sweden could get a visa. He'd also said that Europe was being very uncooperative about letting Turkey into the EU. "They don't want us," he said gloomily. "So why should we go there? Things are getting better and better here in Turkey! Stay here instead! Fight for our own country. We can manage without the EU."

It was coming to his turn in the line. They weren't stopping everyone to inspect their passports. Not those who looked Western European.

He approached one of the female officers and held up his passport for her to see. But she stopped him.

Politi it said on her breast. She was so tall, she almost had to look down at him. She thumbed through his papers and asked something, making curious throaty sounds, and at first he didn't understand; but then he realized she wanted to see his return ticket, too, so he dutifully produced it, handing it to her with sweaty fingers.

"To Sweden?" she said.

"Yes," he nodded. "To Sweden." It said that on the visa.

Then she turned to her colleague. This was bad; she hadn't done this to anyone else. He took out his radio and spoke some gobbledygook into it.

I'm going to shit my pants, he thought, and clenched for all he was worth.

"Please stay here," she said, and keeping hold of his passport and papers, had him stand to one side of the line, which continued to snake forward in the narrow passageway out toward the broader walkways of the terminal.

"Bathroom!" he said, almost panicking.

But she ignored him.

He repeated his plea, but more loudly and more resolute. His bowels were on the point of exploding. She must have interpreted his panic-stricken face correctly. The strange language whizzed over his head like a machine gun salvo, and one of the airline staff came and took pity on him.

He was a little calmer when he came out. But it didn't last long, because two new police officers were there, who each took him by an arm and said that he was to go with them. They dragged him away like some common criminal. Or rather, let him walk himself. He was as meek as a lamb.

They arrived at a room with windows overlooking a large car park. There were more police officers in the room, as well as two men in plain clothes, who were now approaching him.

"Are you Ilyas Bank?" said one of them in Turkish.

"Yes."

"We are policemen from Sweden."

His heart began to gallop. What had happened? What had he done? And Miro was there waiting for him.

"Where are you traveling to?" continued the dark-hard one, with a slight accent.

"To Sweden. My cousin's waiting for me. He's picking me up in his car."

"Where does your cousin live?"

"In…" He couldn't pronounce the place. "I've got it written down here."

He pulled a piece of paper from his back pocket.

"Landskrona," the Swedish-Turk read. "OK, we'll make sure to inform him and to give him your luggage. You can call him yourself and tell him you won't be coming today. You're to come with us to another town in Sweden. The journey will take almost four hours."

"Why… ?"

"Because you were a witness to Carl-Ivar Olsson's death."

Oh, shit! thought Ilyas. Is this dead old man going to follow him everywhere?

Barely an hour later, Ilyas was sitting in the back seat with a sturdy, red-bloated Swede of the larger kind beside him. They wanted to keep an eye on him, he supposed. The policeman called Mustafa Özen was driving.

The car drove onto a long bridge that stretched between Denmark and Sweden, he learned. Nice view. The sun was shining and small boats were sailing in a flock some way away; otherwise the water was quiet, compared, at least, with Istanbul's frenetic boat traffic.

They arrived in Sweden. To a country that seemed clean and somehow desolate. They drove through some flat countryside until the forests took over. Trees, trees, and more trees. They stopped off at a McDonald's in some godforsaken spot and let him go in as a normal civilian.

"What would you like?" wondered the one called Özen.

He pointed to a picture of a McFeast. It was hardly something he normally ate, but he was hungry. His stomach had eased, and he was clearly not meant to die today.

So there he was, munching a hamburger at a rudimentary, wiped-clean, bolted-down table, with a burly Swede on one side and a Swedish Turk on the other, staring into a murky forest.

So this was Sweden.

CHAPTER 53

ÖZEN CALLED TO ANNOUNCE that they had Ilyas Bank. They'd picked him up at Kastrup and had stopped off in Växjö to have a bite to eat.

Claesson looked at his watch. They'd be in Oskarshamn by four, at the earliest.

He called Louise and asked her to contact some kind of carpet expert who could come and value Olsson's stock. She promised to do what she could.

He drove to the hospital. He approached the information hatch, showed his ID and asked them to page Christoffer Daun. While he waited, he read the note that was taped to the glass partition. A wanted notice: If anyone had seen the woman in the picture they were to contact the Oskarshamn police, it said.

Daun was on the ward, he was told, so he took the elevator up to the sixth floor, opened the frosted glass door, and stepped inside. Felt the familiar ill-ease. This was not an environment for him. It wasn't a case of hypochondria or cancer phobia, but of feeling shut in, diminished.

Christoffer Daun came to greet him. He was wearing a light-blue shirt with pens sticking out of the breast pocket, white pants, and sneakers on his feet. And a badge, of military design that you just stuck into a fold in the cloth. Name and rank – although in this case it was profession: *Registered Doctor.*

"I've got a few minutes," said Daun. "We can go in here."

Just then Claesson's phone rang. It was Özen.

"Can we talk?"

"Make it brief."

"Merve just called and said that they'd located Olsson's bank account. Turns out that his payment to the carpet dealer in the Grand Bazaar was all in order. He had a pretty fat account. Her conclusion is that he was straight and paid tax in Turkey and all that."

"OK."

"But then Olsson had also withdrawn a small fortune in lira over and above what he needed for the rug. Roughly two hundred thousand Swedish kronor."

Silence.

"Did you hear me?"

"Yes."

"I haven't asked Ilyas. We'll have to take it later. But who might have it?"

"Thanks," said Claesson feeling suddenly braced, but collected himself when he caught sight of Christoffer Daun's face.

The man looked worn, but still had that baby-like countenance that academics from better social circumstances often had. The kind with a large head and even teeth who'd never dream of replacing the drainpipes on his house.

"I'm not investigating Tina Rosenkvist's disappearance," said Claesson.

Daun's jaws were working frantically, he noticed.

"But Carl-Ivar Olsson's death. I know your wife worked for him. Has Annelie mentioned some special rug or carpet of some kind?"

"She goes on a lot about special rugs and carpets. That's pretty much all she talks about these days. They've gone to her head," he said, but not without a certain tongue-in-cheek irony, as Claesson interpreted it.

"So you can tell me nothing about an old fragment…" he took out the picture, "… which is five, six hundred years old and which might be worth at least one and a half million? Probably more?"

Christoffer Daun stared at the picture.

"I have no idea. This hasn't passed through our home at least. Is this what everyone's after?"

"What do you mean?"

"I'm thinking about that psycho who came bursting into our kitchen and…"

"Started to strangle Tine Rosenkvist?"

Daun shrugged lightly.
"Yes."
Claesson thanked him and left the ward.

CHAPTER 54

CLAESSON RECOGNIZED ILYAS BANK from the ferry at once, and gave a quick thought to the strangeness of seeing him here. In the wrong part of the world, and in a completely different role to that of a seller of hot tea in cute little glasses.

Ilyas Bank was looking uncomfortable, despite his more casual clothes: jeans and a smart top instead of the white shirt and black pants he'd worn on the ferry. Both garments looked new, as did his shoes.

Did Bank recognize him? This would be an excellent test of his memory. Or perhaps not? Rather a test of his own vanity, he realized as he thought it. Ilyas Bank probably met hundreds of tourists every day. If he recognized anyone it was probably through association with a particular event or notable appearance.

"Is he tired, or can we get cracking right away?" he asked Özen.

After a visit to the bathroom and tea and sandwiches and even some little cakes that they'd found in some forgotten corner of the fridge, they sat themselves down at a table with a tape running. The corridor was silent.

"Ask him if he knows why he's here," said Claesson.

Özen became more animated when speaking Turkish; Claesson had noted that back in Istanbul. Now he was gesticulating again as he asked questions. Ilyas Bank cast a quick glance at Claesson now and then to see if he was listening. The fellow was starting to pale, and kept wiping his palms against his jeans.

"Try to make him understand he's in no danger here, that we want him to help us, and we're not out to arrest him...not at the moment, anyway," said Claesson.

Özen explained, sounding calm. Claesson understood nothing of what he said. Turkish and Swedish have little in common, that's for sure, he thought. As he sat there, wholly dependent on Özen and his interpretive skills and honesty, he felt that powerlessness that an immigrant parent without knowledge of Swedish but with Swedish-speaking children must feel. An inverted age hierarchy, the younger now the spokespeople for their elders.

Finally Özen nodded.

"He's ready."

Claesson took out four small color portraits of Magnus Öberg and three other men of the same skin and hair color. He placed the photographs in front of Ilyas Bank and instructed Özen to ask Ilyas to say if he recognized any of them. He could take his time.

Ilyas didn't react immediately, and apparently didn't recognize any of them. It was difficult to identify faces without a body, Claesson knew that. No height, build or posture to go by.

"Him, maybe," said Ilyas after a while, pointing a trembling finger at Magnus Öberg's enlarged passport photo.

Claesson resisted a smile, and produced instead as many photos of exactly the same men, this time digitally manipulated so that each was wearing a cap with the letters ICA glaring in all their redness on the front.

Ilyas Bank studied the photos carefully again, but his body was starting to twitch even faster.

"That one there looks most like the man on the boat," he said, lifting his thick black eyelashes to stare uncertainly at Claesson while identifying Magnus Öberg once more.

"Thank you," said Claesson in English.

Ilyas turned to Özen and said something while continuing to glance at Claesson from the corner of his eye.

"He says that it's strange, but you also look like a man he once saw on the boat," said Özen on behalf of Ilyas.

"Tell him that he might be right," said Claesson.

The mood became almost jovial for a moment.

"Why do you remember me?" asked Claesson in English turning to the young Turk.

Ilyas understood.

"Because of you…" he said, and coughed, running out of words. He resorted to Turkish.

"Because you sat where you sat on the ferry," interpreted Özen.

"So what did that make you think?" asked Claesson.

"It was same place… ahem… as dead man, you know?" he offered in English.

"You mean because I was sitting in the same place that you found the dead carpet dealer in?" said Claesson in Swedish by way of clarification and Özen interpreted.

Ilyas Bank nodded, his cheeks blushing violently, and said something in Turkish. He sounded subdued, spoke quietly, almost mumbled.

"Yes. It was horrible. The worst experience of my life," Özen interpreted, conveying Ilyas's frame of mind by being equally subdued. He even placed his hand on his breast over his heart, in the same way as Ilyas did.

"Did you dare touch the dead man?" continued Claesson in Swedish and Özen in Turkish.

"No. Yes, I tried to feel for a pulse."

"That was good thinking!"

Ilyas smiled gratefully.

"Did he have any pulse that you could feel?"

Ilyas Bank shook his head.

"Did you touch his clothes?"

Ilyas Bank looked uncertainly at Claesson, wondering, of course, what the Swedish policeman was getting at.

"No, I didn't touch his clothes. I ran for help as quickly as I could."

Claesson nodded. He knew that this wasn't his job, that it was the Turkish police's department, but he couldn't help questioning the man now that he had him here in front of him.

"Did you manage to see if the dead man had anything in his pockets?" continued Claesson. "Maybe there was something sticking out or something."

"No."

Claesson noticed that Ilyas had become slightly flushed around his cheekbones, but judged him prepared to stick to his answer.

It was with some reservation that he cut straight to the chase and asked the next question:

"Did you happen to see a bundle of bank notes?"

"No, I've said, haven't I? They asked me that in Istanbul, too, that policewoman. It was horrible, I just wanted to get away from there…"

Ilyas Bank suddenly asked if he could use the bathroom. He all but stumbled out of the room, bent slightly forwards as if suffering an acute attack of the gripes.

It was hopelessly difficult to work out whether he was telling the truth or lying, thought Claesson. According to the science, it was quite simply impossible to determine. All manner of tests and trials had been done. The human psyche was more complex than that, and he liked that. He liked the multifaceted, the seemingly inexplicable.

He reflected that Merve Turpan had reported on the other man on the boat, the one who ran the *kiosk*. He'd hinted to Merve that Ilyas had become less careful with his money after the murder. Bought new clothes, and expensive shoes among other things. He'd also suddenly been able to afford to travel.

And two hundred thousand in your pocket would get you a long way, thought Claesson. According to Olsson's bank statement, he'd taken out that sum in Sweden before he left. He must have gone around with the notes rolled up in his underwear or in some other intimate hiding place on his person. There were specially designed flat belts for that. He'd probably been properly upholstered both front and back! Like the priest with drugs in his underwear.

The money had at least not been used to pay an invoice, as far as they could see. The expensive rug from the dealer in the Grand Bazaar – the one they'd seen neither hide nor hair of – Olsson had paid for though his firm, all legit and above board, with all transactions and papers in order. And there was more money in the company. It was solvent, as they said. But admittedly that two hundred thousand Olsson could have used for something else. For partying and flashing around. For treating himself to the good things in life.

Claesson realized that it was stupid to get hooked up on the money, a small sum in the context, but once a parsimonious Smålander....

Anyway, no one had reported the money missing. If anyone was to do that, it would be Olsson's estate, but they'd probably not gotten that far.

Ilyas returned, but Claesson saw no point in pressing him for more. It was a killer they were after, not a thief. And if their Turkish colleagues wanted to follow that up, that was their business.

It was half past five, and they'd booked a hotel room for Ilyas Bank for the night.

"We'll have to think about what to do with him later," said Claesson.

"It be best for him to be with his relatives in Landskrona, wouldn't it?" said Özen. "And then we'll just bring him over here when it's time for a line-up. At least it's closer to Landskrona than bringing him all the way from Turkey. I don't think he's the type to make a run for it."

Claesson thought.

"No, he's got no reason to. Not if he's telling the truth."

Özen took Ilyas Bank away. The door closed loudly behind them at the same moment as Claesson powered down his computer and did a quick tidy of his desk.

Once upon a time he would've gotten a kick out of clearing the decks when everyone else had gone and the evening calm had started to descend. That was in the days before the family thing. The women in his life had had to put up with it. He never gave it a thought, their tolerance, because to him the priorities were obvious. And if they complained – he'd hear accusations of his egocentricism and insensitivity – he just let it go in one ear and out the other. He'd really not wanted anything else back then.

Veronika knew that he'd be late. She wasn't even at home but at dinner with a nice family with a young son called Otto, a friend of Klara's from preschool.

Louise Jasinski suddenly appeared in the doorway. She must have been creeping through the corridor.

He gestured at the chair, but she didn't sit down, just entered the room and leaned against a bookshelf, as was her habit. A signal that she intended to keep things brief.

"How's it going with the carpet dealer?"

"We're getting somewhere, I think, but it's a bit tricky and now it seems as if everything's related. First Olsson's murder, then that assault in Bråbo that also seems to have something to do with rugs, and where the attacker seems to have got the wrong person. And then the victim is reported missing two days later, which is odd to say the least. And on top of everything, someone's stolen the old rug that I inherited! It's pretty intriguing in a way, you know, but there are too many coincidences and too many rugs!"

"Anyway," Louise interrupted, and took a deep breath so that he'd understand that she had something important to say. "Anyway, forensics got the DNA results today from Linköping. Some of them, that is. There are more to come, apparently. We've not wanted to disturb you. I mean you've been in the interview room, but there's a lot here.

"We know who he is, the man who attacked Tina Rosenkvist. He's called Patrik Lindström, and he's not exactly God's little angel. Clumsy, too. He'd tossed a cigarette butt onto the ground where he'd parked his car… the one that Veronika saw as she drove past on her way to a friend's, or whatever she was doing."

Claesson nodded.

"There was saliva on the cigarette butt," Louise continued. "All we had to do was look through the database and bingo!"

People always leave some kind of trace behind, thought Claesson. But this was sloppy. An experienced criminal should have known better. But then they get all worked up and lose focus.

"He's got several convictions for everything from burglary to assault, although not murder. A known violent criminal, in other words. Seems as if he's been operating as a front man, or a hit man, sent out to find a rug and possibly intimidate or threaten. There's a warrant out for him, of course, but we haven't gotten hold of him yet. Lindström isn't known for being the type to make plans, doesn't do security vans or anything like that. He hits hard but maybe subtlety isn't his best quality, and I imagine it wasn't his intention to nearly kill that Tina woman. He comes from Norrköping, and that jives with the info we got on his dialect, and he's got links to the Stockholm underworld.

"As long as Tina Rosenkvist is missing he's got every reason to lie low," continued Louise. "She might have been abducted by him, or even killed. It's not the alleged lover, Doctor Daun, at least. He was on duty when she went missing. He was at the hospital the whole time."

"I know," said Claesson. "I've spoken to him."

"OK, there were traces of his saliva on the victim's face, they took careful samples when she was in hospital. They probably had an intimate relationship, no matter how much he won't admit it. They drank some wine, that was all, he says, but he'll change his mind, you'll see."

Claesson pondered for a while over dates and the possibility that it was Patrik Lindström who'd been in Istanbul and murdered Carl-Ivar Olsson.

"Have you got a photo of Lindström that I can have?"

Louise went to fetch one. A completely different type from Magnus Öberg. Bigger, broader face, lighter hair and shorter. Height: five foot ten, he read. An ICA cap on his head? Well, possibly...

No! He remembered now that the man had turned up at the carpet shop in Oskarshamn on the same Saturday that Olsson had been murdered in Istanbul. He could hardly have been in two places at the same time. Hadn't Patrik Lindström also asked Annelie Daun when Carl-Ivar would be coming home? Yes, that's right! He shared his thoughts with Louise.

"Annelie Daun didn't exactly give a brilliant description, but now we have a picture to show her."

Louise nodded.

"The widow said that a man named Lennart Ahl had called their house and asked for her husband. It sounds like a made-up name to me. He probably didn't want to reveal his true identity. Just wanted the rug, nothing else."

"Well, I'm going home," Louise said then. "This job of ours can be a real thrill at times. See you tomorrow."

He took the stairs down and walked to his bike. A cigarette butt. So trivial. Yet so classic. He'd been wearing gloves, Tina Rosenkvist had told them. On that point he'd been careful.

But it's not easy to think of everything...

Annelie Daun closed up shop at five o'clock and went back to her mother's apartment. She'd sounded strange when they'd spoken earlier that afternoon, tired and kind of gravely.

The woman who opened the door bore a ghastly pallor, but she was absolutely adamant about not going to lie down.

"I'll never get up again," she said, and slumped down onto a kitchen chair to light a cigarette.

But it clearly didn't taste good, as she put it out at once.

"Where does it hurt?" asked Annelie.

"My whole stomach," groaned her mother, doubling up. "And up into my chest and my back, and down my legs, everywhere."

She sounded abnormally pathetic, in an altogether normal way. Not in that cunning whiny way that drove Annelie up the wall. When she'd so blatantly whine and wheedle to get her way. Compulsive thoughts that needed venting but that were of no use to anyone, least of all her to mother herself.

"You've got to go to the hospital."

"I don't want to."

"Look, you have to."

"No, I really *don't* want to, OK?"

Annelie clenched her jaw and wondered if she should call Christoffer. But she decided not to. She preferred to have nothing at all to do with him. Didn't want to demonstrate any kind of dependency or inferiority, even though they lived under the same roof. Some nights, at least. But that was pretty much all that was left of their relationship. She was searching high and low for an apartment, although he wanted her to stay.

And sometimes she felt sorry for him.

Foolish, stupid Christoffer! He was incorrigible, and obviously took her for a fool that he could simply hoodwink. She'd been both jealous and angry, of course, when she found that wretched piece of red paper, but at the same time, she got a kick out of knowing. A real kick, even, from having read Tina Rosenkvist's doe-eyed drivel on the red notepaper, but hadn't confronted him with it. Left him feeling uncertain instead. She could see how much that made him suffer.

Stupid, stupid man!

But she wasn't afraid of him. Every human being is capable of killing when push comes to shove, she'd read, but she didn't really believe that Christoffer would have murdered Tina Rosenkvist. Missing person posters had been put up, like in the movies. Her gentle face appeared in the most surprising of places. Like at the library, in the ICA supermarket, and in the sporting goods store. What a mess! Fact really is stranger than fiction, she thought.

He was at work now, she knew that, doing the night shift.

Her mother twisted her body and groaned. Finally, unable to take any more, Annelie picked up the phone. But Christoffer sounded surprised and even affectionate, and not at all irritated, as he could often be when she disturbed him at work. He listened carefully and then became very practical, and she needed that. It could be anything from gallstones to kidney stones, pancreatitis or a heart attack, he said. Or a dissecting aorta aneurysm.

"Really?" she said and stared at the hall wall, which was papered in a small floral pattern. "Is that serious?"

"Yes. It means that the aorta is about to rupture, like a dried-out garden hose. But we'll just have to hope it's not that, because then she'll have to go to Linköping. It causes acute stomach pains, which radiate out to the back. Whatever it is, she must come in right away for immediate examination."

"She refuses."

"You mother can think what she likes!" he said in his comforting voice, the one that he'd not used with her for so long that she'd almost forgotten it. But that he clearly still had. "You'll just have to drive her here."

She softened. Everything suddenly felt easier. She didn't have to be alone in the decision about her mother, who was actually feeling a little better when she returned to her in the kitchen. But she still did not, under any circumstances, want to go to the hospital. And maybe it wasn't necessary any more, thought Annelie as she helped her into bed.

As soon as her mother lay down it was if the pain went away almost totally. It feels more tender, like an after effect, she said.

Annelie perched on the edge of the bed.

"Mom, can I ask you something?" she said, seizing the opportunity. "Do you know what Carl-Ivar had in the attic?"

"Pah," said her mother. "Mostly just a load of junk. Old rugs and stuff. Feel free to go up there and see if there's anything you think you might get some pleasure from, though I doubt there is. Take whatever you want."

Was it that simple?

"But don't I have to ask Birgitta and the cousins?"

"Why? It's my attic. It's my name on the contract and it's me who pays the rent, even if Carl-Ivar did give me a little for the storage."

"Yes, but…"

"Unless, of course, you needed help carting the stuff away. Because I certainly don't intend to do it. And I certainly don't want to keep the extra compartment, either. I mean, what do I need it for?"

Annelie stared through the half open blinds. She could hear the birds singing. They were nesting and mating, ready for midsummer, or so they said.

"Mom, do you know what Carl-Ivar was doing in Istanbul?"

"I guess he just liked being there. I suppose he relaxed and went around looking at the odd carpet."

Annelie fell silent. Her mother sounded so warm, and so secretive.

"He had his commitments there, I suppose, I don't really know," she continued, and her voice dropped, as if weighing up whether or not to say more.

And then she continued anyway. "But I know that he met a girl there a long time ago, when he was newly married to Birgitta. He was very fond of his Turkish girl. He loved Birgitta too, but I guess in a different way. It pained him. I don't know how he sorted things out. Maybe he never did. Let the years go, and I've been so preoccupied with my own life, with you to look after and… well, I've been a drinker, boozed my life away, I guess you could say… so I guess I'd not thought so much about how Carl-Ivar was."

Seagulls screaming outside the window. Otherwise silence.

"Do you know?" asked her mother, studying her daughter's face.

"Maybe."

Her mother nodded, as if she already knew the answer.

"But don't tell Birgitta, promise me that. It's not always so easy to tell the truth. This'll have to be just between you, me, and Carl-Ivar," she said, winking in that sly way that put Annelie on her guard.

It's not easy telling lies, either, she thought.

It had got damp and chilly out. Annelie jumped into her car and left Filaregatan. She called Christoffer from the road and told him that the pains had subsided and that her mother was sleeping soundly.

"In that case it was probably an attack of gallstones," he said, sounding untroubled.

"Thanks for the help," she said.

"Are you headed home now?"

"Yes."

She'd slept in the shop one night and at Gabbi's, but it was tiring being on the move, so she'd moved back home and had taken the bed in the guest room. It was actually quite OK. The walls were papered in a cute pattern of dainty little flowers that she'd chosen herself, and she'd hung up white curtains through which the sunlight filtered so beautifully.

"So I'll see you tomorrow when I'm off," he said, and sounded like he was looking forward to it.

Breakfast together. Coffee, tea, and toast. Why not?

She parked the car in the driveway at home. The red Passat wasn't there; it was in the hospital parking lot.

At least there'd be no red letter slipped under the windshield wiper this evening, she thought. If there was, she'd have to assume it was a ghost. Or that she was in hiding, this Tina Rosenkvist. Maybe she was in hiding from Pär.

What a crazy time.

You knew so little about what people can get caught up in. She couldn't be dead, could she? thought Annelie, stepping out of the car, her body aching with fatigue. The stillness enveloped her in a way that surprised her. Fields and meadows greeted her and the gnawing tension ebbed away. This was why she lived out here, she thought. In the Garden of Eden. And the serpent had already paid a visit. She didn't need to worry any longer.

She really should be on her guard, after all she was wearing an alarm and all, but somehow it was as if she just didn't have the energy. Or perhaps the will. Or rather refused to believe that some thug would turn up wanting to get some information out of her, or, even worse, attack her. Not now. It wasn't the right time. It would be like plunging straight into a wasps' nest. The police were involved now, and everyone was just waiting for him to strike again.

Tina had nothing to do with carpets, she was sure of it. She was convinced that her disappearance was down to an unstable and slightly psychotic husband, but that was a thought she kept to herself. It would make people suspect she was jealous.

And she was, too, but her blackness had nothing to do with anyone else. She handled it in her own way. With silence, and that worked. And when it came to Pär Rosenkvist, local opinion was pretty undivided. There was something about him that made most people a little scared.

She didn't go into the house, but down toward the slope at the back of the garden. The grass lay cut in the meadow. Yellow irises brightened up the river bank and the buttercups glowed against the gray stone fence, even though they were starting to close their petals for the evening.

It was still light. Water gushed forth in the brook, brown but clear, so that the stones on the bed looked like soft lumps of clay. A pair of flycatchers flew busily in and out of their nesting box.

She dropped down onto a rock. Everything that had happened just didn't really move her that deeply. Not now. It was so divinely beautiful that she couldn't help but feel consoled.

Maybe things would sort themselves out. Between her and Christoffer. And perhaps she'd be able to carry on working as a carpet dealer, "for real."

She got up, went into the house, and poured herself a glass of wine.

"Cheers!" she said to herself, lifting her glass in salute.

CHAPTER 55

IT WAS GETTING CLOSE TO eight o'clock on the evening. Birgitta Olsson had mechanically hung up the laundry and tidied the kitchen. Now she was sitting watching the news on TV. She should really go out and put the garden tools back in the shed but she couldn't be bothered. The hedge clippers, the rake, the pruners, and the lawn edger – the one with the short handle and that was brand new and sharp-bladed and nice to handle – were lying in the hallway in their long, narrow basket, which she'd placed on a wooden stall by the wall to keep it out of the way and to stop mud getting everywhere. It was unlike her to be sloppy with the tidying like this, but it was as if she just couldn't be bothered since Carl-Ivar's death.

She was sitting in Johan's old room in front of the portable television. Her powers of concentration were not at their peak. But then the news wasn't that remarkable, and her thoughts were mainly occupied by the day's event, that Chief Inspector Claesson, Veronika's husband, had stopped by. Not when Sven was with her, though, luckily enough.

The woman on the quayside. And Carl-Ivar.

The picture had stuck in her mind when she'd seen it that first time, in Istanbul, even though she hadn't let on when she had Claesson in front of her. Carl-Ivar looked so unusually relaxed. Like when he was younger.

The telephone rang. It was by her side, and she turned the volume down on the TV and answered.

It was Chief Inspector Claesson again, wondering if he could ask a question that he'd forgotten earlier.

"Do you recall if that man who called and asked for Carl-Ivar spoke with an accent? The one who claimed to be Lennart Ahl?"

"Yes… He could've been from around Västervik," she answered. "Or Vimmerby. Or further north."

"And where do you end up then?" he asked as if hosting a quiz show.

"In Östergötland," she answered obediently. "Maybe he was from Norrköping."

The Chief Inspector sounded very pleased.

"Was there anything else?"

No, nothing else. She switched off the TV and went to pack her bag. She was due on night duty at nine.

She would've been able to get a longer period of sick leave, the diagnosis would no doubt have been *crisis reaction*, or she'd have been table to take vacation time, at least up until the funeral next week. In a way, she was still numb, but she expected this paralysis would hang around for a long time. She wasn't so much in shock that she couldn't concentrate on her job. Body and soul wanted to return to normalcy, were being drawn back toward living their life again, as far as this was possible, during the time that her grief over losing Carl-Ivar was claiming its due.

But most of all, she just wanted to get away. The house was so silent and depressing, and seeing Sven take off for the golf course with his Nettan now when the evenings were still light wasn't making things easier. Suddenly it was just the two of them that mattered, and then he didn't have eyes for her any more.

She didn't take her bike today, as she usually did. It was quite far to pedal and she didn't have it in her to be alert the whole time, even if the weather had made another u-turn and was balmy and pleasant again.

The vegetation was less delicate and had started to mature, she noticed through the windshield. It was indescribably beautiful.

Once she'd parked and walked into the entrance hall, she spotted the notice. It was stuck on the wall by the information desk straight ahead for everyone to see. She walked closer to it and studied the photograph carefully. It was like a movie. Her anxiety rose.

The police needed help finding this woman, the note informed her. Rosie looked out at her from it. It was a good photo. Tina was smiling kindly, and looked her normal self. Like a flitting butterfly.

That had now flown away.

Once she'd changed and was at her station, she felt happy to be back. Here she was, sitting waiting for the change of shift report, as she'd done since time began. She was wearing her white dress. She was a nurse, not a grieving widow, at least not *only* that. She'd already tired of that role.

Anne-Sofie came in like a warm breeze and gave her a hug. How nice that they were on night duty together, she thought. She hadn't called to check which assistant nurse she'd be working with. They also changed the rotation quite often, so you just had to take who you got, and Sofa was a diamond.

"Do you know who the night doctor is?"

"Nah."

Birgitta picked up the schedule.

"It says that it's Daun."

Sofa rolled her eyes. At that moment, Birgitta felt a powerful sense of déjà vu. The only one missing was Rosie, with her bustling in to report out in her slightly disorganized way. Otherwise, it was exactly the same team who'd been on night duty the last time she worked before finding out that Carl-Ivar was dead. So much had happened since then. As if years had gone by.

"Do they know who did it?" asked Sofa cautiously.

"No, not yet, I'm trying to get used to the idea that they won't ever find his murderer," she said.

She'd also have to get used to expressing her plight in plain words. She couldn't quite make herself say, "My husband's been murdered." Rather: "My husband was tragically murdered." But not even that sounded good.

What do you say?

You avoid saying anything, maybe. People rarely ask about sensitive matters, so it could work. The funeral director had managed that feat with such discretion that she'd hardly noticed.

It was then time for the report, which was followed by several hours of routine. It was an unusually quiet night, with almost too little to do. They grew lethargic, and had lots of time to chat. They couldn't just keep turning the patients in their beds the whole night, they needed to be left in peace to sleep.

They got their meal ready at around midnight. It was still a little light outside. Everyone loves the light, except those who suffered from spring depression, and they chatted about that as a warm-up. And then they plunged straight into the sea of minor tragedies. They started with Göran Bladh, who was still in intensive care, Sofa said. He was on the road to recovery, but they didn't know how he'd pull through, whether he'd just be a vegetable. Time would tell.

They knew how it could be, and chose to cheer each other up with all the cases they could remember where the patient had miraculously fared much better than anyone would have first thought. There were the opposite cases, too. But they were so fond of Bladh that they wanted the best for him.

"Maybe he'll quit the bottle after this," said Sofa. "Realize that he's been given another chance."

So thus far they hadn't mentioned Carl-Ivar. Sofa was sensitive and realized that Birgitta had no need to unload. There wasn't that much to say, either. The papers had covered most of it.

"It must be worse not knowing where your own are," said Sofa. So now it was time to discuss their own Rosie. It was the kind of thing people said, but it didn't matter, thought Birgitta. It was never easy to know what was worse, and she wanted to avoid all kinds of comparisons. But people liked grading things. Making top ten lists over tragedies. The worst tragedy wins.

They chewed over the subject for a while.

"There are those who disappear and never come back. Their relatives don't know if they're alive or dead. And then it turns out they've moved to other side of the globe," said Sofa.

They agreed that that didn't seem Rosie's style.

"You don't just abandon your kids," said Birgitta.

Just as they were about to discuss what everyone already knew, that Rosie had had an affair with… he suddenly appeared. As if conjured up by magic.

Christoffer Daun blinked quickly and looked almost abashed. Had he overheard them?

"Hi," he said. "You alright? I'm just doing a final round before I go to bed. It seems pretty quiet."

This was something new he'd started doing, Birgitta thought. The other doctors usually did the rounds before going to bed, but never him.

It was probably after what had happened. Though Sofa said, once his footsteps had echoed away off down the corridor, that there had obviously been more wrong with that woman who'd died at home. A blood vessel in her head had burst, and no one could do anything about that.

That was lucky for Daun, thought Birgitta. He who's already up to his neck in so much other trouble.

The night passed. When Birgitta jumped into her car, chilled to the bone and deliciously ravenous, she was remarkably at peace. That some things didn't change was liberating.

She slammed the car door shut in her driveway at a quarter to eight just as Sven and Nettan stumbled out of their house.

Sven became flustered and went to get the car out of the garage and pack away the golf bags.

"If you don't get there in time when the weather's nice like this, you have to wait forever for your turn to tee off," chirped Agneta. "It's lovely, isn't it? The early bird and all that!"

As cheerfully upbeat as always. Agneta's piqué top was pink and Sven's orange. Both were wearing checkered cotton slacks.

"Come on, Nettan!" he called from the car.

Of course. Agneta Bromse was off on Wednesdays. Sven never came over to her on Wednesdays.

Birgitta walked inside without looking in Sven's direction. She was aching all over with tiredness. She didn't even have the energy to be bitter.

She made a cup of tea. Got a bit slack and toasted a couple of slices of white, rather than the wholegrain. She didn't know what had gotten into her, but now when Carl-Ivar wasn't alive… Pah! She just felt like something hot, that's all, and since she had a sliced loaf in the freezer for him and his taste for continental breakfasts, it was just a case of popping a couple of slices into the toaster. It'd be a waste to throw it away.

Later, she found her head sinking softly into her pillow. Heavy work, heavy sleep, she thought, and dropped straight off to sleep for the first time since Carl-Ivar's death.

CHAPTER 56

THE TELEPHONE RANG just as Birgitta Olsson was getting her suitcase ready to go and visit her parents in Bråbo. She let it ring until it stopped. Her mother had baked a sponge cake, she said when they agreed that she should pay them a visit. She enticed her with something tasty, just like in the old days. Something freshly baked for their afternoon coffee.

Birgitta tossed in her toiletry bag and a change of underwear, in case she decided to stay over. Her old room under the ceiling was calling her. A yearning for the old and habitual. To snuggle down and have her body relax in a bed that her torso and limbs recognized from before. It was a physical memory, which strangely the body still had. And the comforting sounds coming from her parents puttering around downstairs.

Her mother had started to fret about the funeral, Birgitta could tell from her constant anxious questions and felt instinctively that she had to go and reassure her parents that she wasn't going to have a breakdown.

"That you were widowed first is just not the right order of things," said her mother. And her father had guffawed, though neither coarsely nor jovially. He could have said that it was terrible or tragic, but those words to too big to fit in his mouth. Rather this, thought Birgitta. Or he might have darkened and withdrawn. People's reactions were unpredictable. "The order in which people die is beknownst only to him up there," he said, pointing with a finger into the air.

References to the Great Man in the Sky were otherwise a rarity in her childhood home. Age and their own imminent death made the soul softer and more tender, she supposed.

On the other hand, Carl-Ivar was to have a church funeral, of that there was no doubt. After all, it was in the Christian tradition that they both had their roots. Civil funerals were becoming popular, and times were changing, but the alternative grated now that Carl-Ivar had died in that graceless way. There was a need to neutralize the appalling and macabre, as far as this was possible, with the familiar. She and he up there in his heaven needed this stability, she reasoned.

The phone rang again just as she'd put her coat on. Stubbornly and irritatingly, the signals implored her to pick up.

It was Annelie Daun.

Her mood sank. She just didn't want to talk to Annelie. To discuss the carpet shop. She wanted to run away from it, and had already planned for Johan and Lotta to be there when it was time. But preferably not Magnus, as he got so businesslike, delving into details.

"I'd like to come by now if it's OK," said Annelie Daun.

Birgitta looked at her watch, it was almost 1:30.

"It's not really possible, I'm afraid. I'm just rushing out…I'm actually standing here with my coat on."

"Isn't it anything you can put off?" persisted Annelie. "I want to talk to you now. In private, if possible."

Dear me! She'd certainly made up her mind. As if she'd psyched herself up. It sounded worrying.

"But can't we meet in Bråbo? I'm just off to my parents'… and you live just across the road and can easily pop over."

But Annelie didn't want to. And she wanted to go to Holmhällevägen, preferably at once.

For some reason, Birgitta didn't ask why. She just sensed it wouldn't have been a good idea. Her hand was trembling slightly as she hung up.

And then she picked up the receiver again and called her parents to say that she'd have to go over tomorrow instead. Something had come up that she couldn't get out of.

"Not bad news I hope," said her mother anxiously.

"No, no," she promised.

Then she sat down on the sitting room sofa and waited. Could it be the rug that Annelie wanted to meet her about? The one that that detective asked her about twice by now? Lotta had also been circling the matter.

As Birgitta Olsson stared into space, her gaze fell on the new flat-screen. It was off, presenting a soothing surface to gaze at while she recapped the conversation she'd had with Lotta when her daughter called from Stockholm last Monday. She'd picked up almost immediately that Lotta had something on her mind, and remembered well how the conversation went. "Mom, you know that policeman from Oskarshamn…" she began with contrived jauntiness.

Even at that point Birgitta suspected that there was someone in the room besides Lotta. Was she calling on behalf of Magnus? Her tone was unfocused, as if her attention was being drawn in two directions. Like when you talked to someone on the phone who was reading and answering emails at the same time. The muffled clicks of the keys in the background that snuck into the microphone. She always felt inclined to just hang up.

But she stayed on the line, despite the faint whispering in the background "Yes, and what about him?" she'd asked dryly instead.

"Well, when he spoke to me the other day, he asked about a rug, again.…"

"Did he now?" she'd said, making every effort to sound completely neutral.

"Yeah, he asked if that very special rug that he'd asked about when he interviewed us in Istanbul and that Dad had bought down there in Turkey to take back to Sweden… He… I mean the detective inspector, wondered if I knew if it was in Sweden somewhere… About where more precisely it had gotten to and… and I told him the truth, that I still hadn't the foggiest idea… Dad had so many carpet deals happening that it was simply impossible to keep tabs on them all, I said. But then I couldn't help checking then with Annelie to see if she knew something, but she didn't, either."

"Really?"

"The policeman said that we shouldn't talk about it, and I haven't, other than here at home, of course. But Mom, do you *really* not know where it is?"

"No, I honestly don't," she'd replied. "You know very well that I've never had anything to do with your father's carpet business. But it'd be a good idea to get hold of it now, don't you think? I bet it's worth a fortune! It would pay for the funeral and more!"

She didn't know what had gotten into her. Being nasty like that. Lotta had fallen silent, realizing that there was no point fishing for any more. And Magnus, who was probably hovering around Lotta, was also silent.

Sven had been with her when Lotta called. Nettan was at work and they'd just had some coffee. He sat sill on the sofa, listening of course. Afterwards he'd reacted to how she'd sounded so stiff and artificial, and wondered, naturally, what the matter was. Was there something he could do?

"Pah, it's just an old rug that the kids are trying to find," she'd said. "Or rather, Lotta."

"What rug?"

"And old one… It's pretty threadbare and bleached out, but they say it's very valuable. A rug that Carl-Ivar had apparently invested in over in Istanbul but that has since disappeared to God knows where."

"Oh good Lord, might that have been why he was murdered?" Sven burst out. "Maybe someone wanted to get their hands on it!"

She'd noted something sweat-shiny around his eyes. He'd sprung into life and she wouldn't be able to dodge past him that easily. That powerful energy that he'd made such good use of as entrepreneur and radiated from him. He was raring to get down to things, to roll up his sleeves and take control.

"You mustn't tell anyone," she begged him. "It's a secret that the police are working on, that lead… with the missing rug, I mean. It's a sensitive matter since it's so valuable. It almost makes you think it's flown off," she said a little jokingly.

But his curiosity had been irreversibly sparked.

"May I be so bold as to ask what kind of price class we're talking?"

She held her tongue. The silence became soiled and a little hungry, like it could be when the conversation turned to money. She didn't want to tell him. It was really nothing to do with Sven. Yet it was tempting to outdo him a little; and not just him, but his perfect Nettan, too.

"Let's see," she said lightly. "A few million, I guess, but I'm not that sure."

He didn't give a whistle, but just remained silent, staring wide-eyed at her.

"Well, well, that's not bad for a rug," he said in an almost reverential tone.

The door knocker banged loudly. She ran her fingers through her hair as she liked to do to freshen herself up, but mainly to steady her nerves. Then she opened the door.

Annelie Daun was standing there. She was carrying a large shoulder bag with the strap diagonally over her chest. She looked no different than normal, thought Birgitta. Though you could never be sure given what her husband had been up to. She should be a total wreck.

Birgitta asked her right away to step inside.

"Would you like a little something?"

"I'm OK, thanks," said Annelie.

"Shall we go into the kitchen?"

"That'll be fine."

They'd hardly sat down opposite each other, Annelie in Carl-Ivar's place, when she lifted the bag onto her knee, opened it, and took out a thick file. It was made of warn, gray-marbled cardstock. She placed it in front of Birgitta, who stared at it.

Annelie said nothing, just nodded. Birgitta looked her in the eye, and then lifted her hands up to the file to open it.

A tepid wave of unease rolled through her. And at the same time, a dormant thought awoke in her, like Sleeping Beauty being awakened by the Prince's kiss. But this was a kiss of a totally different kind.

Because she'd had her suspicions, alright.

Chapter 57

CLAESSON LAY STARING OUT at the evening. He'd been reading Emil in Lönneberga to Klara, who'd just shut her eyes. His daughter's warm body close to his. He'd let her lie there a little while more so that she'd really settle. It was a trap, and normally he dropped off, too, but now he had so much running through his mind that he was wide awake. The past day had been his greatest failure for a long time.

The next step of the investigation they'd have to try to plan more carefully, any fool could see that. Some mistakes were admissible, but not too many. He'd said that to Özen in the car on the way home from Stockholm. On the other hand it was nothing to mull over either, just something to learn from and let sink below the surface while your focus was on the way ahead.

He was trying to be the wise mentor for Özen that he was expected to be. Some people never learned to let mistakes and wrongs go. He could give many examples, but was thinking particularly of one person, which he didn't mention to Özen. Having favorites was the worst thing a manager could do. It was Martin Lerde that got his goat. Lerde could go on and on about mistakes, especially other people's, forever, and he wouldn't pass up the chance that presented itself now, of that Claesson was well aware. Having a dig at his boss and his rival at the same time would be too golden an opportunity for him to pass up.

Lerde was a coward, he thought. Gossip behind his back came with the job of being a boss, and, true, Lerde's comments were put elegantly, in the guise of humor, you could say – he was not without talent, that young man. But it still wasn't nice. To make fun of other people was an unacceptable master suppression technique. What was a joke and what was serious? His colleagues gave as good as they got, sure, but it whipped up too much sediment.

He'd have to put Martin Lerde in his place at the next performance review, he thought. Claesson felt how his pulse had dropped slightly. He was done with processing it. Anyway, he knew that he'd forget the whole thing until it was time for the meeting.

After the morning briefing, he and Özen had, rather hastily, shot up to Stockholm, a three-hour or so drive, and back. They enjoyed each other's company, but that wasn't enough. They got a little out of the trip, as one generally does; if nothing else, they got to see the environment in which the daughter and son-in-law lived and worked, world's apart from carpet dealer Olsson's own. Louise Jasinski had promised to make sure that they scrutinized Karl-Magnus Öberg's business affairs a little more carefully in the mean time – those that they could get their hands on, the figures that were public. This was to give the greatest yield of the day.

What they were hoping to do was to meet the Öberg family, and see them in their posh apartment on Sibyllegatan with their own eyes. Broaden the picture, so to speak.

But it was Magnus Öberg himself whose pulse they wanted to feel a little more closely. To squeeze more out of him than they'd managed during the brief interview in Istanbul. And he couldn't question Patrik Lindström. Their Norrköping colleagues hadn't gotten hold of him yet. He was in hiding and had every reason to be so, with charges of assault, possibly aggravated, hanging over him, even if the injured party, for the moment at least, was missing.

Things were starting to pile up. Long periods of routine and petty crime, and then suddenly these two dramatic cases at the same time. It was like that sometimes, oddly enough.

Claesson toyed with some ideas about the woman's disappearance. He had a hunch that it was the husband who'd somehow gotten rid of her. But where? Jealousy could push people to do almost anything. It was DI Peter Berg's brief, with Martin Lerde's willing aid and Louise's sharp, watchful eye on him. That would do, he reckoned, when it came down to it.

This rug, he thought then. He was quite curious about what it looked like, but realized that it was hardly at the top of his list to get his hands on it. It was Magnus Öberg he wanted, first and foremost.

He remembered him as correct, not overly garrulous, but with a professional smile on his lips, a little wider than was appropriate given that his father-in-law had just been killed. All in all not exactly Mr. Charming.

He'd read through the printed-out notes from Istanbul. Öberg had answered his questions, no more, no less. At the time of his father-in-law's death he'd been on business in Germany, in Munich among other places, he'd said. But his alibi hadn't been confirmed yet. He claimed he'd driven there, which seemed a bit contrived, in Claesson's opinion. It would've been more reasonable to fly and rent a car down there. Here was a weak spot.

Claesson had called Magnus Öberg on the Monday, two days ago, that is, and reminded him amicably that it would be advisable for him to send the documents they'd requested verifying his trip to Germany, and as soon as possible.

"Mostly for the records," he said mildly so as not to arouse this sleeping dog.

"Sure, sure! No problem. I'll get onto it right away," Öberg promised.

Not likely, of that Claesson was fairly convinced. So he wanted to catch him napping. To witness that helplessness that struck people when they didn't have time to prepare themselves, to raise their guard.

So suddenly there they were on Sibyllegatan, he and Özen. Claesson had sat behind the wheel on the way up, as he enjoyed driving. Özen would be driving back, they'd agreed.

They pushed the front door intercom code as given on the list beside it. They waited. Studied two thin, elderly women who stood a bit away, for want of anything else to look at. The women were engaged in deep conversation. Both were in their sixties, probably older, being of that spindly type that was hard to determine the age of, what with all the wrinkles. No bottoms filled out their close-fitting jeans; if anything they were concave down there. Both were identically clad in denim suits of some doubtlessly *au courant* label, but the uniform wasn't blue but brown and apricot, respectively. Their jackets were waist short, and fussy in the front. Both wore their hair in a page cut – a term that Claesson had learned from Louise Jasinski – held in place by a little headband. Both were wearing large glasses with toned lenses and leopard-skin patterned loafers and each had a tiny, fluffy dog under her arm. Very interesting, he thought. This was a model of woman that was exceedingly rare where he came from. If they even existed there.

Clearly no one was in. It was almost eleven o'clock.

"Not a time that working people are at home," said Claesson with the wisdom of hindsight.

They slunk away to find Magnus Öberg's office. The GPS told them it wasn't that far off, on Banérgatan. They left the car; they had to consider themselves lucky to have found a parking spot. Anyway, they needed to stretch their legs, they had a long drive home in front of them.

They followed Valhallavägen eastwards, passed a shopping center that was called Fältöversten and that looked quite dull and boring. Outside, a woman of the same mold that they'd spotted earlier but sans doggie, was packing herself and her shopping bags into a taxi with the driver's willing assistance. She was tipsy, to say the least. He could just make out around her lips and teeth that bluish tone that excessive consumption of cheap red wine could cause.

The office was on the ground floor of a thirties' building on Banérgatan. The firm was called Ö&L AB. Who L was they didn't even intend to find out. Perhaps it was the young, pretty but reserved woman who opened up for them when they knocked. She probably wouldn't have let them in if the office interior hadn't been clearly visible from the street. She'd realized, in other words, that they'd seen her.

"I don't really know where he is. I haven't seen him today… We've got completely different jobs… so it's more like we share office space," she drawled and pulled out some of the corkscrew curls in the enormous fuzz of hair that framed her delicate face.

The office was of the minimalistic and neosimple style that you saw in interiors magazines. It was hard to believe that someone worked here. Magnus Öberg worked with advertising or communication in one way or other, didn't he? Weren't they the same thing? Glossy table tops on legs of blond wood, white cube-shaped shelves along the wall, classic black desk lamps.

Another mission unaccomplished, then. He and Özen went for some sushi at a bar around the corner. Inside, it was all go. Sushi wasn't one of Claesson's favorite meals, preferring hot food that was more filling, but this wasn't at all bad. Özen ate with chopsticks, while Claesson grabbed a knife and fork for himself. It felt ridiculous to sit picking at grains of rice in that unaccustomed manner, which he'd never mastered. It was like sitting at a children's party.

They returned to Sibyllegatan. This time a voice answered on the intercom and let them in without too much dithering. It couldn't be anyone other than his wife. Unless, that is, she was the cleaner.

A soft Oriental carpet ran along the ground floor of the block. Some hypermodern strollers stood squashed up against the wall. There were probably constant neighborly spats about them being in the way, thought Claesson. The stone staircase up was broad. There were some beautiful leaded windows overlooking the courtyard representing stylized flowers: hepaticas on the first floor, coltsfoots on the next. The ascended two floors. The elevator was a fine example of some ancient design, but they preferred to use their legs. Free exercise.

It was wife and carpet-dealer-daughter Lotta Öberg who let them in. It was almost two in the afternoon, Claesson noted on the antique pendulum clock that hung on the wall near the tall, white double doors leading into what they took to be the living room. Or *drawing room*, more appropriately.

But that was as far as they got, and they had to stand there, shuffling their feet on the soft carpet. Lotta Öberg had come home to change and was stressed, she said. Was off to an *event* with work. So she had to get into her cocktail dress and powder her nose.

The pictures on the narrow walls in the hallway were nothing to sniff at, Claesson could see that from where he was standing. Nor those he could glimpse on the walls of the main room, where the light shone in through tall windows.

"So what is it you want? Is there a message you would like me to pass on?" She studied them critically.

"We'd just like to discuss some details with your husband," he said with as much calm as he could muster.

"If it's something important you can call him. He's in Germany."

"Aha. In Munich, perchance?" said Claesson.

She stared at him. "How could you know that?"

"He was there before when your father was murdered in Istanbul."

"Is that so?"

She was wearing a white terry robe, like at a spa. The belt was drawn tightly around her narrow waist. Short, blonde hair. Self-assured, slightly sullen air, but she looked good. Although not, he thought with a change of mind. The people he found really attractive were always the warm types. A lithe body and a perfect profile weren't the be-all, end-all.

It looked like she was standing there trying to regain her balance.

"We need to take it up with him in person," Claesson insisted. "When is he due home from Munich, so that we can plan a meeting?"

"Just in time to attend Father's funeral."

"Well, good. Then we can take the opportunity to deal with this little matter while he's in Oskarshamn. So that'll be a week from Friday?"

She nodded.

"In nine days' time, then."

She nodded again, but barely perceptibly.

"So he's got so much to do in Munich that he needs to be away for so long?"

"He's there for a major advertising campaign. It's simply inconvenient to dash home over the weekend and then back again."

"I see," said Claesson.

They turned to go. Claesson laid a hand on the doorknob.

"By the way, you might ask him to send tickets and other documents confirming that he was in Germany at the time of your father's murder. He promised to do so, but he's obviously been busy and not gotten around to it. It's a formality, but important nonetheless."

She didn't comment on that either.

Lying now in Klara's bed, Claesson grew all the more convinced that Magnus Öberg had been standing listening in a closet somewhere in that airy apartment.

He and Özen hadn't been that downhearted when they drove out of Stockholm. Özen had sat behind the wheel, while Claesson directed him to Norrtull and then up onto the E4 southbound.

When they reached Södertälje, Louise called. Yes, Karl-Magnus Öberg had a company registered in his name: Ö&L.

"I know," he said.

"Did you also know that he runs it with his wife?"

No, that he hadn't managed to find out. There were, after all, only two of them in this strange transnational investigation. But OK, that explained the L. Lotta. And it was actually quite clever: ÖL, the letters made, the Swedish word for beer.

"To cut a long story short, they're almost bankrupt," continued Louise. "Revenues small and debts big. The debtor collectors are knocking on the door."

"And a six-figure rug would be a great help?"

"Probably, but there's a lot that has to be paid before he can get around to selling it on the world market, get my drift?" she said. "I've actually been wondering if Öberg was maybe blackmailing his father-in-law."

Claesson's thoughts came to a standstill.

"How do you mean?"

"That maybe he had some kind of hold on him, perhaps something to do with Istanbul. We think that Öberg went there, right? Anyway, everything points to that."

"I'll think it over," said Claesson, and then let Özen in on Louise's theory.

"It's got something to do with that woman on the quayside, I bet," said Özen.

Quite. They hadn't forgotten the woman on the quayside.

They'd haul in Magnus Öberg, sooner or later. There was a point to not getting worked up; it wasn't as if they were dealing with a serial killer. Slow and steady.

So, the funeral next, he thought and started to plan in his mind how they'd place Ilyas Bank. Maybe in one of the pews so Magnus Öberg could feel what it was like to have someone breathing down his neck. No, he thought with a change of mind, it'd be better to have Ilyas sitting in a car outside with Özen so that he could point Magnus Öberg out unobserved.

He broke off his train of thought and dragged himself up from out of the low bed and walked downstairs to find Veronika on the sofa. She was sleeping with Nora against the backrest.

He touched her arm gently.

"Don't you think you might as well go up and get to bed?"

She stared with newly woken dopiness. "Yes."

He went into the kitchen, took a beer from the fridge, and then stood looking out over the darkening garden.

The photographs were lying scattered over the kitchen table. Hours had gone by but they hadn't bothered to switch on the kitchen light. Two candles in the window glowed with erect, steady flames.

Birgitta Olsson blew her nose for the umpteenth time in succession. Annelie had put some tea on. A hot drink was comforting. The late rays of sunshine poked wearily through the foliage. It was half past eight and time had ceased to exist.

"I've always known about it really, in a way," said Birgitta Olsson. "For all these years I've felt that Carl-Ivar was living a life of his own… but I suppose I was never brave enough to find out the truth. I was just too much of a coward to corner him. Or maybe it just never mattered that much," she added with a shrug. "We've lived our lives with each other, he and I and the children, as well as we could. And we've done OK."

She cried again. Tears of despair. She looked down at the photo.

"And I suppose they have, too…lived their lives…that dark-haired woman and the girl. The daughter, Carl-Ivar's daughter. It's just so hard to grasp."

Only thirty minutes ago Annelie had regretted her ploy, but not any longer. So her conscience was clear. Otherwise, it was always the messenger who got shot.

"We didn't have a bad life together, Carl-Ivar and I," Birgitta repeated.

Annelie sat memorizing the story that she'd found the file hidden in the carpet shop. It hadn't been that difficult to manipulate this lie into a truth, it was just to juggle the locality a little. She'd then hidden away the file and taken it home to Bråbo so that police wouldn't find it when they turned the carpet shop upside down, she'd explained to Birgitta. She wanted to protect Carl-Ivar. He'd been like a father to her. Almost.

"Do you know," said Birgitta, whose voice had recovered a smidgen of energy. "There was always something elusive about Carl-Ivar, like a shadow that followed him… And funnily enough I always find an air of mystery attractive," she said with a wry smile.

"I suppose it was that that drew me to him for all those years. That there was something else there, something I couldn't really put my finger on. Do you know what I mean?"

Annelie nodded.

CHAPTER 58

IT WAS THURSDAY and the time was three minutes past eight. Özen and Claesson were sitting in front of the TV screen with the others. The Kalmar district was just holding forth.

They were mainly presenting just minor events. Routine stuff. Tina Rosenkvist continued to be conspicuous by her absence, as did Patrik Lindström. Norrköping hadn't gotten in touch.

The previous day, Rogge and the other canine officers had been out again. New areas, new uprooted trees to sniff under. They didn't know what to think. Was Tina alive or not? Had she just run off? If she had, she'd done so without leaving a trace, which was hard. No withdrawals on her bank card. No air or train tickets purchased, unless she'd paid in cash, which wasn't that common these days.

"It seems pretty bleak," said Rogge. "Still, I really want to believe that she's alive and has somehow just run off. She's got good reason to keep well away from that man she's married to, that's for sure. But the idea of her lying in some woods somewhere…"

"I know," said Louise.

When the subject had been exhausted, Claesson reported on the current situation with the carpet dealer. They still had a suspect, but they'd have to lie low until the funeral. Patrik Lindström was wanted primarily for the grievous attack on Tina Rosenkvist, but it was connected to Olsson's death somehow, that was for sure. The common denominator appeared to be a missing and very valuable rug.

"A jewel in the carpet world that no one's seen hide nor hair of," he said in closing.

"Well, I'm sure it's a hell of a lot nicer than your beat-up old rag, at least," said Conny Larsson.

"Don't be so sure," countered Claesson. "It's not even in one piece, but pretty moth-eaten along the sides if the photograph's anything to go by."

Whether Tina Rosenkvist's mysterious disappearance was anything to do with the missing rug was, on the other hand, dubious.

"I agree with Rogge," said Conny. "Her old man's beaten the crap out of her."

"But it's just depressing we can't find her," said Peter Berg, who was on the case with Martin Lerde.

They had their work cut out for them, in other words.

Claesson went up to his office. The sun was sending oblique rays over the clinic across the road. Özen came in after a while and announced triumphantly that Patrik Lindström really had spent the night at the Marine Hotel. Yet another part of the puzzle in place. He then dropped the passport photo of Lindström onto Claesson's desk. They'd already decided to confront their best and only witness, Annelie Daun in the carpet shop, with it.

"Can you try to get hold of her and ask her to come here, today if possible?" said Claesson.

Özen nodded and left. Claesson got down to opening his mail, but was interrupted immediately by Louise Jasinski, who came in to introduce a charming woman, robustly built, pushing sixty he guessed, who knew everything there was to be known about rugs and carpets.

Louise was a rock, he thought, and gave the woman a quick run-through of what they wanted her to do, which was to value the carpets and rugs in Olsson's shop.

"It will only be an approximation, of course," she pointed out. "The prices depend on who the buyer is, at least when it comes to auction sales. But I can see if there are any rarities there, naturally."

He showed her the photocopy of the fifteenth-century rug fragment.

"Where does this come from?"

"As far as we know it was found in a mosque in central Anatolia," he said, sounding like a real authority on Turkey.

"Really?" She sounded reverential.

"The area's called Cappadocia, I believe," said Claesson and told her what the carpet dealer in the Grand Bazaar had said.

"This is indeed a rare item, of course," she confirmed. "But one would have to examine the fragment properly to be able to give a true valuation…and the price, you know, is always dependent on whether there are sufficiently solvent buyers. The value of a rug of this kind is, of course, high, if it is as well-preserved as the photograph would suggest, but, as I said, you never know until you have it in front of you. I have not actually seen one like this on the open market for a very long time. But at a rough estimate, I would say it was in the six-figure bracket without a shadow of a doubt."

Claesson sat the woman in the visitor's chair. He asked Özen to take the portraits and to come with him, and then dialed the number to the carpet shop. Annelie Daun answered.

"I hope it's OK if we stop by in a while," he said.

"What? Yes, of course, you're welcome. May I ask what it's about?"

"We have with us a carpet expert from Stockholm who we've asked to value the shop's stock."

Annelie Daun probably stiffened, he could tell by her silence down the line.

"It's nothing to worry about," he said paternally.

He and Özen then accompanied the visiting carpet expert to Olsson's shop.

"I read about that horrid murder in the newspapers," she said while they walked unhurriedly past the large concrete block that housed the town's two newspapers, and then the newly built house with the tower overlooking Besvärsgatan.

"Terrible. Carpet dealers do not usually belong to the murder victim category," she said. They crossed Östra Torggatan and then passed by the windows of the bookshop.

Who does? wondered Claesson, but he understood what she meant.

The market was in full swing as they crossed Lilla Torget Square and stalls of brightly colored flowers, fresh baby vegetables, and eggs from free-range hens.

"This seems like a lovely little shop," said the expert before they stepped inside.

Annelie Daun was standing waiting by the table. The women greeted each other with a smile. There was a crackle of static there, thought Claesson. One of those rare occasions when you see two people who've never met really click at first sight. Two similar-minded people, despite the slight guardedness, or rather humility, in

Annelie Daun's body language. It was the older woman who was the authority here, of that there could be no doubt.

It was not without a certain ardor and perhaps even pride that Annelie Daun then showed the expert around the shop and the downstairs storeroom.

Claesson and Özen waited until she came back upstairs.

"We'd like to show you some pictures," said Claesson and laid the solemn-looking faces on the table one at a time.

Patrik Lindström was number two. She identified him almost at once.

"It was him, definitely," she said with certainty.

They left the carpet expert in the shop and walked back to the police station. Claesson took up the latest reports and sat down to read them while his brain was reasonably alert. He always slowed down toward the afternoon. He wanted to recap, to remind himself of what had happened.

The telephone rang, and his train of thought was broken. It was Nina in reception.

"A woman by the name of Birgitta Olsson is here wondering if you can see her."

Yes! He hurried down and escorted her to his office.

"How can I be of help?" he asked once they'd seated themselves.

She hoisted up a black cloth bag with the logo of a gym on the side, took out a cardboard file, and laid it on his desk, right on top of all his own opened files and stapled together reports, which he hastily moved out of the way.

"To give us more room," he said.

She said nothing. And her face revealed nothing either as she pushed the file over to his side of the desk, which was now empty. She just nodded. He lifted his hands from his lap, removed the long-since perished rubber band, its elasticity a distant memory, and opened the file. His eyebrows rose.

This is it! he thought.

"What does M & MS mean?" asked Veronika over the evening dinner at the kitchen table.

"What do you think?"

Cooked food was on the table: gnocchi with pesto, mozzarella, and rocket salad.

"Murder and manslaughter," she said.

He nodded. He knew that she'd sat in his office breastfeeding Nora.

"It's in that file that I keep all the documents on the deaths that I'm still waiting for the autopsy reports on and different bits and bobs from the pathologist. Police deaths are there too, suicide, for example."

Klara poured out her mug of milk, and a white waterfall ran down from the edge of the table, dripping down onto his newly washed jeans.

Crap! he thought, but said nothing; he just got up, walked over to the sink, snatched up a dishcloth, and thought that he'd not get any peace and quiet until he was seventy.

Chapter 59

It was liberating to bike to work on the Monday, Claesson couldn't help but think. A weekend in the shelter of his family had slipped by and it hadn't been only nice and relaxing, but also, in fact, quite strenuous at times. "Well, what did you expect?" Veronika would have said if she could hear his thoughts. He'd get glorious solitude later in life.

What's more, they'd clashed in a blazing argument on the Saturday. There was bound to be some sort of emotional discharge sooner or later, he'd realized. Rarely could you just keep on pushing boundaries and trying people's goodwill forever. And as usual, it was a triviality that lit the fuse.

Crayfish tails.

It had been Veronika's idea to invite Janne and Mona Lundin over for dinner that Saturday, as he'd reminded her calmly and matter-of-factly when she started to howl and launch into him. As a thank you for helping them out with Klara while they sped off to the maternity ward, she'd said. And, of course, because they liked the Lundins.

And he had nothing against that. Not really. But it was just a little over the top, he thought, even though he wasn't so stupid that he didn't realize that Veronika possibly needed to step outside the baby-bubble for a while and have some adult conversation with someone other than him. Of course he understood that! But she didn't say so. She said nothing about her really wanting to have guests for dinner herself. Instead, she said that they should obey some kind of rule of etiquette, and *he* thought rules of etiquette they could forget. Especially when it came to the Lundins, who weren't the type to read the small print in the code of propriety. He was the one working, he was up at nights with Nora, and, quite simply, he was tired.

They discussed this fairly soberly, and he finally gave in. The Lundins were coming over.

And so the crayfish tails. He'd forgotten to buy them when he was at the store.

That did it.

The starter that Veronika had chosen and was going to prepare in accordance with the recipe was based on this very ingredient. And say what you will about her cooking skills, she did not belong to that division of chefs who could easily conjure up something else by digging into the fridge and the freezer and improvising. Her self-confidence was stable in many situations, but not in the kitchen. "And I'm not ashamed of it," she'd say with more or less contrived self-assurance.

Nursing and running around after Klara and sleepless nights had, of course, whittled away at her patience. He, a man filled with a large measure of bad conscience – he'd been in Istanbul instead of on paternity leave, and was now up to his ears in work – could think of nothing other than offering to pop out to buy some crayfish tails an hour before the guests were due to arrive. Constructive and thoughtful.

But it was too late. They wouldn't have time, she said. What with the house in a mess, too. Mouth pursed, she stamped her heels hard against the floor as she scuttled around tidying up the sitting room with Nora wailing over her shoulder. A martyr. He kept out of her way. And that, of course, was wrong. But he hated to plead, even more so as the white-hot wrath seething within her was really quite scary. The wrath that he never managed to penetrate but that had to either dissipate of its own accord or gradually settle, and that could take time. And time was exactly what they didn't have.

The silent threat of a grim mother with a hard, unapproachable face upset Klara, as it was not something she was used to. She cried and ran away to hide. But once Mona and Janne were standing in the hallway, she came crawling out in her best dress with dust balls clinging to the hem. She was allowed to sit up with them for a while. He and Veronika could breathe out. It was over.

Janne and Mona. It was strange, but some people seemed made for pouring oil on troubled waters. Mona's cheerful, uncritical demeanor, and Janne's thoughtful manner. Klara climbed up onto Mona's lap and Mona read her a story. The food arrived, without a starter, without crayfish tails. A storm that blew itself out.

That he then drank too many beers with his colleague Janne and sat talking shop in the kitchen while the women occupied the sitting room, and then stumbled drunkenly into bed and failed to hear the children during the night, were all things that wouldn't score him any more points.

But Veronika was magnanimous enough not to bring it up the next day. In return he took the girls on a long Sunday walk so that she could have an afternoon nap.

His colleagues had spent the entire weekend looking for Tina Rosenkvist, but had taken their search down a notch. Still no sign of a witness or of the slightest clue that could lead them to her, dead or alive.

Apart from a neighbor who claimed to have got up in the early dawn to go to the bathroom and then heard a car start. But he'd already gotten back into bed and wasn't curious enough to drag himself up again to see whose car it was. Someone picking up Tina, maybe? Or her husband, Pär Rosenkvist, taking off under the cover of semi-darkness?

The forensics team had picked through his car meticulously. There were naturally ample traces of his wife, hairs and fluff from her top, since she'd both driven the car and been a passenger in it, so it meant nothing. But there was no blood, no secretions, no flakes of skin to be found anywhere. No signs of violence around the seat or in the trunk.

"We'll find her, sooner or later," said Peter Berg reassuringly, and Martin Lerde nodded as confidently as he always did.

Claesson had called Birgitta Olsson again to ask if she thought that anyone else knew about her husband's other woman and daughter in Turkey, and she'd repeated her reply: she had no idea, but she was pretty sure that no one knew anything. "That would be horrible. If others knew but not me."

She'd been given strict orders not to talk about it to anyone other than Annelie Daun, who already knew, and who they'd also put a gag on.

Özen had contacted Istanbul, both Fuat Karaoğlu and Merve Turpan. They said something along the lines of "as we suspected."

Karaoğlu and Merve had been continually updated with the results of their efforts in far-off Oskarshamn. They were, of course, informed that Ilyas Bank was in Sweden and that he'd be acting as a witness during the forthcoming funeral. Whether or not he'd robbed Olsson on the ferry was something they'd more or less dropped in Oskarshamn, and they didn't seem that interested in investigating that part of the story in Istanbul, either. First off, the money would have to be reported missing. They'd have to treat it as a side issue in the shadow of a murder.

Özen came in to Claesson's office. Merve had been in touch. She'd just met Olsson's daughter at home in Yeniköy, she'd said.

"Did she live in a *very very nice house*?" wondered Claesson.

Özen lost his thread. "How do you mean?"

"Merve talked about those yalis along the Bosporus that she loved so much, didn't she."

"Er, she said nothing about that, but I can ask her when I next talk to her," said Özen fondly. "Anyway, she said it hadn't been hard to get hold of the daughter now that they had an address to go on. Her name's Ayla."

Özen also mentioned a surname but it was far too long and difficult for Claesson to even try to memorize.

"So what do we do now?"

"How do you mean?"

"Maybe she also saw the murderer from the quayside."

Claesson rubbed his eyes. He was terribly tired.

"Yes, of course, she might also be a useful witness. But can't they deal with it in Istanbul? Öberg will be extradited, you know, if we arrest him here."

"Hmph…"

"What do you mean, hmph?"

"Merve said something about how the daughter really wanted to attend her father's funeral."

Of course she did.

"We can't actually have any opinion about that," he said. "We can't stop her going, if that's what she wants. And if she wants to get in touch with Olsson's widow, that's also her own business."

Özen nodded.

Nothing else of much interest happened during the day apart from a sudden downpour in the afternoon, which soaked Claesson as he biked home.

The next day was also fairly uneventful, except for the message that came in saying that Olsson's Turkish daughter was genuinely intending to attend the funeral. Merve had supplied the young woman with all conceivable information about how to contact the Swedish police, preferably Mustafa Özen, and her father's wife.

"She speaks excellent English, Merve says. She's apparently quite highly educated," said Özen, and then gave a slightly bashful laugh. "Merve joked that she herself actually wouldn't mind coming to the funeral, too. For the sake of the investigation, that is."

Claesson gave him a friendly look. "You don't say? Otherwise, you could always spend your vacations in Istanbul this summer."

Özen blushed. It was possibly a thought that had crossed his mind, too.

Claesson could take some flextime and be a more present father and husband while waiting for Carl-Ivar Olsson's funeral. He rode his bike with Klara to the preschool, bought fresh buns on the way home and ate a second breakfast with Veronika when he returned. Some hardcore family stuff, in other words.

The tension ahead of the Friday when Olsson was to be buried and they would hopefully be able to arrest Magnus Öberg took its toll. Thoughts came and went. If Öberg didn't show up and his wife continued to claim that he was still in Germany, they'd have to call in Interpol.

According to Birgitta Olsson, only the immediate family and their closest friends would attend the gathering in the parish hall afterwards. She was unsure, not to say worried, about how many were intending to come to the actual service. "It's caused quite a commotion, you know," as she'd said. "And that always attracts people."

She wasn't wrong there.

He gave Klara an extra push on the swing.

It never rains but it pours, he thought.

CHAPTER 60

IT HAD ALREADY BEEN DECIDED that Özen would go down to Landskrona with Lennie Ludvigsson to fetch Ilyas Bank. This was to happen after the Thursday morning briefing and the meeting with the special team that would be keeping a watch on Olsson's funeral, mainly to arrest Magnus Öberg but also to keep order. Like Birgitta Olsson, the funeral director also thought that there'd be quite a crowd turning up at the church.

There were twelve of them sitting around the meeting room table.

"The funeral is at 2:30. It'll be a cremation service in the Western Cemetery chapel," Claesson said for protocol's sake. "You all know what it looks like there. You drive in from Stengatan and park in the visitors' lot on the right. Though we can count on it being full, and people will have to park wherever there's room. So the car with Ilyas Bank in it, an unmarked car, that is, must get there in good time, as it'll have to be positioned where it can see everyone entering the chapel. At the same time, we must try to be tactical," he continued, "so that we don't disrupt the service or lose Magnus Öberg. There are a lot of bushes around there, so make sure they don't block your view."

After discussing matters back and forth, they decided that Conny Larsson was to be in car number one with Ilyas Bank in the passenger seat and Mustafa Özen in the back to interpret and deal with any language problems.

Lennie Ludvigsson wondered if they could leave now, Claesson nodded, and Lennie left the conference room with Mustafa Özen for their drive to Landskrona.

"I was thinking of attending the funeral myself," said Claesson. "But we'll need one more person in the chapel..."

"I can come, too," Louise Jasinski offered.

"Good."

They discussed deployments and how many police cars they'd need to keep order and be on stand-by.

"But really, what can happen?" wondered Peter Berg. "If Ilyas Bank recognizes the son-in-law from the car, then I assume that you and Louise will just go up to him nice and calmly after the coffee and say that you want a word with him down at the station, right?"

"Yeah, that's the scenario I'm envisioning," said Claesson.

"You might let him finish his coffee and layer cake first," said Peter Berg.

"Maybe," said Claesson. "How do you know there'll be layer cake there?"

"Just an educated guess," smiled Berg.

"But haven't you got nothin' else on him?" wondered Forensics Benny. "Even if he confesses an' you can prove that he was in Istanbul an' even stayed at a hotel right opposite his father-in-law, there's no sayin' that it'll stand up in court… in the best case scenario, right, but if you've got no…"

"Physical evidence, you mean," said Claesson and smiled. It had almost reached the point where it was now the physical evidence that weighed the heaviest. Not the witnesses, that could be word against word, or the confessions; the reason for confessing could lie on a totally different level than just releasing the pressure and embracing the truth and easing your conscience. To have five minutes of fame, for example. Some people's need for attention was insatiable. Negative contexts were better than no contexts at all.

"Maybe. The best thing would be if we could find Öberg's shoes to see if they match the prints that forensics in Istanbul found in a pool of blood on the deck. It wasn't an entire sole, but part of the bottom of some international brand of sports model. Cem, their forensics expert, thought it was a men's size 10 ½ , which is more common in Sweden than in Turkey. And with a little luck, we'd find traces of blood in the tread, even if Öberg used them afterwards. Or what do you think?"

"He might've cleaned 'em, if he hasn't chucked 'em away somewhere," said Benny Grahn. "But otherwise I'd say it's possible, you don't need much to get some DNA with the techniques we've got today. But first we have to find the shoe, like!"

"Of course…" said Peter Berg.

"There must be splashes of blood on the clothes too, but the likelihood is greater that he's dumped them," said Claesson. "We'll have to search his apartment in Stockholm."

"You mean his *rooms*," said Louise.

"Right. On Östermalm you don't have an apartment, you have *rooms*, of course. Like the way people live in summer cottages rather than vacation homes."

They speculated a little about whether Magnus Öberg had any inkling that they were concentrating their investigation around him.

"I bet he does," said Claesson. "Guilty people tend to go around with the constant suspicion and worry of being found out. But I almost regret escalating things by going to Östermalm. His wife must've known that we weren't just passing by, if I can put it like that… Not if we're based in Oskarshamn. But there's nothing we can do about that now. And that's why we've decided to keep calm and not to ask the boys in Stockholm to storm the place with a whole squad and turn over his apartment, sorry, *rooms*, in the search for those shoes. Or a white cap with a red logo on it, for that matter."

Benny Grahn frowned. "Don't you think he's gone and dumped the cap somewhere?"

"Probably. And if we happened to find it in his flashy *rooms* his lawyer will claim that anyone could have a cap like that lying around. They were given away for free for a time."

"An ICA cap doesn't seem to me to be the headgear of choice when shopping or going for a stroll," said Louise. "But I don't know the particular dress code, do I. What do I know, maybe a perky little ICA cap is the latest thing on Östermalm."

"Maybe he'll be wearing those shoes you've mentioned when he comes down to Oskarshamn," said Peter Berg. "Maybe not at the funeral, but otherwise?"

"Right, that's crossed my mind too, and if he does, well, bingo!" said Claesson.

A little later during the day, Claesson found out that the charming carpet expert from Stockholm had been in touch. He called her and discovered that there was nothing whatsoever wrong with Olsson's stock of carpets and rugs.

"But nothing unusual?"

"No, and that's the thing," she said in a slightly apologetic tone, almost as if Olsson owned a mongrel and, yes, of course it was charming in its own way, but.... "There were no rarities or real treasures there at all. Nothing for collectors, in other words. More just your everyday rugs."

Olsson was clearly a more temperate dealer than Claesson had once thought. The carpet expert promised to send a written valuation.

So who was to have this extremely special rug? Claesson had touched on the question several times. Maybe they'd never know the answer. But for some reason he couldn't let go of the idea that Olsson perhaps wanted it for himself and had no intention of selling it. They hadn't managed to dig up a single document, a single telephone call to verify the existence of a customer or client. After the carpet dealer in the Grand Bazaar, the lead just stopped.

His work cell phone rang at a quarter past three. Claesson was told that they'd arrested Patrik Lindström in his home in a suburb of Norrköping. He'd been hiding out in a friend's summer cottage but had wanted to check the mail, pay bills, and do other such worldly things. He should've known better than to go home, you might think, but he was no doubt a little tired of being on the run.

The arrest had gone smoothly, the Norrköping police had said. No fuss, Lindström had no intention of lengthening his sentence by being uncooperative. He could be taken to Oskarshamn for questioning by the next day at the earliest, but then Claesson and his colleagues would be fully occupied with Carl-Ivar's funeral. He'd have to sound him out as soon as he could and ask Peter Berg to do what he could to find out how Lindström was connected with Magnus Öberg. There had to be some connection, thought Claesson. He was sure of it.

Patrik Lindström wasn't the brightest bulb in the box, they'd realized, but he was powerful and had the tendency to strike first, think later when cornered. Touchy and short-fused, in other words. Lindström was only too happy to work for others, for payment. He looked kind and well-kept, with light blue eyes, and that was his asset. He could dupe law-abiding citizens whose guard would've been lowered. On the other hand, he could be difficult to squeeze information out of, Claesson had learned. But that was probably because of the circumstances, what he had to lose or gain by squealing.

Patrik Lindström was the prime suspect in the assault on Tina Rosenkvist. Formally speaking, the prosecutor was the leader of the preliminary investigation, but Peter Berg was responsible for the groundwork and was working with his group in close liaison with the new prosecutor, a woman with a droll nature and a northern accent that was pleasant and soft on the ear. Comical women weren't all that common, thought Claesson, and many of them in the service were, or became, hard and career-minded. But when making this observation to Veronika, he'd received a slap on the nose. "Are career-hungry men so much funnier, then?" she'd said drily.

Before heading off home, Claesson called Birgitta Olsson, really just to ask if everything was alright.

"No new plans for the funeral?"

"No," she said. "What like?" She sounded subdued.

"Nothing special, just wondering. And your children?"

"They're coming with their partners. But the grandchildren are staying at home in Stockholm with some acquaintances. They're not that old."

"And where will they be staying?"

"Where will they be staying? Johan and his Malin live in Kalmar, so they'll drive over on the day, and Lotta and Magnus will naturally be staying with me."

"And no one else has been in touch?"

"Like who?"

"I was thinking the girl… or woman, rather, from Istanbul."

An arid silence met him, and he almost expected her to slam the phone down in his ear.

"I know nothing about that," was all she said.

CHAPTER 61

A LIGHT EARLY SUMMER RAIN fell on the day of Carl-Ivar Olsson's funeral.

Next to the parking lot of the Western Cemetery, large rhododendrons bloomed bright lilac. It was an intense color, almost pompous, like a kind of impertinent protest against the transience of life, against death, thought Claesson. Otherwise, he'd always been a bit ambivalent about these very flowers, but he supposed he was affected by the gravity of the moment. They were magnificent, but it was as if the extravagance was too much and too gaudy for Scandinavia's barren nature and granite rocks, dark forests, black earth.

The cemetery was fairly centrally located and stretched over quite a large area. A verdant part to wander around under tall, straight pines. The newly mown grass smelled fresh and life-affirming.

The stream of people was large. Worryingly so, bearing in mind their mission. According to the funeral director, people had called wanting to book seats in the chapel, which wasn't possible, but everyone who could fit in was welcome once the immediate family had taken their seats. The police helped to direct cars and curious passersby, and were an extra reinforcement to the cars that Claesson's own group had tucked away in readiness. The press and TV were also there. The situation wasn't chaotic, more low-key. There was no bustling, no pushing, no one who came bursting in at the last minute.

Louise had gone inside and taken her seat at the back of the room. The chapel was a relatively modern building from the early sixties, with yellow brick walls and broad, functional connecting roads and paths that gently followed the terrain. A double door was used for burials, a narrower door for cremations, as in this case. After the ceremony, the coffin containing the remains of Carl-Ivar Olsson would be conveyed to the incinerator. The interment of the urn could take place much later.

The service itself was to be held in the main room. There was also a side entrance, but that was only used, they'd been told, by the staff, the priests and other ministers, funeral directors, and cemetery workers.

When he saw the congregation, he had a strong feeling that Olsson probably wasn't a person who'd dreamed of returning unto dust under such sensational circumstances, no matter how locally esteemed he'd been. It was like a celebrity funeral. But many people naturally also wanted to pay their final respects and commiserate his wife and family.

Larsson had parked the unmarked police car with Özen and Bank as best he could so as not to arouse suspicion and not to have their view obscured by the rhododendrons. Claesson and Jasinski, dressed in a classic black pantsuit for the occasion, were to stick to the chapel, it had been decided. They were all wearing earpieces.

Özen had already called in and sighed.

"If Ilyas recognizes the suspect among all the people milling about here, it'll be a miracle," he said.

"We'll do as we've agreed," answered Claesson, his jaws clenched, his lips making the smallest possible movements toward the microphone he had pinned under his lapel.

"OK."

To make matters worse, there were now quite a few opened umbrellas.

Louise had made sure to reserve two seats at the back of the chapel by the aisle so that they could come and go with ease.

Claesson was wearing a white shirt under his dark gray jacket and a pair of unmatched, lead-gray, pressed slacks that he put on maybe once every third year, and always on occasions such as this. Over his jacket he had his dark green Gore-Tex coat, the one he'd had for so long that its resistance to wind and weather, and above all rain, was no longer what it once was. The damp was eating its way in.

He and Louise had arrived early and greeted the priest, whom Claesson knew from previous professional encounters. He was a down-to-earth man, and one who was now informed of their, preferably invisible, presence.

There was a sudden crackling in his ear. "He thinks he's spotted the mark," reported Özen excitedly.

Hot damn! thought Claesson, and bent his head. "Copy that," he said. He knew that everyone else had received the same information. "Where?"

"Walking up the path to the chapel."

"Thanks."

Without shifting his position, Claesson stretched his neck almost imperceptibly while his eyes scanned everyone who was approaching the chapel. The drizzle had started to lighten up. The faces were wet, as were the clothes, but more and more people were folding away their umbrellas. Sometimes things really went your way, he thought.

He figured he blended in well with all the other darkly-clad funeral guests. It had been decided that Louise would remain in the chapel unless ordered otherwise.

A stream of people in dark clothes advanced steadily in clusters along the asphalt pathway. He recognized one or two, and they nodded barely noticeably to each other. Of course they realized why he was here. That Olsson's killer hadn't been arrested yet was public knowledge.

And then they saw him.

Magnus Öberg was walking slowly with slightly bowed head and eyes fixed on the ground. He wife was beside him.

It was definitely him, Claesson confirmed to himself, but found Öberg slightly taller than he remembered him from Istanbul and than his passport details stated – six foot – but that could have been because he seemed to have grown thinner. The shoulders of his elegant dark designer jacket stuck up, the front hung down despite being buttoned up, and his pants flapped freely over his thighs. His black shoes shone.

Claesson took his eyes from the Öbergs, but kept them in his peripheral vision. As he stood there he could feel his chest tighten in that familiar way, and that was one of the main reasons why he hadn't chosen a job that mostly involved sitting on his butt in an office. He didn't need peace and quiet. He needed excitement and to feel his pulse gallop now and then.

It wasn't until the Öbergs had passed him and entered through the doors that he told the others that he'd also spotted their mark, and that this mark should soon be in his seat in the chapel.

They could, in other words, arrest him after the funeral and the coffee in the parish hall. Wait until afterwards out of respect for the family. No fuss, just nice and calm. They didn't intend to lose sight of him, even if the relocation entailed a certain risk. But why would Öberg try to run once he'd made it all the way here? They had to keep their profile low so as not to arouse suspicion. In one sense it was an advantage to already have such a large police presence at the chapel.

Claesson entered and sat down beside Louise, listening to the quiet murmur, the odd echoing coughing fit, the blowing of a nose, voices whispering as the darkly-clad guests slowly continued to fill the pews. He smelled the faint odor of wet clothes.

True to custom, the Olsson family was seated at the front. The widow and the two children with their spouses. Claesson let his eyes drift over Magnus Öberg's neck at intervals and never let him fully out of his sight. Louise and he exchanged the briefest of glances, confirming the situation. They were in control and everything was going according to plan.

He saw Annelie Daun coming down the aisle, her husband on one side looking hollow-eyed and her mother on the other – a haggard woman whom Claesson knew from long ago. Her name was Kerstin Olsson and she was the carpet dealer's alcoholic sister. Some neighbors, he assumed, were also putting in an appearance along with members of the Tradesman's Association, Rotary, and the local folklore society. He could make out some faces he recognized. He was a real Oskarshamnian, as they said. Belonged to the town. It sat in his body like cement.

The chapel was as full as it could possibly get without people sitting on each other's laps. People from the funeral director's office helped to squeeze people together and ushered others demurely and courteously to empty seats, often in the middle of a pew. People had a tendency to sit at the far ends, to block the way.

The chapel was stylish inside, too, thought Claesson as he surveyed the clean, light yellow brick walls. At the front by the altar, daylight filtered in through a beautiful stained glass window. The chapel was restrained in its decoration, with a tasteful, muted tapestry on one wall, simple lighting, and nothing else. He estimated that the room held about a hundred people.

The bells started to ring, and the murmuring and coughing gradually subsided until silence descended upon the congregation.

The rain had stopped and the sun was poking though the window, causing it to glow in all its variegated colors. As if someone up there had a hand in proceedings, he thought.

The organ had just started playing a prelude that Claesson didn't recognize, when he heard a dull bang from behind him. The noise had come from the door, and now walking slowly along the aisle was a dark-haired woman. She seemed diffident, and came to a halt a few steps in.

Just as she was preparing to squeeze into one of the rear pews, Annelie Daun turned. She extracted herself from the front row, walked all the way to the back, and escorted the woman back with her to the family pew. It was a brave gesture. And a clear demonstration, Claesson thought, as he turned to Louise, who raised her eyebrows. They'd both recognized her.

When the service was over and everyone had laid down their wreaths, Claesson and Louise slipped out to stand by the front door of the chapel to watch the guests come streaming out. It took time. A man standing next to them unfolded a large white cotton handkerchief, with which he blew his nose and wiped his eyes. His wife asked something about what the matter was, which Claesson thought a strange thing to say just after a funeral.

"It's the freshly mown lawn," he said.

"Did you forget to take your medicine?" she asked.

Hay fever, thought Claesson. The spring and early summer were a tough time for many.

"Yes. It'll pass," he said through his blocked nose, and wiped his handkerchief over his puffy eyes once more.

"Look, I'll drive you home and we'll pick up your pills and spray on the way to the parish hall. It won't take long. You can't drive with your eyes like that."

They walked off, while Claesson remained where he was, observing how the guests had touchingly gathered in small, slightly lost clusters before moving on to the parish hall. Many of them were going to drive, otherwise it was no more than a fifteen-minute walk.

The sun came and went. It was warm and relatively still and dry. The group over by the driveway had gotten smaller as far as he could see, but not by much. It was all those who hadn't gotten a seat in the chapel but who'd had to stay behind the hastily erected police cordon. Those who'd wanted to pay tribute to carpet dealer Olsson, or at least take part in the grieving for reasons that in many cases were likely to be extremely personal. Things got so blown up these days, thought Claesson. The media, particularly through the Internet, spread the news and inflated the emotions. I guess we need it, he thought. To cry tears of joy at a wedding or of sorrow at a funeral, even when we might not even know the people involved.

And still not everyone had come out.

Louise was standing outside on the other side of the exit. Birgitta Olsson emerged, looked at Claesson, and walked over to the woman who'd arrived late and who was now standing shyly, with bowed head, with Annelie Daun. The two of them were cousins, it struck him.

Claesson had also seen these photographs, but the one that had lodged itself most firmly in his memory was the one taken by chance by a member of the ferry's crew, showing a quayside bathed in bright sunlight. Father and daughter together for the last time.

The woman had a slightly irregular face, with the dark hair tied back tightly from the face, brown eyes under heavy eyebrows, a small mouth with a well-shaped Cupid's bow and a dimple in her chin. He recognized this soft yet resolute chin from Annelie Daun and Carl-Ivar Olsson, if the photos were anything to go by. Her shoulders were broad and her waist narrow. She was wearing a dark brown coat.

Ayla, a beautiful name, thought Claesson. It didn't seem as if they were saying very much, she and Birgitta Olsson. They were just standing there now looking at, now avoiding each other. The features of Birgitta Olsson's face were hard to read, because they were constantly shifting.

Finally, the young woman bowed her head. She was crying. As was Birgitta Olsson.

It suddenly struck him. Magnus Öberg hadn't come out.

He stared intently at Louise, who'd also just realized the same thing. His wife, Lotta Öberg, was there, however, and was greeting, with slight guardedness, her half sister. She was followed in this by Johan Olsson, and then his wife.

"The bathroom," said Claesson and nodded to Louise to wait while he made for the chapel entrance.

Meanwhile, Louise Jasinski thought that she heard Lotta Öberg say something to her mother about her husband. She made out the words "migraine medicine" and "will be along later," no doubt meaning the parish hall. Jasinski informed Claesson at the same moment that he found the bathrooms vacant. No Öberg there, in other words.

The side entrance!

Damn! Why hadn't he deployed someone there? That was very unprofessional, to say the least. If Öberg had slipped out that way straight after the ceremony, he'd have a few minutes' lead on him.

But why would he do that? Was he feeling that things were heating up around him? Or was it something else? And where had he gone? Home to Birgitta Olsson's to get his migraine medicine?

Hardly. But they'd have to send a car over just to make sure.

He took a deep breath and dropped his shoulders. Typical. Everything had been going so smoothly and now this. But there was still no reason to panic, he told himself. They knew were Birgitta Olsson lived. They'd have to pick up Öberg there, either immediately if he *had* really gone there, or after the coffee gathering, at which he should sooner or later make an appearance. And if they were really lucky, he realized, they'd be able to confiscate the shoes with the treaded soles.

He went out to Louise to start directing his people.

CHAPTER 62

NETTAN BROMSE SNATCHED a tissue and blew her nose. She'd passed the Coop supermarket on the way to the funeral and had popped in to buy a family pack of disposable tissues. Sven insisted on his cotton handkerchiefs, and she'd even sometimes iron them for him if she was in the right mood. She preferred tissues herself. It was more hygienic. Crusty old snot-rags were revolting.

There would be more tears, of that she was convinced. There was still the coffee gathering to go and no doubt the odd emotional speech. They agreed in the car that the funeral had been moving. That said, they fell into a collective silence. Nettan thought mostly about the traffic. They were feeling a little harried. Sven blew his nose beside her, and panted noisily through his mouth.

She turned down onto Holmhällevägen and slowed down. There were children living around here. Now that she'd seen the coffin, it became real to her that Carl-Ivar would never again walk down his garden path. She guessed she hadn't really grasped what had happened. That she'd never again get to see him walk down to the mailbox by his gate in his slightly rocking, leisurely way, with his gaze often absently directed at the stone pavement.

People came and went in your life, that was only natural, and you both got accustomed to it and didn't, she thought, as she drove up onto the garage driveway and turned off the engine. A car was parked outside the Olssons', but not right in front of the gate.

"Strange," said Nettan. "Isn't everyone at the funeral?"

"Maybe it's the son-in-law's car, and they drove together to the funeral," said Sven, looking up toward the Olsson house. He simply couldn't keep tabs on every single car, and anyway, the models all looked pretty much the same these days, he thought as he walked toward his own front door with a strong yearning to be rid of all his allergy symptoms.

Just then he saw, despite his red eyes and blurry vision, how the Olssons' bedroom curtains seemed to twitch. Or did he imagine it?

He was just about to take his eyes off the window when, again, he thought he glimpsed a person in it. But who'd be snooping around Birgitta's bedroom when she was out?

He had a nasty feeling that some smart burglar was taking the opportunity to empty the house of jewelry, money, and other easily shifted items while everyone was off at the funeral. He'd read about things like that. Break-ins while families were on vacation and on New Year's Eve when people would certainly not be coming home until after midnight. He also thought about that low-life with the rug trick who'd been at Birgitta's. The guy who'd learned from the city hoods but who was so inept you almost felt sorry for him.

All these thoughts flitted quickly through his mind. Didn't the Olsson's have an alarm? he thought suddenly. He'd stopped in his tracks on the natural pink paving stones, from where he lifted his glasses, wiped his eyes, and put his glasses back. My word yes! There was someone there!

Should he just forget it? It probably wasn't a thief. He hesitated. But someone was very clearly in Birgitta's house, and he wasn't the kind of person to let things be. Not things that really worried him. He liked order, and if something was amiss, he was the man to fix it.

"What is it," asked Nettan, who'd already unlocked the door. "Hurry up!"

"I thought I saw Birgitta's bedroom curtains move," he said in a low voice.

"You don't say!" she almost whispered back. "Then you'd best see who it is. Everyone should be at the parish hall…"

He wavered.

"Do what you want, I'm going inside to get your medicines together," he heard her call from inside the house. She'd left the door open.

Maybe Birgitta had forgotten to set the alarm, stressed as she was about the funeral, he thought as he crept through the hedge onto the Olssons' garden and positioned himself on their front steps. Should he knock? He wasn't sure if that was such a good idea if it did actually turn out to be a burglar. Unconsciously, he reached out his hand and grasped the door handle.

It was unlocked, and the door swung open and a stuffy warmth hit him as he peered into the darkness of the hall.

And sure enough, he could hear a faint noise coming from deeper inside the house, but what astonished him most of all was that the contents of the hall closet were lying partly strewn on the floor. Someone was obviously searching the house for something.

He left the front door ajar and crept a few steps into the house. He saw the sitting room ahead of him, untouched. The kitchen table was empty, and there was no one in the passageway between the kitchen and oven.

"Is anyone there?" he called out in a loud, firm voice on pure impulse, and at once the banging stopped. There was an unpleasant hush. His heart somersaulted. Maybe I should just back away, he thought. But his curiosity was still pricked. His eyes were running, and he breathed in the way he did when his nose was blocked.

He took a step toward the bedroom – the hall opened into a recess there – and pulled up short.

"Oh, sorry," he said when he saw who it was standing there in his white shirt and funeral pants. The son-in-law had, however, removed his jacket.

Sven made to turn on his heel and leave with some apologies on his lips, but the sight of Birgitta's son-in-law standing there in her bedroom sent, with a moment's delay, all the alarm bells in him ringing. This was not right. It was quite clear that something was very not right indeed. The son-in-law had opened all the clothes closets and the linen closet and parts of their contents were lying scattered in jumbled heaps all over the bed.

"Are you looking for something?" he said, fixing Magnus Öberg with his eyes. OK, he was a big shot in Stockholm, Sven recalled, but he didn't care about that. The man just didn't belong in Birgitta's bedroom!

And at that moment, the son-in-law didn't look like a big shot. Sweaty face, eyes flitting about nervously. As if he'd been caught with his hand in the cookie jar, as people said when Sven was growing up.

He felt his advantage quickly grow as the silence grew.

"That's none of your business," Öberg finally answered, stressed.

I see! Insolent, too, Sven thought coolly. Then he remembered the telephone call he'd accidentally overheard once at Birgitta's. Had been something about a rug, hadn't it? It was the daughter who'd called.

Was it that rug he was trying to get his hands on now? The one that was worth so much?

Sven gave pursed his lips authoritatively. "You have no right going through Birgitta's closets," he said with gravitas.

"And you have no right coming in here uninvited," returned the son-in-law coldly, and seemed to pull in his stomach so that his upper body swelled, as if he was prepared to punch Sven at any moment.

Sven felt his fear like a hunk of ice in his gut. But it neither crawled up his spine nor rode on his back. He clenched his jaws, noticing that he became fired up as he did. This bastard wasn't to go around believing that he could act as if he ruled the place! "I'm calling the police," he threatened.

"Like hell you will!"

Sven felt that it was time to leave. He swung round and stepped quickly into the little hall. A pair of winter boots that clearly belonged in the closet stood in his way.

Just as he lost his balance, a hand grabbed hold of his jacket and then one of his arms. At the same time, the front door blew shut, and all of a sudden the situation became dangerous. Nettan wouldn't hear if he shouted. But she'd probably come soon enough anyway. Wondering where he was.

"You're going nowhere," hissed the son-in-law and the grip on Sven's arm tightened. A fist landed on his jaw.

Sven's mouth was bone dry, but now suddenly he could taste blood. His throat stung, and his heart was pumping so wildly that his legs became weak. He tried to tear himself free but he felt almost paralyzed. He couldn't do any more, he was too old and out of breath to fight. Finally, he managed to slip out of his jacket, but it was too late. As he turned his head, he saw through watery eyes that the son-in-law had grabbed hold of something. A lawn edger. He held it over him, preparing to strike.

"No!" was all he could manage as he tried to protect his face with his hands. He gasped for air, and his breath came heavily, almost like a hiss. Magnus Öberg swung the sharp edger down toward him. He was done for, that much he realized.

Again and again, he struck like a man possessed. Chopping at the scalp, face, neck. Hewed open huge gashes, chop, chop, chop. Pain and blood. His nasal bone splintered. Broke off. The eyes, no, not the eyes! Red. Lips, teeth, crash, smash. Throat and neck again.

The taste of blood was Sven Bromse's last sensation before the darkness descended on him.

She sat huddled on the steps, a middle-aged woman with a frozen face, refusing to budge.

"I reckon it's the neighbor," said Conny Larsson quietly. "Her old man..." he said with a jerk of his head toward the door.

Claesson nodded. Louise was standing next to him. Both understood.

Larsson and Özen had arrived first. Ilyas Bank had been told to stay in the car. Since the call had come in, the various emergency vehicles had started to gather.

They were cordoning off the area, and the forensic team's minibus stood ready with its back doors wide open. Forensics Benny and his two assistants had climbed into their overalls and plastic shoe covers, and had started to rig up the lighting indoors.

"Take care of her and put her in one of the cars, and stay with her," said Claesson to Police Sergeant Lena Jönsson, who'd arrived in one of the patrol cars.

The woman was in such a bad way that they could hardly get her onto her feet. Larsson helped his younger colleague to virtually carry her off.

Agneta Bromse was her name. It said so on the mailbox, Claesson and Louise were informed.

"So then it's Sven Bromse who's lying in there," said Özen.

They opened the door and looked in.

"Nobody's goin' over this threshold!" ordered Benny Grahn.

"We can see well enough from here," Claesson said dryly.

The man was lying heavily on his back, his head and face horribly disfigured. The worst thing was his missing nose, which had left a mere hole in the middle of his face. A method used a long time ago, thought Claesson as he swept his gaze over the floor and walls. Desecrating one's adversary by cutting off his nose, even if it was on a marble statue, although whether this was a fabrication or just a matter of the nose being the most vulnerable to weathering, he didn't know. One ear was also missing, and his eyes were so mashed that their aqueous jelly was dribbling out of the orbits. There were huge gashes in his scalp, the flesh sticking out from his skull like bloody flaps. His stomach heaved, and he focused instead on the garden edger that lay on the soiled carpet. Öberg must have simply dropped it and fled. Just taken the car and driven away.

But they'd find him.

"OK," he said quietly to Louise Jasinski. "We've got our work cut out for us now. Looks like he's totally lost control."

Just as he was about to turn away from the door, he caught sight of the shoe rack under all the coats.

"Benny!"

The forensics technician looked up. Claesson nodded at the sports shoes that stood there.

"OK," said Grahn and turned them over with his gloved hands. "10 ½."

Claesson nodded.

"I'll take 'em with me. Naturally," said Grahn. "If we're lucky, it's via blood that Öberg will be tied to both murders."

Through blood will he be tied to the murders, thought Claesson as he walked away. It sounded like some macabre line from Shakespeare. Or like a cool headline.

CHAPTER 63

BIRGITTA OLSSON LOOKED out through her parents' kitchen window, past the geraniums that had got so tall. Midsummer was approaching.

Lasse was on his way inside. She could only see his head sticking up above the lilac bush. He generally kept to his own house, and she hardly ever went there herself. It was a bachelor's hovel. Admittedly, it wasn't particularly simple, not so as to break your heart with pity, but she got the impression that he was ashamed of exposing his life. The mess and the smell.

Although he wasn't starving or neglecting his health, he couldn't hold his drink any more. Most things fade with time, she thought. Life's tolerant sides. And Lasse was a hard worker, and many of the locals called for him. But still their father would never think that he'd made a man of himself. But that would also soon be a thing of the past, what their father thought.

Things were as they were.

Perhaps Lasse wanted a bit of company, and that was fine with her. She lifted the thermos. Yep, it still sloshed. Her mother had gone to lie down, and she had no idea where her father was.

Lasse stepped out of his shoes in the hallway, the big, heavy shoes that clumped. He then stood in his socks in the kitchen, pulled off his cap, and ran his hand over his crown, groping for the words.

"Hi," he ended up saying.

"Would you like some coffee?"

"Yes. Please."

She set out some cups, a loaf of bread, some butter and various toppings.

"So you'll be staying here, then, Sis?" he said once he'd sat down to tuck in.

"Maybe. But not in this house…not with Mom and Dad." She made a face as if to stress the word *naturally*. Her aversion to becoming a maid or a nurse to her parents she kept to herself, but she was watching her words. Many people had no doubt seen Lasse as their father's menial. "I guess I'll find a cottage somewhere. After all, I know this area, it's my home," she said, batting him affectionately with her hand.

She'd never go back to Holmhälleväg. Once the hall had been cleaned properly, she'd sell. She guessed Agneta wouldn't want to hang around, either. She'd stopped chirping. There was no one left to call her Nettan.

It was terrible. She'd been helped not to feel ashamed in front of Agneta. She wasn't the one who'd attacked Sven. But Agneta was firmly convinced that the entire Olsson family were a bunch of dangerous criminals.

Birgitta was training herself not to think about it. So she smiled. Lasse smiled back, but tamely; his teeth were not a source of pride for him.

"But you'll stay on at the hospital?" he said.

"I was thinking of it." She took a gulp of coffee.

"You're a good girl, Sis."

"I don't know about that…"

He spread a thick layer of butter on his bread and slapped on three slices of polka-dotted salami. German sausage of the best kind, she thought, and watched him eat with large mouthfuls.

There was something he was wanting to say. She waited.

"Well," he said when he'd warmed up, and rose from his chair to walk out to the hall. He returned with a soft bag made of some kind of black textile.

"I found this in the barn."

She stared at it. The truth will always come out in the end, she thought.

"It's mine."

"What is it? I peeked inside but it doesn't look like anything worth keeping. An old blanket or rug or something. Do you want it, or shall I drive it over to the tip?"

It was nice to be around people who didn't know everything, she thought.

"Lasse, I can deal with it myself. Give it to me."

It gave her a sensation of stability to have the soft bag there by her feet. Maybe she'd ask Annelie to help her value it and to get in touch with an auction house. But she'd have to do it on the sly. She could do without any more attention.

They'd gotten past the warm-up. The air was slightly muggy, but the oxygen was still adequate. Claesson, Özen, and the defense lawyer. Magnus Öberg had been reduced to a mere shadow of his former self.

He clearly wanted to testify. Wanted to confess, unburden himself of everything he could, that much they'd understood. Liked letting the words take control of the thoughts.

"Can you tell us what was going through your mind?" asked Claesson.

"When it came to the neighbor, I guess nothing. I'd say I've never thought so little in my entire life. I'm not really sure what happened, I just went berserk. All I knew was that I had to get my hands on the rug and then that old bugger came in and started asking questions. I was desperate for money, quickly. I was…."

Öberg stared helplessly at the wall while seeming to struggle with the angst that was probably billowing up.

"It sickens me to think about it," he said in a near whisper. "I'm not usually a violent man, but I've been under such pressure of late… the firm, the debts, Lotta and the kids…that my whole life would go down the tubes." He lifted his glass and moistened his lips with a little water. "I thought of Mom and Dad, the bankruptcy, the shame, the… Well, I was struck by panic, that's all. As if someone was controlling me from the outside."

He drank some more water.

"Look, I knew Patrik Lindström could turn just like that and totally flip out," he continued. "Er, we've known each other since military service… I hadn't actually had much contact with him over the years, but I got in touch with him now. He was the only one I thought capable of doing me a favor, or whatever you want to call it, because I could hardly have gone down to Oskarshamn to look for the rug myself."

He told them that Lindström had agreed to the job of getting hold of the valuable rug for a cut of the sale price. Magnus had called

Lindström when he'd returned from Istanbul, but had said nothing about having killed Carl-Ivar Olsson. Lindström, for his part, had been eager to stress this in earlier interviews.

Lindström wasn't interested in being embroiled in a murder inquiry, he'd explained. Claesson had pointed out that if he'd opened a newspaper and read about a murdered carpet dealer in Istanbul, surely he'd have put two and two together. But Lindström didn't read papers, he said then, and that was possibly the case.

And anyway, he couldn't believe that Magnus Öberg had killed his own father-in-law! There were bound to have been other maniacs in Istanbul only too happy to help out, he said, and Claesson let the matter drop for the time being.

According to Lindström, Magnus Öberg had only told him that there was a valuable rug being taken to Oskarshamn, that the widow had carried it home from Istanbul, and that it either had to be at her place or in the carpet shop. Or possibly that it had been sent by courier to one of these places.

"Is that true?" asked Claesson.

Magnus Öberg nodded.

"Yes. I missed the rug in Istanbul, didn't I, so I called Patrik and lied a little. Said nothing at first that Carl-Ivar was dead. He did his job pretty much as he liked. It was the way he worked, he said. That was why he stole a rug that he'd seen Annelie carry home from the post office. In the end he became like a bloodhound, obsessed with finding it, and I lost control of what he was up to… And I grew worried, of course, when I heard that he'd almost strangled the wrong woman… the one's who gone missing… Well, so, then I thought that we'd best just give up and walk quietly away. But at the same time I was thinking of the rug, of all the problems that the money would solve…"

He shrugged and asked to go to the bathroom.

They had a brief recess, and asked for some coffee and tea.

"Can you tell us how you knew about this valuable rug… what you knew about your father-in-law's life?" said Claesson once they'd resumed the interview.

"It was ages ago… perhaps five or six years, that I happened to be in the carpet shop. This was a long time before Annelie started working there. My father-in-law had a dentist's appointment and wondered if I could hold down the fort while he was away. There wasn't that much to do there, so I just wandered around the carpets for a while. And then I noticed a letter."

"Where?"

"In one of the desk drawers downstairs. I couldn't help having a read."

He was snooping around, thought Claesson.

"It was a letter containing a photograph of someone called Ayla with an unpronounceable surname." He fell silent again.

"Did you read the letter?"

"Yes. She wrote that her mother had died and that she needed money to pay for the funeral. I didn't understand at first, but then I started to rummage around the desk drawers and found a whole heap of files of letters and photos and then I realized that my father-in-law lived a double life."

"So what did you think?"

"I thought it was repugnant… but also quite appealing."

A crooked smile.

"Did you tell anyone that you'd discovered his… his secret?"

"I told him, no one else."

"How did he react?"

"He got scared."

"What happened then?"

Magnus Öberg fell silent.

"What happened?" insisted Claesson.

"I promised to keep quiet. It wasn't the same day I discovered what he was up to that I decided to confront him with it. First, I thought I'd do the honorable thing and keep it to myself, but then… I think it was some time just before Christmas, that's why we were in Oskarshamn. I was in the carpet shop one day and so I told him that I knew. He couldn't protest, because at that moment a customer came in. I imagine she could feel the tension in the air…"

"So you promised to keep quiet?"

"Yes, if…"

"If what?"

"If he gave me some money. I was in a real fix and needed money for the business, which had been doing pretty badly at times."

"And he gave you money to keep you quiet?"

"Yes."

"How often?"

"Oh, I don't know…"

The defense lawyer squirmed on his seat.

"But this time, when you went to Istanbul, what did you have in mind to do?"

"I'd found out where he was staying, it was in one of the letters, so all I had to do was book into a place nearby so I could keep an eye on him."

"Did he know?"

"Maybe. I can't say for sure."

"Tell us more about Istanbul."

"I hadn't been there before, but had managed to sniff out the fact that he had some weird rug deal going on there. He'd boast about rugs and carpets and his contacts in Istanbul… and spoke about some precious item he was going to be bringing home with him.

"Well, I understood that this was one exclusive rug, so I booked a flight at the same time as his. I knew everything about the date and itinerary through Lotta, she and her mother talk almost daily. Naturally, we didn't take the same flight, Carl-Ivar and I. He flew from Kastrup and I flew from Arlanda, and I didn't arrive until the day that Birgitta was leaving."

"So you didn't meet her down there?"

"Oh, no. I made sure of that. She'd have smelled a rat at once if she'd seen me there! But once she'd left, I called my father-in-law on his cell phone and told him I was in Istanbul and that I was thinking of supplementing my spending money. And he offered me what I wanted…"

"How much?"

"What, about two hundred thousand… not lira, kronor, though I'd get it in euros."

"And he agreed?"

"Sure. So we decided on a restaurant in the old part of the city where he'd hand over the money."

"But then it dawned on me that I could possibly get more, after all he had that rug too, didn't he? And so I kept an eye out for him from my hotel window and watched him come out and take a taxi and he had that bag in his hand. The rug, I thought. And then I wondered where he was off to, I mean we were meant to be meeting the next day. Was he thinking of slipping away? Although I knew it would've taken him time to rustle up that kind of money. I mean, it wasn't as if he was some sort of bank robber, exactly. So the next morning I called him and asked him what was happening, and he just said that everything was worked out and that he'd be taking a ferry from that place where his daughter lived, Yeniköy or whatever the place is called, to that quayside in the center…"

Öberg poured himself a Ramlösa soda water and took some gulps.

"I don't know what got into me, but I was all wound up… I really needed that money. I also needed a weapon, but shooting isn't really my thing, and you can't on a boat anyway, I thought. Otherwise I was thinking I could stick a knife in him down some dark alley. But then what happened, happened. I bought the knife… and… it came in useful."

Magnus Öberg suddenly looked exhausted.

"Can you continue? Or shall we take the rest tomorrow?"

"No, let's carry on."

"Did you get hold of the rug?"

"I thought so, but Carl-Ivar had ripped me off." He smiled crookedly. "The last thing the old man did in life was to flip me the finger."

"I don't get you."

"It all went incredibly quickly, the knife was far more effective than I'd reckoned with, and it was nasty. I just had time to search through one jacket pocket, where I found his cell phone, which I threw over the side, and so then I just grabbed the bag… but the money he was supposed to hand over to me in the restaurant I never got my hands on."

"You reckon he had it on him?"

Magnus Öberg shrugged.

"I have no idea."

What became of the money will be hard to follow up, Claesson thought. Luckily for Ilyas Bank, perhaps.

"You said that Ayla looked right through you at the funeral. Did you meet her in Turkey?"

"No, but I'd seen photos of her. I thought I was the only one who knew of her. I blanked out when I saw her at the funeral, I thought she'd recognize me as much as I did her… It was like seeing a ghost!"

"What was in the bag?"

"A toiletry bag, a shirt, socks, underpants."

"And that wasn't what you'd been expecting?"

"Hell, no!" He drummed his fingers on the tabletop. "So I figured that my mother-in-law must've taken the rug home, I mean, if it was anywhere it must be at her place. I was gripped by panic, I didn't know that you… might have been… after me…"

He swore, this well-bred murderer, Claesson thought. But did so in such a polished Stockholm accent that it sounded more like a quaint detail.

Afterwards, the group gathered in Claesson's room. Özen, naturally, and Louise Jasinski, Peter Berg, and Martin Lerde. Their forensics man, Benny Grahn, was out of the building.

"You've done well," said Louise Jasinski.

It was a strange sensation to receive praise instead of giving it, thought Claesson. But not a bad sensation in the least.

"Have you got time for a beer? It's time to knock off for the day," she continued. "I can spread the word."

Claesson didn't really have time, and should soon be on his way home. But then again, a quick one wouldn't hurt.

EPILOGUE

ANNELIE DAUN WIPED the sweat from her brow. She'd declined all help to empty the attic. She had all the time in the world, now that the carpet shop had closed down.

She understood Birgitta, Lotta, and Johan, that it was easier just to discontinue the business and not to stir up the family relationships any more with some financial settlement.

What Ayla thought about it she didn't know, but whatever it was, she was entitled to her share of the estate. But Ayla was back in Istanbul and her job as a teacher at the university.

The chest, of course, she couldn't lift herself, and she had to get some removal men over to do it. But it was to go back with her. She'd already measured it to see if it'd fit into the guest room. It would be tight, but it could be shoehorned into place. If she draped a *kelim* over it, no one would ever think of opening the lid. And if anyone did, they'd never appreciate the value of what lay within.

She had plans. High-flying carpet plans.

But first she'd have to bide her time. At least for a while. Maybe sell off one or two carpets at a major auction, but not too often. It would arouse suspicion. The money she'd invest in her own shop. A carpet shop selling rugs and carpets that people could afford. One like Carl-Ivar had had, yet different. Her own style.

Carpets that were kind on the eye and exceptionally soft to walk on.

ACKNOWLEDGMENTS

The book is set in Istanbul and Oskarshamn and its surroundings, especially in Brådbygden, the delightful village further inland in Kristdala. Go there and see its beauty with your own eyes. I did!

I would like to thank Chief Inspector Anders Pernius for his warm reception at the police station, which I'd never visited before, and for answering all my questions. The police station in the book is my own impression of this workplace rather than an authentic depiction of it.

Thanks Lars Henriksson, forensic technician in Helsingborg, for always being there for me.

I'd also like to thank Mustafa Özen of Cappadocia, and Raija Öbrstedt of Landskrona, who have taken me to Turkey several times. A special thanks to Raija, who opened the door to the world of carpets to me, and who has given me the two rugs that actually feature in the story.

Thanks Fredrik Nygren, in Stockholm, who helped me understand how a carpet dealer might think and act. It's always great talking to you!

Thanks Andrea Karlsson, who helped me with the Turkish names and who threw ideas around with me about the differences and similarities between Turkey and Sweden.

My portrayal of Oskarshamn isn't totally accurate, and at times I've stretched the truth a little. And anyway, a town is in a constant state of flux: streets are made one-way, buildings are torn down and new ones built. But on the whole I've tried to describe things as they are.

I'd like to thank the staff at the tourist office in Oskarshamn yet again for being ready and willing to take my calls. And likewise, thanks Ann Margreth Kvarnefors and Stefan Jutterdal, my friends in

Oskarshamn, who were only too happy to send photographs of places that I needed to revive in my memory.

I'd also like to thank Annika Seward Jensen, publisher, for her valuable comments, and Katarina Ehnmark Lundquist, editor, (we know each other by this stage) for her sterling, not to mention enjoyable, cooperation.

LUND, AUGUST 2009

Karin Wahlberg